The Wind and the Blood

Other books by Jim Prothero:

Theology and C.S. Lewis:

Sunbeams and Bottles: the Theology, Thought, and Reading of C.S. Lewis
Simply Mary: Meditations on the Real Life of the Mother of Christ
Gaining a Face: the Romanticism of C.S. Lewis (with Donald T. Williams)
The Form of Faith: Reflections on my Life, Romanticism, Meaning, and the Christian Faith in the Early 21st Century
Sacred Land: Finding Faith in Desert, Mountain, and Forest
The Stable Door: C.S. Lewis, Belief, and the Paradox of Recognition

Fiction:

The Sun is But a Morning Star
Maggie of Long Hollow
The Wind on the Grass
Ana Sanchez and the Coyote Murder
Ana Sanchez and the Hidden Assassins
Ana Sanchez and the Kokopelli Mystery
The Coming of the White Wolf Girl
Darkness Before and Danger's Voice Behind
There Darkness Makes Abode.
Substance and Shadow, Light and Darkness

More information at jimprotherowriter.com

The Wind and the Blood

A True Story of the American West Without the Damned Nonsense

JIM PROTHERO

RESOURCE *Publications* • Eugene, Oregon

THE WIND AND THE BLOOD
A True Story of the American West Without the Damned Nonsense

Resource Publications
An Imprint of Wipf and Stock Publishers
199 W. 8th Ave., Suite 3
Eugene, OR 97401

www.wipfandstock.com

PAPERBACK ISBN: 979-8-3852-6721-7
HARDCOVER ISBN: 979-8-3852-6722-4
EBOOK ISBN: 979-8-3852-6723-1

VERSION NUMBER 031126

To my father,
A Colorado boy who taught me
To love the Rockies, the Plains, and the Southwest

Clifford Prothero

1920–2004

Contents

1.

Going Back

1832–1833

I AM SAM PLUNKETT. I am a renegade, and I don't mind saying it. I have killed ten white men that I can remember, and probably more, and never feared the law. They had it coming. I am Irish in my blood and Cheyenne in my heart, and I'll gladly fight to the death any man who says a word against either of my peoples.

I was born on a farm near Grayson, Kentucky on the second day of the year in 1819, and it amazes me to this day that I have seen another century. I'm not sure it will be any better than the last. My family story is pretty mixed. About 1832 I came to the Rocky Mountains when I was fourteen. It's an amazing fact that I did not get killed and scalped, which I owe to the man who was my real father, Jack Rather. I reckon you've heard lots of stories about the old West, though people sure mix it up, tell a lot of lies to make it look like a romantic adventure. I don't. I was there. And my experience is different, for a good reason. You see, I fell in love with a woman of the Cheyenne nation, actually two of them. And because of that I have seen and been grieved by more hatred from white people than you ever thought was possible. You see, if you ask around the streets of St. Louis, Chicago, or Denver, any normal white man will tell you that Negroes are stupid and untrustworthy, that Indians are bloodthirsty and ignorant savages. This is just what pretty much everyone believes, even here in 1902, though things are beginning to change. The strangeness of my thinking is catching on in a few places. Mr. Grinnell is writing books about my people.

You see there's what everyone believes, and then on the other hand, there's what I know. My experience taught me different.

But I have both fear and hope for the American nation. Sometimes I just want to go back to Ireland where my people came from and have done with this place, but I'm too old and I have children and grandchildren here. Like it or not, I am American. And that includes a lot of things. But my history changed me in ways I never would have guessed and I feel like a stranger in this land. Really it burns down to one thing that sticks in my craw.

That sense of the normalcy of a white man, and the oddness of any other kind of man, like I say, is what almost everyone I've met believes; it is the sea in which we all swim. A couple of months ago, I read some fellow named Pratt in a speech called it "racism." I don't know if that's a good word for it. I, for reasons my story will tell, have learned that racism is a brutal lie. But whatever you want to call it, I have seen a lot of it—more than I ever wanted, more than I thought I could bear without killing somebody quickly. Up till this, my eighty-fourth year, I have held my peace and kept my Green River knife out of sight. My eldest granddaughter disagrees. She thinks it ought to be condemned in the streets, shouted against from the hills. She's as stubborn as her mother is, and her grandmother was. As always, when we disagree, she wins, clever girl.

I was never much good at my letters, so my eldest granddaughter, Lisa, is writing this down for me. She has been through as much as I have, maybe more. I'm proud of her bravery, a part-Cheyenne, part-Mandan, part-French, part-Irish woman living in a white man's world. But we were sitting on the porch the other night here at the ranch, and we decided my story needed to be told. If there's any hope for America at all, we're going to have to stop hating each other, for the way we look or talk. You'd think after the war to save the Union in the 60s we'd have figured that out. To be honest, at 84 years, I don't have much hope. Lisa has more, and so she labors to take my rambling stories and weave something sensible out of them, taking my Kentucky accent and turning it into proper English.

I should say, Lisa is my eldest, but that I have sixteen grandchildren all told. I had two children with Asimoni, four with Singing Night, and one with Greta: five girls and three boys. Some of them, as my old father, Jack, would say are "gone beaver." There's a special kind of pain when a man watches his children pass from this world. It ain't right. But I'll get to that part in order.

When I was fourteen, I lived with my aunt and grandfather in St. Louis. My mother had died three years before. I learned from a mountain man that my father, Richard Plunkett, was alive in the Rockies. It's a long story and it's been told elsewhere, so I won't labor it here. But that mountain man, Jack Rather, helped me find my natural father. Richard Plunkett was a disappointment though, and I learned that he had deserted my mother and me, for pointless jealousy, and for whiskey mainly. I also learned that Jack had loved me and loved my mother for years, and Jack saved my life several times before losing his own. So, I call Jack Rather my true father and no man is going to tell me otherwise. The other thing Jack did was introduce me to the *Tsistsistas*, the Cheyenne people. I guess I'll start this story about the time I left St. Louis the second time.

I had gone back to that town after Jack's death to make things right between my grandfather, my Aunt Mary and myself. And I was glad I did. You see, I had run off from them and planned never to see them again. But I grew up some in the Rockies, so I went back and apologized to them both. They were mighty pleased. I decided to winter with them in St. Louis and think about where the stick floats. Lisa is after me to explain that. That's mountain talk for knowing what is what.

For though they wanted me to stay, I had seen the Rockies, and those shining mountains haunted my soul. I reckon they still saw me as a boy. Grandfather kept talking about apprenticing me. But what boy was left in me was clawed out when I was almost killed by a grizzly bear in the Uintah Mountains. I had no more silly dreams and illusions. I knew a man had to hunt or work so as not to starve. And I had in the mountains done a lot of both. My schooling was poor, but that was pretty common. But it meant I wasn't fit for any but the poorest paid and hardest working jobs on the St. Louis waterfront. Grandfather talked about passing the tobacco shop to me, but how can a man who has seen the sunrise over the Tetons get cooped up behind the counter of a tobacco shop the rest of his long days? I knew I couldn't stay in the settlements, and made up my mind to spend the winter of '32-'33 there and no more.

In the end, they accepted my declaration that I would leave in the spring without much protest. I said it quietly, without drama or much emotion really. Even they could sense that I had made the transition to manhood in the months I'd been gone, and they knew that there was nothing in St. Louis to hold me. And if any other thing about me made them certain, it was the fact that the left side of my face is a mass of scar tissue. My left arm is much the same, though it now works well enough. That bear worked me over good before Jack killed him. And I came close to dying. There's something about dancing with death that wrings the silly boy out of you forever. I had gone to the mountains with foolish ideas and dreams of finding father, and of living a life of adventure and romance. I was as visibly scarred on the outside as I was inside. No white woman would ever have me back in those days, at least no self-respecting white woman.

I had come back, having lost everything, but most of all, my childhood. It was in the quiet way that I talked, the long stretches of silence I had come to prefer that Grandfather and Aunt Mary never got comfortable with. The West changes a man. She is a powerful and sometimes cruel mistress. Many a man cannot say no to her. I could not. But there was one more thing.

I also remembered a Cheyenne girl that I'd met when Jack took us to the village of his wife. In English, her name was Spirit, in Cheyenne, "*Asimoni.*" And I could not stop thinking of her. Oh, hell, why not say it. I was in love. Yeah, I was 15, but in other ways I was older. On a cold and rainy day, three days after New Year's Day, 1833, and the day after my fifteenth birthday, I rode my pinto mare to a big mansion in St. Louis on the hill, where the rich folk live. There I hoped to find a man Jack had introduced me to, Bill Sublette, and his partner, Bob Campbell. I tied off my mare in front and walked past the white picket fence and up the white steps to knock on the door. I guess I figured I was a sight in that part of town, where men wore frock coats and pantaloons. I was dressed in buckskins with my worn, broad-brimmed hat, with moccasins on my feet, my big Green River knife in a holster behind my back, on my belt, and Jack's .50 caliber Hawken rifle in the crook of my left elbow. Unlike when I used to be a boy in this place, my new look got me a lot of respect. No one seemed to doubt that I could use the rifle or the knife. People looked at me with fear and got out of my way. My childhood friend, Bill Robinson, who was now a blacksmith's apprentice, came to see me when I first got back, but we had nothing to say to one another. He left after 20 minutes, making poor excuses for going.

Finally, the door opened. A butler in a frock coat stood there. At any other house, I reckon they'd have told me to get out and called the sheriff on me, but this fellow must have seen trappers before. He asked me to come in, took my name, and said he'd go see if *monsieurs* Sublette and Campbell were available to see me. The butler returned after a couple of minutes and ushered me into a parlor. Bill Sublette was there, all right, a big-boned, tall man, heavily muscled, with long, blond hair over his shoulders, but going bald on the top. He wore a frock coat and a cravat, which did not look like they fit him. He was standing to the left of the table. To the right, a man clearly older, whom I did not recognize, sat at the table looking at accounts and maps in front of him. His beard and hair were thick and colored somewhere between black and copper. There were many creases in his face. He wore old buckskins, like mine but dark with grease and use.

The tall, blonde man spoke up. "Bob, this here's Jack Rather's cub, young Sam Plunkett. Sam, this here is Bob Campbell. Reckon you've heard of him."

"Yessir," I replied.

"Sorry about Jack last summer. He was a brave man. And you showed yourself to have the hair of the bear in you. My brother, Milton, can't say enough about what you did that day."

"Weren't nothin'," I replied.

Bob Campbell's eyebrows shot up. "Weren't nothing? I heard you carried a wounded man almost twice your weight a hundred yards under heavy fire. I'd call that something." It was more like thirty yards, and I did it for Jack, and I really don't remember much about it. Still, it had given me a reputation amongst the boys in the mountains, and I intended to cash that in. I think I nodded to Bob Campbell, by way of recognizing what he'd said. I had become silent, like a lot of the men of the mountains. Something about all that beauty and all that death and destruction up there took a man's words away. I cannot even now explain it. Lisa has to drag words out of me. But she's a school teacher, and she can whip her old grandfather into speaking. So, I speak for my oldest granddaughter, my best love on earth. I would do more than that for her. And the world will never know how much I have done for her, though I think she even now suspects.

"So," Billy Sublette said, re-initiating conversation, "What do you have in mind, young Plunkett?"

"I was hoping you had work for the spring hunt."

"Jack were a free trapper," Campbell commented. "You gonna give that up for the life of a company man?"

"Lots of places are trapped out. Free-trapping don't pay. I need to make money. Money is in the brigades and Blackfoot country."

"Well," Sublette commented, nodding, "That's true enough and it speaks well for you to have seen that when many a man is too stubborn to see where the market is. But why do you want money more than freedom?"

"I need to buy about ten good horses and take them down to the South Platte, end of summer."

"Why . . . ?" Campbell began but then stopped.

"He wants a native bride, Bob, I'll be bound. He needs horses for the bride price."

"Yessir," I answered. I wanted there to be no misunderstanding when I took my pay and horses and left at the end of Rendezvous.

"Fair enough," Campbell answered. "What about the fall hunt?"

"I'll rejoin you where and when you want. I just need about two weeks to go to the Platte."

"Alright," Bill Sublette answered. "Your lady Crow? Shoshone?"

"Cheyenne," I replied.

"Of course," Sublette nodded. "Shoulda knowed. Jack's woman was Cheyenne. Ok, young Plunkett, you have a deal. We will pay you the standard company wage minus the price of ten horses and see you in the fall. Let's decide where and when at Rendezvous. Meantime, this is the standard contract. Can you sign it?"

I reckon he didn't know if I could read and write. I can. A little. I was able to dip the quill pen in the ink bottle and sign my first and last name. Sublette said, "Come back to this house about the beginning of March and we'll know where and when to meet. By the way, you prefer to ride up the Platte I suppose. We need crew to go up with the keel boats."

"I done all the keel boating I care to do in this life," I replied.

"That's fine," Campbell replied. "I can use you in the ride up the Platte. See you in March, young Plunkett."

After that, the butler showed me out. I went and told Grandfather and Aunt Mary that I had a job as of March, and that if they would have me, I would stay till then. Grandfather said they would have me as long as I would stay. He said it a little sadly. I felt it. But I did not belong there anymore. Still, I knew that when I left this second time, I would never see them again. Life is like that. You never know who you're going to ride with or when your trails will part.

I did not waste my winter in St. Louis, and after asking around, found a trader by the name of Joe Barden who traded sometimes with the Cheyenne and who knew a few phrases in Cheyenne language, and the basic words for yes, and no, and good morning, and thank you, mother, father, and the like. I paid him to teach me all the Cheyenne he knew. It wasn't much, but it was a start. As he was pretty good at hand sign language, something all the plains tribes knew, I paid him to teach me that as well.

On March 20 I took my possibles (Lisa makes me say those are my equipment), my Hawken gun I inherited from Jack, my pinto mare, and rode up the Missouri with the Rocky Mountain Fur Company as an *engagé* as far as Lexington. On the 7th of May, 1833, we rode out, heading west on the Platte River.

I have always loved the Platte River country. Down in Missouri, the Platte is slow, and sluggishly shoulders its way through marshes of heavy grass and a few trees. Except in the winter, the air is moist and heavy, like a wet blanket you can't get off your shoulders. But as you leave the hot, muggy, Missouri River country behind, you come on to the dry, clean, wind-cut plains. And the grass sings, like it's being scythed by the wind again and again. And there's almost always a wind, unless a big storm is building up and the wind dies down for a bit before building up again, and raging and blowing you off your horse. And the grass has a smell that I can't quite describe: a sort of burnt, savory smell, like well-roasted buffalo meat, or maybe a fire that is burning a sweet-smelling wood. It makes you want to wrap the sea of grass around you like a warm coat. Here the Platte runs clean, with few rapids, wide, deep, and slow. Around it grow groves of cottonwood trees and thick stands of wild grass, so that you can go up or down the Platte and if you're careful, no one traveling the other way will even know you were there. It was a great place for ambushing someone.

For us it was the Road to the West. Sure, the Missouri was that, and had long been. But the Missouri River ran far north, almost to Canada and reached the Rocky Mountains in the dangerous Blackfoot country. If you wanted to trap, the Platte was your road. I cannot count the times I have traveled it. And I'm only saddened today that it is now hemmed in and bundled up through all its long length by ranches and towns. The first time I saw it, the Platte was wild, unbound, and free as the wind that ruffled the surface of its waters. It was the road to freedom, to the opening up of life. I will love the Platte best of all rivers till the day I die.

This was my second trip up the Platte, but it was not like the first, which was quiet and open. I was now a company man, and we had orders to drive and protect the livestock. In some ways I was right sorry to have done it. I had at least for a time, given up the freedom of a free trapper. Jack would have scoffed. There were 55 of us in three parties, driving cattle and sheep to boot. It may have been safe from Indian attack, but it was slow and noisy. And it was, except for an attack one night by a mad wolf, uneventful, plodding up the sweet banks of the Platte, mile after mile, week after week.

Most of the boys on the trip were company trappers and I already knew a few. There were some interesting greenhorns, that is, people new to the mountains. There was a Scotsman, Sir William Drummond Stewart, Baron of Grandtully. He was not only an adventurer, but a writer of books. I reckon he'd laugh if he knew I was writing this memoir. He liked to ride along side of me, mainly, as he told me, that he preferred an Irishman as a companion to all these English-bred Americans. He tried to explain to us that we could not call him "Sir William" till his father died and he inherited the title, but the boys didn't make these kind of fine distinctions, and with his grand Scots accent, and Brit ways, they started calling him "Sir William" and the name stuck. He gave up trying to correct us.

Then there was 'Doc Ben.' Doctor Benjamin Harrison was a doctor and son of a famous politician and army general back east. Despite the fact he was only 27 years old, he looked a lot older. Like my scars on my head from the grizzly, Doc Ben had scars on his mind and heart. The death of his wife had driven him to whiskey, and whiskey had driven him to get clear of the settlements for a while. I hadn't the heart to tell him that once we got to Rendezvous, whiskey would flow like water. He was no mountain man, but he made himself useful treating the sick and the injured and did his best to save the man that got bitten by the mad wolf. He used to tell me that a good surgeon might be able to do something for the scars on my face. I told him that I was proud to look on the outside the way I felt on the inside, and he never mentioned it again. A few times I did wish my old friend, Antoine Charette, were with me. However, he never returned from Quebec and I was sure that I would never see him again. I figured the Jesuits, no doubt, absorbed him and set him to work among the people of Quebec.

We poked our way up the south bank of the Platte, then past the fork to the North Platte, turning up the Sweetwater River to almost the foot of the Wind River Mountains, then struck off southwesterly across South Pass and struck the Green River above Horse Creek three days later. Heading down to Horse Creek, we rode into camp and set up on July 5. I told Doc Ben that I would not be drinking whiskey and that I would help him not to drink too. I had tasted whiskey and didn't mind it, but the thought of what it had done to my mother's husband, the man that should have been my father, put me off for a time. And I did not think much of the behavior of most of the boys in the mountains when they got a powerful drunk on at Rendezvous. I guess unlike most of the boys, I pulled into Rendezvous ready for bad things to happen. After all, at Rendezvous last year I'd learned that the man who fathered me was a faithless drunk. And I lost the man who was my real father. I had no reason to think that Rendezvous was going to be good.

2.

Rendezvous

1833

I WAS WORKING FOR Milton Sublette, Billy's little brother. He was blond and thinner than his big brother, and he ran the store. The store was three barrels and four planks, two planks between each. Milton sat on another barrel behind the planks and dispersed trade goods and what passed for whiskey to the trappers one at a time as they came in. No money changed hands, only *pleus*, or bound stacks of beaver fur, which Milton wrote down in his big account book. Then Milton would let the trapper spend their credit on whatever Milton could give them, from horses, to firearms, to traps, to watered-down whiskey, and finally to foofuraw. Lisa reminds me to explain mountain language. Foofuraw is hand mirrors and beads and trinkets and other pretty and useless things an Indian woman might value. Jack had bought foofuraw for Menoke, his Cheyenne wife and my second mother. Some trappers with native wives did the same. The others bought foofuraw to pay to buy a roll in the bushes with some drunken fort Indian girl.

Lisa is after me again to explain. When I came to live with the Cheyenne, they had a term that all the plains tribes used in their own languages: "fort Indian." It was a term of contempt for a man who abandons his family and the ways of his ancestors, and hangs around a fort or trading post of the white man, begging for whiskey, and selling everything of value that he has, including his wife and daughters. This brings me to mind a couple of things: one, the deadliest weapon the white man ever leveled against my Cheyenne kin and other tribes, was not the cholera or the smallpox, though that takes a close second place, and certainly not the United States Army, that took 50 years to defeat the strong warriors of the plains when they had the numbers and weapons to do it in 10, but whiskey. With soldiers or disease, you could take the life of a Cheyenne, or Sioux, or Shoshone, or Crow warrior. With whiskey, you could destroy his heart, mind, and soul, and make him beg you to keep doing it, till the whiskey finally took his life.

The second thing is that there have been many things in this life that have made my heart bleed. Few have done it worse than to see some proud warrior destroy himself with whiskey and stoop so low as to sell his women into prostitution for horny fur trappers or other white men. I think this was the point that I decided to never touch whiskey again. And I felt bad, because my job was to sit with Doc Ben just behind Milton Sublette, and when a trapper ordered a Hawken gun, or traps or a horse from the corral, Doc Ben and I would fetch it. Milton did the dealing and wrote the records. Doc and I did the hauling and fetching. We also did the watering down of the whiskey, something I quickly came to hate. But I volunteered to do it all so Doc Ben didn't have to come near the stuff. I kept telling myself it was a job and I was getting paid. But I did not like it none.

Occasionally, if Milton had to walk back into the trees aways and take a piss, it fell to me to sell stuff at the marked prices to trappers who came up, if they already had credit. If a trapper wanted to bargain his furs, I had to tell him to come back when Milton was around. But if a trapper just wanted another jug of watered-down whiskey or some foofuraw, I could handle that. I found my ciphering and writing were up to keeping Milton's records straight. So, after a while, Milton began to trust me and take longer breaks.

Doc Ben and I worked from midday till sundown. A couple of other fellows helped Milton in the mornings. And occasionally Henry Frapp or Bob Campbell, or one of the other Rocky Mountain Fur Company partners would take over and give Milton the day off. But mainly it was Milton who did the trading.

And Milton didn't talk to us much more than he had to, so that I found a friend in Doc Ben. He and I kept together, and eventually Sir William, the Scotsman, joined us. We three were almost the only sober men in camp. You may have heard stories of the old rendezvous. One writer my Lisa read to me called them "mountain Saturnalia." My Lisa had to explain to me that a Saturnalia was a drunken riot where every man and woman did everything they wanted to and without inhibition for a short time. That fits it pretty well. I had seen it once, the year before, but I had Charette, Jack, and Menoke with me then, and I didn't see so much of it. Here boys who spent their whole year on little food, little warmth, and on the edge of death, came in, got roaring drunk, fired off their guns and ran around doing the craziest things they could think of. Some of it was harmless, even funny, like the horse races, the singing, dancing, and the laughing. And I have to admit that when some boys sat around the fire, telling lies to each other, making 8 foot grizzly bears into 20 foot grizzly bears with two heads, I had a good laugh. Some boys just got blind drunk till they run out of credit with Milton and fell asleep in the bushes. When they woke, they drank some coffee, packed up and rode out. You couldn't have shining times if you were sober, a thing that struck me as odd.

But often times two fellows got in a fight, and if one got killed or maimed, no law came after the winner. It was rough luck on the dead man. Murder was alright, so long as you were drunk. And I already talked about the fort Indian girls. I have no more to say about that. But all the boys in the mountains would agree that the main thing was that they were free. That was more important than anything, even the life of another trapper, or the soul of some whiskey-soaked Indian girl. Free. Free. Free. That was their religion.

I got to brooding on this and thank God, Doc Ben was there and we got to talking. I told him how I was feeling about Rendezvous. I said, "Maybe I shouldn't be so hard on the boys, but it ain't right, Doc Ben."

"I see you're a philosopher, Plunkett."

"Hell, Doc. I had three years of schooling. No, it were four. Last time that ol' teacher man cracked me across the knuckles for a ciphering error, I got up and left. Grandfather never could make me go back."

"Well, that is some consideration, but you are a thinker even if you walked out of school. And most schools don't teach you to be educated, I am sorry to say. They teach you reading and writing and arithmetic, that is, ciphering. A good teacher will teach you how to think, logic. Take for instance this Rendezvous. You are not drinking, so you can think. And that tells you right off that thinking and the way these men are behaving don't fit each other well. They drink, perhaps to keep from thinking. From what you tell me, their lives are lonely and violent. They build up a certain amount of emotion behind the dam of their souls, and they come here to open the flood gates for a while."

"I reckon that makes sense," I said. "And I don't mind a good drunk. My father, Jack, was a good drunk when he drank and didn't hurt nobody. The man that is my natural father, he were mean and jealous. If there's any evil in a man's soul, drinking seems to bring it out."

"Well, I have to agree with you there. By the way, I saw him."

"Who?"

"Your natural father, as you call him."

"When?"

"Yesterday. You were out fetching two horses for Milton. A red-haired trapper came up and Milton called him Plunkett. Milton bought his furs and sold him two jugs of whiskey, and a lot of powder and shot. Then Milton said you were around and asked if he wanted to see you. The man just glared at Milton and walked off."

"Well, that's alright, because I don't care to see him neither."

Doc Ben wanted to know why and I told him the whole story of the year before. I won't tell it now, because, like I said, it's been told elsewhere. Sir William came up as I was beginning, and I had to start over for the both of them. I hadn't told no one before, and even though we rode up the Platte for a month or two together, this was the first time I felt like I could trust them. We were probably the only three sober men in a hundred miles. Even Milton had kicked back with a jug. After I had told them about my pap, Richard, and how I was feeling about all the drunkenness, Sir William said,

"Well, lad. It speaks well for ye. But don't be too hard on these boys. They all have a rough life from what ye've told us of the trapping."

"Why aren't you drinking, Sir William?" I had to ask.

"Ah, lad. That's no' whiskey. That is alcohol and water and something for color. I've had the real Scotch whiskey. I'll no' be drinkin' this crap."

"I think the young man," Doc Ben said "is wondering about the dark side of a man that shows when he is drunk."

"And there's plenty of that," I added.

"Ah, well, Sam," Sir William said, nodding, "There is that."

"They talk about their freedom all the time," I complained. "But their freedom seems a lie when they're just free to be evil."

"You see, Sir William, that is pretty thoughtful for a young man like our Sam. I told him he was a philosopher, and he laughed. He hasn't finished much schooling. I told him thinking was something else beyond reading and ciphering."

"Yer right there, Doctor."

This was just the first of our talks. Doc set about really educating me. He had two books with him and he would let me read some, then we'd talk about it. One was the Bible, but that book is powerful confusing. I was reading in the Gospel of Matthew, somewhere around chapter 25, and pointed out to him that not many a preacher man ever talked about the things there, much less lived them.

"That's a sad truth, young Plunkett. I've noticed it too. Sometimes I think what passes for Christianity in this country is just people doing what they like and finding the Bible passage to excuse it."

"Sorta like all these boys getting drunk so they can do the things they'd normally be ashamed to do," I responded.

"Yeah, hate to say, but I think you have a point there, young philosopher."

The other book he had me read from was by a couple of English poets. I said my grandfather didn't care much for the English, but Doc Ben encouraged me to read it out to him anyway. I liked the poems. One of the poets, a fellow named Wordsworth, wrote about the beauty of the natural world that was the way I felt when I looked on the Rocky Mountains at sunrise. The book was called *Lyrical Ballads*, and I came to like it a lot, especially a poem about some place called Tintern Abbey. Other poems were about poor people whose hearts were good, but who were destroyed by the cruelty of the world. I could understand that.

While Doc Ben was educating me, two major things happened to me in camp. For all my fine talk, I almost killed a man. Twice. It happened like this. One evening as the sun was going down, I was headed to the north side of camp to hear some boys tell tall stories and lie to each other. I was passing by a small thicket of trees and bush. I heard some grunting from there, and I knew some free trapper was rolling some fort Indian girl in the bushes. Nothing much new about that. I kept walking. Then I heard something that made me freeze. The girl was crying out, her shouts muffled, maybe by a hand over her mouth. This wasn't some drunk fort Indian girl. This girl was being raped. I know I should have thought it out more, but I was in that thicket in a moment. You see we had some fort Indians in camp, but we also had a lot more of the honorable kind of Indians in camp, Shoshone mostly, Nez Perce, Flathead, and a lot of Crows. Maybe this girl was out walking and this drunken trapper grabbed her and took her to the bushes. I never found out.

What I saw was a big trapper in buckskins, with a dark, bushy beard, long dark hair, on top of an Indian girl. He had his right hand over her mouth and with his left, he was trying to pull up the skirt of her buckskin dress, while hitching down his own buckskin pants. He had pretty much got her skirt up over her belly button. She was trying to cry out in a language I didn't know, and with both hands was trying to pull her dress back down over her hips. I came up on him fast and with my right foot kicked him on the side of the head, causing him to roll off the girl. She sprang up in an instant and dashed off toward the Shoshone camp. I didn't really expect her to stop and thank me, and besides, I was busy.

The trapper stood up, glaring at me. "Wha' the hell you do that fer? I was having me a wimmen!" He reached behind his back and pulled his Green River knife out, swaying a little, with his pants wrapped around his thighs and his male parts dangling out front, half extended.

I put down my Hawken gun (we never went anywhere without our gun) and pulled my Green River knife. I suppose I had the drop on him and should have pointed my gun at him and told him to pull up his pants and clear off. But there is something like a mountain code of honor when it comes to fighting. And I had been trained.

Last year I'd almost been killed by a keelboat captain with a Green River knife. Jack had to shoot him. Since that day, while I traveled with Jack, he would teach me how to fight hand to hand with a Green River knife. They're big knives, maybe really small swords. And there's an art to it that has to do with balance, with looking for mistakes your opponent makes that leaves him open for a killing thrust. Jack taught me this for every night when we made camp for over two months. He had a couple of sections of a heavy branch that he'd chopped off the same length as a knife, so he could "stab" me with the wooden practice knife, and leave a bruise. I had one and he had one. Yeah, he showed me the moves, but then he'd practice them on me. Every time his fake knife scrapped across my throat or jabbed me in the ribs, he would cry "Yor gone beaver, Sam!" It was painful, and I remember wishing a lot that he would give it up, but he didn't until I found that I could nail him once in a while and call those damn words back at him. After almost three months, though he still won more than he lost, I was a good opponent. Only then did he stop getting at me about using my knife. Now in this moment, with this big, drunken trapper in front of me with a knife, looking ready to kill me, I thanked Jack in my heart for all those painful lessons.

That's when I remembered the last lesson Jack taught me about hand-to-hand fighting. If you don't win, you're dead. So win. Fighting clean is a luxury a man of the mountains cannot afford. Also, never draw out a fight. You only get tired and sloppy. Win fast and be lethal. I knew that. And, what's more, this fellow had a weight advantage on me. I needed to be careful. That big fellow came at me slashing back and forth sideways. I knew from Jack's training that this was a bad move, because half the time your knife is way to the left or way to the right and your center is wide open. I could have killed him right then by timing it right when his center was exposed, so that my blade shoved straight into his chest, "up to the Green River" as the boys say, that is up to the hilt, where the knife-maker stamped in the company name into the steel just above the hilt. The boys would have shrugged and said 'rough luck.' No law would come after me. And this big fellow would be safely dead. In hindsight, maybe I should have ended it there.

But in an instant I knew what to do. As he came close and his blade went wide to his left, I jumped in right on him, skin to skin, put my Green River to his throat, pinned his knife arm, and kneed him in the manhood as hard as I could. He went down like a felled tree, maybe because his manhood were so exposed, my knee must have given him whole new worlds of pain. I kept my Green River at his throat, grabbed his knife and tossed it deeper into the bushes. I got up right in his face and said really soft. “Mister, I don’t know who you are, and it ain’t none of my business if you want to roll some willing girl. But she’d better be willing.” His eyes were wide with terror and pain.

Then I jumped up, collected my Hawken rifle, and got the hell out of there before he could do or say more.

When I got back to where Doc Ben, Sir William and I were camped near the Rocky Mountain Fur trade goods, I was shaking. They were sitting by our fire pit. I sat down and told them what happened, while I tried to calm down.

“You are a young knight, Plunkett, preventing a rape like that,” Doc Ben observed. “But it might have been wiser to kill the man.”

“Aye,” added Sir William. “Now he’ll come after ye.”

“Let him,” I said. Though I did not see that man again that summer.

But I seemed to not be able to stay out of trouble, as Doc Ben observed. After my run in with the big trapper, I stopped going around to the different fire-rings in camp. I didn’t want people discussing me to my face. Sir William and Doc Ben scattered out and brought me the news. The big trapper’s name was Morton. He was a free-trapper and dangerous in a fight when he was sober. I had made a bad enemy. But he had cleared out, probably embarrassed by having been beaten and spared in a knife fight with a pup, as he would have put it. I would have to watch out for him. Sir William told me that about one third of the men he talked to thought I was right to interfere, another third said it was none of their business what I did, and the last third thought I should have let a free-trapper to do what he pleased. He was a free man after all.

“That ain’t freedom,” I said.

“What do you mean, Sam?”

“Well, I don’t know nothing, but it seems to me that to be free means to be free to do what is right.”

They both looked at me puzzled, as we sat of an evening around our campfire near the other Rocky Mountain Fur Company men.

“Well,” I explained, “I’ve been thinking about it. And it seems to me that freedom is a good thing, but not the best thing. Got to keep all those sorts of things in balance. If you try to make some good thing the best thing, the only thing, why it gets all twisted.”

“I don’t follow,” Sir William said, sitting up and focusing on me.

“Well, if I said kindness, or justice were the most important thing, well, things would get all confused. If kindness were the best thing, why we’d let every criminal go and let every thief get away. And if justice were the most important thing, we'd be hanging men and women everywhere without any pity. Freedom is wonderful, but if it means you can rape an Indian girl, then it ain't freedom. It's something else."

Sir William and Doc Ben looked at each other silently.

"Did I say something stupid?" I asked, a little irritated.

"On the contrary, young Plunkett," Doc Ben said, "You just said some of the wisest words I've ever heard. Are you sure you didn't finish school and go to Harvard?"

I put my head back and laughed at that.

The next day, when I got off, I decided to stop being afraid of what the boys might say and grabbed my rifle as soon as I was off work, and walked around the wider camp. That is how I met the man who has been one of my greatest friends, Jim Beckwourth. I came through some bush on the north side of camp and saw something I hadn't seen since St. Louis when I was a boy: a black man. This one was dressed like a mountain man, and he stood backed up in some rocks, with his Green River out. Around him on three sides were three white trappers with their knives out. I came upon them pretty much as a surprise.

The big white trapper in the middle said, "Come on, boys, let's carve up this lying black sumbitch once and for all. I'm tired of his jaw."

I cocked my Hawken and leveled it at the big white trapper's head. "I wouldn't if I were you, mister."

He turned and looked quite frightened to be looking down the barrel of my Hawken rifle.

"You're that Plunkett pup what licked ol' Morton. Why don't you mind your own business and leave us to ourn?" he told me.

"Can't do that, mister," I replied.

"This black sumbitch has got me riled. I mean to fight him."

"That's just fine, mister, but you can do it by yourself. Your friends can clear off."

"Well, what if we come after you, Plunkett?"

"Well, then I'll blow a hole through your head like a melon and me and that black fellow can fight the other two fairly, knife to knife, one to one. Sorry, mister, but I just like even odds."

The man glared at me with hatred, then finally said to his companions, "C'mon boys. Let's clear out. I'm not finished with you, Beckwourth, nor you Plunkett."

As they left I kept my rifle on the big one till they were out of sight.

"I coulda took them *vide-poche* white boys," the black man told me with no small irritation. "I didn't need no white savior."

“No matter. I’da done the same if’n you were white or green or blue.” I don’t know why I said it, but it seemed to me that the issue was fairness. You want to pull your knife and fight, fine. Do it like a man, one on one. Coming with a gang like that is what bullies used to do on the waterfront in St. Louis when I was coming up. I used to fight them and get pretty bad beat up. But they went away with bruises too. I just didn’t like any kind of bully.

“So, you’re the Plunkett that kicked ol’ Morton in the manhood and almost killed him?” the black man asked.

“’Fraid so.”

“You sure like trouble.”

“You too. What did you say that got them riled?”

“I just told a story they didn’t like.”

“That all?”

“Yeah. You may not have noticed but lots of white men won’t cut a black man no slack. Especially if those white men come from south of the Mason Dixon Line.”

“Yeah. I had noticed.” And I had already been thinking a lot about how whites assumed they were better and smarter and morally superior to Indians. I began to extend my thinking at that moment, and wonder about black men. “What’s your name?”

“Beckwourth. Jim Beckwourth.”

“Sam Plunkett. Pleased to meet you.”

“Say, weren’t you Jack Rather’s boy?”

“Yup. That’s me. How come I ain’t seen you around?”

“I’ve been staying with my Crow relations.”

“Crow?” I snorted.

“I heard you were like Jack, hanging ‘round those damned Cheyenne horse thieves.”

“Horse thieves? They were just taking back the horses the Crow stole from them!”

“Well,” Beckwourth stopped and thought. “I owe you a favor, so I’ll spend it by saying no more about the Cheyenne.”

“Fair enough,” I replied. “Just stay outa trouble.”

“That’s what I should tell you, young Plunkett.” And he nodded, put his Green River in its scabbard, picked up his Hawken rifle and went into the bush in the direction of the Crow camp.

When I reached my camp later in that night, Sir William and Doc Ben were waiting for me. They’d already heard the news that was racing around camp like a wildfire: Jack Rather’s pup, young Plunkett was the avenger of Indian maids and black men.

"Oh hell," I swore, "it weren't nothing like that. I just made that man fight Beckwourth one on one and he backed off. I hate bullies."

"Be careful, Sam. There isn't a more irrational passion in the hearts of some of the boys around here than their hatred for Negroes."

"It ain't right," was all I could think of to say. "I didn't stop him from fighting. I just told him he had to do it one on one."

Sir William interrupted, "Doc is right. You Yanks go crazy when you see a black man. Be on your guard."

"Well, I don't, and it doesn't much figure. Rendezvous is breaking up tomorrow and I'm getting away from those *vide poche* cutthroats. By the way, you didn't catch their names did you?"

"The bully was Will Powers. Never learned who the other two were. Yer right, he's a coward. Doesn't like to fight one on one. But he'll sneak up on ye and cut yer throat. Watch out for him, Sam. But no more of that," Sir William told me. "Doc and I have something for ye. As this is our last night here in camp, we prepared a goin' awa present fer ye, Sam."

They pulled out a big sheet of paper, the kind that Milton Sublette used to keep track of business. On it, written in a pretty fair hand, I assumed by Sir William, it read:

University of the Rocky Mountains
Awards the Bachelor of Arts Degree

In Philosophy
to
Samuel J. Plunkett

July 24, 1833

Sir William Drummond, Chancellor
Dr Benjamin Harrison Vice-Chancellor

Verum utcumque quaerere
seek truth at all costs

"My Latin is a bit rusty," Sir William admitted, "but I think it's correct."

"University of the Rocky Mountains?" I asked.

"Yes, we formed it this morning." He handed me his tube-shaped case in which he normally carried his spy glass. "If you roll it up and put it in here, this will keep it safe."

"Why 'J' for a middle initial? I don't think I have a middle name. If I do, nobody ever told me."

"Well, it looks more formal. So, we took the liberty of naming ye after yer father, Jack."

I liked that idea and to this day, I sign legal documents as Samuel J. Plunkett. Samuel Jack Plunkett. I just like it. "Well, I don't know what to say."

"We do. We've learned a lot on this trip, mostly from you. We're not trappers. I came seeking adventure, and Doc, well you know why Doc came. But you have been the most pleasant surprise in this riot called a Rendezvous. Doc and I wanted to thank you."

I knew why Doc came. Then he surprised me even further when he put his Bible and his copy of *Lyrical Ballads* in my hands and begged me to keep them.

"Plus, we reconsidered Sublette's offer to go up the Yellowstone River and ride a keelboat back to St. Louis. Seeing as how you spent your Rendezvous making enemies, we're going with the party of twenty or so that are riding down the Platte. We'll ride with you as far as you go that way. So, if Morton or Powers were planning to jump you tomorrow, they'll have to face more than twenty of us."

"I'm grateful," was all I could think of to say.

3.

Native Bride

1833

NEXT DAY, CAMP WAS all a bustle, tipis coming down, wagons loading up. Milton let me pick ten of the best of the remaining horses and gave me my $7 worth of pay that remained in shot and powder for my Hawken. I rigged the horses up to a line, and Sir William, Doc, and I rode out with the party heading down the Platte. Just before leaving, Henry Frapp, one of the older and better brigade leaders, came up and told me that if I wanted to work the fall hunt, I was to come to him at the beginning of October on the Green River near the Uintahs. Jack had taken me through that country a lot and I knew it well. He told me to keep a calendar on a piece of buffalo hide, this being the 25th day of July, and I did, and still do to this day, even though my Lisa brings me printed paper calendars. By October 1st, I was to look for his brigade south of the Flaming Gorge of the Green River. I told him I'd be there.

We rode northeast across South Pass and picked up the Sweetwater at the southeast tip of the Windriver Mountains. There was no sign of Morton or Powers, and we followed the Sweetwater to the North Platte and down for a week. When the North Platte converged on the South Platte, I bid a sad farewell to Sir William and Doc Ben, knowing full well I'd never see them again in this life. I turned southwest and started following the South Platte up toward the Front Range, shining in the distance. I was very nervous, with a train of horses and alone, but thank God, no Pawnees nor Crows found me, nor any free trappers with thievery on their minds. On the third day I came upon a big cottonwood grove on the south bank of the river. I could see the tops of tipis above the trees and cooking smoke coming out. Jack had told me that only White Coyote kept his village on the Platte among the Cheyenne this time of year, but I couldn't be certain. Still, I had to try.

The custom among the Cheyenne on approaching a village as a friendly, is to sing a song in Cheyenne. I didn't know much Cheyenne at this time in my life and all I could think of was an Irish song, "The Blooming Flower of the Grange," that my mother had sung me. I am not much of a singer, but I began belting it out as loudly as I could. Just as I thought, about five warriors rode out to me, armed. As they grew closer, I felt a sense of relief. They were clearly Cheyenne. Some white folks say that all Indians look alike. Well, folks that say that are just showing their ignorance. Cheyenne look like Cheyenne. It's in the straight ridge of the nose and the rounded face and the cheekbones. Plus, their beadwork on their leggings and the way they wear their hair, all are far different than Crow or Shoshone. And they smell like Cheyenne. I know this sounds strange, but Jack assured me that as I stayed in the mountains, I would find that my smelling got good. White men smelled like white men, or just like cheap soap. But bathing was a luxury in the Rockies in those days. Most Indians wore some kind of bear grease or something to protect the skin from the sun and keep off mosquitoes. And each tribe did it differently. Trappers had learned to smell the difference long before they saw the warriors.

So, when Cheyennes rode out to see who was singing the strange song, I was powerfully relieved to see they were Cheyenne. I had been to White Coyote's village before but I always had a guide. This was a risk. The singing, I knew, was some protection. If I had been attacking, I would have come silently, so already I had cooled down the situation by singing. Then the warrior riding to my left said some words out loud to the others in Cheyenne with the name I recognized: "*Maovese*." They began to smile and say again "*Maovese, Maovese*." I pointed to myself and said "*Maovese*." This had been my name when I was here last year. It translates "Red Hair" in English. The Cheyenne are real practical about names, as Jack had told me. I was so relieved. I had found the right village.

By the time I entered the ring of tipis, people were coming out and laughing and talking and saying "*Maovese*" and pointing to me and chattering away in Cheyenne. I was news and a welcome break from the daily routine. A woman emerged out of a far tipi to my left and before I knew it, she was tugging on my knee to dismount. I recognized her, the woman I most wanted to see on this earth. I slid off my horse and she hugged me without stopping.

I had found Jack's Cheyenne wife, Menoke. As she hugged me, I said the Cheyenne word I'd learned and had been practicing for this moment: "*Nahko'eehe*," or ' my mother.'

She said into my ear, "*Nae'ha*," which I knew meant, "my son," in English.

I had made it home.

It wasn't till years later that I learned that Jack had told her in Cheyenne language, when we first met, that I was his son, never explaining the way Jack had lost my mother, or how Richard Plunkett had been my natural father. So, for Menoke, it was simple: I was her husband's son, and therefore I was her son. My gear was unloaded and my horses dispersed by boys into the village herd. I was not worried about this. The boys that managed the herd knew every horse and whom they belonged to. I had not lost anything.

With Menoke holding gently to my left arm, I was marched triumphantly through the village and to White Coyote's tipi. White Coyote was Menoke's brother and a chief of the village. As I stepped through the circle opening, I prepared to step to the right, as is courtesy on the plains, to allow the man of the tipi to choose where you sit. But Menoke switched to my right arm and tugged me over beside her, sitting me down on the buffalo robes. I suppose it was her way of saying that I was no guest, but family.

As my eyes adjusted to the light, I saw White Coyote, a strong, middle-aged Cheyenne warrior that I remembered as Jack's friend, and I guess brother-in-law, and his wife sitting beside him. And sitting beside his wife, looking at me in wonder and maybe panic, was Asimoni, his daughter. She was more beautiful than I remembered. And I had thought that bringing the horses and asking for her hand like Jack told me, would be enough. Now I wasn't so sure. And what if this beautiful Cheyenne girl did not want to marry a *ve'ho'e*, a white man, like me? Menoke and White Coyote talked quite a lot and she seemed overjoyed at my coming.

I knew I had to try. I waited for a pause in the conversation, and said, "*Nea'ese*," which is 'thank you.' Then I began to sign. With my hands I said "Me come see mother" I added to the last by pointing at her. Then I went on "Me work mountains live here yes?"

White Coyote smiled and nodded, then signed "Yes."

"*Nea'ese*," I added, then signed. "Help me learn speak?"

Menoke laughed and squeezed my arm, answering in a torrent of Cheyenne that must have been her saying yes, she would teach me to speak Cheyenne properly.

Then I hesitated and you could see they all felt my hesitation. But I signed, "Me ask big ask." Dare I go on? I swallowed. I reckon I looked like a hunted deer for a moment. But Jack would have told me to be bold. I decided I had come to risk this thing, and there was no turning back. I had practiced this speech forty times in St. Louis. I signed "Me ask marry daughter yes? Me bring ten horse give you." Jack had explained to me the year before that to marry the girl, the main thing was to bring her father a gift of many horses and be proven in battle. My carrying Jack away in Battle of the Big Hole was proof that I was a warrior, and no Cheyenne would have missed the fact that I came into camp leading ten fine horses.

Everyone in the lodge gasped a little. Asimoni, looked downward and would not meet my eyes. White Coyote looked thoughtful. At last he signed, "Me think tell tomorrow. You eat now sleep here welcome." And that's what we did. I had thought Menoke would still have Jack's tipi, and that after my bold asking, we could retreat to it and let the request simmer. But then Jack had explained to me that a tipi required a man to hunt to support it. A widow fell back on her family, as Menoke had done, and he was feeding her. We would have to stay here. This was even more awkward than I thought. Asimoni ate and slept but never again looked me in the eye all that evening.

When I woke in the morning, White Coyote, or *Evokomo Okohome* as I should call him in his own language, and Asimoni were gone. Deer Kicks, his wife, or *Vao'tseva O'hoh'ta'xe*, in Cheyenne, and Menoke were making a buffalo meat stew. They talked to each other freely in Cheyenne. When Menoke saw me awake, she spoke to me and gestured for me to come over to that other side of the tipi and sit and eat, which I did. When I was finished, we went outside to the camp, which was moving with morning chores. Women were working jobs around camp or taking bags and sticks and heading out to collect roots and berries. Boys were down amongst the herd, managing the horses. Men were walking down to the herd, mounting horses and maybe ten of them rode off to the southeast with bows, probably on a buffalo hunt.

Menoke walked me over to the area behind *Evokomo Okohome's* lodge and I could see there were ten long lodge poles stacked, with a buffalo hide cover. I recognized a bit of the design on the cover: this was Jack's tipi. We went about setting it up next to *Evokomo Okohome's* lodge, and as we worked, I would point at things and ask, "*Henova'eto?*" a phrase I had much practiced in St. Louis, meaning, "What is it?" Menoke seemed pleased that I was trying and gave me Cheyenne words for all the pieces of the lodge as we put it up, as well as words for pull or lift up. It was quite a lesson. I repeated every word she gave me until she seemed satisfied with my pronunciation.

But I knew the situation needed a good-faith measure on my part and right away. Once the exterior was up, I signed to my mother, "I go hunt return." She smiled and went on with furnishing the interior. I fetched my Hawken rifle and my possibles from the first tipi lodge and walked down to the horse herd, where the boys smiled and chattered at me. I walked amongst the horses till I found my favorite pinto mare. Jack had bought her for me and told me not to name her in case I had to eat her, but I couldn't help it. I had begun to think of her as "Jane" and couldn't stop. Don't ask me why she was Jane, because even today I couldn't explain it. Jane snorted when I walked up, I suppose because of seeing my familiar face. I stroked her head for a while and talked to her before leaping up on her bareback. I had a saddle for her that I bought in St. Louis, but I had become accustomed to riding the Indian way, bareback.

I rode off southwest, up the river, watching the horizon for at least two hours, hoping that I'd see something. Like before, you get clear of the settlements and you can smell the savory smell of the grass, and hear the wind singing to you like it was a person. I laughed to myself in contentment and rode on across my old friend, the open plains. But I had learned patience in hunting from Jack and didn't panic when I saw nothing but a distant buffalo herd running. About an hour after midday, I saw a herd of pronghorn antelopes to the south. I slowly rode to the west further, testing the wind, making sure that when I tacked back toward the antelopes that the wind was in my face. If the wind was moving and I could feel it on my back, then I had failed, for the antelopes would smell me and run off. I waited a long time for the wind to be right. When it was pretty clear it was going southwest, upstream, away from the village, I started to close the distance between myself and the antelopes. This part of the hunt took at least another two hours and the day was getting late when I knew the wind was right. I rode up to the herd slowly and was lucky to find a small rise between me and them and pretty close to the herd. I dismounted Jane and told her to wait there. Jane was a smart horse and I didn't have to stake her. She fell to eating grass and ignored me.

I crouched down and got up to the top of the rise on my belly. The wind was still in my face and I thanked God that it was so. The Hawken was loaded. I sighted in on the nearest buck, out in front of me maybe 50 yards. I was a little worried that firing into the wind on this long shot might take some velocity off my round. But that couldn't be helped.

I squeezed off the shot and thank God, the buck went down as the rest of the herd ran off. Three hours later I rode into camp singing my Irish song with the buck over Jane's withers. The boys danced around me and the men shouted "*Ha hou!*" in celebration of a successful day's hunting. I was so relieved. All my hopes rested on being a hunter the Cheyenne could believe in.

Menoke, my mother, came out of Jack's tipi as I rode up and gave out a trilling cry I've heard Indian women give when they celebrate. I felt so good.

Really, that may have been one of the best moments of this long life of mine. She took the antelope from me and set to work in the messy business of cleaning and cutting. I took Jane back to the herd and gave her to the boys, and then returned to the lodge. I was nervous. I had staked so much on this native bride. But I was odd to these Cheyenne: white, scarred, and I couldn't speak. I could think of nothing else to do. Apparently, the long day's hunt and my edginess were exhausting enough that I fell asleep on the robes in Jack's now-furnished tipi lodge.

When I woke, Menoke was setting up a feast. I figured that we had guests and I would get an answer, so I took my small knife and hand mirror and went down to the river bank and shaved my chin and the right side of my face. Over all the years I lived in the mountains and on the plains, I have always shaved. Most trappers did not, and were even proud of their beards. But Indian men grow little facial hair and shave what they do grow. It was to Cheyenne men, in part, a gesture of respect. The other reason was that the scarring was so bad on the left side of my face that only a couple of stray hairs grew there, so if I did grow a beard, it would only be on the right side. And that would have been odd-looking. So, in all my long years, I have never grown a beard.

When I came back, Menoke had put on her best dress with the bits of colored shells and the dyed upper part. She pointed for me to sit at the center of the back, opposite the door. This was an odd sensation for me. That was Jack's place, the place of the master of the lodge. But Jack was gone. And in that moment I felt a pang of loss as I sat down in his place.

Fortunately, when White Coyote stepped through the opening and stepped politely to the right, I knew what to do, as Jack had taught me. I gestured him to sit on my left, the place of honor. This he did and Deer Kicks, and Spirit—Asimoni, followed. Now here my Lisa is getting after me not to be confusing and using the Cheyenne name and then the name in English. So, we have decided that I will remain with the English versions of the Cheyenne names just to be clear. So, my dear Asimoni will be Spirit, and my mother, Menoke, will be Willow, which is what her name meant in English.

Anyway, so Willow served the antelope steaks and everyone ate. She did a lot of talking and White Coyote nodded to me and said something that sounded like a compliment. I guessed he was pleased that my first hunt with the tribe had brought in game. Spirit, who was the center of all this, sat by her mother eating and never once looked up at me. I learned years later that this was the Cheyenne idea of modesty and emotional control. At the time, I was just worried about how scared she was, and that was probably true as well. God knows I was scared out of my mind as I sat there in Jack's place, trying to be calm and play the master of the lodge.

When most of the eating was done and my nervousness had grown to the point that I am sure I was sweating, heavily, White Coyote signed to me that he had spoken with Spirit and that she had agreed to be my wife. He thanked me for the gift of ten horses and accepted them. There was a little more talk and then he signed to me that she would come tomorrow. Then they rose, thanked me, and left. Willow was overjoyed and said a hundred things to me, none of which I could make out. And out of nowhere, tears came to my eyes. She stopped and asked me a question, looking perplexed. But all this had brought Jack back to me and I missed him dreadfully and without warning. I made signs for pain and for Jack's Cheyenne name, Lost in Snow, pointing to my heart. A sadness crossed her face too. And she pointed to herself and nodded. We both missed him painfully, and no language barrier concealed it.

Still, now that the lodge was quiet and the guests gone, I was rather stunned. I had done it. A thousand ways for this to go wrong and it had gone right. How often does that happen in this life? Jack would have been proud of me, I just know it.

In the morning, mother, Willow, was busy setting up the sleeping robes in a different fashion after breakfast. Hers were moved to the right side, the guest side coming in the entrance. Mine were moved to the far opposite side, the family side, and the robes doubled. And this brings me to an interesting point about love and being social in the Cheyenne world. Lots of Cheyenne rules and ways are based on the simple fact that you are living in a buffalo skin lodge maybe 15 feet in diameter, and you are there in winter all day and all night for days on end. It is mighty easy to get on someone's nerves. So, the Cheyenne and other plains peoples build social walls inside their minds and with their behavior, while in their lodges. There are no bedrooms or honeymoon suites in Cheyenne homes. You learn to roll over, go to sleep and ignore couples practicing the way of a man and a woman together. This will strike white men as very odd, but then I have noticed that white society is far too worried about sex in one way or another.

At this time, of course, what little I knew about it was from spying through whore-house windows in St. Louis as a boy with Bill Robinson. I had some idea how things worked. I didn't know what the Cheyenne would expect. And frankly, I was still waiting for some sort of wedding ceremony, in spite of what Jack told me. But there wasn't any ceremony. When White Coyote accepted the ten horses from me at the feast in Jack's lodge, the marriage was official. I went out hunting again that day just to do something to let out all my nervous energy. I followed the party of buffalo hunters from my village and watched at a distance as they ran down an old cow and killed her from horseback with arrows. It was pretty skillful riding, I had to admit, and it kept me distracted. I came home to Jack 's tipi about mid afternoon and Willow was cooking fresh antelope from yesterday's kill. As she cooked we went through all the words for all the things in the lodge, me pointing, she telling me the Cheyenne word, and me repeating it several times until she was satisfied with my pronunciation. So I didn't know what to expect when suddenly Spirit appeared in the doorway, in her finest beaded dress, looking frightened.

To my surprise, Willow did not speak to her but looked at me. I had at least the presence of mind to point to the spot next to me on my right, as I realized that she was now family. She carried a rolled bundle of buckskins, which turned out to be all her things and her other dresses. She was moving in. It got very quiet and I couldn't understand why Willow hardly looked at her and did not speak to her. I later learned that one of the Cheyenne taboos is that a mother-in-law does not speak to a daughter-in-law, nor the other way around, this being one of the major friction points in any family. There was a way to lift the taboo if everyone was willing, and when I found this out some six months later, I asked for the ceremony that lifted the taboo. But the air in the lodge was charged with unspoken energy.

Imagine my surprise when Willow said good night to me, tamped down the fire, rolled up in her robes and was soon asleep. I looked at Spirit, sitting next to me, so beautiful. To my surprise, she reached down to her hem, pulled her dress up over her head and crawled under my buffalo robes. I figured I at least needed to take off my deerskin shirt and crawled in next to her. Under the blankets I could see the beauty of her brown skin and her rounded breasts. My own desires burst into flame. But I realized she was trembling. And something more came as a surprise to me. Cheyenne women wear a soft rope chastity belt over their privates. I could see Spirit's. She was looking at me and I suppose waiting for me to take it off and do my business as a husband had a right to do. But I loved this girl and she was afraid. My desires would wait, I told myself. I wrapped my arms around her and realized she was crying. I held her and we slept that way till morning.

I woke and both women were working, fetching water, preparing food. But it struck me odd, for Willow would wait for Spirit to direct her. But since they did not speak to each other, Willow would speak to me in Cheyenne, asking some question I couldn't possibly understand. Then Spirit would do the same back, addressing the answer to me. And Willow would respond by going to fetch water or to turn the meat on the fire, or whatever was required. I did not understand the mother-in-law to daughter-in-law taboo and didn't for some time. It all seemed comic to me, but life went on.

After breakfast I looked at Spirit and signed "I return." I went out with both my Hawken rifles. I had a .30 as well as a .50, and I thought today I was going for buffalo. The .50 was the better gun, but it has quite a kick, and you want to be solidly behind it. And I was thinking that if I was going to try to take down a buffalo, I didn't want the .50 to buck out of my hands at a high speed gallop. So I loaded up the .30. Also, I took my saddle down and put it on Jane. It had two scabbards, one on each side where you could keep a rifle, and I figured that running with buffalo, my saddle riding was a lot more stable than my bareback.

As I rode out, I found that five young hunters had seen me heading to the horses with two rifles and were interested enough to grab their own horses and follow me. I made a hand gesture, a beckoning, inviting them along. They laughed and rode up beside me. I made the sign for "buffalo." One warrior pointed to the east-northeast and we trotted out that way for a while. Finding no herds that way, I decided to try south and they followed. Nothing. By this time it was late afternoon. I turned west and started back toward the camp when we all heard a rumbling to the south and west. I squeezed into a canter and we all followed the sound. It turned out to be a small herd, only a hundred or so animals. I kicked up to a gallop and Jane took me directly into the herd. I came up on the right side, trying to not eat so much dust. I had the .30 in my hands, primed and ready.

My companions worked mostly the other side of the herd with their bows and I saw a bull go down. I had come up by a large cow and she was starting to pull away. All this was a trick of balance, and dangerous. An ounce of weight here and an ounce of weight there was the difference between getting a kill, or falling under the hooves to be trampled to death. I leaned way over with the .30, balancing and counting on having to compensate for the kick of the rifle. I fired into the cow's head where I thought the brain would be and just inches away. The kick was considerable, but it helped me center my weight back up over Jane's withers. The cow vanished and I veered off to the right, slowing and turning back. When I reined Jane to a halt, there was the cow dead on the prairie. I dismounted and did what Jack had taught me last summer.

You see, the Cheyenne and most Indians believe that no animal is stupid enough to ever get caught. They offer themselves to the hunter. It is a gift. So a hunter stops and thanks the animal for the sacrifice. I knelt down, still holding the .30 in my hand and thanked this buffalo. I sure hoped she understood English. The other hunters rode up to where I was and seeing I had a kill, they let out sharp yips and shouts of triumph. One of them rode back to the village. The rest of us got to the messy business of cutting, and cleaning, and hauling. Some women rode out from the village to aid with the work, though I made sure to do as much as I was able to do. I had done this with Jack last summer and was able to get a lot of the animal skinned before the old women, laughing at me, shooed me away so that they could cut the rest correctly. The whole village would share the meat and everything was done properly and fairly. It was close to dark when the products of the buffalo I'd brought down and the one the other warrior had brought down were finally hauled into camp. There was a dance where one of the warriors danced with a buffalo head mask over his head, lots of shouting, laughing, telling of what must have been jokes, and the pounding of the drums. We all ate till we could eat no more, and Spirit sat on my right side, holding my hand and giving me looks of pride.

That night under the robes, Spirit pulled off her dress again. This time she wasn't trembling, and she looked at me expectantly. But I still didn't just want to take off her chastity belt. I pulled my hands up to where she could see them and tried signing "me no take you give." A confused look crossed her face, and I felt a damn fool. My sign vocabulary was limited, and I wasn't even sure she knew much hand language.

But I remembered the hushed up story in my family, how my mother was raped in St. Louis not long after my natural father abandoned us. Maybe that's why I responded so forcefully when Ol' Morton was raping that Indian girl. I hated rape. I hated the idea of anything being forced from a woman. I didn't want to take anything from Spirit. She had to freely give it to me. I could see on Spirit's face that she was working all this out in her mind and I could see when it finally hit her. Understanding bloomed in her face like a flower. Her eyes opened wider. I would not force her to do anything she did not want. She didn't say anything but it washed over her like a wave. And then there was such a look of love and appreciation on her face. She kissed me several times, more and more passionately. Somehow, this kindness I was giving her touched her heart and broke all the final fear and ice. She slipped the chastity belt off past her knees and kissed and caressed me and we didn't need no teachers to figure out what to do next. It was beyond beautiful. I fell asleep so happy.

Now before Lisa finishes this chapter, I need to say something about what she read back to me. I don't want no fool to think that I'm telling lies or making the lives of the "noble savages" of the Plains sound high and righteous, or some other horsecrap like that. In my 84 years I've found that men of all races are good and bad in about the same proportion. The white people surely treated my Cheyenne relations badly, but that is just human. There ain't too many good guys and bad guys here like my grandson reads me in those fool dime store novels he collects about the Old West. It was not like that. The only purely evil man I ever met was John Chivington, but I'll save that story for later.

Sure, there were some wonderful things about living in the old way of freedom with the Cheyenne. And though every warrior was as about as free a man as God could have created, you did not hear them go on and on talking about it. I never heard any Cheyenne loudly demanding his or her rights. And a warrior was a hunter, and he expected to share his catch with the whole village. There wasn't much difference between rich and poor except in how many horses you owned. If there was food, all shared. Nobody got uppity about their rights and their property.

On the other hand, it was an incredibly hard life. Lots of times the village went for weeks without a successful hunt. And Crow and Pawnee not only stole horses, but could attack at almost any moment. Most Cheyenne men expected to die in battle. Getting old was a rare thing. That was why when we did catch food, there was celebration and sharing. Life was too hard not to care about or depend on your neighbor. I guess they had the advantage of living in small enough villages that every man and woman and child knew each other, and there was no room for being indifferent. Like I say, just staying alive with all your neighbors to help was a trick. Bringing down even one buffalo was an affirmation of life. Lisa gave me that last phrase because I could not think of the right way to say it. For the Cheyenne, starving was normal and feasting a rare and wonderful moment of joy. And the Cheyenne at this time, before the dark times came, were good at living with joy. It was not to last.

4.

Fall Hunt and First Child

1833–1834

I STAYED ALMOST TWO months more, and by the time I was ready to ride west as I had promised Henry Frapp, my Cheyenne was good enough that I could say most of the things I wanted and understand anything told me, if that is, they didn't talk too fast. I found myself often asking people to say things again more slowly. But I spoke Cheyenne. Lisa wants me to say here that from now on, I will narrate what my Cheyenne kin said in the English language, even though they were actually talking in Cheyenne. It will keep things from being too confusing for the reader.

But the fact that I now understood that my hunting justified the tipi worried me. I asked White Coyote about this and he told me not to worry, that he would keep my mother and wife fed while I was gone. I could see why Jack had loved this Cheyenne man; he was one of the smartest and kindest human beings I have ever known. And I am proud that he was my father-in-law. Deer Kicks, my mother-in-law, would smile at me, which is about as far as we got. We weren't allowed to speak to each other. But she must have been satisfied that I was treating her daughter well.

So, as I got my gear ready for the ride to the Green River, I felt a sadness. Spirit sensed it and told me that she understood why I must go, that I had promised. My mother, Willow, said the same. Many of the boys in the mountains had native brides and did this sort of thing all the time. Still, I felt uneasy. I compensated a little by bringing down a big buffalo bull two days before I left and Willow was able to jerk a large portion of our share, meaning that my women would be able to eat for a month after I was gone. I told myself I was doing it to earn money for my family, but I didn't see what a Cheyenne needed money for. I reckon I needed it for shot and powder and other gear, but I wondered if there wasn't a better way to obtain those things.

But the real kicker was when Spirit, with her hand on her belly told me, "Red Hair, husband. I am with child. You will be a father soon." If she'd hit me with a tree limb, I couldn't have been more stunned. I was 16 years old by then, but older in experience, and in the eyes of white people I was still just a boy. The Cheyenne saw you as a man or a woman when you proved you could act like one, and did not remember birthdays, and kept little track of the years they'd lived.

All this was swimming around my head as I looked back over my shoulder at the village disappearing to the east behind me and Spirit and Willow watching me vanish into the prairie. I cut north cross country and picked up the North Platte west of Horse Creek. There wasn't much sign on the trail. Things had been quiet between the Crow and my people for a time. Lisa is after me here again to explain that "sign" is what trappers called tracks and broken twigs and other indications on the ground that something living had passed by. We became very good at reading sign. The alternative was to blunder into a hostile war party and get scalped, or to frighten away game by stumbling on them accidentally, and end up starving. By this time, with Jack's teaching and my experience since, I was pretty sharp at reading sign.

I followed the Sweetwater down to the Green and rode south through the Flaming Gorge, coming into the eastern reaches of the Uintahs about September 25th.

In case you're wondering why I took the long way around instead of riding due west, what most modern people don't realize what with roads and railroads going in straight lines from one place to another, in the old days on the Plains, water was scarce. Some folks called the plains the "Great American Desert", though actually that's a better name for the country between the Salt Lake and the Sierra Nevada mountains. Rivers were the first roads. They meant you didn't have to carry water skins. Dry camping and crossing between rivers was dangerous and tricky. Plus, if you knew where a river went, it was hard to get lost in dry country. And lastly, animals too stayed near rivers, where the grass was lusher and they could drink. So the hunting was better. And once you were in the mountains, not only were river valleys the only roads, but if you were hunting beaver, you would find them nowhere else.

As I rode west, day after day, I was surprised how much the solitude of these days alone bothered me. This was something I used to not mind quite so much. I had become accustomed to living in a village full of almost 200 people. I was changing. And I began to doubt again whether brigade trapping and leaving my Cheyenne family was such a good idea. But I also realized that my best days in the mountains had always been in the company of Jack and Charette, or Sir William and Doc Ben. I was lonesome. But that's the curse of the boys that live in the mountains. And I told myself brigade trapping was safer than free-trapping, which was certainly true. Plus, it paid no matter how many beaver you caught, which to my mind was important. as the trade was going away. Over a year later, I heard that the other RMF brigade that had gone north, had been robbed by the Crow. So, the safety even in brigades, was not a sure bet.

All these things were on my mind as I left the Flaming Gorge behind and followed the Green River south around the eastern edge of the Uintahs, a set of mountains I knew well. I found sign of the trapping brigade and followed it with ease into Henry Frapp's camp on 29 September, 1833. There were about 20 of us, working south methodically down the Green River and up any tributaries for a ways, without going too far up big rivers like the Yampa. It's cold work. You spend the day wading in cold water setting traps and recovering traps with dead beaver in them, then skinning the animals and treating the skins so they will not rot. Then they are bundled into *pleus*, or packs of beaver fur a couple of feet thick. Jack and Charette had taught me this work well last season and I knew it well, but just as Jack and I had discovered last year, the beaver were few and far between and most of our traps lay empty.

One of the few amusements was a member of our party, a trapper by the name of Bill Williams. He was tall and skinny with red hair like mine and a full beard. He walked in a jerky fashion, like his legs didn't quite work. He didn't talk much to anyone, and for people as unfriendly as fur trappers, and we do shine at being unfriendly, Bill Williams was even more unfriendly. In camp everyone called him "Ol' Solitaire." The boys in camp told me he had been a preacher to the Osage Indians and "went renegade". That was the first time I heard that term, but not the last. He had married an Osage, but she had died. He went west to trap and trade and then married a Ute, the tribe whose country we were now in. He'd been a guide to the military and was rumored to steal horses in California, drive them into the mountains and sell them. He was also rumored to have eaten one of his wives when they were starving, trapped in a blizzard, and she'd died before him, though I did not credit that rumor. He kept to himself, but there was more pain and sorrow in his look than the kind of cruelty I had already seen in the looks of some other men. Maybe he was a little crazy, but I began to wonder if all of us up here weren't a little crazy. The oddest thing I found about him was the way he shot his Hawken rifle. He didn't steady his rifle and squeeze off his shot like most folk. Instead, he'd point it generally in the direction he was aiming, the rifle swaying back and forth. Then he'd pull the trigger at the right moment. Somehow he always hit what he was aiming for.

But my moment came in a conversation, like many, after a hard day wading in cold water to check mostly empty traps. Old Joe Charly looked at me, having discussed Bill Williams and his Indian wives. "I hear, Plunkett, you've got an injun woman."

"That's right."

"Crow?"

"Cheyenne," I said, offering little.

"Wagh, Cheyenne. They is friendly critters now, but don't you get on the wrong side of them. They are fine warriors, and dangerous. Someday they're going to be as much trouble as the Sioux or the Blackfeet."

I shouldn't have said it, but it slipped out before I thought, "We won't be no trouble if people don't trouble us."

"Wagh! 'We'? Us? Sounds like you've gone renegade, Plunkett."

I just laughed. Renegade. To be someone who has betrayed their own people and gone over to the other side. Well, maybe that was beginning to happen.

"Well," Charly went on, "I hope ol' Cheyenne Sam here don't lift my topknot." I laughed, not because it was funny, but because they did, and I wanted to let up the tension. And that is how I got my nickname. Lisa tells me to explain here that "topknot" was mountain slang for your scalp. Then Will Coleman, a younger trapper just up from St. Louis this year added, "Maybe you should look up Will and Charles Bent, and their partner, Ceran St. Vrain. I hear tell they're down on the Arkansas, trading with the Cheyenne and the Arapaho."

"Thank you kindly," I replied. "I just may head on down there."

I don't remember the rest of the conversation, but it's not important. The conversation went on about other topics, since my native wife was now boring to them, and the favorite topic was always that the beaver were getting scarce and the trade was going. We seemed to talk about little else in the end.

So, when it started getting cold in the second week of November, I told Henry Frapp I'd be pulling out, and that I wouldn't be back in the spring. I didn't see the point. They could not afford to pay us if we couldn't catch enough beaver, and Frapp knew I understood that, and simply nodded. By this time, we had started working our way east up the Grand River, (Lisa reminds me that it's now called the Colorado River) and were preparing to hole up for the winter. Frapp and ol' Bill Williams himself gave me directions how to go straight to the Platte to find my Cheyenne village. I packed up all my gear on Jane, mounted up, looked at the boys and said, "Watch yer topknot, y'all."

"Watch yourn," they politely replied, and I reined Jane upriver and rode off. That was the last time I worked for the Rocky Mountain Fur Company. But it was no matter. They went under at the rendezvous the following summer.

I followed the north bank of the Grand east-northeast up into the Rockies for about two weeks till I was at the headwaters. There I went north over a very high pass and found a stream running downhill on the other side to the north-northeast, building another river, which Bill Williams had called the Cache de la Poudre. Lisa wants me to translate that name from the French, which was still the second language up in the mountains. A cache is a storage place, usually in a cave or dug into the ground, or a skin bag slung from a tree limb. And poudre is French for powder. Some French trader must have buried some of his powder along this river and that's how it got its name.

This river wound down eastward out of the mountains and to the Platte, sure enough. It was beginning to snow when I reached the village site and found it deserted. The sign on the ground showed that the village had moved southwest, up the South Platte, beyond where the Cache de la Poudre entered, and toward the mountains. This made sense, since it was probably less windy and not as cold right up against the Front Range, and the hunting would be better since our hunters could hunt both the Plains and the foothills of the mountains through the long winter. I followed the trail and was singing myself into the village three days later. And I'm pleased to tell you that I had learned the proper enter-the-village song in Cheyenne and didn't have to sing an Irish ballad like before. This new site was a good village site and years later I realized that the open prairie where we camped, twenty years after that became the north side of what was to become the City of Denver.

I cannot tell you how glad I was to hug my mother and my wife, who was already very pregnant and walking off balance due to the roundness of her belly. Spirit enjoyed it when I put my hand on her belly and felt the baby kick inside. Holding her close to me at night and feeling the baby in her womb is one of the deepest and most sacred memories I have all these long years. This was also the time when White Coyote tactfully told me about the mother-in-law taboo and suggested that I could request the lifting of it. I did so immediately, and my home became much easier, since Willow and Spirit had always got along well. They no longer had to resort to the fiction of talking to me when they meant to talk to each other.

I told them that the work with the Rocky Mountain Fur Company was no good anymore and I would not be leaving for the spring hunt. I wanted to be home to greet my first child. They were both glad, but it was Willow who told me that this was wise. Then I asked her if she had heard about other *ve'hoe*, that is, white men, trading along the river to the south of us.

Willow told me, "Yes, we have heard that the white men trade on the river to the south with White Thunder's village. My son, we could go there if you wished, and you could work with the white men and still have your family around you."

"You mean leave our village?" I asked, a little startled at the suggestion.

Both of my women laughed at me. Willow told me, "We do not have to stay in any one village, and my brother will understand. Our tribe has about fifteen villages spread out between the Flint Arrow Point River to the south and the river in the north, the River of Gun Powder. We do not camp as a tribe except once a year at the Medicine Lodge dance. This year you will see it. You can meet White Thunder then. For the tribe is to meet here, on the Fat River, once the mid-summer moon comes. You will see. His village is one of the Hevataniu Band villages. Our village here is the one village of the Ivistsinihpah Band, who were my mother's people. But we can go to any village you wish."

Lisa is after me here to point out that for the Cheyenne, unlike white people, descent was traced through the mother. So, when I married Spirit, I married into the Ivistsinihpah Band of the Cheyenne nation. I found out that there are ten bands, from the Hevataniu, or Hairy Rope Band to the south, to the Omissis, the Eater Band far to the north, closest to the Crow.

"Why do we only meet once a year?" I asked, wondering why a tribe would split itself and risk attack weakened by division.

Spirit shook her head at my ignorance, "Surely, Husband, you must know that all the horses of our nation would soon eat up all the grass in a single place and all our hunters destroy all the game. We are a great nation, and we cannot live together all the time or the land could not support us."

Willow and Spirit had much work to do over the months to fix my ignorance, but they undertook the task with diligence. There was much snow that winter of '33-'34 and we spent lots of time together, the three of us, in Jack's lodge. But I was happy. It was far better than sleeping in the open under tree branches like most of my fellow trappers were doing. And I was out hunting any day that the snow wasn't coming down in buckets. Willow brought out Jack's old snowshoes and I felt honored to wear them. I found the foothills and the shallow canyons held deer, so I went there most often.

Lisa tells me that I need to mention the people in the village more. I made five fast friends, that first day that I went to hunt that buffalo, waiting to hear if Spirit might be my wife. If you recall, I told you that five warriors followed me and rejoiced when I brought down that cow. We started hunting together regularly once I learned to talk in Cheyenne. Their names were Laughs at Night, Four Thunders, Many Horses, Red Mountain, and Stands to the Left. Cheyenne names are always practical, and in each case, the name came as a result of a vision or something they did or something distinct about them. That's why I was Red Hair when I lived with my Cheyennes. I could have just as easily been "Scarred Face" or "One Ear", since that bear ripped up the left side of my face and pretty much took all of my left ear that stuck out above the skull.

But I should not have named them. Lisa knows why—it is against tradition to name the dead. But I will break Cheyenne taboo and name them anyway. They were the best friends a man could ever have and I name them to honor them. And if their spirits come to haunt me and hover about me, so be it. I welcome seeing them in any form. And all names are actually like this; we white people have simply forgotten what our names mean and choose names for our children mainly for the sound. Grandfather once told me my name, Samuel, means "God has heard me." I reckon God has heard me, because I have been howling out prayers for over 80 years now.

Anyway, me and my hunting friends worked the foothills of the Rockies all that winter and spring and brought home plenty of game, thank God. That is never a given. Starvation was pretty normal to the Cheyenne. And on the 12th day of March I came into my lodge after a long two-day hunt, and found Willow hovering over Spirit, who looked exhausted, lying in our robes. But in my wife's arms lay a little baby girl, wrapped in a soft, deerhide robe. This was my first child, and I named her twice. I named her after my birth mother, and for the meadowlarks that sing on the prairie. So she had an English first name, a Cheyenne name, and an Irish last name. That's a mouthful for such a little girl, but I didn't care. She was Kathleen, Yellow Bird, which in Cheyenne is *Ve'kesheovast,* Plunkett. I thought of her as Meadowlark, which in Cheyenne is "yellow bird." I couldn't wait to hold her. It was maybe the most joy I have ever felt.

5.

My Last Rendezvous and My First Horse Raid

1834

Spring came late that year, leaving lots of wet, muddy snowfalls that killed the first flowers. Spirit went around with my little daughter in her cradle-board on her back. It was the sweetest thing. With the last snows, the hunting became easier and not so cold. My five friends and I went out and brought in quite a lot of game. But preying on my mind was Rendezvous. I did not really want to go. Plus, I knew Ol' Morton and Powers might be looking for me to even the score. I figured I could probably take them, one at a time, but I didn't really want to have to kill anyone. And Powers would probably bring two or three to help him, being the coward that he was.

I decided to share these thoughts with Willow and my wife. Willow asked why I felt I had to go at all. I explained that Rocky Mountain Fur Company owed me for the fall work, which would be paid in powder and shot and other gear I needed in the mountains. I finally decided I would go in just when things were starting, try and get my pay in the morning when most of the boys are sleeping off their drunks, and clear out minutes after arriving. I had seen two Rendezvous now and I really didn't care to stay for another one.

So, around the end of May I rode north up the Front Range, going creek to creek, like climbing a ladder. Once I found the North Platte, I took it northwest the usual way till I found the Sweetwater and cut cross country to the Green River. Going down the Green I found the Rendezvous on about

June 18 at Ham's Fork. It was near end of day when I saw it so I rode back into some trees several miles north and camped as quietly as I could, making no fire. I was pretty sure no one had seen me. I was wrong.

In the morning I got up at sunrise, broke camp and mounted up on Jane. I rode southeast till I picked up the Green and rode into camp as a few fellows were cooking bacon, leaving smoke plumes from their cook fires, but mostly all was quiet. Milton was at his counter made of boards and barrels as usual and a couple of fellows I knew, Billy Fontenelle, and Saul Jacobs, were sitting behind him doing the job I had done last summer. I dismounted and walked up.

"How you doing, Milton?"

"Pretty poorly, Cheyenne Sam," he answered. I think I startled to hear my nickname, but that was the moment I realized the name had stuck. "But I won't bore you with my troubles. I see you have no *pleus*, so you probably want to settle up for the fall hunt."

"Yessir."

He looked through the big accounts book that I had got to know so well. "Well, it's about $10. What will you have?"

"Gimme a couple of strings of beads and two mirrors and split the rest between powder and shot," I told him.

"Ah, foofuraw for the little woman," he smiled. Like I had done the summer before, Billy and Saul dug out the foofuraw, powder and shot and delivered it up on the boards.

"You hear about your pap?"

"Jack's gone under," I answered. "You know that."

"No, I mean Richard Plunkett."

"No, I don't have no dealings with him."

"And you never will. Gone beaver. Blackfeet killed him last fall in the Bitterroot Valley, took his scalp. Damn fool was trapping by hisself in Blackfoot country. Thought you'd want to know."

I nodded, I think, feeling more emotion than I cared to about the man who had ruined much of my young life. "Thanks for that, Milton. Hope things go better with you."

"Oh, I'll survive if I don't murder my damned brother."

"How do you reckon?" I couldn't help but ask.

"The son of a bitch went and called in all our debt because we were trying to get around him. Rocky Mountain Fur is gone under. We had to sell out to American Fur and those boys. These boards won't be here next year."

"Sorry to hear. You'll find something."

"Oh, I will. But it will be a while before I say two words again to Billy. You watch your topknot, Cheyenne Sam."

"Watch yourn, Milton," I replied politely, and taking my wares and packing them onto Jane's saddle I rode out north of the camp in the early morning, figuring I'd got out clean, just like I planned. Lord, I was wrong. My first night's camp was on the Sweetwater. They struck in the morning, just as I was cooking up some venison. They came out of some cottonwood trees from downstream, crawling up close, then standing up about thirty yards away. It was Morton and Powers both and before I heard them, they both had their Hawken rifles aimed at my chest.

"Wall, Plunkett," Ol' Morton laughed. "I'm figuring to scalp you and cut off your manhood to boot. Then I'll kill you."

Powers laughed. I figured if I dove and they missed, I could get one of them before I went under. I was telling the Lord Jesus and His Mother that I would be seeing them soon in the silence of my mind. My hand was on my Green River knife in the scabbard at the back of my belt. There were a tense few seconds and then a *whick! whick*! sound. An arrow went through each of their throats and their eyes opened wide in shock. Blood ran down, dark, rich, and red from the arrow wounds. Powers briefly made a gurgling sound, and they both toppled over in a couple of heaps.

"What the hell?" I gasped.

Slowly, five Cheyenne warriors stood up from the grass to my right. It was Laughs at Night, Four Thunders, Many Horses, Red Mountain, and Stands to the Left, my hunting friends. Laughs at Night walked up to me and said, "Red Hair, you are so careless sometimes. I saw these two white men follow you yesterday. Why didn't you?" Meanwhile my other friends went over to the corpses and collected their Hawken rifles, shot, and powder. Four Thunders asked me, "Red Hair, will you teach me how to use this thing?"

"Gladly, my friend," I said, still in shock.

Then Four Thunders and Many Horses reached down with their knives and scalped Morton and Powers. Many Horses claimed the second Hawken rifle, its shot and powder. I can't say I care for scalping, white or Indian—and yes, the white men I knew did as much or more of it—but I felt only gratitude for these friends that had just saved my life.

"Why did you follow me?" I had to ask.

"Your mother asked us to," Red Mountain replied. "She was worried and it looks like she was right to be. We will teach you to be more alert. But now we are hungry and you have breakfast."

I invited them all to the fire and we made a small feast of the venison I had. It depleted my supply more than I had planned, but I knew with my five friends along we could find more, and I cannot put into words how glad I was to see them. I think this is the moment that I ceased to be white in my mind the first time. We were laughing and talking avidly in no time. Laughs at Night went and fetched their five horses from where they had staked them out of sight. We had a very merry feast and used up all my supplies, but I was only glad.

But then came the dirty work and following that, my even bigger surprise. Day was getting warm and the flies had found the two corpses. Red Mountain announced to me casually that I could keep Morton's and Power's two horses. Then I said,

"I reckon I should bury them." It seemed decent.

They all laughed at me. But you have to understand not only the Cheyenne world view, but the white American world view as well. In the white American mind, all Indians are barely human, uncivilized, heathen savages and worthy of being killed without a second thought. I have seen plenty of that over the long years. And even though Morton and Powers were two evil men, white Americans would assume they were Christian and deserved a Christian burial in spite of their sins. They were real, fully human people, unlike Indians. I had been raised that way.

In the Cheyenne mind there were three kinds of humans: there were Cheyenne; there were allies, like the Lakota and the Arapaho and a few white men, like Jack and me before we married into the tribe; and there were enemies. You didn't honor your enemy, in fact, you scalped them. And as for honoring the dead, the idea of digging a big hole and putting bodies in that hole was foreign to them. If you wished to honor the dead, you put them in a tree, and let the sun, and other natural forces pick the bones clean.

To them, in spite of my pale skin and red hair, I was a Cheyenne, and they had saved my life as a friend and fellow tribesman. My enemies were their enemies, and Morton and Powers deserved to be left to the vultures and wolves. I began to see all this while they watched me in amusement. "Well," I stammered in Cheyenne, "I don't want them here by the river."

"Red Hair," Stands to the Left reasoned with me, "If you leave the bodies like this, most white men will think the Arikaras or the Blackfeet killed them. If you bury them like a white man, they will all suspect you killed them and some of them will hunt you down."

It was a good point. All I had to do was erase my own sign, and the killings would never be traced to me or my friends. But it still bothered me. I said with some irritation "I don't want them found at all." Here again, Lisa asks me to remind the reader that rivers in those days were like roads and that except when hunting, or short-cutting between rivers, no one went into the wide open spaces where there was no water. That didn't happen till years later when white engineers and builders drew straight lines on maps between two points when building a highway or a railroad, and sent men out into the water-less lands to build them.

They all laughed again, jumped up from where we'd been eating and talking, and set to work. Laughs at Night and Red Mountain mounted up on their horses after each tying a rope around a corpse, covered in their saddles and unwanted gear, and they dragged them off to the south in the middle of the plains, probably a mile or two. They didn't come back for a while. Me and everyone else broke off a cottonwood branch and went all over the camp, erasing any sign that we'd even been there. And Lord, they knew how to do it. Many Horses doused and scattered all the remains of the fire. Then they worked backwards to the river bank so that when they had finished, they were standing in the water where they had put the horses in the shallows. Even I was impressed as to how much sign my friends destroyed. When Laughs at Night and Red Mountain came back, they took the lead lines of the two horses they said were now mine, and we mounted up in the shallows of the river, where they all stopped and turned to me.

I knew we were going to wade for a while to wipe out the last of our sign, but Many Horses looked at me and said, "Red Hair, you have put us to a lot of trouble because you are so careless. We thank you for the two rifles and the scalps of your enemies, but it is a shame to come this far north and not visit our old 'friends', the Crow, and relieve them of some of their extra horses."

Here again, I was caught between the white and Cheyenne worlds. In the white mind, Crows were friendlies and Cheyenne possibly hostile, and inter-tribal warfare was discouraged because it interfered with white trade on the plains. And we white men get mighty worked up when someone stands between us and a profit.

In the Cheyenne mind, the war with the Crow was ancient and honorable. And I was a Cheyenne warrior, expected to stand up for the tribe. I said in English, "Oh what the hell." They looked puzzled, so I switched to Cheyenne and said "Let's go!"

We rode about a day west in extreme caution, since once we crossed to the north bank of the Sweetwater, we were in the heart of the Crow country and liable to be attacked at any moment. And make no mistake, as a white, the Crows would not have attacked me alone. With a party of Cheyenne, I had surrendered any claim to neutrality, and my red scalp could soon be hanging from a Crow lodge pole if we weren't careful. Many Horses and Stands to the Left rode up with me and played a game, or maybe it was training. We'd be riding along hearing nothing but the wind on the grass and the hooves of our horses when one of them would say, "Did you see that rabbit?" or perhaps "What is behind us?" Half the time I couldn't answer the question, but as Jack had done, they kept after me and after a while I did see the rabbit hiding 30 yards ahead to our right and noticed a frozen herd of antelope behind us waiting to bolt if we approached them. My ability to see and notice had been decent by white standards. It got trained to a higher standard on that trip.

We found ourselves soon following the Wind River, though we kept it about a couple of hundred yards to our right to avoid being easily spotted. The river wound in and out of pine stands and open meadows where the Plains teased the edges of the splintered ice and rock slopes of the mountains to our south. About 20 miles westward, upriver, we saw the Teton range appear in the V created by the Wind River Range to our left and the Absaroka Mountains to our right. The southern reaches of the Absarokas came down from the north, near the sources of the Yellowstone and Snake rivers. After a while, a dark spot a mile or so ahead looked to be a thick grove of cottonwoods on the river, a prime place for a village. Smoke wafted from several places in the grove, a clear sign of cooking fires.

After going up to the river's edge and watering the horses in the river and filling waterskins, we headed back south from the river bank about a mile into the plains in the foothills of the Wind River Range, found a small, thick grove of pines and aspens, and waited out the rest of the afternoon mostly watching the smoke coming out of the trees to the west of us. I spent it teaching Four Thunders, Many Horses, with the other three watching, how to load and fire a Hawken rifle and hit what you are aiming at. They were rather excited to hear that they could take down a buffalo at 50 yards lying in the grass. I warned them about the serious kick and about pulling to the right by too vigorously pulling the trigger. We would have practiced firing off a few rounds, but this close to an enemy village, we dared not make any sound. I did promise Red Mountain, Laughs at Night, and Stands to the Left, that over the next year or two, in gratitude for their saving me, I would find a way to buy them Hawken rifles as well. Years later I learned that providing rifles to almost any Indians was highly illegal. I didn't give a damn.

When the sun went down over the mountains to the west, Stands to the Left and Red Mountain vanished into grasses in the long summer twilight, coming back an hour later. While we waited, Many Horses played the training game with me to see which of us spotted them coming back the soonest. I lost. I was going to have to get better at this. By this time it was fully dark. It was suggested by Red Mountain that I would stay in camp with the horses because I had the least experience and the biggest gun, should the Crow come at our horses while the others were gone. I was to stay on watch, make no fire, and guard our seven horses, being ready to ride as soon as my friends returned in whatever state. I agreed to this. I had no practice stealing horses.

But Many Horses wasn't having it. "Red Hair is a warrior of our people! He has a right to take a horse from the Crow as much as any of us."

I thought this was risky, but they all agreed and I figured I was along for the ride no matter what. Plus, though I doubted I'd be stealing any horses, I liked the idea of being in close to help them in case the alarm was raised and a swarm of Crow warriors came after us. So we walked our horses quietly in the dark the mile to the camp, taking the last hundred yards an inch at a time. We found a far part of the cottonwood grove away from the camp and tied off our horses there. Red Mountain had found the horse herd on the far side. At this point I asserted myself a little and said I would follow them and stay closer to our horses on this side of the village to cover their retreat if necessary. They nodded and accepted this. Then they vanished like smoke. Ok, I know that sounds like magic, but it sure seemed like it. They slipped down into the grass and behind trees and I just could not find them anymore and it took two seconds. Damn, I was impressed. I was going to have to build up my watching and stealth skills. I moved in further to the village and stopped behind a tree about 20 yards from the southernmost tipi.

It was a big tipi and there was a roan mare behind it, tied to a rope that went under the cover. I knew this meant that this horse was special, and I had a strong sense that I had seen this horse before. Men sometimes kept their best horses tied to their wrists in their sleep and just outside their lodges, instead of in the village herd. Stealing such a horse was highly risky. But then the line leading to the horse went slack. I heard a stirring in the lodge and got down low in the grass and tried to stop breathing. The front flap opened in the dark and instead of a Crow Indian, to my astonishment, Jim Beckwourth stepped out. It was hard to mistake him, even in this dark night with little moon. He was not armed, not even with his knife, but he hooked a left turn and started walking straight toward me. I swear to the Lord Jesus the hair on the back of my neck stood up. I did not want to kill him and firing my rifle would have set off every Crow warrior in the village. The Cheyenne did consider horse-taking as a form of war, which is why it wasn't stealing to them, but it was a non-violent form if done right. We fully intended to liberate a few horses and be gone like a wind without a trace. Getting into a full-on fight could only go badly for us.

As he came right up to my tree I froze and hoped. He shoved the front of his buckskin pants down and suddenly I felt that I was being showered with tiny droplets of foul-smelling water. He was peeing about a foot to my left, but I was getting the bounce off it. The other foul smell I caught was the intense whiskey on his breath. He muttered a few things I couldn't make out, packed up his manhood back in his pants and sort of staggered back to the front flap. I swear to this day it was Jim Beckwourth. I read his book what said he was east of the Mississippi about this time, but I was peed on by the great Jim Beckwourth.

Anyway, just by the door flap, he tripped over a tipi peg in the ground and fell over on his face. He did not get up for a long time. I was certain he was passed out and I hate to admit that I was rather provoked at him for making water on my head. If I hadn't been so provoked at him, I would have just cleared out of there. I moved as quietly as I could to the back of the lodge, picked up the horse's lead line, which was attached to nothing, the owner being passed out drunk in the dirt in front of the lodge, and began leading the roan back through the trees to the rendezvous point. When I got there, only Many Horses was not there and they all had new horses. They stood silently looking at me in wonder to see that I'd come away with a horse as well. I don't think they were expecting that. I had managed to surprise them. Many Horses showed up soon after with a pinto horse and taking multiple lead lines we began walking our own horses and our new acquisitions to the southeast, following the south bank of the Wind River. We went that way, slowly, soundlessly, for almost a mile, then we dropped into the shallows of the river to hide our sign, mounted, and picked up the pace considerably. We knew with daybreak the missing horses would be discovered and we would be pursued. It was part of the game. We did the same when the Crows stole horses from us. The trick was to get away with it. And I have to admit here now, though many will shake their heads at my lax morality, it was a hell of a lot of fun. So here we were, splashing south in the dark with a sliver of a moon, as fast as we could trot, each of us riding one horse and leading another, except for me who led three horses. Go figure that, will you. It almost made up for the fact that Jim Beckwourth pissed on my head.

6.

Medicine Lodge Dance

1834

So, THREE DAYS LATER we rode into the village, having eluded any Crow pursuit. The men of the village yipped and cried in celebration and the women did their trill. It was quite a parade as we rode through the heart of camp. I had a good laugh when I saw the astonished faces of my wife and mother looking at me leading three strange horses at the tail end of what had clearly been a successful horse raid on the Crow. I had just gone to cash my chit with Rocky Mountain Fur and ended up being the most successful horse-raider. Go figure. Makes no sense.

Back home I thanked Willow, my mother, for sending out my five friends to watch me. And I admitted to her that two white men had ambushed me good, and only my five friends had saved me. Spirit scolded me in a way that showed me how much she would miss me if I went and got myself killed. And we had some very tender moments over the following few days. Nevertheless, I met with my friends for a week or two and really worked on seeing and smelling and listening out on the prairie.

But that didn't last long because a miracle happened. At least it felt that way. We were camped on the Platte a day's ride east of the mountains. When I woke on the fifteenth day since I returned, a large camp of Cheyenne was setting up north and a little east of us, and not right on the river, which would have been normal. When I say large, I mean a full village like ours with maybe 200 people in it. The following day, two more villages showed up south and east of us. Willow explained to me that our village was to be the west village in a vast circle and that each band had a traditional place to set up in the circle, which would remain open to the east.

Cheyenne from other villages came to ours and were invited in to talk and feast. I thought I would stick out, but apparently Spider People, that is white men—sorry, but that's what Cheyenne called us white people—had married into other bands and I was not so unusual or remarkable as to get much attention from visiting Cheyennes. I was relieved to discover this, though by this time with weather and sun on my skin, I was almost as dark as any Cheyenne, and my Cheyenne language was fluent. Only my hair gave away the fact that my origin was from the Spider People.

Lisa tells me I have to explain this name. In old Cheyenne legends there are talking animals, like the stories of most tribes. For most tribes, Coyote is the creature who is always trying to trick other animals and always tripping himself up instead. But for the Cheyenne it is different. In Cheyenne legend, the spider is the creature that is always spinning webs trying to trap others, but she is so foolish that Spider always traps herself. Spider always tries to trick other creatures and always in the end gets her comeuppance. When White Coyote's grandfather and his people first met the Lewis and Clark expedition maybe 30 years before I married into the tribe, Americans seemed to them to be like the Spider in the story. That's how we got our name, "*vehoe*", which is the Cheyenne word for both 'spider' and 'white man.' French white people were considered a different breed and had a different name, "*mai-vehoe*", or "red Spiders." Those white Americans who came from the east are Spider People. I have to say that when this was all explained to me, I felt something like shame. The Cheyenne had seen through us the moment they met us. Sweet Medicine told them we were coming.

Now Lisa tells me that I have to explain Sweet Medicine. According to Cheyenne legend, long ago when they still lived along the north shore of Lake Superior with their friends, the Lakotas, a child was born to the tribe named Sweet Medicine. He had special powers and performed miracles. He taught them how to live proper like. And before he vanished, he warned them of the coming of the horse, and of the coming of the Spider People, who would all but destroy them. I don't know much about legends, and I ain't no priest, like Charette, but I sometimes have wondered if the Lord Jesus didn't show up not only in Israel, but other places on earth as well. I wonder if he wasn't Sweet Medicine. But what do I know? I do know that from what I read years later, when Lewis and Clark visited the Cheyenne on the Missouri River, there were a few hundred of them, living in a small village of mud domed houses and growing vast fields of corn. And I understood in part why they had left their lives as river-side farmers, gotten horses, and followed the buffalo herds out onto the plains in the last two generations. They had grown into a mighty people.

The circle of villages grew over the next few days. Where the river flowed to the northeast, the gap was left. So, if you'd been on a mountain and looked down at the vast Cheyenne camp, it would look like the letter C with the opening on the east where the South Platte flowed out. Between our village and the Omissis and Hevataniu on each side of the circle were individual villages of the other seven bands. On the north bank were two full-sized villages of the Omissis, our brothers to the farthest north. And south of the Platte, there were three villages of the Hevataniu, our brothers to the farthest south. In between were our village of the Ivistsinihpah, and on each side between the Omissis and the Hevataniu, were villages. So, on the north side were the Wuhtapiu, the Suhtai, and the Hoivimanah. To the south of us were villages of the Issiometane, the Hofnowa and the Mahsihkota. And the Hevataniu were at the end. My mother told me that the Suhtai were both Cheyenne and a separate tribe, that had joined the Cheyenne in their wanderings generations ago, around the time they lived together in the Black Hills.

The entire Cheyenne nation was camped there, and though I couldn't count properly, it was easily three-thousand souls. Some of those villages were small, little over a hundred souls. The Omissis and the Hevataniu dominated the tribe in population, with multiple villages, all of which had more than 200 people in each. And in the circle around the Platte in the center there were at least two-thousand horses, including ours. Still, the boys kept them accounted for in a way that amazed me. Those boys could tell you where every horse was and who they belonged to. And no Crows dared to come try to steal them while we all camped there. Nor did the Pawnee dare to attack from the east. When the whole Cheyenne nation met together, it was mighty and dangerous, and our enemies drew back. And I understood what my wife told me, how the whole nation was too rich in horses to camp for very long together. The horses would eat up all the grass and we would hunt the surrounding country into barrenness. My Cheyenne kin were always aware of how they affected the earth around them. They called her Mother and treated her like their mother too. I ain't seen much of that from white people. We destroy a place in nature, leave it behind, move off to some new untouched place and do it again. We're too busy trying to get rich. The name "Spider" fits us, sadly.

Many Horses came to me at this time and asked me to assist him as he had committed to dance in the Medicine Lodge Ceremony. I didn't know what this meant at all, but I would have died for him, much less helped him for some dance, and I said yes. He smiled at me and said, "You will have to begin to dress like a man." Then he left. I told this to Spirit and she had a giggle-fit, which made me uncomfortable, because I knew the laughter was at my expense.

"What?" I asked with some irritation.

Spirit giggled again and looked at me in a flirty way. "It is that you hide your manhood like a Spider."

I could not make any sense of this. Then she did something only a wife dared do, she caressed my manhood and said, "You have a good manhood, but you hide it." I grew even more perplexed.

She said, "I will make you a proper breechclout and leggings, and you will not go around like a Spider any longer, acting as if you were ashamed of your manhood. See? You have a daughter. You are a man."

This is how I came to understand that for Cheyenne men, the breechclout, that long rectangular piece of soft deerskin that wraps through a belt front and back and under a man's crotch, was more than a piece of clothing. It stood for male fertility and prowess. Cheyenne were too modest to go around naked like some tribes I've seen. But the men let the world know that they had a manhood, to say it quite frankly. I am seeing my Lisa blush as I say this. Well, her old grandfather at least can make her blush. I must not be entirely useless. And that outward assurance of manhood was the breechclout. Spider men, that is us whites, were thought odd because we closed the space between our leggings and made breeches, or as people have started calling them, though I don't know why, "pants." Cheyenne thought this laughable. And Many Horses didn't want me helping him if I was dressed like I was ashamed of being a man.

So next day, I walked over to Many Horses' lodge in my new breechclout and leggings, and I have to tell you, they are mighty comfortable. I was expecting to feel strange about it, but that did not happen. My other friends were there and a couple of other warriors besides. We all sat down while Night Star, Many Horses' wife, served us buffalo stew. The eating done, Many Horses explained that he was to make the pledge for the Medicine Lodge Ceremony. He had asked Four Thunders, a warrior of the Wuhtapiu band, to be his instructor. They would carry out the ceremony between them, and we were not needed for that. But he had to pay Four Thunders and for that he needed our help. We went around the circle and starting with Red Mountain, told our host what we would give him to pay his instructor. I was about halfway around and I was having a hard time knowing what to give. Stands to the Left offered up five eagle feathers he'd been saving. I had no eagle feathers. Stands at Night offered up some trade blankets he'd gotten down to Bent's Fort. I had no trade blankets. Another fellow offered a new-made sturdy bow, and then they all looked at me. Fortunately, I had a moment of inspiration.

"I offer the three horses I took from my enemies and from the Crow," I said, hoping to God Almighty that this was the right thing to say. Several of them sucked in their breaths. Horses were wealth, and I was rich owning four. I'd just handed that over to Many Horses. There was a lot of nodding at me and smiling and I can't tell you how relieved I was that I'd made the right choice. Plus, it was the only thing I'd had to give. I learned later that one horse would have been generous. Giving my friend three was beyond generous in Cheyenne eyes. Just to make sure it stuck, right after our meeting broke up, I went down to the herd and explained to the boys that I had given Many Horses the three horses. Those boys were sharp and you could see it in their eyes that they were tabulating the transaction. There would never be any confusion about the exchange of horse ownership.

When I told all this later to Willow and Spirit, I could see they were both proud of me. And that to me was worth far more than three horses. I mark that as the day I truly became a Cheyenne.

The Medicine Lodge Ceremony was an eye-opener for sure. I did not understand the way they dressed, nor the songs they sang, or the way they painted their bodies. But I did finally understand that the old man, Sees Rain Coming, kept the bundle of four sacred arrows in his lodge, because he was the Sacred Arrow Keeper for the whole tribe. We, the Ivistsinihpah band, were not only the central band between north and south Cheyenne. We were that because we kept the Sacred Arrows. It was sort of like being Washington DC, because we were in the middle and the national treasure was there. We were neither north nor south. If we'd had a president or a king, he would have been an Ivistsinihpah. But the Cheyenne never even had something like a head chief. They were far too democratic to even consider the possibility.

Unlike the Lakota version, the Sun Dance, our summer sacred dance did not include piercing the skin of one's breast with skewers and pulling at thongs attached to the central pole of the sun lodge. But it was plenty painful and exhausting without that. I will tell you about how I felt watching it, now that such dances are almost no more and the earth no longer turns from season to season as it should. But Many Horses came to my lodge and walked with me out to the horse herd, to see his new horses, or at least that's what he said. But I knew it was really to explain his decision to me.

"Red Hair, you have not grown up with our people and this may look strange to your Spider eyes. But you must understand why I do this thing. I care too much about my people and I know hard times are coming. You know this too, I believe. What I am about to do will be very painful, but

I make this sacrifice willingly for my *Tsistsistas*, my people. For if young men do not sacrifice for the people, even for the whole world of *Hestanova*, that world will stop turning as it should, from summer to winter, and back, from youth to love to old age and honor, and all that survives will live in a nightmare of madness, where men and women lose their reason and their sense of right and wrong, good and bad. It is against that thing that I offer my sufferings."

I remember nodding that I understood, but I didn't really—then. Now I understand it all too well. And he was right about the hard times. I knew that thousands and hundreds of thousands of poor and hungry Spider People lived east of the Mississippi, ready to do anything to anyone for land and hope. And their hope was in moving west. I had seen them. Hell, I had been one of them. I had seen the floodgates opening. The collision between them and the *Tsistsistas* was only a matter of time.

That very day the Medicine Lodge rose on the north bank of the Platte inside the circle of villages. Sees Rain Coming moved his lodge next to it, taking with him the Sacred Arrows. The Medicine Lodge was not a tipi, but rather a large skeletal building made of cottonwood logs and branches. It was circular, about forty feet in diameter, with walls of log frame covered over with old buffalo-hide tipi covers, rising up maybe eight feet high. The roof, if you want to call it a roof, was a shallow cone made of cottonwood limbs that met over the central pole, which was a tree trunk planted in the ground. They made no effort to cover it, so other than the cover of the leaves on the smaller branches of the beams, the inside of the lodge was open to the sky.

But I knew, and though I couldn't explain this, I could feel that in this forty-foot circle was the whole universe, stars and the Earth and the Moon and all the hopes and fears of all of humanity. The Cheyenne word for this place was "*Hestanova*." I won't describe all the dances or the magical way Many Horses and the other young pledges were painted, or the whistles they blew on or how they danced continually for hours and hours, far beyond exhaustion and past the place where you start seeing things you don't normally see.

White people, looking at this, would only snort and laugh and say rude words about "ignorant savages." But it reminded me of something in the New Testament that I'd been reading, the copy that Doc Ben had given me. People had the Lord Christ right in front of them and they couldn't see nothing but what they expected to see. They only saw a rabble-rousing con man, and so they killed him. People haven't changed a whole lot in 1900 years I figure.

I didn't stay the whole time, for it was exhausting to watch, though not nearly so exhausting as it must have been for Many Horses and the four other warriors who I didn't really know, who danced with their instructors and the Medicine Priest watching. I came and watched and went back to my tipi at least three times. The dancing went on for days. But as I sat there amongst my friends, silently watching, I felt like the ground was moving under me and there was a humming in the air that was there but almost too soft to hear, and yet too loud to bear. I knew the Earth not only turned through the seasons, but being a Spider with a bit of science, I knew it was like a ball turning. I had never told this to Many Horses, but I think he would not have been surprised.

Then I went home, reeling and walking like I was drunk. I staggered into my tipi and Spirit looked at me. I said nothing. She seemed to understand, maybe that I was drunk with the power of the Medicine Lodge ceremony. Willow was at the ceremony. Spirit came over, took my hand, pulled me down to our robes and we were lovers yet again. After that, I think I slept for almost two days. You'd think I was the one, not Many Horses, who had been dancing endlessly. Spirit seemed to understand this, though she did not discuss it with me. The Cheyenne seemed to understand that not all things are rational. Some things are just magic.

And now, as I finish this, I must tell Lisa, and you, whoever is crazy enough to read this, that I have a problem. I'm not saying that the Cheyenne, the *Tsistsistas* people, had found paradise on earth or were better than run of the mill people. But they had some good things in their lives and bits of wisdom I don't see around me these days down in Denver in 1902 of this modern, up-to-date era. They weren't gods or saints. They had their troubles. And the days I'm telling you about didn't last.

You know some folks will read this and see the glory of the Indian people of the high plains, those horse lords of freedom. I suppose there is some truth, to that, though to listen to Buffalo Bill's show and those fool magazines about the Old West my grandson reads me, you'd think it had lasted forever till the white man came along. But old White Coyote admitted to me that he had been born in what is now the Dakota Territory—wait, it's been South Dakota for fifteen years now, hasn't it? Anyway, he said he was born in what whites call the Black Hills. And his grandfather farmed corn and lived in a mud dome house on the Missouri River, and saw Lewis and Clark. And though White Coyote had no son but me, I being next generation, saw the Cheyenne people almost destroyed and exiled to two lousy reservations far from their old homes for the most part. The glory days of the Plains Indians lasted a generation, maybe two.

7.

Working for the Bents

1834–1835

Once the Medicine Lodge ceremony was over, the lodge was taken down. It was too sacred to be left standing around and used by other tribes, or animals, or worse, by Spider People. And then I had an eye-opener. White Coyote, Sees Rain Coming, and two other leading warriors of our Ivistsinihpah band went out one afternoon and assembled with about the same number of chief men from the other villages in a large circle in the center of the villages on the banks of the Platte, mainly close to our village. I was not invited, and I had enough sense to stay clear. Willow explained to me that each summer when the tribe assembled, the 44 peace chiefs would sit down and consider what to do about matters having to do with the whole tribe. They took all afternoon into evening and most of the next day. The thing was that the Omissis and the other northern bands were still living along the headwaters of the Cheyenne River, south and mainly west of the Black Hills. The Hevataniu and a few other bands like ours had ventured south toward the Arkansas River, interested in the trade with Spider People down there and the Kiowa and the Comanche, as well as with our friends and allies, the Arapaho. So, our people were stretched out some five-hundred miles between the Cheyenne River and the Black Hills to the north and the Arkansas River to the south. There were fears that being so spread out would invite attack from our old enemies, the Pawnee and the Crow. And there were also fears that the Comanche and Kiowa might stop being friendly and trading horses and go over to being enemies. White Coyote told me later that all the Peace Chiefs charged White Thunder and the leaders of the southern bands to make peace with the Comanche and the Kiowa, if possible. The Omissis showed little interest in moving south with the rest of the tribe, so in the end, no solution to the stretching of the tribe presented itself. Unlike the American Congress, there were no factions nor parties, outside of the bands themselves, and they didn't vote on anything. If they reached consensus, they would all act. If not, they would meet again next summer.

A new location and a date—by the phase of the summer moons—was set for next year's tribal assembly and Medicine Lodge Ceremony, and the Peace Chiefs adjourned. When I was coming up in Kentucky and getting what little schooling in St. Louis that I got, I used to hear a lot about American democracy. But the most democratic thing I ever saw with my own eyes was the meeting of the Cheyenne Peace Chiefs.

The following day, all the lodges in all the villages began to break down and pack up. White Coyote took me to meet White Thunder in the Hevataniu village and White Thunder invited us to stay with him. Though I told White Coyote before we left that we would return in the late fall to winter with the Ivistsinihpah. So late in the day, riding in the lead on Jane with Spirit, with little Yellow Bird in the cradle board, and Willow mounted up behind, the travois and our lodge on Willow's horse, we moved south along the circle of villages and met up with White Thunder and his people before heading south. I had three horses again, because Many Horses gave me back the roan I stole from Jim Beckwourth and Morton's old horse, which was bigger and better able to pull the travois. He thanked me for my generosity, but said I needed the horses more than he did. I got pretty emotional saying goodbye to him and my other friends. I promised to try and come up in the fall. They told me the village would be on the North Platte River by that time. They were hoping to get more horses from the Crow and have a good fight.

With White Thunder's band all around us, we forded the South Platte and followed the Front Range of the Rockies south, keeping it on our right. I felt strange but all sorts of women rode up to Spirit and Willow and walked their horses alongside, talking. We may have been from another band, but Cheyenne was Cheyenne as far as these people were concerned. The warriors looked at me, but no one rode up to talk to me. I understood. Until I started bringing in game to eat, I was a question to these hunters, and they would wait to see what this Spider who married into the *Tsistsistas* was made of. We rode south for ten days, crossing several creeks, and dropped into a country that was lower in elevation, and drier, more desert-like. On the ninth day we hit a large, wide, shallow river, flowing east from the Rockies. From maps I'd seen at Rendezvous, and what the boys in the mountains had told me, this was probably the Arkansas River, heading east to the Mississippi. We turned east and rode along the north bank.

Late on the tenth day, we saw on the horizon a large, rectangular structure rising out of the plains on the north bank, tucked in amongst the cottonwoods. Rectangular meant Spider People. It was plainly adobe, with walls a good 30 or 40 feet high. On the west end that we were approaching was a large, wooden gate, standing wide open. They clearly feared no attack. Our band of Cheyenne stopped a half mile short along the north bank of the river and spent the rest of the day setting up tipis and settling the horse herd.

I was thinking of just walking into the post the following morning, but it didn't happen that way. Laughing Bull, a *Hevataniu* warrior in our band, stepped into my tipi and told me that White Thunder wanted to see me and to bring my wife, daughter, and mother. Then he stepped out. Willow, Spirit and I all looked at each other, puzzled, and I was afraid something might be wrong. But we left and walked over to White Thunder's tipi and entered, stepping to the right. I was absolutely stunned to hear the first voice speak to me in English, the first time I'd heard it since Rendezvous, almost four months back.

"Well, I'll be damned, you were right. It's Cheyenne Sam hisself."

Seated on White Thunder's left were two white men in their 30s or 40s. One had a long nose and a long, sloping forehead, with eyes that seemed to squint all the time. His hair was black, long, and combed back down his neck, shining with bear grease. He had a bushy moustache, but no beard. The Spider next to him had the same sort of squinty eyes, a low forehead, high, prominent cheek bones and a toothy smile behind thin but prominent lips, and clean shaven. His hair was also long and black, greased and combed down the back of his neck. Next to him sat two Cheyenne women, who by their faces were clearly sisters. On White Thunder's right sat his wife, Tall, by name, a Cheyenne woman of greater years, but who looked much like the two younger women, or they like her. It was obvious that they were all family.

White Thunder addressed me. "Red Hair, these are the Bent brothers." The English name "Bent" sounded funny, inserted in a Cheyenne sentence, sort of jarring, because the two languages sound so different. Cheyenne flows like water and English crashes like stones in a rock fall. Apparently these two white men went by "Bent" and had no Cheyenne name, or if they did, White Thunder did not use it. He went on. "This one is my son-in-law. My daughter, Owl, is his wife." Here he gestured to the Spider on my right, the clean-shaven one. "You two are Spiders in our tribe married to our women. I know you wanted to meet these brothers. Please, all sit down. We will talk and eat."

I thanked White Thunder in Cheyenne and we sat. Spirit and Willow leaned over to Tall and began talking rapidly about things that women enjoy discussing. Tall was very taken by my daughter, Yellow Bird, in her cradle board. Spirit took her out and let the older woman hold the baby, which led to much laughing and talking in silly voices to the baby, and letting little Yellow Bird reach out and touch their faces. Owl and Yellow got up and sat next to their mother to join. The clean-shaven white man beckoned me to come and sit by him. I did. Again, when he dropped into English, I was almost startled. I hadn't heard much of the language in what seemed now like a very long time. In fact, the last English I'd heard was when Morton told me they were going to kill me. Not a particularly good memory.

"I'm Will and this is my brother, George. We heared you were coming down this way. Say, weren't you Jack Rather's boy? I was sure sorry to hear that Jack went under."

I nodded and swallowed because even thinking about Jack gets me feeling sad and choking. But I pushed it down and replied. "Yessir. The trade is going for free trappers. Beaver are near gone. But I reckon you already know that. I been living with the *Ivistsinihpah* but I need to work and earn my possibles. I heared from the boys that you built a post on the Arkansas. So we came after summer break-up. I was hoping you had work."

George and William looked at each other and made slight nods. William spoke up, "Well, you know where the stick floats and you obviously are fluent in Cheyenne. How's your sign?" He meant my sign language. I answered him with my hands, adding that I did not want to go to any more Rendezvous because much evil was there.

George nodded again and William laughed. "Well, I guess that answers that. Yeah, Cheyenne Sam. American Fur has got Rendezvous all tied up anyway. I can see why you don't like it. Down here in the southern Rockies, the trade all goes out of Taos. The road between Taos and St. Louey runs right through our fort. Plus, boys with bear, buffalo, and what few beaver pelts are left, can come here quicker than go all the way over the Sangres to Taos, or all the way up to Rendezvous, almost to the Blackfoot country. Plus, the Arkansas River is sort of the border between the Kiowa and the Comanche on the south, and the Cheyenne and Arapaho on the north. They're all getting along right now, good thing. And our trade is booming. And in case you be wondering, we built our fort on the north bank because, like it or not, the Mexican government knows we're in US territory. South bank is Mexico. It's a border for the Indians and us to boot.

"Anyway, we need hunters and we need people we can rely on to deal with the Cheyenne and the Arapaho. And we get Comanche and Kiowa too. They all know sign but it would be good if you could learn some of their talk, especially the Arapaho. They don't like white men generally, but being a married Cheyenne, you could get past that. You could parley and trade without fear of losing your scalp. What do you say, young Plunkett? Want to work for the Bent Brothers?"

"Oh, yessir, I do. I was hoping you'd offer."

"Good, good. Then you're hired. Come up to the fort tomorrow morning and I'll show you around. A big train of wagons is due to come in midday, if the Comanches didn't raid them, and we'll need help unloading and general dealing. The run between here and St. Louey can be pretty grueling, so be ready for some sorry-looking people. If it weren't for us, they'd barely make Taos at all."

And I was to find out the truth of those last two remarks he made.

In the morning, I got up, collected my Hawken rifle—like I said, we never went anywhere without a loaded rifle—and stepped out of my tipi.

I walked up to Bent's Fort, and passed in through the gate. The place was buzzing with Cheyennes, and at least three other tribes. White men were there, but they were scarce. A bunch of white fellows were piling up buffalo hides onto the beds of two mule-pulled wagons and looked at me with curiosity. The fort itself inside was two long, rectangular, two-level, adobe buildings about 120 feet apart, facing each other, with wood porches and wood-framed windows on both levels. The space between them was the yard, where all the work was going on. At each far end, a wood wall connected the two buildings and that's where the two gates were. After over a year of silence on the windswept plains, the coming and going and the commotion seemed loud to me. But the white fellows were outnumbered by Indians 2 to 1. I didn't see either of the Bent brothers and asked one of the white fellows where they were, in English. Again, it felt weird after so many months to speak the language. They pointed to a door in the porch in the middle of the south building and I made my way over there. A crowd of Indians stood around the door.

I recognized the Arapahoes, about three of them anyway. I signed greeting to them and they returned the sign. They recognized me for a Cheyenne, even if I did have red hair. And our people are allies. Like I said, if anyone tells you Indians all look alike, they're just showing their ignorance. Arapahoes don't have quite the cheekbones we Cheyenne typically have, and the colors they use on their breechclouts and leggings are far different. The majority of that group were proud, tall, well-dressed warriors wearing loudly colorful breechclouts and leggings. They looked a little like Shoshones, so I knew they were Comanches. It's just a certain look in the shape of the face, and the vastly different way they wore their long hair, and not just their bold colors. Plus, they were the tallest Indians there on average, though not much taller than us Cheyennes. There were about 30 of them and five others from a different tribe that I guessed to be Kiowa.

The Shoshones were a peaceful tribe, that lived around South Pass and the Green River country and west toward the Columbia. But most boys in the mountains knew that in the years just before the fur trade really got started, a lot of Shoshone warriors, tired of being peaceful, split off the tribe, took their women and children and headed south. These were the Comanche, a tribe that was anything but peaceful. They would trade at Bent's Fort and walk in and out like friends, as proud as princes. But if they caught white men, Spiders, out on the trail, they might just kill, rob, and scalp them. My people were at peace with them for now, so I was safe from a fight with these young bucks. That and the fact that another 30 or so Cheyennes from my village were there pretty much made me untouchable for those Comanche. But I could see why the 44 Peace Chiefs wanted to stay at peace with the Comanche, and not be weighed down with a running fight from three directions.

The Cheyenne, like most plains tribes, relished a good fight. We weren't afraid of the Comanches. But too many enemies meant wars that could not be won. Already the Crow on the northwest and the Pawnee on the east were pressing us. That was enough enemies, thank you. That's not to say we were afraid. We did raid Comanche horses all the time. But both we and the Comanches avoided a pitched battle. Plus, for the Comanche, tangling with the Cheyenne meant tangling with our allies, the Lakota, and the Arapaho. Lisa tells me that in that respect, the plains were something like Europe, a complex knot of tense alliances, giving each other the wary eye. We kept a wary eye on the Comanches, and took their horses when we could. But both of us avoided a pitched fight.

I opened up the door and went into a dark, cool office. The adobe walls were bare, and the room smelled strongly of dust. The Bent brothers were there, George sitting behind a crude, wooden desk and William standing beside him. They faced a mountain man who had his back to me. As I came in, William laughed and said, "And here is the fellow now. Sam, come meet your new partner."

The mountain man turned and I was looking at a short white man in buckskins, with a badger-skin cap resting like a bird's nest on the top of his thick, long, black hair. Though he had a face with a few wrinkles, clean-shaven, he didn't seem that much older than me. He nodded silently, which is about as friendly a greeting as you'll get from us trappers, talking not being our long suit.

"This h'year is Jeremiah Coleman, out of Taos. You'll be working with him, Sam. We need you two boys to take two wagons of buffalo hides down to Taos and get them to our partner, Ceran St. Vrain. Coleman knows the way, so you don't have to worry about that part, Sam. St. Vrain will load you up with as many trade goods from our list as fill the two wagons, and then you are to come back. You got two wagon drivers."

I was perplexed. It didn't seem like I had much to do if Coleman knew where the stick floated and the wagons had drivers. "So what do I do?"

"You, Sam, be a Cheyenne. And there's a good chance you may be attacked. However, those Comanche boys might think twice when they see a Cheyenne riding with the train. They like trading with your people and they don't want White Thunder down on them. Your job is to ride along, fight if you have to, keep your topknots, and our goods." Then William rolled out a big map and showed me how we went up the Arkansas to the Front Range and followed it south over Raton Pass. "Coleman knows the trail across the Sangres and he'll teach it to you." (Lisa reminds me to say that is short for Sangre de Cristo range). "Taos is here, on the west side. And don't be surprised if you see some familiar faces in Taos. Lots of boys in the mountains have given up on Rendezvous and are working out of Taos." There was a little more instruction and Coleman and I left the office. We walked past the crowd of warriors and I followed him to a recess in the wall near the west gate.

"Meet me here in the morning," Coleman said. I nodded and went back to my tipi to prepare my possibles for the journey.

8.

The Bloody Road to Taos

1834

The wagons, four of them, came in the next day and it was bad. The Comanches had hit them on the trail, probably as a way of getting a discount on the goods they would have to buy if the wagons made it to the fort. There were several wounded men and they had left two behind dead on the plains, as well as a wagon the Comanche had taken. The Comanches tolerated Bent's Fort. They did not tolerate other white men. And they were happy to let white men know it in lethal fashion. I understood why the Bents wanted me along on the journey to Taos. It turned out that two of the wagons, loaded with trade goods, were the wagons Jeremiah and I were to take to Taos. The fellows who had driven the wagons from St. Louis refused to go out again, they were so scared. That's how Jeremiah and I ended up with Bert and Antonio.

Antonio had a Mexican name and even looked dark with cropped black hair, and a tight-cropped black beard. I don't know why, but he spoke always under his breath in a throaty, bass voice. And every time he spoke, it was about someone he hated, who had done him wrong. He hated all Indians, but especially Comanche, the Bents, though he took their dollars, Mexicans, Spanish, Negroes, fur-trappers, buffalo hunters, what he called "Frenchies", and all the women who had ever denied themselves the pleasure of his bed. I never did see him with a woman—I don't think any woman ever got near him twice. But the rest were "whores" for refusing to act like whores for him. I once caught him listening to someone else talk in Spanish and it was obvious he understood them, but I never heard him speak a word of it. He was big and muscular, with a beer gut, and nasty in a fight. I am pleased to say I did not have the privilege of getting to know him any better. The best I can say for him is he knew how to drive a team and care for horses or mules, the only creatures on God's green earth that he had any feeling for.

Bert was worse. Bert liked to work into every conversation that he thanked the Almighty he was a white man, which was usually followed by a contemptuous glare at any non-whites within range, and a spit of tobacco juice into the dirt. Old tobacco juice fouled his considerable gray beard, but he never thought to clean it or shave. His hair had gone almost completely gray. And he was a creature of a single mind. You could be talking about trading, or the weather, or even about taking a piss, and Bert would somehow turn the whole conversation into thanking the Almighty for the color of his skin. Plus, Bert picked fights for the pleasure of it. He was big and strong and good with horses. I couldn't think of any other reason why the Bents kept him on the payroll. When Jeremiah and I met Bert and Antonio, they didn't have to say anything, but you could tell they were none too pleased with being sent to Taos under the direction of a half-Cheyenne renegade. They had no love for Jeremiah either. Apparently, this odd-looking man had already made a name for himself in the trade and was well on the way to getting rich. Bert hated rich people as well. I may as well describe Jeremiah. He had a narrow face and large eyes, and a Roman nose that made him look like maybe he had some Native blood in him. His chin was cleft and though he had a day or two of growth on his chin, it was obvious that unlike most trappers in the Rockies, he shaved regularly, like me. He appeared to be around 45 years old, and had the air of assurance of a veteran of mountain life. I didn't mind letting him take the lead. I sensed he knew what he was doing.

We headed west at first light two days later. Bert and Antonio had a covered wagon each with a team of two big horses. Jeremiah and I rode ahead and behind, trading positions every few hours. We followed the north bank of the Arkansas the first day and made it pretty much to the foothills of the Rockies. Bert and Antonio made a separate camp and fire on the far side of the wagons, with the horses, and that was fine with Jeremiah and me. We didn't care much for their company either.

That first night camping, Jeremiah and I sat around our fire with our loaded Hawken rifles on our laps. I was expecting him to not say much, as us trappers are folk of few words. But he spoke.

"I knew your Pap, Jack, right well. He had the har of the bar in him."

I was pleased to be working with a friend of Jack's, but I couldn't think of anything to do but nod. Even to think of Jack brought a knot to my stomach that surged up into my throat and cut off any words I might say.

Jeremiah didn't seem to mind that I had nothing to say and remained silent himself for quite a while.

"He ever tell you that we trapped together fall of '30?"

"No," I said. I knew that after Richard abandoned Jack, he'd trapped alone or with some friends he never named, but I was pleased to have discovered one.

"I heared stories of what you did for Jack up in Big Hole. Jack would be proud you know. Anyway, I meant to tell you where the stick floats so if I go under you can finish the job."

This old mountain veteran go under? Not a chance.

"Once we cross the first set of hills, we'll be in the Eagle Nest Valley. It is wide and grassy. We follow it south and find the stream that comes into it from the south. That stream will wind up into the mountains a long, long ways. We follow it to its source, then go due west about a day through the forest. We'll hit another stream starting and dropping down to the west. That's Taos Creek. We follow it straight into Taos. Now, when we get there, you let me do the talking. Some riders will come out and ask us questions, because they mean to charge us a tax. But we only tell them these wagons belong to Ceran St. Vrain. He's a Mexican citizen and they can't tax him the same. So, no matter what they ask, just say *Este carro pertenece a St. Vrain.* You got that?"

He made me repeat it several times. I felt a kind of shock that he could even believe that I might be the only survivor. Here was one of the most experienced men of the mountains. It was a lot more likely that he'd bury my carcass. My thought escaped. "If I go under," I told him in a halting voice, "lay me out up in some tree in the Cheyenne way. And let my woman know."

I thought that he'd laugh at me, as speaking the meandering thoughts of a greenhorn cub, but he just accepted it and nodded.

Some more words just burst out of my mouth, though I wished I could take them back the moment they were out. "But you ain't gonna die, Jeremiah. You're too . . . you know the way of the mountains."

He thought about that for a second, then said, "My best friend in the mountains was Jed Smith. Lord, he had the har of the bar in him. You know he was one of the owners of Rocky Mountain Fur before it was called that. He took men to California and came back by Oregon. A great man, and he knowed the way of the mountains better than most. Plus, he loved the Lord Jesus, and wasn't a poor sinner like me. He wanted to make some money and go back to the settlements and marry a girl and live proper like."

"But how does anyone leave these mountains?"

"Oh, I know most of the boys feel that way. Most of the boys in the mountains are like your pap, Jack, in that they fell afoul of the law one time and came out here to escape it. But me, I was like ol' Jed. You know, Sam, I got a woman waiting for me in St. Louey, name of Rachel Moore. I write her love letters. One more big haul and I'll have the money to go back and marry her like I shoulda years ago. Some men come to the mountains to escape the law; and Jed and me and a few others, we come to escape poverty. But I will bless the Lord the day I can walk into a church again and worship. Jed and I both felt that way. Not many boys in the mountains do."

"I have a Cheyenne wife and she and her people are my whole life now. I've never had family like this before."

He put his hand gently on my shoulder, "Well then, Sam, you be true and loyal to her and them above everything and everyone. Don't even let Americans get in your way."

I nodded, having no words to say, but I never forgot what he told me. And I stuck to it, by God. I stuck to it.

We headed out the following morning. Once we crossed to the south bank of the Arkansas, we really had to be alert. I am sure some Comanche scout spotted us. They'd probably watched us from the moment we left the fort. It was for them, a matter of cold calculation. The markings I had painted on Jane were clearly Cheyenne, and my leggings and breechclout were Cheyenne as well. Except for my long, red hair, I looked and smelled Cheyenne. The Bents had been counting on this. Yes, Cheyenne and Comanche were raiding each other's horses, but we weren't fighting hand to hand battles. Attacking us just might mean a big fight with White Thunder's Cheyennes, and maybe the whole Cheyenne tribe. The local Comanches didn't mind stealing our horses, but feared the Cheyenne enough not to want to risk war.

As we worked our way south along the Front Range, I did spot their scouts, lying in the grass to the south or east of us on at least three occasions, and Jeremiah spotted two more. I thanked my friends back in White Coyote's village for their training me to scan the horizon better. It saved my life that trip, I am sure. Not that this made any difference on the attitude of Bert and Antonio, who continued to glare at us every time I looked. Four days out, camped up in Raton Pass, Bert, fairly drunk on some whiskey he'd stowed, came over and unloaded his opinion on us.

He cussed me out for being a stupid, cocky "renegade". Then he continued by calling me a "red Negro." Of course he used another word for 'Negro', that starts with N, but I will keep my promise I made to Jim Beckwourth never to use that word again. Jeremiah didn't even look up at him, while Bert went through this preaching of hate. Jeremiah just kept chewing on dried buffalo strips. I had heard this term before as a way of piling contempt on Indians, but though I didn't touch a drop of whiskey, I just had enough when he called me that. I was up in a flash and the razor-sharp edge of my Green River was at his throat, and I was about to send this varmint to Hell ahead of schedule.

"Mister, I've had just about enough from you. . . . "

"Sam," Jeremiah said patiently. "Don't kill that trash. He ain't worth the trouble."

I had made up my mind to do it, but there was something in Jeremiah's voice. I was still looking at Bert very close in the eye, the stink of tobacco and whiskey on his breath. The man was clearly terrified, his bloodshot eyes wide open and staring at me. And I realized that all this hate he had for people that didn't look and talk like him was deep down his terror of anything different from the way he was raised. The rest of the world simply scared the crap out of him, people who weren't white or didn't have white ways. And for that, he hated us.

I calmed down a notch, but I still really wanted to kill him. I thought about all the trouble with the Bents it might cause and trouble for my people, especially in White Thunder's village. That's something the Cheyenne taught me. When you are Cheyenne, you carry the weight of all the people on your shoulders. No Cheyenne would have talked about being free like the boys at the Rendezvous did, and done what they pleased, raping, or stealing, or killing another Cheyenne, or going off to earn glory in war in a way that put the whole tribe in danger. You weren't an individual nearly as much as you were one of the *Tsistsistas* people. You were not alone; you were a member of a body of people, to whom you owed everything. Every decision you made as a warrior was for the tribe, not you. I think in the end, this, and Jeremiah's patience, kept me from killing Bert right then and there.

I said in an angry whisper, "Next time I hear from you, Bert, anymore about your being white, or what you think of Jeremiah and me, I will come and cut your throat. Then I will lift your worthless scalp and put it in the mud back of my lodge and piss on it for a year. Now get the Hell out of here before I change my mind." Even drunk, he turned and ran back to where he was camped with the horses and Antonio.

In the morning, when we packed up and saddled up, neither Bert nor Antonio would look us in the eye, nor say anything beyond "un-huh" for yes and "no." I was happy for that. Let them fear me as a crazy, murdering, renegade, son of a bitch. We rode south out of the pass and Jeremiah led us into some high country in the Sangre de Cristo range, the southernmost range of the Rocky Mountains. Next night we camped in some high meadows. Jeremiah told me that we would be in Taos in two days. Eagle Nest was a meeting of streams in a broad, grassy valley that ran north-south between two tall lines of peaks to the east and west. Jeremiah said we'd go south of the peaks to the west and a river would take us right into Taos. That was the plan.

They hit us in the morning, after we'd been running south up the Eagle Nest Valley for a couple of hours. There had to be fifty of them and they didn't look like any Indians I'd seen before. They didn't come riding in on horses, for one thing. And there weren't any feathers or much war paint. They were down in the sage brush and I didn't see them very clearly at first. Most of them wore a breechclout and a bandana wrapping their long, black hair. They were heavy set, shorter and stockier than my Cheyenne kin.

Jeremiah was out front and saw them first, turned and rode back at a gallop to the wagons, but it was too late. They were around us on both sides. Arrows came in from every direction. From where I sat in the saddle on Jane, I saw Jeremiah's gray gelding down and I thought he was gone beaver. An arrow sliced past my nose maybe an inch or two in front of me. I got down fast off the right side, with both the .50 and the .30, one in each hand, but it wasn't enough. Jane shrieked like horses do when they're hurt and crashed down in front of me with an arrow through her neck and blood welling out. As Jack once told me, the last act of a good horse is usually as a portable barricade from Indian attack. But I was down behind Jane and that was fine with the Indians to my east who had shot at me. There were others on the west side and I didn't dare get up off my belly. I guess my luck held because I wasn't all that interesting to these warriors. They wanted the wagons. Bert and Antonio were killed by multiple arrows almost instantly and I can't say I mourned their passing. Still, I had failed in my job and that galled me.

But Jack had also taught me that for most Native tribes, boys are too valuable, and you kill a few warriors and more often than not, the rest figure their medicine is bad and pull out. I didn't dare get up over Jane's midsection and shoot, but I could see motion in the sage to my right, to the west. I lined up the .50, Jack's Hawken, took my aim nice and slow, and let her rip. There was a yelp in the brush and I guess I'd hit my man. Some fellow popped up and charged toward me, probably figuring he could get me before reloading. I hit him square in the chest with the .30 and pulled out my pistol. Nobody else popped up, but several arrows went just over me and thudded into the leather of my saddle.

This kind of fight is not at all like the fool version in my grandson's adventure stories of the old West. Nobody fired off round after round just to pin down an opponent. Nobody rode boldly through a hail of arrows untouched. That's a damn fool way to get killed. And arrows these warriors had a lot of, and they could afford to pepper Jane's corpse with arrows. But shot and powder were too dear for anything that wasn't a kill shot. While they were missing me, I got both Hawkens reloaded lying flat on the ground, which was not easy. Just as I finished the .30, another warrior popped up, crying out and charged me. I shot him in the gut with the pistol and saw the blood and gore fly out his back as he fell dead. Like Jack had also told me, there wasn't much pleasure in killing a man, and it was downright ugly. I never did like it.

Just about this time I saw one of their warriors out in front of the wagons go down and heard a .50 Hawken go off just as he did. Jeremiah was alive. Thanks be to God! I think they would have got us and lifted our scalps, but right then the second wagon, the one nearest me, started forward and I heard the team of horses neighing loudly as the warriors whipped them into a frenzy. The wagon veered west into the sage and grass and the horses ran it off out of range before Jeremiah or I could respond. This seemed to be the signal for the warriors. They had got something for their pains and at least four of them were dead. I guess they decided to cut their losses when they got the wagon and its load, and they all just melted into the sage. Jack was right as usual; Indians don't like to throw young men into a slaughter. They're just too valuable. And taking out Jeremiah and me would have cost them at least another four warriors. It got real quiet. Just the same, I stayed on my belly for a good ten minutes to be sure. Then I gave Jeremiah a holler.

"Jeremiah! You alright?"

No answer.

"Jeremiah?"

No answer. I made sure both rifles and my pistol were loaded, and then with them crawled on my belly through the sage up to the first wagon. The horses knickered. I took a chance and stood up, going around front of the horses and inspected them. One had a surface wound but nothing serious. Bert's corpse was on the wagon seat, penetrated with at least four arrows, and the flies had found him. He didn't smell very good alive; he was starting to smell worse. Antonio's body was nowhere to be seen. They must have hauled him off in the wagon, scalped him and dumped the body during their exit.

Jeremiah was laying in the brush beside the corpse of his horse. I ran up to him and kneeled down. He had an arrow deep in his left shoulder and was struggling to stay awake and deal with the considerable pain. "Don't smell them no more," he observed. "They even dragged off their dead. Guess we ride in the wagon."

"Jeremiah! You're hurt."

"Yeah, well, I reckon so. I wonder if you might help me up into the wagon."

"Of course. Maybe I can take out the arrow." I put my hand on it, but he stopped me.

"No, it's too deep. My best chance is a doctor in Taos. Get me in the wagon and you'll have to drive. Remember what I told you."

I helped him to stand and he weakly made his way to the back of the wagon, leaning on me, and crawled in, laying down among the buffalo robes. I made sure to collect his Hawken and his truck, and I rolled over both Jane and his horse and recovered our saddles and as much of our food, shot, and powder as I could under the dead weight of the horse corpses, and dumped them in the back of the wagon. I said farewell to Jane and told her she was a good horse. Then I rolled Bert's heavy corpse off the seat and he thudded to the ground. Sorry, Bert, that's the best I can do.

I made sure both my Hawkens were loaded, and Jeremiah's as well, and had them all handy from the wagon seat. Then I jumped up on the seat and took up the reins. I'd seen it done a thousand times, but I'd never taken the reins of a wagon before. I shouted and slapped the reins on their backs and sure enough, they started to move. After a while I realized that if someone as stupid as Bert could do this, it wasn't going to be hard for me. I felt a little bad for not burying Bert, but not much. Even if I'd had a shovel, it would have taken me hours to get him six foot down. And if I just covered him with rocks, or dug him in shallow, the coyotes would dig him out just the same. Sorry Bert, but you've got an appointment with the coyotes. Funny, I had never heard Bert say he hated coyotes in all his lists of things he hated. But Jeremiah might live if I could just get him a doctor, so Bert was out of luck.

I thought I'd better keep Jeremiah awake, or he might slip away like my mother did in her sleep. So I talked to him as I drove the team up into the woods and hills along Eagles' Nest Creek.

"Who were they?" I asked.

"Apache. From west of here. They like to come down onto the trail and snag goods. And they attack in big groups."

"Reckon they'll come back?"

"Probly not. Lost too many warriors to us the first time. Their medicine is bad. They might wait and try to catch us on the way back in a few days."

"That's what Jack woulda said. Bad medicine and they pull back."

Jeremiah groaned and fell silent. I whipped up the horses and followed the creek.

We got out of there and rode through the rest of the day into the night to get some serious distance between us and the attack site. I followed the creek into the mountains, but after some hours, the horses were exhausted and I had to rest them. First stop I checked on Jeremiah and watered the horses in a flat ford of the creek. Jeremiah seemed to be doing alright and I had this image in my head of how we'd laugh at this adventure, once we reached Taos. But we had to reach it. I set the horses going again.

At the second stop I went back to check on Jeremiah. When Eagle Nest Creek had trickled down to nothing, I had gone west cross-country the way he told me and found the headwaters of Taos Creek. I wanted to tell him, so I stopped the wagon and crawled back to where he lay. But he was gone. I checked the pulse three times, but there was nothing and frankly, his body was cold. No mistaking it. Thankfully, his eyes were closed, unlike most dead people. He must have fallen to sleep and died. I stood there in the dark, leaning on my Hawken. I might have wept. I don't know. I did let the horses have a longer rest, since there was no hurry now. I found a leather bucket in the wagon and watered the horses from Taos Creek, which was roaring over its rocks next to us. I wrapped a robe around Jeremiah and broke off the shaft of the arrow, so he could be covered and lie in peace.

Then I got up on the wagon bench, took the reins, and slapped the horses into motion. I pulled into the east side of Taos as daylight was breaking.

9.

Taos and Señoritas

1834

COMING DOWN THE VALLEY from the east, Taos didn't look like much—a scattering of odd-shaped adobe houses clustered around the place where the road from the east met the road that ran north and south. There were more trees than elsewhere, though the pines, spruces, and firs we'd been riding through in the mountains gave way to more junipers and cedars and scrub oaks around the town.

As we got closer, and the rumpled cluster of houses started to look like something, I got tense. I can't tell you how nervous I was. Just as I drove up alongside the first adobe, two riders popped out and hailed me. They looked like all the drawings I'd seen of Mexican vaqueros, with the chaps and shiny, silver buttons, except that they weren't wearing the big, broad-brimmed hats. One rode a gray and the other a black horse. They didn't seem to know much English, so I tried the phrase Jeremiah taught me. I had some French I'd learned from Charette, but no Spanish till years later.

"*¿A donde va a usted?*"

"*Este carro pertenece a St. Vrain,*" I replied.

"*¿Tienen ustedes permisión . . . .?*"

"*Este carro pertenece a St. Vrain,*" I repeated, evenly.

They asked a few more questions that I didn't understand, and I kept repeating myself. By this time I was well into town, with adobes on each side of me. The second rider, who was looking bored, said something to his friend that sounded like "*Olvidelo*" and they rode off down a side street. I followed the west-leading street through the sagging adobes till it stopped at a T intersection, puzzling where to go next. A Mexican fellow was walking along the street on my right side. I looked at him and said, "'Scuse me. Ceran St. Vrain? St. Vrain?"

He looked at me and said something in Spanish, which I didn't understand, and then waved me to follow him, which I did. So doing, I turned the horses to the right and we rode up to the north for a short way. About four houses up, he stopped, turned and faced me and pointed to a wide, fenced yard of a large adobe on the west side of the road. I did remember to say "*Gracias!*" as I turned the horses into the yard and stopped them in front of the adobe.

I dismounted, walked over to the wooden door, and knocked. After a bit, it opened and a large, heavy-set Frenchman stood there. He reminded me of my friend Charette just a bit, except that his hair and beard were almost completely gray. He wore the mountain uniform of greasy old buckskins and moccasins. He took at look at me and the one wagon, and said "Who the hell are you?"

"Sam Plunkett, sir. The Bents sent me."

"They said they were sending Coleman."

"He's dead, sir. He's in the wagon. I'm very sorry."

"So, you're Cheyenne Sam, huh?"

"Yessir."

He stepped out and shut the door behind him, coming around the back of the wagon. Seeing the roll of buffalo robe, he stepped up into the bed and uncovered Jeremiah's face. Then he pulled enough robe away to find the arrow embedded in Jeremiah's shoulder.

"Well, Plunkett. What the hell happened?" He asked, not looking at me, in a clearly French accent.

"Apaches hit us in Eagle Nest. Killed the drivers and took the other wagon. Jeremiah was alive then. I was trying to get him here to find a doctor, but he died 'bout the time I found the headwaters of Taos Creek." I felt like maybe I was going to cry, and I didn't want this tough, old mountain trader to see me. All I could think of to say was, "I really didn't want him to die."

This seemed odd to me, such a brief description of all that happened, but the Frenchman just looked at me over his shoulder and nodded, like someone was telling him the weather. It occurred to me that this sort of thing was pretty common. In the end, I didn't have to explain much and he had probably guessed why I didn't have my own horse or Jeremiah's. I knew lots of men were killed in the trade but most were trappers dying in one-on-one fights with Indians. I hadn't known how extensive or deadly the raiding of trade goods was till this moment. I had figured only the Comanches were raiding trade. In this moment, I realized everyone was in it for themselves, free-for-all. Everybody raided the trade of others and the American and Mexican law made feeble protests at best. Navajos against Mexicans; Apaches and Comanches against Americans; Cheyenne and Arapaho against Comanches; Comanches against Cheyennes; Apaches against Comanches; Comanches against Mexicans; Americans against Mexicans. And free-booting scoundrels of mixed race attacked just about anyone.

The Frenchman didn't seem too upset, though he was somber. He crawled out of the wagon and stepped down, looking at me.

He smiled a small smile. "Cheyenne Sam, huh? I have heard about you. I am Ceran St. Vrain. Sorry to meet like this, but from what I hear, this isn't the first time you've seen a good man die in these mountains."

"No sir."

"Yor pap, Jack Rather, was a good man. Had the har of the bar in him. They say you do too. Looks like you handled this, bad as it was. Come on in. I'll have Juan and Carlitos take care of the wagon and Jeremiah. We'll give him a proper send off."

"Sir?"

"Call me St. Vrain."

"St. Vrain. Jeremiah said he had a woman in St. Louis. I seen some letters in his possibles. I would like to write to her if it can be done, but I don't write much. She should know. Jeremiah would want her to know. But I . . . ."

"I'll write to her, Plunkett. Good of you to think about that. Come in."

And that, pretty much, was my report in. As he led me through the front door into a broad room, I realized his remark that I had "handled it," was an expression of approval that I had come through a difficult situation and done the right thing. I had been expecting to be at least scolded, if not fired for having failed so badly and having lost my partner. But St. Vrain knew the mountains, and must have figured that what could have been done, I had done. It was an odd feeling, after a disaster, to get a pat on the back for rescuing the situation as much as possible. I guess he figured that taking on a mob of Apaches and coming out alive was good work on my part. Anyway, it sure struck me as—hell, I don't know the word. Lisa says it's "ironic" and when she explains to me what that means, it sounds about right.

"Welcome to my home," St. Vrain said, leading me in and shutting the front door behind me. "That door over there leads to your room and I will let you get some rest. Grab some vittles over by the fire, if yor hungry. Big dinner tonight. I have just killed a pig. We will talk about sending you back with four wagons, and you can use your credits to replace your horse. I gotta go scare up Juan and Carlitos and take care of the wagon now." Then he left me alone in the big room.

The house was adobe walls no more than 8 feet high, with a roof of crosshatched logs with cut boards running across perpendicular. Lisa gave me that word. Half-circle tiles made up the roof above the beams. The dirt floor was covered by a thick mat of trampled straw. The furniture was rough wood, tables and chairs, but handsome. There were a couple of paintings hanging on the wall in the main room, portraits of a Spanish gentleman and a lady. The main parlor ran maybe twenty feet wide, unhindered from the front door to two wooden doors at the back, about 30 feet at least from the front wall. I was not accustomed to the idea that so much space could be dedicated to living. I lived in a tipi 15 feet in diameter. Three quarters of the way down the left, past a wooden table, a door appeared and I followed St. Vrain through it into a smaller room with a wooden desk and a bookshelf behind it. The wall had a window looking out onto the back where there was something like a veranda and two Spanish ladies, or so they seemed, sitting on chairs, smoking cigarettes.

I went through the door he indicated and found what was basically a windowless store room, not a bedroom. But then most boys in the mountains were so used to sleeping outdoors or in small cabins, they were uncomfortable with any kind of luxury. St. Vrain figured me right. I found some buffalo robes in a corner and was asleep in seconds.

I slept about four hours I figure, though it felt like more, and when I woke, I was in the dark. By the light crack at the bottom of the door, I could see that I was laying on a buffalo robe on the ground and a candle in a candlestick lay on the floor next to me in the dark that someone had put there. Also my saddle, my .30 and my .50, and my possibles were all stacked near the door. They must have been unloaded from the wagon while I was asleep.

I sat up and let my head clear before looking around in the dark. Standing up, I walked toward the door and opened it, letting the light spill in. I walked out into the central room again. Over by the back corner on the far wall was a kitchen, that is, a fireplace with a rotating iron hook, a table, a large tub of water and some scattered chairs made of un-sawn pine logs. The fire was cold but on one of the chairs sat a Mexican lady, and lord, she was pretty. She hit me like a wave in a river bounces off a boulder. She wore a large, soft, red skirt and a white blouse that was low cut so that you could see pretty much all the tops of her breasts right down to almost the nipples. The separation between her ample breasts was nothing I had to guess about. She had hair black like a moonless night, flowing down over her shoulders, a fine, thin nose, large brown eyes and full lips that blushed red. The smell of tobacco hovered around her and I knew she was one of the ladies that I had seen smoking outside the window. And it hit me that this might be the boss's wife.

"Good morning," I said, reaching for the most polite thing I could think of to say.

"Eet ees afternoon," she replied in a Spanish accent. "Who are you?"

"Sam. Sam Plunkett. I came this morning."

She looked me up and down for quite some time so that I became a bit nervous. "Wha happen to your face?" she added.

"A bear," I replied. I wasn't offended. I was used to people noticing it by now. She continued to look me up and down and I was about to excuse myself and go outside to look for St. Vrain when another woman entered from the opposite side door. She looked much like the first, though she was a bit older and her blouse covered her bosoms more completely. I thought to myself that this second woman must be the boss's wife. I made a clumsy bow.

Back then I didn't speak any Spanish, like I speak it now. But I remember what they said and later was able to piece it back together.

"*¿Lupita! Que haces?*" the older woman demanded.

"*Miro a este hombre. Me interésa,*" the young beauty replied.

"¿Te has presentada a el?"

"Ya no."

Then the older woman turned to me and said, "I am sorry, Meester Sam. I am Maria Dolores St. Vrain, an' thees ees my seester, Lupita. My husban wai's for you back of the house." Then she smiled a lovely smile at me, which dissolved in a moment when she turned her eyes on her sister and unleashed a rushing river of angry and rapid Spanish which was an unmistakable scolding. The sister, Lupita, got up suddenly, pouting and angry, and stormed out of the room into the door where the Señora had come from. I guessed the proper bedrooms were attached to the house on that side.

I was soon outside. Hell, I almost ran. St. Vrain and five trappers I'd never seen before were at the outdoor table studying a crude, hand-made map. St. Vrain introduced me all around and they nodded, which is about as friendly as trappers ever get. One fellow stood next to me as we poured over the map. He was considerably shorter than everyone else, with dark hair to his shoulders, deep, penetrating blue-gray eyes and like me, he had no beard. St. Vrain told me his name was Kit Carson and he seemed almost my age.

St. Vrain asked me to point out the place where Jeremiah and I had been attacked if I could find it on the map. That was easy because it was just below where Eagle Nest Creek turned south, and I could see that on the map. Then he had me relate all the details of the attack, including the way we were ambushed from both sides. When I'd finished, he spoke. "So boys, looks like the Jicarillas (Lisa reminds me to say that these were Rocky Mountain Apaches) have been waiting for wagon trains. So I plan to teach 'em a lesson. We're all going back that way in a few days with four wagons. And we're gonna make them smart. Maybe they'll be a little less likely to raid our wagons after we lesson them some."

Carson spoke up, "St. Vrain. What if only two boys ride with the wagons and the rest of us trail out of sight. When the Apaches hit, we come in behind them and make them pay."

"Hmmm. Not a bad idea. But we don't know where they'll hit us, or even if they'll hit us. It's gonna be a trick to stay out of sight but keep close to the train."

"I think they'll hit us in the same place. They can get there and they know they have good cover there. We go and try it and assume they'll try the same thing again. Already got one wagon that way. All we have to do is spread out just before we reach this part of the valley."

"Alright, Kit. We'll do it your way."

The meeting broke up and a couple of the boys took me over to help them dig a grave for Jeremiah. I was glad to help, though I remembered him asking me to be put up in a tree, the Indian way. But I wasn't about to argue with St. Vrain, and having bodies in trees in a town like Taos probably would have caused a problem. So I just pitched in with the boys. Using ropes, we lowered him in the hole, wrapped in a trade blanket. St. Vrain said some words about him being a good man and asking God to welcome him home. One of the boys had made a wooden cross out of two pieces of pine tree limb tied together. They hammered that in the ground and we all wandered off to get our gear ready for the ride in a few days.

With my thoughts on my short-lived friendship with Jeremiah Coleman, the whole business with Miss Lupita had pretty much slipped my mind. So, I was almost totally unprepared for what came next. After we finished up, Kit and St. Vrain walked off somewhere, leaving me. I decided to look around a bit.

I was walking in the wood of scattered oaks a few yards to the west of the house, on the edge of town, when I heard my name. I turned to my left, thinking myself stupid for having let down my usual guard because I was in the settlements. No mountain man should ever let anyone get within a quarter mile without being aware of it, Indian, Spanish, or white. But you couldn't do that in a city or town, with so many people wandering about. You'd go mad.

To my left, there was Señorita Lupita, dressed attractively, as always. She walked up to me without a further word and began to kiss me, hard, forcing her tongue into my mouth. She withdrew a second, running her hands through my hair. Then she began to kiss me again, even grabbing for my crotch. I confess that I was too shocked to move for a several seconds, but then I started to back away and say "No, no, no, no, no!" I may not be much, but I love my woman and would never betray her. I turned and ran back to the house, which was deserted, thank God. I went to the store-room where I was staying, lit the candle, closed the door, and sat there a while, trying to make sense of it all by the dim light of the candle. I stayed that way until I heard St. Vrain's voice in the main room. I came out and there were no women in sight. St. Vrain asked me to help him with the wagons and the *pleus* in them we were preparing for the run to Bent's Fort, and I was relieved and happy to do so. I didn't see no more of Lupita that day, thank God.

Over the next few hours, eight more tough-looking old trappers showed up, arriving in ones and twos. I didn't know any of them. But hearing them talk to St. Vrain, I realized he'd hired 13 of us to go back to Bent's Fort. And he was telling them there was a good chance we'd have a run-in with the Apaches. That seemed to be something they were glad to hear. They were all spoiling for the fight.

After I helped St. Vrain and the new men load the four wagons with beaver *pleus*, he took me over to his outlying shed, which was full of all the possibles a mountain man could dream of. I bought two .50 Hawken rifles off St. Vrain. I didn't tell him I was fixing to give them to Indians. Didn't have enough money to buy the third, because I needed a new horse. St. Vrain walked me over to the stable in town and told me to choose a horse that he'd pay for with my credit against what the partnership of Bent and St. Vrain would be paying us.

I named my new horse Ann Marie. I have no idea why that name. I never met any woman named Ann Marie. I knew I would get attached to her and then lose her in the next fight. Still, I wanted to have a name to mourn, even if I had to eat her. I know I'm a fool, but that's how I feel. Don't name them—you might have to eat them. This is the only piece of Jack's advice I routinely ignore. Of course, Ann Marie was a big pinto mare with a round, even back and a canter as smooth as glass. I must have looked at 20 horses before I picked her and bought her. By this time, I knew what I liked in horses.

That night, St. Vrain, as part of payment, took the boys off to drink at the tavern in Taos. But so much valuable fur and equipment was sitting out in the yard, he said he needed two of us to stay back and watch it. Kit and I volunteered to stay behind. I hated whiskey after my experience at Rendezvous. And I didn't want to drink it now. Kit and I were sitting in one of the wagons on a stack of buffalo hides, talking softly, our Hawken rifles across our laps and stopping frequently to listen for anyone trying to sneak up on us.

"Kit, why'd you volunteer for this?

"Don't like to be out of control, especially around men bigger than me. Most men are bigger than me."

"Taller, maybe."

"Why did you?"

"I hate what whiskey does to a man when he's had too much. If there's anything bad in him, it comes out. I don't drink anymore with the boys."

"Well, that's true enough and I can't blame you. Say, Sam, I hear you have a Cheyenne woman."

"Yup."

"How is that?"

"Pretty fine doin's. She's a good woman and true. She's already given me a beautiful daughter. And, frankly, no white woman would have me with my face all carved up."

"How'd that happen?"

"About three year ago, a griz went after me. My pap killed him but I got carved up."

"Hmmm. I'm thinking of a native bride myself."

"Cheyenne are good folk and true."

"I've had some good doin's with the Arapaho."

"They're our allies. They're good folk too."

Kit paused for a moment. "I reckon those Apaches are going to be waiting for us. Hope you're ready for another scrap with them."

I thought about this. No Cheyenne warrior turned from a fight unless his medicine was bad. "I'm ready," was all I said.

At this point some critter moved in the bushes and made a slight noise. Probably was nothing worse than a racoon, but Kit and I stayed silent for quite a while. Then we got out and started patrolling the house and the yard as quiet as possible. I did hear Lupita singing in Spanish inside the house. I whispered to Kit that I would be sleeping outside this night with him and the boys, even though St. Vrain had offered me the storeroom. The night remained quiet and nothing else happened, which is a good thing if you're on watch. Always better to be bored and safe than excited and under threat.

The next day, the four wagons got hitched up to teams of mules in the yard across from St. Vrain's front door by four Mexican wagon drivers. The drivers shifted the loads inside with high-stacked *pleus* of beaver and buffalo pelts, balancing the weight between the four wagons. All thirteen of us trappers settled down to checking and re-checking all our possibles, cleaning our firearms, taking in extra powder and lead. Horses were watered and fed for the last time. Saddles were checked, cinches tightened. St. Vrain supplied everything. If you wanted something, you asked and it appeared, though St. Vrain wrote it down. You had to work it off. Still, the boys would rather be fully equipped than short-supplied in the wilderness. I asked for extra shot and powder, and St. Vrain only nodded as he brought it over to me. I thought about what Kit had said.

We saddled up and rode east out of town around mid-morning. Mrs St. Vrain and Lupita waved at us as thirteen mountain men, including me, Kit, St. Vrain and the others all surrounded the wagon, guns at ready. I confess I did take a quick glance back at Lupita. She puckered her rose lips and made a kiss at me. I turned and urged Ann Marie into a canter and did not look back again.

Those two young Mexican fellows who tried to charge me a fee coming into town were waiting for us just east of town. But they made themselves scarce when they saw us going out with St. Vrain in the lead. They weren't up for a fight I guess. Thirteen grim-looking mountain men armed with loaded rifles just wasn't worth it for them.

The following day we made the Eagle Nest Valley. Sitting on Ann Marie looking north from the edge of the forest, I could see the creek snaking north into the distance and the low hills to the northeast that led to the plains. To the east and west, the valley rose up from its shallow dip toward the stream in the center and jutted into pine-covered mountain slopes. I strained to look, but I could not see anyone or anything in the spot I knew to be where Jeremiah and I were attacked. But I could smell that smell I remembered during the attack.

"I think I smell Apache," I whispered softly to Kit.

"Me too," he replied.

St. Vrain had five of us dismount on each side and tie off our horses in the woods we had come to an end of. Kit and I were on the far-left flank, the west side, with three other trappers to our right between us and the wagons. St. Vrain and two other trappers slowly rode ahead with the wagons. Five other trappers were stationed on the other side of the trail. So we together swept before us something like a half mile of grass and brush. But all of us were trained like Indians, and moved almost unseen and unheard through the grass. We were told to stay up with the wagons, but at a crouch and as out-of-sight as possible.

Kit and I had been moving silently through the brush for about ten minutes when I saw motion in front of me and dropped. Kit must have seen me because he hit the dirt right after me. The three other boys down the line on our side saw us and did the same. I thanked my Cheyenne friends for training me to observe, because it probably saved our lives that day. The Apache smell was getting strong and then I saw a head move. That's why I dropped. I signed to Kit that they were maybe twenty feet in front of us. I think we all thought they'd hit further down the valley, north of us, like they did the last time. Kit signed back that we would stand up and shoot on the count of three. He passed it down the line using sign language. Then he held his hand up; one finger, two fingers, three fingers. I rose to the top of the bush I was behind and with my luck that Apache buck I first spotted was standing and taking aim at the wagons with his bow. About a dozen other Apaches were doing the same. I shook hands gently with my Hawken, like Jack taught me, and it roared. The Apache buck's head exploded with a broad splatter of blood, and he went down. I saw four others go down as well, but then I was expecting that.

In the mountains, shot and powder are dear, and trappers generally feel that it's an insult to the man who made your gun to miss a target. In those fool books my grandson reads, both sides are banging away constantly until combat breaks off. And they fire just to lay down a hail of lead on a target in the rough hope that one of them will find the mark. Our battles weren't like that at all. If we fired, someone went down. And we got out of sight and reloaded. Maybe years later, after those lever-action rifles got out into the mountains, people might reel off a lot of shots, but I'm not so sure. Ammunition is expensive, as well as heavy to carry, and when you're out, your weapon is almost useless. Plus, those repeating rifles had a way of heating up till you couldn't hold them, if you just kept firing and firing. I think the reality was more like what I remembered. A shot here and there—whoever had surprise and position quickly killed their enemy—then retreating on the other side.

That day, with five of their warriors killed in less than a second, the Apaches decided luck was not with them, or their medicine was bad as they would have seen it. They melted into the grass and were gone. We moved forward cautiously to make sure and found four of the bodies. Like I say, I don't much care for killing a man. I found the Apache I'd killed with half his head blown away. I looked away. I remember what Jack had told me about the Indian mind set that honored a man who died in clean battle. Still, it didn't make me feel much better.

A little farther on we found a hollow rimmed with grass, where they'd staked their horses, and they were definitely gone. We walked back the better part of a mile, to the edge of the woods and retrieved our horses, catching up to the wagons that were moving undisturbed down the trail to the north. About a half-mile on we found the wreck of the wagon the Apaches stole from Jeremiah and me. We found Antonio's body too, or parts of it anyway.

And as I suspected, the coyotes chewed up Bert's corpse and scattered it pretty widely. I was almost sorry for Bert. Almost. All the merchandise in the wagon was gone, of course. We stopped long enough to assemble what was left of Antonio and Bert and dig a deep hole and bury their remains.

When we crossed out of the mountains and onto the plains, heading north to the Arkansas River, I could smell the Comanches too, and I even saw them twice, thanks to the training my friends gave me. But they must have decided we were too expensive, there being thirteen of us, all heavily armed, and me clearly a Cheyenne. I could see that St. Vrain's plan had been to teach the Apaches the same lesson. The Comanches watched us but never came close. Ten days later we rode into Bent's Fort with all four wagons, and our scalps, and some good stories. And I almost ran to my tipi, to my Spirit, and bedded her that night feeling like a loyal husband who just maybe deserved her open arms and cool, naked skin.

10.

My Second Great Loss

1834

SEVERAL THINGS HAPPENED ABOUT the same time to change my mind and fortunes. First, Asimoni, I mean Spirit, told me the first morning I woke in my own bed that she was pregnant again. That kind of thing gets a man to thinking. The Bents didn't send me back with St. Vrain and the twelve other trappers. So, I said goodbye to my new friend, Kit, at the gate and watched them all go. I had asked to stay closer to the fort and they needed hunters to keep the fort fed, so that was fine. I rode out every day for maybe a month to take down buffalo and antelope. Much of the meat I brought back to the fort, but also much of it went to White Thunder's village. I was very welcome there, and Cheyenne was Cheyenne, but I was really missing my good friends up north. I talked this over with my wife and mother and they said they would be fine with whatever I wanted to do. So, after about three months of hunting, I told the Bents that though I thanked them for the employment, I was going to rejoin my family up north in the village of the Ivistsinihpah people. I had all the possibles I would need for at least three years, so there was no reason for me to stay. And I wanted my children to grow up amongst the Ivistsinihpah. They said they understood and asked me to stay another couple of weeks till St. Vrain came out with another group of wagons, because then they could hire one of the trappers that came with him to take my place as a fort hunter. I agreed.

White Thunder too was agreeable, and gave me his blessing to go. He understood the bonds of family and when I told him about my five friends, he said, "They are your brothers that no family gave you." I thought about it, and he was right.

Late in April, Ceran St. Vrain came through with four wagons loaded down with furs and about seven other trappers, including Kit. Kit agreed to take over my place as fort hunter, and told me privately that there was a girl in the nearby Arapaho village that took his fancy. The next day, doing what I could to pack things up. Kit came by and helped me. I was with my wife and mother and actually, since women are the experts at breaking down a tipi, they were doing all the real work, while I held onto my toddler daughter. Men are generally useless at this kind of work, though I could have done it. But women took pride in what they could do, and I would not rob them of that. Kit wished us well and rode out with another hunter to do his job. It was years before I saw him again.

In about an hour, we were ready, and the travois were made up on two of our horses. I was standing watching, after having worked for the move all morning, with my little girl, Meadowlark-Kathleen, squirming in my arms. Spirit and Willow were finishing up, lashing the last of our possessions to one of the horses or another. At times, various Cheyennes would stop by and wish me well and I thanked them. These Hevataniu were fine folks, but I was determined to go home. Then, much to my surprise, St. Vrain walked up to me.

"Hello, Sam."

"Hello St. Vrain. Come to see us off?"

"Actually, no. I come to ask a favor."

"Oh," I said, struggling with the squirming toddler in my arms.

"I would like to travel with you as far as the Platte and a little beyond. I need to look at the valleys of the Front Range near the headwaters of the Platte and I think you know those valleys better than most boys in the Mountains."

"I have hunted them year-round. I expect I do know them."

"Will you teach them to me?"

"Certainly. We could use another man in case there is trouble on the way."

"Fine. When do we leave?"

"Well, I was hoping to leave here in less than an hour . . . "

"Fine. I am ready to go."

And so, St. Vrain joined us. Looking back it seems huge and like the whole earth was moving beneath my feet. At the time it was just one more detail, and I was glad to have a second Hawken gun on our side if we were attacked. And we were.

I have noticed in this blessed, or maybe cursed, long life of mine, that when disaster strikes, it always seems to happen after a long stretch of peace and quiet. It strikes like a lion, who waits under cover of trees and pounces on the deer from behind, biting into its neck. I had taken a zig-zag course up the Front Range, showing St. Vrain my favorite hunting places. We were past the South Platte, and had found the old site of our village had been long abandoned, as my friend had told me it would be. We had taken a small creek that ran north and mostly west, and followed it into the mountains a ways. I knew this creek well, and it led into what I had always felt was the most beautiful valley in the foothills of the Front Range, green, rolling, with patches of woods and meadows and deer in plenty. I was almost reluctant to show it to St. Vrain, but I figured he'd find it anyway. We rode along, in the quiet, with nothing but the singing of the wind in the grass. In less time than a thought, arrows were slicing past us at high speed.

They were Pawnee, though why they were this far west is a mystery to me to this day. They had that characteristic way of shaving the sides of their heads and leaving a tall ridge of hair down the middle. I had met them before, friendly in those days, because I was white. Jack bought my first horse, Jane, off some Pawnees. But I guess as we rode along, with Cheyenne lodges packed on Cheyenne horses, and smelling Cheyenne, these Pawnees thought we were the enemy. And, except for St. Vrain, we were. But St. Vrain and I were all covered in buckskin, so it was probably difficult to tell if we were really white. Doc Ben once said he thought us mountain men were really just a tribe of white Indians in the mountains. I've thought about it since. In some ways, I think he was right. And it makes me wonder, if white ways are so wonderful, why did boys like me and other mountain men go to all this trouble to move west and become renegades?

It came silently, the hail of arrows. St. Vrain's horse went down, and he rolled off it, being well practiced about how to respond to ambush. He managed to grab his powder, shot and Hawken rifle off his dead horse and jumped up behind me on Ann Marie. We galloped into a thicket of pines and dismounted, dragging the travois with a great rattling sound. I'm sure we left parts of my lodge behind, but there was no choice. We got down behind some logs and St. Vrain and I got ready as the Pawnee started to close in on us. "Hold them off," I told St. Vrain, and putting down my Hawkens, I went to my pack and pulled out my .30 Hawken and the three .50 Hawken rifles I'd bought, bringing them over to where St. Vrain was behind a log. I must have surprised him. His eyes got big, but I didn't have to tell him what to do. We loaded up every gun, plus both of us had pistols. Then we waited. I heard my daughter whimper behind us but Spirit, like all good Cheyenne mothers in danger, pinched her nose and Meadowlark fell silent.

The Pawnee did what both St. Vrain and I knew what they'd do. A few of them started creeping out, bent over, in the open toward us. St. Vrain and I raised our rifles and two Pawnees went down. That seemed to be the signal for the rest to charge us, because they must have figured that we would be reloading. They were wrong. We fired another six times and six more Pawnees walked the Hanging Road of death. That was enough for them. They must have thought we had friends nearby who reinforced us, plus their medicine was bad to lose so many warriors so fast. They picked up their dead while we were reloading, and carried them off. Later, we realized that they had high-tailed it out of there. But I had other things on my mind.

As I was reloading, I heard Willow cry out. I turned and saw her lying ten feet away. She had an arrow deeply embedded in her right side, just above the waist, I rushed over to her, but there was nothing to be done. She was bleeding heavily. How she stayed on her horse at a gallop and made it to the thicket, I'll never know. Damn, but Cheyenne women are the toughest women in the whole wide world. There wasn't much to be said. I'm sure I was weeping, though I don't remember. All I could think of to say was "Mother! Mother!" She caressed my face with her bloody right hand, saying, "My son. My beautiful son." And then her hand dropped and her eyes stared over my shoulder at nothing. She did not breathe, nor move.

I don't know how long I sat there, stunned. Spirit started to wail very softly, as we were still in danger. Her long hair, in two braids, came well down, past her breasts, but she handed me our daughter, took out her knife and cut off her braids to the length of right below the ear. This was one of the ways Cheyenne women mourn, for their hair is part of their beauty and to lose it is a sacrifice. For me, holding my baby girl helped me to somehow come out of the trance I was in, so that I finally heard St. Vrain say to me softly, "Sam? Sam? We must set her to rest and move on. The Pawnee are gone."

His face was full of sorrow. He was no stranger to death of a loved one. "It's time," he said. "Let us honor your mother in the Cheyenne way. I checked on the Pawnee. They have fled. We actually killed seven. They won't be back." I was grateful for his gentle way. I was also grateful that he chose to say nothing about me taking three .50 Hawken rifles to the Cheyenne. Traders like St. Vrain frowned on arming Indians.

There, in that most beautiful of Rocky Mountain valleys, we made a platform in a hidden pine tree, and placed Menoke, Willow, beloved wife of Jack Rather, and the best mother a fellow could ever have, gently out on the platform with her eyes closed and her hands folded. I stood at the base of the tree and said the only prayer I could remember, the Hail Mary. You know, it's funny, but I really got the impression the Blessed Mother was standing right beside me at the base of that tree.

Nevertheless, we couldn't stay long. We found the dropped elements of my lodge and retied them to the horses. St. Vrain removed his saddle from his dead horse. He rode on Willow's mare, and we got ready to move north. Just before I mounted up, I stood one last time and swore to the Virgin Mother of God that I would return to this valley and live here someday. And right now, sitting on the porch of my ranch house, with my granddaughter writing this down, we're less than a quarter mile from my mother's tree. Do I go and visit it? Well, granddaughter, you've often wondered where I go when I get quiet and wander off sometimes. It's the tree above our little cemetery now. But even though Menoke lies below in the ground beside Jack, her husband, the tree is always special to me. Next time I'll take you with me. Tomorrow even. And we'll see my mother's tree.

Two days later, we pulled into White Coyote's village on the north bank of the North Platte. When the riders came out to meet us, they got quiet really fast. My wife's hair told them that we'd had a death. And everyone knew that Menoke should have been with us, so it wasn't hard for those people to figure out who was dead. By the time our column of horses entered the village, the word had spread and I heard the keening wail of mourning coming up from the women. Menoke, or Willow, had been well loved and was the chief's sister. Many women were in the act of cutting their hair as we rode by.

White Coyote walked up to meet us and put his hand on my leg when I reined up Ann Marie. I looked in his eyes but could find no words, in English or Cheyenne. He nodded and looked away. Spirit and St. Vrain and I began to assemble my tipi next to White Coyote's, doing the work wordlessly. Would to God I had taken that arrow for my mother. At one point I just stopped and sat down on the ground while St. Vrain and Spirit finished the exterior. Spirit, as always, read me like a book. Plus, she needed to arrange the interior, and no one could tell her what to do. She came out and put Meadowlark in my arms, who found an interest in playing with my nose and mouth. St. Vrain sat down beside me, got out his pipe and smoked silently. My daughter, as she did many times after, somehow pulled me back to the present.

Finally after a time, St. Vrain tapped out his pipe and put it in his possibles sack. "I will need to buy a good horse. And I think I will go first thing in the morning."

"Alright," was all I could manage to say.

"Thank you, Sam for showing me that country. I promise though, I will keep that last valley a secret. After all, there were no beaver in it."

"'Preciate that," I replied. "Let's go see about the horse now," I said, getting up. I figured if I wandered around for a bit, I'd find my friends soon enough. But it was Laughs at Night and Red Mountain who were looking for me. They didn't say anything about my mother, but then they didn't have to. I could see the grief in their eyes too.

Speaking in Cheyenne, I told them "This is St. Vrain, my friend. He killed four Pawnees to save my family." That, I knew would establish St. Vrain as a friend of the Cheyenne. "He leaves tomorrow and the Pawnee killed his horse. He wants to buy a good stallion."

Red Mountain lifted up his chin and said, "Ha hou! Four dead Pawnees? I will give him a stallion in thanks for saving the life of my brother, Red Hair, and his family, and for beginning to avenge the death of Menoke."

I translated this back to St. Vrain, who said he was grateful, and he would always fight for his friends. I translated this to Red Mountain, who was pleased. Meadowlark had fallen asleep in my arms, so we all of us walked out to the horse herd. Red Mountain had the boys on watch cut out a big, tall chestnut stud, not very old. "I stole him off some Spiders, so he will take your saddle," Red Mountain explained, and I translated. Then he took the lead line and handed it to St. Vrain, who did know enough Cheyenne to say "*Nea'ese*", thank you, and then St. Vrain walked the horse back to my lodge. Laughs at Night waited till St. Vrain was gone, then said, "Red Hair, come to my lodge this night. We brothers will meet. We need to do something about these Pawnee. We will help you find your revenge."

As he said it, my energy came back to me suddenly. "Yes. Yes. I want to talk about that." Then I returned back to my lodge. Later that evening I found Laughs at Night's lodge and went in. His wife had gone and my five brothers were seated around the fire, with Laughs at Night in the spot of honor at the back, as it was his lodge. I was carrying a large bundle wrapped in a buffalo hide. There was an empty place and I crossed my legs and sat in it, putting my bundle down in front of me. Laughs at Night spoke first.

"Welcome home, Red Hair, though I wish it were a better homecoming. But what do you bring?"

"My brothers," I began, "a winter ago I gave two Hawken rifles to Four Thunders and Many Horses, and was honored to do it. I made a promise to my other three brothers that I would in time find each of them a Hawken rifle in gratitude for saving my life that day. I have been able to keep my promise. So tonight . . . " At this point I unwrapped the bundle and they could plainly see the three .50 Hawken rifles laying there. I stood, picked up the first rifle and lay it across the upturned palms of my hands. Red Mountain was to my left and I offered it to him. "Take this, brother. It is a new rifle, but it has already killed a Pawnee." Red Mountain took it reverently and then let out a "Ha hou! Already blooded! Thank you, my brother!"

I took out the next rifle, and walked it around to Stands to the Left, who was sitting opposite of me. Handing him the rifle, I said again, "Take this, brother. It is a new rifle, but it has already killed a Pawnee." Stands to the Left took it more quietly and nodded his thanks. I got the final rifle and walked it over to Laughs at Night, handing it to him, saying, "Take this, my host and brother. It is a new rifle, but it has already killed a Pawnee."

He also took it reverently and nodded his thanks. "Thank you, Red Hair. None of us ever doubted your promise, and now it is fulfilled."

I sat down again at my spot and said, "The rest of this bundle is shot and powder. I have divided it into five bundles, one for each of you, now that you have rifles as good as those of the Spiders. I am finished, my host. I will listen to you now."

Laughs at Night nodded again, and then asked me "Tell us, Red Hair, how you were attacked and how your mother died."

I obliged by narrating in as much detail as I could about the attack in Menoke's valley. When I had done, it was Many Horses who spoke first. "It seems obvious to me that this Pawnee war party was sent out to find our village and did not, only because we had moved. This was no mere horse raid of two or three, but a full war party with a heart to kill many of our people."

"This was my thought too," Red Mountain added. "The village is in danger if our enemies have come this far west to attack us. But their trail will still be fresh if Red Hair will take us there and we pick it up. We may yet be able to avenge Menoke thoroughly." They all looked at me.

"Let me send off my Spider friend in the morning. Then let us ride there and begin."

Many Horses spoke, caution in his voice. "Your people were once the Spiders, Red Hair. And the Spiders are at peace with the Pawnee. Will this be a problem for you?"

I looked him in the eye. "They ambushed us and killed my mother. I will have no problem killing some more of them. We ride tomorrow."

11.

Bloody Revenge

1834

EARLY IN THE MORNING St. Vrain rolled out of his robes in my tipi and packed up his new horse. "Thank you, Sam, and I sure am sorry for your mother."

I couldn't speak of that easily, so I just nodded.

"Remember," he added, "our trade runs through the land of the Pawnee."

I held my face as stone, watching him riding off to the south. But he knew what I intended to do. I was grateful he didn't give me a moral lecture; he just reminded me of the implications of my own living to an angered Pawnee tribe. And he was right. But that wasn't the biggest blockage in my heart.

Here's another place where I was in conflict. I was raised Catholic and Fr. Larson back in St. Louis was a kindly man and a good priest, not to mention my friend, Charette. I know some folks who had hellfire and brimstone priests, and don't go to mass no more. Not me. I was fortunate in the Catholic priests I knew. So, I was taught by good men, that revenge belonged to God. At the time I still considered myself a Catholic, and as a matter of fact, I still do.

But the Cheyenne have a very practical view of revenge. They see it as a deterrent. And in the boiling waters of the high plains, where traveling tribes swirled around and bumped into each other and imposed on each other's hunting grounds, a deterrent was about all you had to keep the game from getting too scarce to feed your family. That's why the Comanches did not attack me months back. They weren't at peace with us and regularly stole our horses. But they did not want the whole weight of the Hevataniu Cheyenne coming down on them, so they did not kill us.

My friends well knew that if a large war party of Pawnee came upon us and slaughtered us once, they'd be bold enough to do it again. In my case, St. Vrain and I had made them pay dearly, but that might not be enough to discourage more aggression. The Pawnee had to be made to feel it was too deadly to anger the Cheyenne.

Now you can tell me retaliation just brings more retaliation, and that's true enough—in the way white people make war. We go in, take heavy losses and bear it, just so long as we wipe out our enemy. White people make war to conquer; Indians tend to make war to intimidate.

For my Cheyenne kin, and other tribes around us, boys were too few and too precious to sacrifice so easily. Battles like Gettysburg would have puzzled my Cheyenne kin, who would have thought that when General Lee lost so many men for no gain on the second day, he should have figured his medicine was bad and vanished. If the Cheyenne had fought at Gettysburg, there would have been no third day and no Pickett's Charge. But then, the Cheyenne would have never massed all their warriors and marched into enemy territory in the first place. That would have seemed like an unnecessary sacrifice and even mass suicide to them. In fact, only once did the Cheyenne gather that many warriors in a fight, and that was against Crook and Custer. But that's for a later part of this story.

On the plains, the highest honor in war was not to kill your enemy, but to intimidate him, get him to clear out of your hunting grounds. You tapped him and got away unhurt. Some folks call it "counting coup." We didn't call it that. We just thought of it as showing the enemy that they were courting danger by angering us. Do that enough and people stop coming after you. The intent was warning, not slaughter. And more often than you'd think, the message got through. Certainly, there were killings in a battle, followed by scalping, but it was a higher honor to intimidate your enemy and get away alive. That was what the Cheyenne thought of as war, until tangling with the US Army taught them different.

But this time, I wanted more. Maybe it was because after all, I'm still a Spider, at least on the Irish side. I wanted blood for the blood of my mother. My brothers all understood and respected that without explanation. They would have thought me odd if I'd felt any other way. So, when St. Vrain had ridden off west, headed for the Green River, we all met at Laughs at Night's lodge and painted our faces. That was a first for me, and I could only paint the good side of my face, but I did it without hesitation. I felt like I was applying resolve to my soul when I painted berry juice on my face. When you paint your face for war, you commit to action. You are wearing your resolve and there's no backing down.

When I returned to my lodge for final preparations, Spirit looked at me and I saw a bit of fear in her eyes. But Cheyenne men went to war all the time. She didn't seem surprised, just a trickle of the thought must have been going across her mind that I would not come back this time. I said, "I will return and I will see my second child." She smiled a little, mainly I think because she appreciated that I was even trying to calm her fears. I loaded up both my Hawken guns on Ann Marie, who was tied off outside my lodge, mounted up and rode to the east end of the village where my brothers were gathering. Once I got there, Many Horses and Red Mountain had yet to arrive, but about ten more of our warriors sat ready and waiting. By the time we formed up, there were thirty-two of us, over half of the village's warriors. Laughs at Night was acknowledged as leader, for several reasons, including that he was a Dog Soldier. We set off in the midday heat, heading first to Menoke's valley. We picked up the Pawnee trail and headed east, down St. Vrain Creek, down the South Platte and to the confluence of the North and South Platte. After that, we traveled along the north bank of the Platte, following the Pawnee sign till it got mixed up in the sign of other tribes and of white travelers. But no matter. We knew well enough how to find the Pawnee.

The Platte is a lazy river. It's got plenty of water for this dry country, but it meanders between brushy banks, dotted with occasional cottonwood trees until it broadens out and soaks into the Missouri down by the Spider settlements. This means that first, it's the major highway from St. Louis to the Rockies, and you're bound to meet some party traveling up and down it rather suddenly as you pass through some brush or come around a line of trees. And it's not just the Spiders (Lisa is after me to call them Americans). Fine. Americans. Just like I came up it with Bob Campbell, Doc Harrison, and Sir William only a couple of years ago now, you would meet trappers going up, or sometimes floating down in a bullboat full of *pleus*. Lisa is after me to explain that a bullboat is a tiny boat that looks like an upside-down umbrella with no handle. It's made of green, flexible branches covered with buffalo hide as a hull, and tied together with buffalo sinews. Most of the boys in the mountains knew how to make one. They would make them to sail as far as the Missouri. But before my granddaughter interrupted me, I was going to say that the Platte was the road between the Cheyenne and the Pawnee, and that meant it was also a war road. This is what St. Vrain had reminded me of. Being a trader, he'd rather it remained peaceful. And he was reminding me that I too traded in furs. And my real point, that Lisa got me away from, is with all that brush, it was a pretty good place to get yourself ambushed if you were not really careful.

So, as we followed the Platte, we did it slowly and carefully. Though Laughs at Night never chose me for reasons of his own, at which I could guess, we always sent two scouts out ahead for several miles and only when they came back with a report did we move east, following the north bank, even then riding so we stayed hidden in the brush. We did encounter two trappers on the south bank on horseback, going west. We froze under cover as they went by, but watching them, I could tell they'd smelled and then seen us. They were probably making a note of a large Cheyenne war party heading east, and set about making their own way west as quickly as possible. We trappers tried to stay out of battles between tribes, and I was pushing the boundary of behavior expected of a white man in the Rockies to be doing what I was doing. I didn't care.

We traveled for four days like this, or maybe it was six. Can't recall exactly. But it was Many Horses who came back from a scouting trip to report Pawnee on the north bank about a mile ahead, though he didn't say miles. The Cheyenne at this point were still unfamiliar with Spider ways and he probably said something about how long it took to walk there. Never mind. They were a mile ahead. We had the advantage and initiative, which is everything in ambush warfare. Whoever spots the enemy first usually carries the day. We all clustered together and talked softly. I know it wasn't my place, but it was my mother they killed so I said, "Let's use the rifles to set up a different kind of ambush."

Laughs at Night looked at me and said, "Explain."

I knelt down and drew in the mud under our moccasins with a broken off twig. "Here's the river. They're here. We're here. Most of us could go north then swing around and come in from the north on foot and flank the ambush. That pushes them here, toward the river. Those of us with rifles will hide in the brush here by the bank and as the enemy backs toward us, we let them have it."

Everyone looked at my scratches in the mud and they started nodding.

"Very well," Laughs at Night said, "We will follow Red Hair's plan. Sees the Moon will lead the attack from the north and the six of us with rifles will take cover near the bank and wait." My five brothers and I found a log near the river that provided good cover and loaded our Hawken rifles. I had two pistols and gave one to Red Mountain as well. And I laid out powder and ball for five more loads on the log beside me. I had the .30 in reserve, but I planned to use that only if we got in a bad way. Then we waited, silently. War is like that: long stretches of silence and tension with moments of explosion and death, that go as fast as they come. I even began to wonder if the Pawnee had pulled back and our warriors had found no one, when shouting erupted to the north and east of us. I recognized the battle yells of our Cheyennes.

Like dress and smell, every tribe is different. The Pawnee yells responded. I cocked the hammer on my Hawken. The shouts drew closer and then a dozen or so Pawnee were backing up toward us. I thought of Menoke and squeezed the trigger on my Hawken. The other Hawken guns roared as well and six Pawnee went down like felled trees. The others weren't slow to realize their peril and charged us. I got one with my pistol. But one Pawnee buck was running hard at me, and carrying a stone hatchet, and it was too late to grab for my .30. I rose in one motion from my cover, pulling out my Green River. Just then, the rest of our war party showed up, but I didn't see much. I just know somehow I deflected his hatchet blow with my left forearm, and sliced his neck deeply with the Green River knife in my right hand, so he went down and was bleeding out. He only lived a couple of seconds after that. I took a glance around. All the Pawnee were dead and our war party was scalping the dead. Anger still boiled in my heart. For all I knew, this might be the very warrior that shot the arrow that killed my mother. I had never scalped a man before, but I imitated the motion of my fellow Cheyenne, and the scalp came off with a "thwap" sound. I held it in my left hand and looked at it. Laughs at Night was standing looking at me.

"It is not enough, is it?" he observed.

I knew what he meant. The hole in my heart for Menoke was still aching. "No," I answered.

"But," he continued "you still think like a Spider. You want justice. And this is not it. Do not look for it. What matters is that when the Pawnee find this war party, they will be furious, but they will not approach us lightly again to kill our women. It is not justice, but it is a price we can pay for a little more safety. Put that scalp on your lodgepole so you do not forget what I have told you."

And that's what I did. Spirit watched me do it, and it was not unusual to her, but I think she was concerned about the boiling in my heart. But she didn't have to be. I went on no more war parties though I went out and hunted regularly with my brothers. I did not speak of Menoke again, like the Cheyenne I was becoming. The Cheyenne never speak the name of the dead again. To speak of the dead is to call their souls back from the Hanging Road, when they have no body to come back to.

Lisa is after me to explain the Hanging Road. The Cheyenne look up in the night sky and see what Spiders call the Milky Way. They figure it's the road to the afterlife. Menoke was walking the Hanging Road to the next world, or Heaven or whatever you want to call it. I figured I'd see her there soon enough. Maybe she was having a talk with the Blessed Virgin. I wanted to think so, and I left it at that. I know that sounds odd, but I discovered almost instinctively that though the hole in your heart never heals, the only way to not go mad is to let it go. I think that was half the reason that the Cheyenne do not name the dead. And I know I'm naming the dead a lot in this telling. Well, hell. Let them come and surround me. I'd rather be haunted by their ghosts than know most of the men and women still breathing in this world.

So, I guess you could say I calmed down. And when I did think of Menoke, I stepped outside and looked up at my lodgepole to see the dark Pawnee scalp hanging there. And then I remembered what Laughs at Night told me about justice. In the end, it was the Catholic side of me that made sense of it. The only justice is from God. The rest of us are too ignorant to hand it out correctly. The fact was, the Pawnee left us alone for over a year. That's what Laughs at Night had predicted, and he was right. No one else's mother had to die.

In late February, Spirit gave me a son. His Cheyenne name was just 'Red Hair's boy' for years, as Cheyenne let a young man find his name as they come of age. But I named him Jack as well. Eventually through a vision, he earned the name "Flies Straight," but for me he was always Jack. Holding my children in my arms was the most healing thing for me. And like it says in the Bible about Isaac, I was consoled after the death of my mother.

12.

Smallpox

1837–1838

For about two years, I was just another Cheyenne. I did make a couple of trips down to Bent's Fort and Taos, to pick up more powder and shot and other possibles, but generally I stayed close to home. Laughs at Night proved right again. About a year and a half later, there was a big Pawnee raid, and my heart was pierced again. Red Mountain, my dear brother, seeing the other Cheyennes retreat behind him, decided he would be what Spiders call the "rear guard." He staked himself out to fight to the death, and it allowed the rest of us to make cover and set up a defensible line. He must have killed at least ten Pawnee before they wounded him so bad he could no longer stand up. They killed and scalped him. I was there, having just jumped behind some logs and reloaded my Hawken. I have seen a lot of men die, and I have killed my fair share of them myself. But I cannot tell you the pain I felt seeing bullets passing through Red Mountain and little sprays of his blood leaping out. At the end, a large spray of blood and gore exited from the middle of his back and I knew they'd shot him through the heart. I think I screamed, but the sound of the fighting drowned it out. I saw a Pawnee lean over and scalp his body. And even though my round would have been better spent against the Pawnees that were pressing us closer, I took in wind, and distance, aiming a little high to account for the drop of gravity as my round began to lose energy. And I fired. That was the best damn shot I ever made. I saw a spray of blood and brains blow out like a red dynamite explosion from the top of the Pawnee's head and he went down, just as he began to wave Red Mountain's scalp in triumph. Shortly after, the deadly effect of so many of us Cheyennes having Hawken guns caused the Pawnee to retreat rapidly. Like I said, Indians don't like taking heavy casualties. It ain't worth it. They vanished like smoke. When we were sure they were gone, my remaining brothers and I picked up Red Mountain, and his scalp, and took him to a nearby cottonwood grove, where we constructed a flet for him on a low branch and laid him to rest for his journey up the Hanging Road. We mourned him, but for the Cheyenne, to die the way he did was the best way to live and die together. We praised him for living and dying with courage and for sacrificing himself for the Cheyenne people. It was not like the way I had felt at Menoke's death, she who hurt no one and was killed by an arrow in ambush. Red Mountain's death was not so bitter for me.

But it did make me restless, and I left Spirit behind and rode south for a couple of months. I should add that every time I went south to Bent's Fort, I made sure to spend a couple of nights in my valley. I even began my first cabin there on my second trip, what was eventually to become this ranch. It was only maybe 20 ft by 10, and I use it as a woodshed today, but that was my first ranch home.

When I stayed with St. Vrain in Taos, he showed me my valley on a map. He'd named the creek after himself, which angered me until he explained that if he named the creek after me, all sorts of people would know where my valley was, that is, where I could be found. This made good sense and I agreed. I was also relieved to hear that Lupita, his wife's sister that had grabbed my crotch, was married to a wealthy Mexican rancher in the area. He kept her under tight wraps, because she had a reputation for flirting and more, with any man she liked, which was most of them.

But back to the raid, it set White Coyote and the elders to talking. You see, we Ivistsinihpah were the center of the tribe. We were the most Cheyenne of all the Cheyenne. We were like Washington DC to the Spiders, or to the Americans, as Lisa insists I say. Two-thirds of the tribe had joined the Hevataniu band down on the Arkansas River and one-third was up on the Cheyenne River around the Black Hills. Some of the Omissis had even moved farther up north, as far as the Powder River and the Tongue River. Only us in the middle kept the Cheyenne connected as a single tribe at all. But the summer Medicine Dance was not well attended in the last two years, being too far for many Cheyenne, and the Council of the 44 Peace Chiefs wasn't meeting as a result.

When I returned from Taos, I had dinner with White Coyote. He and I discussed the stretched-out Cheyenne tribe. He said it was plain that we were breaking into two tribes: the Southern Cheyenne and the Northern Cheyenne. And even the smaller bands down on the Arkansas were intermarrying with the more populous Hevataniu, so that they really ceased to be anything but Hevataniu themselves. Meanwhile, in the north country, the Omissis were growing and having babies at a rate like the Hevataniu down south. Besides us Ivistsinihpah, only one band had split loyalties: the Suhtai, who had once been a separate tribe that joined the Cheyenne. They were split between north and south bands.

White Coyote told me that the Pawnee raid had the effect of convincing him and the elders that we could no longer safely hold our middle position on the Platte in an effort to keep the tribe together. Our village was too far from our fellow Cheyenne, north and south, and they could not come to our aid when the Pawnee attacked. The elders had decided that the Ivistsinihpah would break camp and go south to the Arkansas River, to join the Hevataniu and the other Southern Cheyenne bands. But he said that I was to pass the word among the younger people, that those who wished to stay in the north were welcome to leave and go to the villages of the Omissis if they preferred. I asked my brothers to dinner in my lodge, and when Spirit took the children and left, we talked freely about what we would choose.

I know you're thinking that I went south to be near Bent's Fort. Well, I did go down that way plenty of times, but my four remaining brothers, Laughs at Night, Four Thunders, Many Horses, and Stands to the Left, all thought that life among the Hevataniu sounded too tame. The Northern Cheyenne were threatened by enemies on every side. They all intended to go north and were grateful for White Coyote's wisdom that he left every family free to decide. So, I talked to Spirit, and though it meant leaving her father and mother behind, we chose to follow my four brothers and their families, indeed many families, and go north, effectively becoming Omissis.

After 20 days of travel north of the Platte River, we reached an Omissis village on the Cheyenne River south of the Black Hills and were welcomed. The chief was named Tall Horse and he was a good and wise man. They were wintering on the Cheyenne River and planned to go up to the Powder River once spring came. I, my wife and two children and my family, settled in, setting our lodges together as an extended family with my four brothers and their wives and children. Before too long, we had become experts at hunting the valleys in the south end of the Black Hills. We also saw many of our allies, the Lakota, both in camp and on the hunt, as well as our closest friends and allies, the Arapaho. In January, an Arapaho village came and pitched their lodges next to ours. I began to wonder if someday the Northern Arapaho and the Northern Cheyenne would become one tribe, and the Southern Cheyenne and Southern Arapaho become another tribe. Turned out that I was half-right. But that's later in the story.

But the event that changed my life in so many ways happened shortly after we became part of Tall Horse's village. One day I returned from hunting to find not only my Spirit and my two children, but a young woman named Singing Night sitting with them. When I came in, Spirit handed baby Jack to Singing Night and after I'd laid down my Hawken and shot, she took me outside for a walk around the camp.

"Husband, I want to ask you for something."

"Anything, my love."

"I want you to take another wife."

To say I was stunned would be to put it mildly. I stopped walking. "What? Where are you going?"

She laughed at me, something she did often. "You are thinking like a Spider again. I am going with you. But Singing Night has lost her husband. She can be my sister."

Lisa tells me that I need to do a lot of explaining. First, the Cheyenne occasionally had men with two wives. Never more than two. And they generally were sisters, since the Cheyenne figured that sisters would already have an established pecking order. Harmony is important if you live year-round in a 15 foot wide tipi. Singing Night had been Red Mountain's wife. She was a close cousin of Spirit. What's more, unlike the beauty of most Cheyenne women, with strong bodies and full breasts, Singing Night was somewhat skinny and for all I could tell at that time, had small breasts. Village gossip said there were no babies in her womb, as everyone assumed Red Mountain could produce sons on any woman. Now she was a widow, and lived on the goodness of Many Horses, who was her cousin from a different side of the family. But this arrangement was strained, and Many Horses' wife, Night Star, did not like having Singing Night around their lodge. Anyway, for a Cheyenne woman, a second wife was a sister to help them with the many chores, and that seemed to be Spirit's attitude. What was hard for me to figure was that Spirit had no sexual jealousy in the matter. I asked her, "It won't bother you that I sleep with my second wife?"

She laughed again, "No. She is like a sister to me, who had no brothers or sisters."

In her mind, sisters shared, even husbands. Here again, my Spider raising ran hard up against Cheyenne values. And again, I sided with the Cheyenne. And I always will.

"Well, all right then," I told her, and she headed back to my lodge, after telling me, "Go see Many Horses."

I walked over to Many Horses' lodge and was invited in and fed strips of buffalo meat, an honor. I asked him, "I have come for your advice and permission. I have thought to take Singing Night as a second wife, but I don't know who to ask or give horses to. But my wife desires this thing."

Many Horses nodded. "It is a wise choice. I and your wife are the only family she has left, and I approve as well. You need not give any horses, for her father is dead. The wife of our brother, Red Mountain, should not live her life alone. Thank you for bringing this to me. Your heart is good and strong to ask it. May she give you many children." He then spoke to Night Star, who bundled up some trinkets and dresses and handed them to me. And with that, the thing was done, or so I thought.

I walked back to my lodge in a fog of bewilderment, carrying Singing Night's bundle. And I realized I had not only obliged my wife's desire, I had solved a problem for the tribe. For though there were unmarried men still, they preferred an unmarried girl and not a widow, and a woman needed a man to support her. So, widows were a burden at times. Plus, Singing Night, as I said, was skinny. When I was a boy in St. Louis peeking in the whore-house windows, I got a good idea of the white man's idea of feminine beauty: big breasts, wide hips, with a thin little waist in between, usually produced by a high-compression corset. The Cheyenne would have thought the skinny waist strange. They knew that wide-built, more muscular women survived child-birth a lot better. Skinny women died at the first birth. But Singing Night was not only skinny, her left hand was malformed, so that she had a left thumb, but her other fingers had never separated before birth, so that she could grasp things in her left hand, but not do any fine work, having only a single wide finger to oppose her thumb. To some Cheyennes, such a thing was frightening, and everyone thought Red Mountain noble to marry her with such a defect. But she had been a good wife to him. And I thought her a might pretty, even if she was skinny. But that wasn't the last surprise. Like a lot of peoples in this world, a marriage ain't properly a marriage until there is sex.

So, when I got back, Spirit was standing outside the front entrance hole, waiting for me. I simply said, "It is done."

She smiled and hugged and kissed me. Then she called for the children and picked up her digging stick and root bag, and taking the Yellow Bird by the hand, and carrying Jack, walked off to the prairie where many women were digging for edible and tasty roots. It was engrossing work and I knew she wouldn't be back for hours. I went into my lodge and Singing Night was sitting there. She stood up and smoothed out her deerskin dress with her hands, but not looking me in the eye.

"What have you to tell me?" she asked, her voice trembling.

"If you would permit it, I would take you for my wife," I said, handing her the bundle, "And this is now your home."

Still not meeting my eyes, she nodded and took the bundle, putting it to one side. We stood there for a long time it seemed. Finally, I said what I had said so clumsily my first time with Spirit. "I will never take from you anything you do not wish to give with your heart."

That was when she looked up and met my eyes, with a bit of surprise in her face. She was not going to be forced. My declaration took a while for her to take it in. Then she looked up and looked me in the eye for some time before saying, "I desire that we be lovers, husband." And she reached down and took off her deerskin dress, from the bottom up over her head, and unfastened her rope chastity belt. I slipped off my breechclout and belt and we became lovers. I found that she was quite fond of love-making, not showing the quiet pleasure that was typical of my first wife, Spirit, but that she seemed to explode with pleasure at least twice, as a man did. This was a lot more rare with Spirit, who seemed satisfied that I explode with pleasure, though sometimes she did too. Singing Night may have been skinny with a mis-formed hand, but she was a good and passionate lover.

It took me some long time to accept the fact that I was a double husband, but in the end, it seemed to work well. As the months went by, my wives enjoyed each other's company and worked well together. The children loved having double mothers. And I made sure to never give one wife something that I didn't give the other as well, so there was no competition. And, as I said, the Cheyenne build mental walls sleeping in a tipi, so that on the nights I laid with Spirit, Singing Night went to sleep and stayed on the other side with the children. And on the nights I laid with Singing Night, the opposite was true.

And I learned one more thing. The gossip around camp had been that Singing Night was barren, for she gave Red Mountain no children. But six months after Singing Night moved into my lodge, she became pregnant. What do you know about that.

But though I cannot think why, joy is often followed by great tragedy. I pray about it, especially since I have a devotion to the Blessed Mother. But God, nor St. Mary don't do a whole lot of explaining. It hit us by surprise. First, one afternoon, an Omissis warrior named Dances to the Left came back from dealing with the Lakota, saying he felt ill. He laid down in his lodge and soon developed red sores all over his body. By the second day he was dead. The Cheyenne were panicked. No one knew what this was. But I knew. My birth mother had me inoculated for smallpox, and I'd seen it before. Without planning to, I became a leader in the camp. I told everyone to stay away from others if they came down with the deadly rash. It was hard. Wives longed to go to their husbands who were sick. But I physically stopped them in several instances. I told them I had been given the Spider's medicine and could not get the disease. I cared for the sick and the dying. I removed their bodies outside the camp and with their blankets and anything they had touched, I made a great fire in a hollow by the river, and burned the blankets and the bodies. I told them that the disease would spread if I did not. It went against the Cheyenne grain to dispose of the dead this way, but after a pause, they began to trust me. This is probably because I gave them hope, and the disease was merciless and quick to kill. So, with my direction, we kept infections to less than one in five in the village. Some whole families were wiped out, true, but mainly I was able to limit the deaths to about one per lodge and in some cases, none. That felt good.

But imagine my horror when Singing Night found me in the center of the village, her belly swollen with child and my other two children with her, and told me Spirit had the disease. I told them to stay there, and ran home. It was true. Spirit was covered with the pox and barely conscious. I did everything I could for her. She lived maybe two more hours. I had to wrap the corpse of my beloved in her favorite buffalo-hide blanket and carry her to the burning pit.

After that, I don't know how I functioned, going through the necessary motions without mind or heart. I recall just barely, carrying her blanket-wrapped body to my burning pit and laying it with others. I recall the blaze of fire that turned them all slowly into ashes. And I recall that I could not bear the thought that any more of my family might catch the dreaded pox from things in my lodge that I should have burned but didn't. In the end, I took out my guns and powder and trapping gear, which Spirit never touched anyway, and torched everything else and my entire tipi, just to keep Singing Night and my children safe. It hurt my heart even more because it was the tipi that Jack made for Menoke, but my family had to be safe. We slept a few nights under some trees in new buffalo hides. And Singing Night and I began building a new tipi.

When the disease finally ground to a halt, the village had lost only 33 men, women, and children. I became revered as a great Medicine Man, for I had saved us from worse losses. Yet I was numb with pain, as I had been at Menoke's death. But there was no enemy to hunt down and scalp this time. I did hear later that whole tribes were all but wiped out by this pox. The mighty Blackfeet, who had single-handedly kept the Spiders out of their country, were now a pitiful handful of survivors and the northern Rockies were wide open for the first time anyone could remember. The Mandan and the other Missouri River tribes almost vanished completely. Rumors went from tribe to tribe that white men started it by giving the Mandans infected blankets. I don't know if that was true, but it was plenty likely.

13.

To the Arkansas

1839–1841

AFTER MAYBE TWO MONTHS, the smallpox did not again disturb us, but other things weighed on my heart. To the good, I found that not only was Singing Night a wonderful mother to the children, who felt sorely the death of their first mother, but I found that I truly loved her body and soul, as I had Spirit. We would all have been bereft almost to the death without the warm heart of Singing Night.

On the other hand, every place I went in this village, I kept expecting Spirit to pop out around some tree or someone's lodge. The village was haunted for me. And the more I thought about it, the more I thought the family down south should know what happened to us. But beyond all this, I was restless for no real reason I could think of. I formed a longing to see my valley, Menoke's valley, on what the map called "St. Vrain Creek." Beyond that, it seemed good to me to maybe visit with White Coyote again and tell him the news, as well as let him visit with his grandchildren. And it wouldn't hurt to work for the Bents for a bit and stock up on shot and powder and maybe get Singing Night some foofaraw, to show her how much I loved her. So, we packed up our new lodge. I said farewell to my four brothers, and promised them I would return. I also said farewell to Tall Horse and thanked him, assuring him I would return. He did not ask me any questions. He seemed to understand the death of my first wife was rocking my soul in some pretty heavy waves.

After a slow journey of a week or two south, we hit on St. Vrain Creek and rode up west into Menoke's Valley. I found my log shed, still in good shape but needing some minor repair. As a test, I moved us in there, instead of setting up the lodge. Singing Night found living in a rectangle bizarre and the children thought it an adventure. But it was warmer than the tipi and the winds did not penetrate nor shake it much. So, Singing Night got used to it, especially after I added a rock fireplace. Fall was starting to turn into winter, so we decided to stay till spring, and I began building what was to become the ranch house we now live in. Winter is a good time to cut trees and horse-drag them easily across the frost-covered pine needles and grass. I modeled it on St. Vrain's house in Taos, with a big central room with a fireplace for cooking, and three bedrooms on either side.

This really perplexed Singing Night, who as a Cheyenne, could not conceive of private rooms for couples and individuals to sleep in. I'm sure she wondered if she had married a madman. But then I was still half-Spider, so she let it go at that. It was a milder winter than most, and I had the walls and roof up before spring. I didn't cut holes for the windows, though I knew where I wanted them to go, because I had no glass to put in them. It also had a big covered porch out front, another thing that perplexed Singing Night, where to this very day, I still sit and talk in the evenings to my granddaughter. In fact, that's what we're doing right now.

The inside had a lot of work to do, but I just sealed it all up, figuring to return later. We could have moved in there but there was a second reason that we didn't and that it went up so fast, and I should have told that before now. We'd been living in the log shed about seven weeks when I scented on the wind something like a white man, but then I also smelled Crow. It was a sunny day, but cold enough to snow, with a small breeze gently whipping the branches of the pines and spruces. That's a good time to get scent. I told the children and Singing Night to stay quiet and stay inside, picked up my loaded Hawken, loaded my pistol and put it in my belt, and stepped out front of the cabin. I could hear hooves trotting near. A figure emerged out of the pines. Mountain man by look, Crow by smell. Damn, if it wasn't Jim Beckwourth. He had his own horse and was pulling a second horse, a buckskin, heavily loaded down with traps and his other truck that the poor horse was having a hard time carrying. Lisa reminds me to explain that "truck" here is mountain talk for your gear.

"Well, hell!" he yelled as he rode up, "If it ain't Cheyenne Sam. You gonna shoot my ass, you damn Cheyenne?"

"Nah," I said, using English for the first time in months, "Wouldn't waste the round. How you doing, Jim? And what brings you here? I heard you went back to 'Merica. What'd you go and do a damn stupid thing like that for? Ain't no respect for Black folk back there."

He stopped his horse and dismounted, giving me a friendly slap on the shoulder. "Well, I figured I'd make some money down South. Yor right. Was stupid. Glad I left again. Anyway, I figured some of these trapped-out valleys might have some beaver what snuk back in. But I been getting bear pelts mostly. They sell better anyway. And I smelled buffler cooking on some white man's big, smoky fire. I see the white man is still in you. Yor building sompen big here," he said, gesturing towards the first few rows of logs that defined my growing house. "Hey, over in your horses there! That looks like my horse!"

My horses, Ann Marie, the roan, and a third I'd bought for Singing Night and the children, were tied off at the side of the house. And I felt embarrassed that I'd made such a big fire in the fireplace in the small house, something no Cheyenne in their right mind would have done. I guess I felt somehow safe in My Valley.

"You mean the roan?" I asked.

"Uh huh."

"It is yours."

"You damn horse thief! So it was you who done stole my horse!"

"Well, you pissed on my head and I was riled."

"I never pissed on your head!"

"You surely did. I'm still trying to wash it out. Whyn'cha come on in and I'll tell you the whole story. I'll even feed you some buffler."

Though he seemed a little riled himself, he pulled his horses over next to mine and tied them off. When I came in there was fear in Singing Night's eyes and wonder in the children's. I explained in Cheyenne that Jim was a friend and a work partner, and he would not harm them. Jim and I sat down and after offering him a big chunk of buffalo meat, I told him the story of how my friends saved me from Morton and Powers, and how I was obliged to join them on a horse raid. Then I told him about almost running into him outside his lodge, how he pissed on my head when he was drunk, and how that got me riled. I apologized for taking his horse and said he was welcome to have the roan back. I could buy another horse.

He had been glaring at me, and then his face was hard to read, like he was about to choke on something. Then, he exploded into loud laughter, falling backwards and rolling on the floor robes, guffawing. It took him several minutes to regain control. And it had such a powerful effect on me that I too began to roll around in uncontrollable laughter. We finally stopped because we were exhausted. Singing Night was looking at me like she'd thought I'd gone mad, but she said nothing. Jim and I sat up and began to eat normally.

"Well, I cain't say I'm sorry that asshole, Powers, is dead. Yor Cheyenne friends done both you and me a favor there. Tell ya what, Sam. I'll take my roan back and leave you my buckskin. She's not really that good as a pack horse—she's too small and slow. But she'll be fine for you carrying women and children. My condition is, winter's comin' on fast and I don't cater much to the idea of spending it next to a tiny fire under a stand of trees. I see yor building that house. That suits me fine. So, we trade horses, and I help you get the walls and roof up, so long as you let me winter in there. What'dya say?"

My mouth was full, so I reached over and shook his hand. The whole thing had gone better than I'd hoped. Most men I know would shoot you for stealing their horse.

Lisa asks me to explain something here. Singing Night and the children had seen other mountain men come visit me and talk to me in English before. That wasn't the shock of it. Lots of the boys in the mountains, in spite of the fact they like being alone best, occasionally get people-starved and go see another trapper to jaw for a while. Since I was always known to be with the Cheyenne, I was a lot easier for these boys to find and also they could do some trading while in my village. It made me almost popular. You could always find Cheyenne Sam quick enough. Boys in the mountains came and visited me in my Cheyenne villages all the time. So Singing Night wasn't surprised by that.

And the fact that Jim was Black didn't matter to her either. In fact, I do believe my Cheyenne people never did really notice the difference between White and Black people, until large all-Black army units, the "Buffalo Soldiers", came along. Even then, for the Cheyenne, the Black man was just another kind of White man. And that strikes me funny because white folks make such a fuss about the difference between Black and White. I will say that like most Indians, my people did make a distinction between Mexican, French, and American. After all, as I've already said, French folks were "Red Spiders" and Mexicans were either "Hairy-nose Spiders" or "Rascal Spiders." I don't suppose my people had a lot of good relations with the Mexicans of Santa Fe.

But I'm off on a coyote trail here. Singing Night had never seen me talk so avidly and laugh so hard with another white man (as she saw him). That's what shocked her. She had never been taught to hate Black people or think of them as inferior. And that struck me after a time. Hate is taught. And what was I teaching Kathleen and Jack?

Jim and I just got along, if for no other reason than that I threw away all that I'd been taught coming up in St. Louis about Black people. As I had done for the difference between White and Indian, I just swept it out of my mind with a broom, like so much dust and horse-crap, and left the door to my mind open. Other trappers were men in the fur business, offering up gossip as readily as they ate up anything I could tell them. They talked low and soft and when they were done, they nodded, got up and left, telling me "Watch yer topknot." That's how I'd known that Jim went back to the South, which seemed the last place a Black man would want to go in the 1830s. Jim and I laughed and told loud stories, and laughed some more. Singing Night was mighty perplexed that winter by the loud ways and the rough humor of Jim Beckwourth.

She was never comfortable with Jim all that much, maybe because his Crow smell, or maybe because she sensed what was to come. She was very relieved that he wintered in the other house, and she didn't have to see him all that much. Me, I enjoyed the company. I was a little riled in later years when I heard that as part of his loud brag on entering a camp, something a lot of mountain men did, he included with his victories and hunting achievements, that he was "the only man to piss on Cheyenne Sam's head and live to tell the story". He could have left that part out. But I figured it was more of the way he bull-shitted White folk, to keep them from bothering him. I've had many trials in this long life of mine, but it would have been far harder to have been an everyday Black man than anything I ever had to face.

That winter, with the ice making pulling logs easy and Jim to help me, the main house went up like I said with everything but windows. There were heavy snow days where we had to stop for a while, but many more days cold, and crisp, where we made progress. We got the roof on and Jim moved in, testing the rock fireplace and chimney, which we still use today. Jim and I built this house, I am still proud to say. Wish I could show him what this house has become, but it's too late for that. We also threw together a small stable for the horses. Feeding them was a constant job, with the grass buried. But fortunately, they could eat the inner bark of some trees. But it was a lot of work harvesting it.

Naturally, unless it was snowing heavily, we were out hunting on days we weren't building the house. That's when Jim saved my life. I should have died at least five times by now but that Jack, and my brothers, and Jim saved me. They're all gone and I'm old and cantankerous, but thanks to them, I'm still here.

I had already been torn up by a grizzly bear when I was young. Jack saved me then. This time was almost the same. I took down a buck deer in the snow and was getting ready to haul it away when this large grizzly sow showed up through the trees not ten yards away. She must have smelled the deer blood on the crusty snow, and thought to take my kill. I could have run or backed off, but the bear was so close, I figured she was spoiling for a fight that I could not win. Plus, it's impossible to outrun a bear in good weather, much less deep snow. My Hawken was unloaded and I didn't have my pistol.

All I had was my Green River knife. I dropped my Hawken into the snow bank at my feet, and reached for the knife, but I had no hope. Every year a few of the boys in the mountains got chewed up or killed by grizzlies. Some of the boys, like Jim, hunted them, which was probably the most dangerous thing you can do. You see, if you hit a griz, with even a .50 caliber shot, and you don't kill them, why, it just makes them mad, and your problem just got worse. Ten yards might seem a good distance, but a griz in the snow can run as fast as a horse on dry ground. I had maybe a second or two to live.

Then a heavy pounding shot rang out over my right shoulder, some distance back in the trees. The griz went limp and fell into the snow, unmoving. I heard Jim coming out of the trees behind me, "Damn, Sam, you shore do like to bring trouble. What would you do if I didn't save your white ass all the damn time?"

I laughed, "Ah, you'd get bored if I went under."

"Most likely. Say, I am gonna make a lot of money off that bear hide."

"Hope you do. And thank you, again."

"I reckon yor welcome, long as you don't steal my horse again. Damn Cheyennes can't help but be horse thieves."

I ignored this. It was Jim's way of bull-shitting me and I think it meant he actually liked me, but like most men, couldn't speak his feelings directly, especially to other men. I was examining the bear and realized that Jim shot him through the left eye and into the brain. That was a tough shot to pull off and one of the few shots that would be a quick and guaranteed kill. I had to comment, "Damn, Jim, right through the eye. That's a hell of a good shot."

"Yeah, well, it was the only kill shot I had. Cain't half miss with a bear. Don't have to tell you what it's like getting carved up by a bear."

"No sir, you don't. But, damn."

"Well, yor welcome again."

I don't want to talk no more about Jim that winter of 38–39. Makes me too sad. Spring came and we packed up and headed south. Jim said he wanted to work for the Bents, so he came along, though Singing Night didn't like it none. We reached the Arkansas River after a week or two of riding, and Jim left us. From where we found the river, about where the town of Pueblo is today, and far east, the north bank of the Arkansas was just one Cheyenne or Arapaho village after another, for miles and miles. Jim really didn't want to mix too much in the villages, so he rode for Bent's Fort. For Singing Night and me, it was like the Medicine Hat ceremony had been, with all the tribe gathered. We spent a day in White Thunder's Hevataniu village, and found out where to find the Ivistsinihpah village further down river. Next day we pulled in next to White Coyote's lodge and set up our tipi. We were welcomed warmly by the whole village. For Singing Night's mother had been Deer Kicks' sister, so even without marrying me, she was family. The first night we ate with White Coyote and Deer Kicks, and I relayed the news, including how I lost my dear Spirit. I told White Coyote we'd be staying for a while, and that I wanted my children to get to know their grandfather and grandmother well. He and Deer Kicks were very pleased with that idea and so everything was settled, and Singing Night was happy to be in the village with people she had grown up with. White Coyote took Jack with him out onto the prairie often, and Kathleen became inseparable from her grandmother, Deer Kicks. It was very good and it did my heart a service to see the young folk learn to love their elders. That is a Cheyenne value, indeed a value among many tribes, that I didn't see often enough amongst white folks.

And I'm sorry to have waited so long to mention it, but little, skinny Singing Night, with her deformed hand, swoll up mighty big with her first child. She delivered him the Cheyenne way, by herself, in the bush, in the course of her daily chores. He was a little boy, but large for an infant. And funny thing, after the birth, Singing Night was heavy like all women after child-birth, for some time. Then she went back to being skinny. And contrary to Cheyenne wisdom, her skinniness did not keep her from having babies and surviving. She was a woman who beat all odds—except the last. But that comes later.

My boy had no real name yet. He would get that with his vision. But then, well I'll save that telling for later. He looked like a right Cheyenne with dark hair and brown skin. But he had my birth mother's shinning blue eyes. We called him Sky in his Eyes in Cheyenne. I called him Andrew in English. I now had two sons and an elder daughter, Kathleen, who helped her mother with the babies, as well as spent a large part of her day following her grandmother around. And I must say that White Coyote and Deer Kicks were the most attentive (Lisa gave me that word) grandparents you could ever want. They spent much of their time teaching my children the ways of the Cheyenne and helping Singing Night with the babies and the chores. And once Andrew was born, Singing Night was eager to return to being passionate lovers.

In the end, I gave up my plans to return to my brothers among the Omissis in the north. I could not bear that my children miss their grandparents so quickly, and Singing Night was clearly happier with the Ivistsinihpah people she grew up with. Plus, the Bents had Jim and me hunting for the fort and running down to Taos together every few months, to work with St. Vrain. That meant I was seeing a lot of my other good friend, Kit Carson. And I was piling up the credits and could buy anything I might possibly want. That was altogether a lot to give up just to return to the north country.

So, we stayed among the Ivistsinihpah clear into the spring of '41. Yet, the thing I recall most of all this was how much Jim and I became good friends. After a while, he set up his own store in Taos, and every time I went down there, we had a good laugh together. Lord, I miss him now.

14.

Charette Again, and Rumors of War

1841

In the spring of '41 the Bents told me in passing that Jesuit missionaries were among the Salish people up in the northern Rockies, in lands claimed both by the Americans and the British. I thought about this a long time. Singing Night was happy down south and the relationship between White Coyote and Deer Kicks and my children was strong and close. I increasingly could not justify taking them away back up north. But the news that Jesuits were up there moved something in my heart. When I was with my true father, Jack, another man had been with us, a runaway Jesuit priest named Charette, who in many ways had been as much a father to me as Jack. If there was even a chance that he was up in the northern Rockies, I had to go see him.

It was at first just a longing, but the year before, in '40, the Cheyenne and our allies, the Arapaho, sat down with the Comanches and the Kiowa. White Thunder and my father-in-law, White Coyote, were some of the chiefs from our side that sat down to talk. It was agreed that we would be at peace, and not fight or raid each other anymore. The Arkansas River would be our boundary. Already the Cheyenne were camped for miles and miles along the north bank. This would become permanent. Of course, this did not stop the Kiowa and the Comanche from raiding the supply trains coming down the Santa Fe Trail to Bent's Fort. When I told White Coyote after this, that I wished to see my old friend up in Blackfoot country, he decided that I could also go and inform the northern bands of Cheyenne of the treaty with the

Comanche and Kiowa. Suddenly, my longing became a reality and I was going.

But that took some preparation. I would be going through Crow country, and looking and smelling like a Cheyenne would be a bad idea. I had to work to look and smell like a white man again. This meant making myself some deerskin trousers and packing away my breechclout. I also had to come up with a different kind of bear-grease than the Cheyenne used. I put away the beaded shirt that Spirit had made me, and let Singing Night make me a new deerskin shirt with no Cheyenne bead patterns. I bundled up my Cheyenne clothes and took them with me, since I figured that when I was done, I'd look in at the village of Tall Horse, or other Omissis villages up north. I would pass the news of the decision of the southern chiefs to the northern chiefs, and convey back any of their concerns. White Coyote readily agreed to keep my wife and children fed, since he was enjoying being a grandfather so much. It wasn't hard to convince him.

My route took me through Crow country and I took a trip down to Taos to consult Jim on the safest way to do that. He drew me a route and coached me on what to say when confronted. He agreed I should look the white man as much as possible. The route would be to go straight north, hopping the rungs of the ladder, that is, all the rivers running east out of the Front Range, until I found the north Platte. As when I'd gone to Rendezvous, I followed this northwest till it branched off onto the Sweetwater. Then across the plains a little north to pick up the Wind River to Togwotee Pass. Once over the pass I'd be in Davy Jackson's valley and know it by the three tall peaks that horny French traders named after a woman's breasts. Further north up there would take me to the Yellowstone River and Coulter's Hell, a strange valley landscape of boiling pools and the stink of sulfur, with occasional spouting of boiling water. Northwest from there I would go down the Gallatin Fork, up the Jefferson Fork to the Big Hole Fork of the Missouri. Then over the pass would be the Bitterroot River and the heart of Blackfoot country. Such a journey even five years ago would be a death wish, as it was for my natural father. But the mighty Blackfoot had been humbled by the pox and I was told that it was hard to even find any Blackfeet, much less have to fear them now. If I followed the Bitterroot north long enough, I would find a broad valley with an inland lake, as large as a sea. That was Flathead Lake, "Flathead" being what the local whites called the Salish tribe. Somewhere in that valley, I would find the Jesuits.

I made passionate love to Singing Night one last time and left early in the morning in mid-April. I did stop in Menoke's Valley and saw that the cabin and the outbuilding were untouched. But it got me to thinking more about them on the long, lonely ride. And it got me worried; the white man's curse—owning property that others could damage or steal. The Lord talked about it in the Gospels, and now I was feeling it. The thought occurred to me that there would come a time that I might move my family permanently to Menoke's Valley and St. Vrain Creek. I resolved in any case to winter there, if I could talk Singing Night into leaving White Coyote and Deer Kicks. That might be hard to do. Her first husband, Red Mountain, had pulled her away from her family once already. I didn't know if I had the heart to do it a second time.

One thing that I did see was up on the North Platte. 35 wagons headed west up the north bank of the river. Their off-white canvas covers flapped in the prairie wind, like big leaves on a branch. I felt an unexpected chill. In my blood I knew that trouble would come of it. I rode down to them with no fear, looking like the white man again. Old Jim Tarkenton was leading them, a trapper I'd known from the Rocky Mountain Fur Company days. He had ridden with me and Ben and Sir William up the Platte all those years ago. I reined up next to him and we talked a while. He, of course, wanted to know what I'd seen, especially out to the west towards South Pass. But coming from the south, I wasn't much help to him.

As I was talking to him, three men rode up to us, wearing blue military shirts, and with saber scabbards dangling from their left hips down their legs. Soldiers. I'd seen blue-coats before, riding here and there in St. Louis. One time I'd seen a whole company of dragoons, what they later called cavalry, riding through town. It was impressive. But it made me nervous, this child don't mind saying. Old Jim introduced me to the cavalrymen as "Cheyenne Sam, what knows the injuns better than most in these parts." The soldiers nodded to me politely.

The senior cavalryman asked Old Jim if he thought that these wagon trains might cause trouble with tribes hereabout.

He shrugged, "Crow? Reckon not. Sioux and Cheyenne, wall, Cheyenne Sam here, he knows more than me 'bout that."

The cavalrymen all looked at me expectantly.

"If they drive off or kill buffalo, there'll be trouble, Jim," I offered.

"Reckon you might talk some peace to your tribe?" he asked.

"Naw, they wouldn't listen if it's the buffalo. That would be war."

Jim fidgeted a little and looked around. The cavalrymen looked stern. Old Jim sighed, "Reckon I'll keep this pack of greenhorns away from the herds."

"Sound wisdom," I said, then asked, "Where you taking these greenhorns?"

"Oregon country. Willamette Valley, down the Columbia, and turn south when you hit the Willamette River. Good country, good farmland.

Thinking of staying when I get there. Maybe marry a woman and open a store. The fur trade is gone, and as you tell me, the Injuns are getting riled. It's gonna get ugly 'round here, I reckon. Which way you headed?"

"Well I come from the Arkansas and gonna take a look around up where the Salish live."

"Blackfoot country. It true the pox killed them all?"

'Not all, but close."

"Serves them devils right. You don't see me shedding no tears."

I thought about all the death and horror I'd witnessed when the pox cut through my village and took my beloved wife. "Reckon I don't much care for the Blackfoot myself, but I'd wish the pox on no man. Seen it with my own eyes. I hope to God I never see anything like that again."

I could tell he was a bit offended at my not joining in on his hatred for Blackfeet. But at this point in my life, I was already disgusted by white folks hating Indians because they were Indians. And I wasn't in the mood to make nice about it. He stopped talking and looked away. Mountain men don't talk a whole lot and the look-away was a common way to indicate they had no more they cared to say. The cavalrymen were looking uncomfortable. Time to clear out, I figured.

I said, "Watch yer topknot, Jim."

"Watch yourn."

And with that I rode off north.

Once I was up on the Wind River, I saw one Crow buffalo hunting party on horseback. They stopped to talk to me for a short time in hand sign and broken bits of English, and then went about their business. I was very glad to have erased my Cheyenne look and smell. I saw no Blackfeet at all, not even sign that they had been hunting in their valleys. At the end of July I rode into a Salish village and was guest of the chief. We spoke in sign, as my French was limited. He told me they had been visited by the French priests, but that the priests had gone north to another village near the north end of the lake. Two days later, I rode into that village and was just dismounting when I heard my name called out in English. "Sam? Sam Plunkett? *ça ne peut pas* être ! »

I turned and saw my old friend, Antoine Charette, in a dusty, long black robe. His hair and beard had gone half gray. He ran over and embraced me. He took me out away from the village and we found a log by the river where we could talk. I caught him up on all that had happened to me since we had parted ways in St. Louis, that is, all the things I've told you in this book that Lisa is making. He simply told me he'd gone back to the Jesuits, and they had forgiven him and put him back to work in Quebec. But when these Italian Jesuits came over, meaning to take a mission to the Indians of the Rockies, he volunteered to guide them. The US-British North America border was not very certain back in those days, and anywhere north of the Columbia, the Missouri, or the Snake, the British were working the fur trade. It wasn't for another seven years before the two governments agreed on a north border, and then all the missionization those Italian Jesuits had brought turned out to be on the American side of the line. But no matter. I had a few days with Charette.

Our talk went long, and it even turned into a confession, since I had no priests out with the Cheyenne. In those days I didn't get confession very often. Now, in my old age, I go once a month. And to this, my 84th year, I am still a Catholic, though not a very good one. Charette gave me a simple penance but added, "Sam, I know revenge is the mountain way, but it is not God's way. I fear that it has latched onto your soul. Beware. It will eat you alive if you let it."

I knew he was right. I had thought of it often. As a matter of fact, I still do. I stayed two more days, but began to feel that I was distracting Charette from helping his fellow Jesuits, and frankly, helping the Salish. The other Jesuits, who spoke no English, were friendly enough with me. But I could see in the way they stood around me that I was becoming a burden. The smallpox had hit the Salish hard. They needed the help the Jesuits had brought. They didn't feel as bad about the Blackfeet though, as they might, for as hard as smallpox hit them, it had all but wiped out their Blackfoot enemies, and they were as free of the Blackfoot pressure as they been in many generations.

When it came time to leave, Charette embraced me in the French way, and planted a kiss on each cheek. I was very sad, for Charette felt almost as much a father to me as Jack had. But his life had gone down another road, and it was selfish of me to expect him to drop everything and tend only to my needy heart. I mounted up and rode away sadly, knowing this man who was one of the few that was dear to me, and that I could absolutely trust, was separated from me as if by a high wall. I never saw him again in this life. I imagine he rests in some Jesuit cemetery in Montreal. But if by some odd mistake, in the next life some devil forgets to send me straight to Hell, when I'm suffering down in Purgatory, with a faint hope of Heaven, I know it will be Charette's hand that will reach down and pull me out and up.

Going south, once I hit Coulter's Hell, I turned east and headed toward the Bighorn Range, picking up the Shoshone River. Touching the west side of the Bighorns, I worked my way down to the south end of it, stocked up on water and cut cross-country to the southeast. I saw no Crow the whole time, and was relieved. After five days I came upon Devil's Tower, a big butte sticking up out of the prairie, with vertical columns scored into its flanks. My Cheyenne kin tell a story about it, how some little girls ran from a hungry bear and sang a song. The mountain rose out of the prairie beneath their feet, taking them out of the bear's reach, and the bear clawed the columns into its side as it rose. The white man in me would quickly laugh at such a simple story. The Cheyenne in me could see how such a thing might just be possible. After all, any man who has seen a grizzly, especially as close as I have, has known just how big a bear can get. And I had known that danger maybe five times, and had to be saved twice by another man each time. I camped there a couple of days and changed back into my Cheyenne clothes, and changed my bear grease. Now I looked and smelled Cheyenne again, and I have to tell you, it made me feel mighty comfortable to do so.

As if my People could sense me coming home, the first day after I broke camp at Devil's Tower, I ran into a hunting party of five Cheyenne warriors. I did not know them, though their accent told me surely that they were Omissis. They had not seen a Cheyenne with long, red hair before, though my clothes and my fluent Cheyenne told them that I was a fellow tribesman. One of them looked at me constantly, and finally said "*Maovese*?"

"Yes," I laughed. Turns out he grew up amongst the Hevataniu and his father had brought him north just this first year of his manhood. As a boy, he had helped manage White Thunder's horse herd when I was working for the Bents, and he confessed to me that he recognized my horse before he recognized me. They told me the chief of their village was Sleeping Wolf and they had been ranging far into what used to be Crow country, going west as far as the Bighorns and the Tongue River further north, a place the Blackfoot had also once claimed. With our Sioux allies, we were moving into these ranges which were far from the wagon trains of Spiders down on the Platte, and gave our people safety. As we all rode back to their village, they told me all the news of the north. Tall Horse and my Omissis village had moved north of the Black Hills to get away from the Spiders. I was closer to home than I had imagined. Our war parties, allied with the Lakota and the northern Arapaho, had ranged farther north and west than we'd ever been able to go before. The hunting up here was good and the Spiders were few. They seemed to be fixated on passing through our lands to the west. But they disrupted the buffalo herds along the Platte and the Sweetwater, and many of the young men were thinking about war with the Spiders to stop this incessant string of wagon trains cutting through our lands. The boy who recognized my horse, Antelope Jumps, pointedly asked me: "If there is war between our people and the Spiders, what will you do?" The other men, older and more politic (that's the word Lisa gives me) gave him a stern look for asking such a rude question of a fellow Cheyenne.

But I had thought of this very thing for weeks now, ever since I'd run across Old Jim Tarkenton and those army officers, with that wagon train on the Platte. I had my answer ready without hesitation.

"I'm a Cheyenne," I said, and fell silent. The others nodded approval.

One of the warriors, Laughing Stallion, made me his guest for two days and I waited there for Sleeping Wolf to convey my news of the Comanche-Kiowa treaty to all the villages of the Omissis. After a few days, Sleeping Wolf returned and no chief objected to the treaty. Then I rode home to Tall Horse's village, where I was the guest of my brother, Many Horses, for about a month.

But my heart was troubled, and it was Many Horse's wisdom that helped me see my way forward. I told him about my desire to be in the north, and my family's desire to be in the south. And I told him about my Spider house, my log home in Menoke's Valley, and the pull it had on me. He listened and said nothing for a few days.

Then, around the end of August, he said "Go. Look to your Spider house for a time. Then go home to your woman. After you do these things, you will know what to do next. The truth is that this Red Spider priest was also your father, and you have parted with him forever. It is a small kind of death. You are grieving though you do not know it. You have known too much grief these last few winters. But grief is coming for us all. What you tell me about the bluecoats and the wagons concerns me. War with the Spiders is coming. And you will feel torn, despite your loyalty to our people. We may need your help to outwit the Spiders, for you understand their minds in ways the rest of us cannot. So do not despair. You are a brave warrior, beloved healer, and credit to your people. Go in the morning."

And so I did, but not without thanking all my four brothers and Tall Horse. It took me almost a week to reach my house in Menoke's Valley. And I stayed there only another week, making repairs, chasing out small animals and stocking up on venison for the trip south. I made it to the Arkansas River just as the late fall rains began. Singing Night ran to my arms as I walked through the entrance of my lodge, and my daughter and sons all pressed on me in one big family hug. But there was another in the hug, for Singing Night was more pregnant than I thought any woman could be. She could barely walk, her belly was so big. Deer Kicks was actually doing most of the woman's work in my lodge. Two weeks later, Singing Night woke up lying next to me in the dark, unable to move or even go outside to deliver her babies like most Cheyenne women do. Her screams of pain must have woken the whole camp and Deer Kicks and several other older women appeared in my lodge door almost instantly. Two older women ordered me to gather my children and take them to White Coyote's lodge. I did not argue, and White Coyote and I sat up and talked softly while the children slept around us, listening to Singing Night's muffled screams in my tipi next door. We could hardly concentrate, but I told him the northern chiefs were in agreement with the Comanche-Kiowa treaty. He nodded and said he would pass the word on to White Thunder and the other southern chiefs. And so, after so many years, the Council of the 44 Peace Chiefs met indirectly and decided a tribal matter through my efforts and travels.

I was amazed as small a woman as Singing Night could cry out so loud and long. Like I said, most Cheyenne women can go out to the trees around a village and squat down and deliver a child without a sound. I don't know any white woman who can do that. But sometimes a birth is difficult, or even deadly, and all the older women come charging in when a young mother is in trouble. I knew I would not be able to think straight if Singing Night died this night, in childbirth. But I knew such things were not unusual. It might just happen. I thought to myself that I would run mad if I lost two wives. As I found out later, I was wrong about that, but I'll tell the story in order.

About 3 in the morning by Spider time, the screams died down and I began to sweat, thinking that I'd lost my wife and new baby to an impossible birth. But shortly after, Deer Kicks came through the entrance smiling. "My son, you have two beautiful new daughters." I should say that when Spirit died, the taboo of mother-in-law speaking to son-in-law was lifted, and Deer Kicks had talked much with me in the last few years. I suppose as she was my present wife's aunt, and nearest living thing to a mother, we should have kept the taboo. But I think we both had learned that we liked each other, and what Spiders would call a technicality (Lisa gave me that word) wasn't worth bothering over.

"Two daughters?" I asked in amazement. "No wonder she was so big." I rushed over to my lodge and found another older woman bathing Singing Night's face and hair with a wet piece of deerskin, as Singing Night held two infants to her breasts, where they rooted for her nipples and fed, before dozing off. In time the first twin out became known as Red Girl, and her sister became Star's Child, because of her delight in watching the night sky, like her mother. I also gave them Spider names, white names: Red Girl was also Charlotte and Star's Child was also Clara.

I wrapped my arms around them all and all four of us. I kissed my wife again and again that night. Then I slept from exhaustion in that pose. There are few things more powerful than a father's joy.

15.

War with Mexico

1846–1848

I SHOULD SAY SOMETHING more about Singing Night. She was given that name as a little girl because she was enchanted with the stars, and would stand out in the cold night, singing to them to make them happy. She never grew very tall, or broad, the way most Cheyenne women do. Some women seem to stop growing about 14 years old and never resume. She always looked like a skinny child. That's why her birthing twins and surviving it was a miracle. Thick-set Native American women may not have been fashionable by European standards, but they sure did well in unaided childbirth. As for Singing Night, her left hand, as I said, had one large odd-shaped finger and a thumb. Her parents believed no man would marry her because of her plainness and her deformity. But my brother of the heart, Red Mountain, could see that she was a good woman, even if shy and not beautiful. So, he married her. I would not have encountered her much except that my dear first wife, Spirit, thought that all would be better for everyone if her cousin, Singing Night, were my second wife. And when the pox took Spirit, Singing Night stepped up and proved herself to be the finest woman a man could want for a partner. In some ways, she was better at reading my heart and thinking about what we needed than any other woman I ever knew, including my other wives.

That's why one day, without me saying anything, she said, "You want to go back to the square wood lodge, I know."

"Yes," I agreed, stunned that she'd read what I was thinking before I could say it.

"Let us ask Father and Mother if they will join us."

By Father and Mother, she meant White Coyote and Deer Kicks. I am sure I stood up with my eyes wide open. Why didn't I think of that? So, we did. And in the end, not only did White Coyote and Deer Kicks want to join us—about ten other families of Ivistsinihpah missed the old home country around the Platte so bad, that they also asked to come along. So, in that fall of 1841, a small band of Ivistsinihpah left the Arkansas River valley and went north across the prairie until we reached the South Platte River. And I led them. We found where St. Vrain Creek runs into the South Platte and went up creek until my log home appeared between the pines and aspens. And the log house was the center of our tiny village. I counted and there were 59 of us, including elders and children, and besides myself, 15 young warriors. So, we were capable of some kind of self-defense. And for the next eighteen years or so, we spent over half the year there, going down to the Arkansas only for the winter. And a few winters we even stayed up at the ranch house village.

But that first time was the most memorable for me. Using all the credit I had stored up with the Bents, I had gone down to Taos and purchased sixteen sheets of glass, each about a foot square. I wrapped these carefully in buffalo robes and took them with us to my log house, or what I now call the ranch house. For I still live there today with my Lisa, and we're sitting on the porch right now with Lisa writing and me palavering on. Anyway, with these panes of glass I made four windows in the house, cutting out two-foot squares in the log walls, putting in cross pieces to hold the glass, and putting four pieces of glass in each window hole. Singing Night and the children were amazed, as if I'd performed some Spider magic trick. They had never lived in a home where you could see out a window, and I'd never even taken them as far as Bent's Fort to see windows there. I didn't figure it was safe for Cheyenne children in the fort. Singing Night had seen the windows in Bent's Fort, but she never imagined it was something I could do to our home. The rest of our small band inspected the windows closely with something like awe. But I already had a reputation as something of a Medicine Man for my work saving lives in Tall Horse's village during the pox. I had just performed another act of mysterious power. It was a long time before they stopped inspecting these windows and we had any privacy in the house.

I knew it wasn't magic, and the glass I bought was of poor quality, with waves and wrinkles in it, so that it let in light, but you couldn't clearly see what was outside. I replaced it all years later, which is why we have decent windows in this house today. I'll tell you one thing: it sure spoiled Singing Night, because with the log walls and the fireplace, we were a lot warmer at night and on cold days, than any of our kin. She didn't like wintering in a tipi after that first winter in the ranch house. I spoiled her.

But it had another effect that I never would have foreseen. The families we invited that first year, being Cheyenne and having a Cheyenne sense of community property, kept showing up every year thereafter. Other families who hadn't been there the first winter, joined us later. Nostalgia for the days when the Ivistsinihpah lived in the center of the Cheyenne probably had a lot to do with it. But today there is a Cheyenne-Arapaho reservation in western Oklahoma, and another Cheyenne reservation in Montana on the Tongue River. My house on St. Vrain Creek, became for a long time the third and unofficial Cheyenne reservation, even after the white folks of Colorado thought they had pushed the Cheyenne and Arapaho out of Colorado forever. In fact, even here in 1902, I still get Cheyennes stopping by to stay for a few weeks, on their way between the Montana and Oklahoma reservations. They consider this Cheyenne land. I have no problem with that. The people of Denver sure did have a problem with that, but that's another part of the story and I'll get to it in time.

I remember these years well, but there isn't much to tell really. Kathleen Yellow Bird, my sweet eldest daughter, was a girl of seven when we first went to the valley. She was wide-eyed and awestruck, and I knew she loved this valley as much as I did. To her I showed Menoke's tree and told her that her grandmother rested there. I knew that in spite of her age, she would deeply understand that. And she did. Jack Flies Straight, my oldest son, was a rambunctious six when we first moved. Little Andrew Sky in His Eyes was only three and it was all his big sister could do to keep him from rambling off into the woods and into danger. The twins, Charlotte Red Girl and Clara Star's Child were still learning to walk. But my Singing Night had help from Kathleen as well as Deer Kicks, with all these children running around. Singing Night herself after the birth of the twins, finally stopped being skinny. Having babies will do that to you. It didn't matter to me. I loved her completely and we were often lovers, now that we had our own bedroom in the cabin and privacy for the first time in our intimate lives. She never did lose her passion for sex. Times were happy though uneventful. What is there to say when you have one good day after another? You thank God; that's what you do. We seemed to live protected, as if Menoke's Valley could shut out time and evil. For eight years we were allowed to believe it until the first blow fell.

If anything, with her breasts larger and some real hips on her, I found my wife even more desirable. In 1845 she became pregnant again and we had our fourth daughter, Anne, whose Cheyenne name was Running Doe because as a two-year old, she was so fascinated with the deer in the valley.

She would walk right up to them and for some reason the deer let her get extremely close before dashing away when my baby reached out and touched them.

Another thing I had not foreseen came to pass. Because I was not in the center of thousands of Cheyenne, Jim Beckwourth visited me every year at the ranch house. The children came to know him as "Uncle Jim", who told good stories and was funny. I can even say that Singing Night got used to him, though she complained that he stank like a Crow. In the end, he made her laugh so much, she even came to like him a little. This was because I had been teaching her what she called "Spider talk", that is, English, and she could understand Jim's humor. The children loved him, for I had been teaching them to speak English as well, and they would listen to his tall tales with wonder on their faces. The other Cheyenne in our little village got used to him after a time, though like Singing Night, they thought he stunk like a Crow. They thought of him as a white man and friend of mine, so he was accepted. They just assumed that white men, Spiders, came in all colors. They were incapable of the basic racial hatred so common to so many Americans. I'm not saying they were saints of some kind, but the boundaries of hatred for them ran to Crow and Pawnee. Black white men were not worth more than a curious glance and a shrug.

And it was not only Jim. In 1842 . . . or was it 43? I can't recall. Anyway about 27 mountain men and bluecoats just showed up in my valley. Leading them was Kit; Kit Carson, my old friend from Taos days. He had changed a lot. When I first knew him, his short stature and youth made him look like a boy. But he was clearly older now and even had a grizzled moustache. He got off his horse and almost ran up to me.

"Cheyenne Sam! Shor is good to see you!"

"And you, Kit. Who'd ya bring?"

"This is Capt Fremont and his men. Most of them are map-makers, not soldiers. Don't let the uniforms fool you."

"Well, come on over to my fire-pit and set a spell."

I made them welcome. I'd just brought down a buffalo and we had a big roast and feast. Their commander, this fellow named Fremont, was a soldier with dark curly hair and curly beard, that had hired Kit to lead him around. He was mapping all the country. I am sorry now, but I got real quiet when he said that. We were all sitting around a big fire I'd made in the yard behind the cabin, enjoying buffalo meat, and when Fremont told me, I just got quiet. I didn't even know why myself. But everyone around the fire got quiet too, then the conversation went somewhere else. In the morning, Kit came up to me while I was feeding the horses.

"What's wrong, Sam?" he asked.

"You realize what happens when your bluecoat friend maps all this country, don't you?"

Kit didn't say anything for a long time. "You know it's coming, Sam. You can't stop all those poor and hungry folks back east. They're coming."

"I'm a fool then. I was hoping it would stay like this forever."

"No," Kit said. "But Fremont pays good, and I need a way to make a living and stay in this country, just like you, as long as I can. I'm going to love it till it's gone."

I just nodded. I wish I could have blamed him and told him he was wrong. But Jack taught me to be honest with myself and others, to a fault even.

"Where's yor 'Rapaho wife, Kit?"

"She's gone beaver some years back. She were fine. Then I married one of your women, Cheyenne. But she didn't last two years. Had enough of me, so I did her a favor and threw the stick. She's free now."

Lisa is after me to explain "throw the stick." Cheyennes almost never divorced. But if they did, the ceremony was simple enough. A man went to his men's society with a stick and explained that he was shedding his wife. Then he threw the stick. Everyone else would do their best to evade the stick. If it hit them, then they took over the wife. Apparently, in Kit's case, his Cheyenne woman was more than happy to be free of him. Why, I never knew. He just threw the stick in her presence and she got to walk away like it never happened.

He continued. "Got my eye on a Spanish girl down in Taos. Gunna go see her when I finish up with Fremont. Like a woman, Sam, this here open country is going to be gone someday soon. I want to love her, and it, while I can."

"Sound wisdom, Kit." I turned and wordlessly shook his hand. Then he walked out of the stable. Later that morning, Kit and Fremont and his boys rode out. I never saw him again.

By 1846 passing trappers told me that the Americans were going to war with Mexico. I was uneasy. For as the Arkansas River was the border between the Cheyenne and the Arapaho on one side, and the Comanches and the Kiowa on the other, it was also the border between the US and Mexico. Bent's Fort on the north bank, was the last stop in the US before you waded through the shallow ford of the river and found yourself in Mexico. And two-thirds of the Cheyenne nation was camped on the north bank of the Arkansas, running east and west for miles and miles. I was afraid that the war would spread and engulf my people, who didn't think much of the American Spiders, and just as little of the Mexican Spiders. I heard news that a Gen. Kearny and hundreds of blue-coated American soldiers had passed through Bent's Fort on their way to take Santa Fe and Taos. I was troubled.

So, when Jim Beckwourth rode into my little village around the ranch house in early March of 1847, I could smell trouble on him. It was written in his face. Various mountain men had brought me news that New Mexico was in American hands and the war was not going well for Mexico. American victory was in sight. But what Beckwourth told me gave me a serious chill. The folks of Taos, Mexican and Indian, had risen up and killed the American governor, my old friend, Charles Bent. St. Vrain was calling all mountain men to join with American forces and help retake Taos for the Stars and Stripes.

Well, I hadn't lived under the Stars and Stripes in fourteen years, though looking back on it now, I had been living in the Louisiana Purchase lands all that time. Still, it felt like I was living in Cheyenne lands. Americans were an odd breed I somehow felt I'd left behind. Oh, I'll grant you, I thought of myself as Irish, and that is another form of white man. Yet, somehow, that did not quite feel like American. Many of the boys in the mountains stayed clear of me because they thought I was a renegade and just another Cheyenne with red hair. And they were right in a lot of ways. But Bent was a good friend and had been kind to me in numerous ways. And he was in the mind of our tribe a Cheyenne, because his brother had married into the tribe. I did not tell the others in the band that, or they might feel honor-bound to avenge him, and this sounded to me like a rally of white Americans. I asked Jim how he felt about that.

He shrugged and said, "I been livin' with white men all my life and making my way around the edges that those folk will let me have. What's different? St. Vrain is a friend. Bent was a friend. I'm goin'. You comin' Cheyenne Sam?"

I was pleased that he didn't include me in "those folk", which meant white men that gave him trouble, which included a lot of folk. I did not look forward to being surrounded by Spiders again. Still, St. Vrain, Charles Bent. Aw, hell. I hated it, but I would help avenge my friends.

"Gimme an hour," I told him and began packing for the trip. Singing Night was not happy that I would leave her and our children to go into a nest of trouble, but she said nothing. I promised her to return. I also changed into the deerskin trousers and beadless shirt that Singing Night had made for my trip north, so that after about an hour, I had Ann Marie packed up and looked like the white man. I looked at Jim, sitting on the big roan horse of his, and I said "Shit. I look like a white man."

He shrugged. "We can't all be lucky."

We rode south and on the eighth day we rode into Taos, New Mexico again, coming in from the east through the forests and passes from Eagle Nest, where I'd driven Jeremiah's body into Taos when the Apaches killed him. When we got into town, Taos was full of mountain men patrolling the streets between the dusty adobe homes, with their Hawken guns, glaring suspiciously at the locals, who avoided the trappers and made only quick dashes from their homes to the market and back. But some of the glares came at Jim and me, a black man and a renegade. And I think I began to feel just a small bit of the constant hate Jim caught for being black. We camped like many trappers, in the square in Taos, but off to the southeast corner, away from most of the other trappers, who built a big fire at the center of their camps in the center of the square. I might have been welcome, but I would have heard the word "renegade" more than I cared to. So, I camped with the black man and was at home. But we weren't alone. A French trader named Philippe Broussard and his 15 year old son, Lucién, camped with us, seeing as "Frenchies" weren't all that welcome by white trappers either. Philippe was dark-skinned, obviously part Indian, and Lucién was pure Indian, his mother being a Mandan. We kept our own company and were glad.

Jim got to talking, as was his habit, and he told Broussard all about my life, including how he'd pissed on my head and I stole his horse. The existence of my little village round the log ranch house came up. Broussard asked if he could visit when all this was done. I said sure. He told me his Mandan kin and his wife were all dead of smallpox and he was not comfortable in St. Louis, or even Montreal. The Mandans had long been friends of the Cheyenne, so I told him he'd be welcome. I can see the puzzled look in the eyes of my granddaughter, Lisa, who is writing this down. Yes, my love, that Lucién is your father, and Broussard was your grandfather.

The court trials of the rebels ended in a day or two, and as sure as the sun comes up, all those fellows were to be hanged. At the hanging, all of us trappers, heavily armed, marched behind the prisoners in files and rows, like a bunch of soldiers, down through the angry crowd of Taos Mexican town folk, and stood in ranks beneath the scaffold, which was a wide platform with an overhead beam and five trap doors that gave way altogether when you pulled a lever. I was standing near St. Vrain, who though a Mexican citizen and of French blood, was angry at the death of his friend and partner. The prisoners came up, were hooded and a noose was put around each of their necks. They shouted in Spanish or Pueblo language as the trap doors were released, the sounds stopping as their bodies jerked violently at the end of the rope. The corpses would dangle a while, ropes squeaking as the bodies swayed and twisted in diminishing motion after the violence of the fall. Women in the crowd sobbed for their husbands, sons, and brothers.

Then the soldiers on the scaffold took the bodies of the dead rebels down and fetched five more fellows to string up till they went through maybe 20 to 25 prisoners. The crowd dispersed silently after the last one, and St. Vrain dismissed us and thanked us for our support.

I didn't stay around. Jim wanted to stay in Taos a while, but I'd had too much. Too many of those Mexican and Pueblo faces on the scaffold looked like people I knew and loved. My knee-jerk fear and hatred of dark faces, well, I guess I never had it. I hadn't finished my growing up in St. Louis and my lessons on who to hate were incomplete. I was sorry to have participated, even if it was to avenge Charles and support St. Vrain. Broussard said he and his son felt the same, so we saddled up and rode east out of town, out through Eagle Nest. As I rode along that shallow, green valley, I told the Broussards the story of my fight there and St. Vrain's revenge. He was impressed that I knew Kit Carson. Nine days later I walked through my front door and Singing Night, as was her custom when I went away, threw herself in my arms. But the most startling thing that happened was when the Broussards walked through the front door after me. For young Lucién spotted Kathleen Yellow Bird, my eldest daughter, a pretty, dark-eyed girl of thirteen, and he could not look away. Broussard didn't notice, but Singing Night sure did and gave me a look.

And the world shifted a little. It's one thing to be a father of small children, to be a herder of young ones, to be the center of all things family. It's another thing to watch them grow up, marry, have children of their own so that instead of being at the center of the family and the motions there, you find yourself out on the edge, watching your young people take your world in their hands and leave you behind. Anyway, this first moment made me lay up all night thinking that somehow in the moment of that love-lost stare of young Lucién, the next world was coming upon me. And then I thought of Kit and Fremont's maps, and I was sure that the world I knew was vanishing like smoke from a fire.

16.

Greta and the Cholera

1849

I CAN'T RECALL NOW exactly why in the spring of '49 I went up to Tall Horse's village, leaving my family behind. I often went to see my four brothers of the heart among our Omissis kin. This must have been one of those times. At this time, Tall Horse had moved the village to the north side of the Black Hills and a little west, along some of the streams that fed into the Belle Fourche River. I had been there a month when the cholera hit. We didn't know what it was, but all around camp, people of all ages and sexes were coming down with mighty powerful diarrhea. All died within days, and some within hours. Many people fled camp. I stayed and helped, knowing that I might be next. But somehow, I never got the cholera. This wasn't because I was Irish, for the disease killed all races and tribes. Years later I learned that it had killed something like a third of all people on earth. We didn't know what to do, so I did what I did with smallpox, and taking charge of the village, burned the bodies as fast as possible.

I did notice that people got sick not long after drinking from the river. I didn't know if that meant anything, but Many Horses, Stands to the Left, and Four Thunders went with me to a spring we knew high up in the Black Hills to the south of us, and taking every water skin we could find, and a string of horses to carry them, we brought the skins back full of spring water. We told the people to not drink from the river. After two days, we took the water skins and made another run to the spring. So long as we kept doing this, a few people slowly recovered and no new cases started up. But for most, we were too late. Our brother Laughs at Night had drunk from the river just before we made the run south to the spring. And when we returned, they were burning his body with the others. I once had five brothers; now I had three. As the disease died down, I got my truck together and left to home, fearing that I would find nothing but bodies in Menoke's valley.

As I drew to the south and to the North Platte, I saw in the distance a westbound wagon train stopped along the south shore. This was not an unusual sight anymore, much to the annoyance of my Cheyenne kin. But this wagon train was standing still, save for the horses that blew and swished their tails in their traces. As I drew near, I could smell the powerful and nauseating stench of death. Many of the wagons had loosed their horses for some reason, though no loose horses were around, only the sixteen or so still strapped in their traces. No doubt they'd wandered off. Maybe the survivors had mounted them and ridden to the nearest settlement. I never found out.

I forded the river nearby and came up on the wagon train from the west. Ann Marie got nervous at the smell. I dismounted and staked her to the plain. Walking near the twenty-two wagons with their stench, I could see they were full of dead bodies, men, women, and children, from infants to white-haired old men. It was a horror to see. cholera, or as I thought of it at the time, the Unseen Killer, had killed every soul in the train, so far as I could tell. Vultures circled overhead because I had interrupted their feast. I could describe what I saw at length and give you such an image of horror, but I don't want my Lisa to carry that image. It was mighty grim.

I will tell you that I found one wagon with a woman in it. She was lying in a puddle of her own excrement, as they all were, which made the foul smell worse still. She was a slender woman of maybe 30 years, with her black hair covering her face. She muttered names and other things I could not understand. She was wearing a soiled print dress. I climbed up into the wagon with a deerskin rag covering my nose and mouth. I gave her a long drink from my water bag, and slicing through the material with my knife, I pulled her away from her dress, which was soiled with excrement. This meant that I had to cut away all her clothes, as they were all ruined. The wagon she was in was without a horse team, so I wrapped her in a buffalo robe I was carrying, and moved her to another wagon with no corpses in it, that had a connected team of horses. She was skinny to begin with, but the disease had wasted away her flesh, and her already-small breasts were almost flat against her chest. Her ribs showed and her arms and legs were almost skeletal. I thought she might die any time, but as long as she lived, I would fight for her.

I went around to the other wagons and freed the remaining horses. As horses will, they gathered in a herd and began to wander off. I was too busy to herd them home, so I let it be. I tied Ann Marie off to the wagon wherein I had placed the dying woman, and taking the reins, woke that team and moved the wagon off a ways. Then I walked back and made the biggest fire I could with spare wood from the wagons and buffalo chips. Once the fire was roaring, I took a burning brand and set each of the corpse-filled wagons alight. It was the best I could do for them and there was no way that by myself I could bury that many folk. I didn't stay around, though I said a Hail Mary for them. I rode that wagon south and up over my secret pass into Menoke's Valley, pulling Ann Marie tied behind.

But I did not go straight home. I rode up to the head of the valley, where St. Vrain Creek fell from crevices at the top of the valley. I carried the half-dead woman up to the spring at the top and for the next day or two just stayed there, feeding her water and bits of venison jerky mashed up into a paste. My passing didn't go unnoticed, and Sun Horse, one of the young men of my village, found me and the wagon. As he drew closer, I told him to stay away. I explained the disease and the deaths among our people in the Omissis village, and that this Spider survivor I found and even I might be affected by the Unseen Killer, so that I must stay away a few more days to make sure I did not bring it to my people. He told me that no one was sick as of that morning. I told him to tell Singing Night what I'd said.

Two days later, the skinny Spider woman and I were both still alive, so I put her back in the wagon and drove it up to my ranch house. Singing Night made a bed for the woman near the fire and helped me to feed her. This kept me distracted, so I didn't know that one of our families had just come up from the villages along the Arkansas River and moved into our camp. Within hours the diarrhea began to rage around our village and people began to die. It was Lucién Broussard who ran into my house and warned me. I rushed out and began to do what I'd done in Tall Horse's village. All water was taken from the springs, and no one was to drink from the creek near the village. Any water we had was poured out. I created a great fire and burned the bodies. After two days, the deaths and new infections subsided. We lost 15, a small loss compared to many places as I learned later. But my heart, and Singing Night's heart were shattered. For our dear little boy, Andrew Sky in his Eyes, my little blue-eyed, eleven-year-old boy, so full of life and curiosity, had drunk from the stream before I knew that cholera had entered the camp. I wept, sobbing like a child, as I placed his body amongst the others to be burned.

But I could not do it. Instead, I dug a grave under Menoke's tree and placed his lifeless body in it. Earth burial is foreign to the Cheyenne mind, but no one questioned me. And I was the chief and a medicine man, so they did not presume to understand my ways. But still, I could see they thought it odd. Me, I still had enough Spider in me that I wanted to be able to visit our boy, as I was not able to do with Spirit. I covered him over and made a stone marker with his names on it, carved in crudely with my chisel.

Like I said, it doesn't sit right with a man to watch his children go before he does. I grieve for Andrew still, even here in 1902.

In a way, the near-dead Spider woman, going in and out of consciousness in her buffalo-robe bed by the fire, helped me work through the grief. I had no time to wallow in my pain. Her needs and the needs of the village came first. I organized regular water-runs to the spring at the top of the valley and it was almost a year before we dared drink from the creek running near the village again.

About a week after the cholera subsided, the white woman came to a place where she was aware of her surroundings enough that she could speak. I could see in her blue eyes that she could actually see me, and there was fear for she did not know where she was or who we were.

"Where am I?" she whispered hoarsely.

"You're in my home. You're safe here."

"Who . . . ?"

"I'm Sam. I found you at the wagons. They were all dead. I brought you here." And I gave her some more water and stew that Singing Night had made for her. The woman swallowed the water and the food. "All dead?"

"All dead." Her eyes filled with tears. At that moment, Singing Night leaned over my shoulder to bring me more water and food for the patient. "Indian," the woman said, startled at the sight of my wife.

"Yes, my family are Indian. This village is Indian, Cheyenne to speak clearly. But you are among friends. No one will harm you. We have already brought you back from death."

She ate what I spooned her and seemed to take this all in.

"What is your name?" I asked.

"Miss McKiernan," she whispered.

"You got a Christian name?"

"Greta."

"Where were you going with that wagon train?"

"Oregon. I teach school." Saying this many words was an effort for her.

"Did you have a husband? Children?"

"No," Greta whispered. "Nobody will have me."

I thought this a peculiar answer and I wondered if there wasn't more truth in it than she meant to let out, for in a state of half-consciousness, folks tend to forget to cover up and lie. But as she recovered, knowing the Spider ways, I could see the truth in her admission. She was tall and skinny, even before cholera almost killed her. Men like women with full breasts and wide hips, and Greta had neither. Her eyes were a pretty blue and her black hair long and straight, but she had a "weak chin" as I heard someone call it, that is, her chin didn't come out very far and her mouth was small. And she had a Roman nose, thin but prominent. She was not pretty at all. And for a woman no man would court, there was only teaching school if she wanted to make an honorable living. I wondered if she'd gone west because there was nothing for her in the east. The wagon train would have accepted her with hopes that when they stopped and settled, that she'd open a school in their new town in Oregon. Well, I suspect one or two men escaped on horseback, maybe more. But most of that community went up in flames on the North Platte, having been consumed by the cholera. They would never see Oregon.

Eventually Greta regained strength enough to sit up and eat. It was about this time she realized she was naked. I could see in her eyes the terror that I had seen her naked body. It was not proper in her mind, I reckon. I stepped away and let Singing Night tend to her more, in order that she'd be more comfortable, even if Singing Night only knew ten words in English. Singing Night made her a deerskin dress, and though I could tell she was wondering if such clothes were proper for a young lady, she really had no choice. Before long, she gave up attempts to put her hair in a bun, and wore deerskin with her hair long. It was quite a mix of looks, the prim schoolmarm dressed like a Cheyenne woman. She began to help around the house, working with my daughters under my wife's supervision. And the girls, who knew English, translated and taught Greta some basic words and sentences in Cheyenne. They found Greta to be kind and humble, and bonded with her quickly.

The hauling of water from the top of the valley was quite a lot of work until we felt safe enough to take it from the creek again. And learning to cook over a fire without a stove seemed to be a challenge, but Greta rose to it. I could tell when she really finally got her strength and resolve back, because she managed to tie her long, dark hair up in a bun, and keep it that way. And that was a shame, because though she didn't have no pretty face, with her hair down, there was a grace and beauty about her.

One evening when just she and I were sitting on the porch as the sun set, she did work up the courage to ask me a question she'd been burning to know.

"Mr. Plunkett," she started. Once she got her strength back, she felt only proper addressing Singing Night as "Mrs Plunkett" and me as "Mr. Plunkett." She even called Kathleen "Young mistress" and the rest of my daughters "young lady" and my son "young sir".

"Mr. Plunkett, when you found me and the wagon train, were you . . . my dress, I mean . . . it . . . ."

"Sorry Greta, it were fouled with filth and disease. I cut it off you to save your life."

"So, you saw . . . "

"Yes, I did see you natural-like, but I'll have you know I wrapped you in that buffler robe just as quick as could be. I did not wish to invade your privacy, if you take my meaning."

She paused to digest this thought and finally said, "That was very decent of you, Mr. Plunkett. I see how as a gentleman, you had no other course of action."

"Me? A gentleman?"

"Yes, Mr. Plunkett, far more the kind gentleman than many a well-dressed young man that I've encountered in Ohio. Tis a pity you are not educated."

"Well, wait right here, for I have something to show you." When I came back, I put my copy of *Lyrical Ballads*, and Bible with my rosary wrapped around it, the rosary that was my mother's, in Greta's hands.

She sucked in her breath in astonishment.

"I do read some. A little every day if I can."

"And you read Wordsworth?"

"Yes, ma'am. Don't understand all the words, but I like the way he thinks and sees his world."

"And you read scripture?"

"That's a little harder to understand. But I do try. I only had four years of school."

"Mr. Plunkett, this is a miracle. Out here in the wilderness to find a gentleman with a passion for books and learning. And a rosary? May I ask if you are a Catholic?"

"Yes, ma'am."

"But where can you hear mass?"

"Only if there's a passing priest. One of my dearest friends in the world is a Jesuit, Fr. Antoine Charette. I went up and saw him a couple of years back, but he's in Montreal by now. Still, like Wordsworth, I find the Lord is throughout these beautiful forests and in the sunrise. Maybe someday I'll find a priest saying mass but till then, the woods will have to do."

"Then I must conclude that as we all lay dying in those wagons, I was granted a miracle. I prayed to the Blessed Virgin and dedicated my life and death to her. And she sent you. You are an angel of mercy, Mr. Plunkett."

"Reckon she wants you alive, then," I replied. "But I'm glad to be of service to her."

"Do you also have a devotion to the Blessed Mother?"

"I reckon so. I can always feel her near, even right now."

Greta looked stunned and made a small, knowing smile. "As can I. I've never told anyone. They would have thought me mad."

I don't know why I chose that moment to speak my mind, but it was out before I could stop it. "Sad and a bit lonely, I reckon, but not mad."

She looked down to the ground and I felt I had hurt her feelings.

"Sorry to speak out, Greta, but I never did know when to shut up. I was meaning to ask what you intend to do, now that you've recovered."

"I don't rightly know, Mr. Plunkett. Are we far from any town or city?"

"You're in the heart of Cheyenne and Arapaho lands. I think there's a fort some 20 days east down the Platte, and they say there's another up the Platte a ways. But Ft. Laramie is only a couple of buildings, I'm told. The nearest thing like a town is Taos, ten days south, in New Mexico. I could take you down to Bent's Fort, but that's just an outpost among the tribes of the Arkansas River. And I reckon the plague is still going around outside this valley. It may not be safe to leave for some time."

She nodded. "I am sorry to be a burden to you, Mr. Plunkett."

"Wagh! You ain't no burden, Greta, but I was hoping there was something you might do for me and my family while you're here."

"If it's honorable labor of any kind, I will undertake it. I fear I am not a great cook like Mrs Plunkett, though I do try to learn."

"Well, with six children round the place, I try to teach 'em English, but I can't give them no book learning. And someday, we might have to live in the white man's world, and I would not have them be defenseless and ignorant. You say you're a school teacher. How 'bout starting a school in my home?"

"Isn't it five children, Mr. Plunkett?" she began, then corrected herself, "Oh, I'm terribly sorry. Your son, Andrew. Do forgive me!"

When she mentioned that, I felt searing pain for my little Andrew. "That's alright, Greta. He passed before you came 'round again. You had no way of knowing. But I have 5 now. Still, if you want to earn your keep, I'd be mighty grateful if you schooled my children."

"And I'm vastly grateful to you for my very life and the kindness you and your family have showed me. I shall have to make my own materials, but may I use these two books?"

"Yes, of course. And I'll help you find the tools."

So, it was settled. We used the shed, the first building I built, and I added a wing to it. It became the school. A second wing with a fireplace became Greta's house. Even some of the Cheyenne families sent their children. I found a way to make sheets of aspen bark and wood charcoal into paper and pencil, and writing and reading the English language was being taught for the first time in Menoke's Valley. Singing Night thought it odd at first until I explained that the children would have to be wise in the Spiders' ways in order to survive. She accepted that and supported it whole-heartedly. She even went to Greta and had Greta teach her to speak a basic English, so that she too might be able to adapt to whatever came our way. And sometimes, when the sun slanted through the trees of an evening, Greta and I went out and recited a whole rosary in the beauty of those woods.

But my heart burned and bled for Andrew for a very long time after.

17.

Wedding, and Going South Again

1850–1852

THE SCHOOL WENT WELL, though after the work started to get hard, my son often sneaked off to manage the horse herd with the other Cheyenne boys. I bribed young Jack with the offer of his own horse from my stock if he finished four years' level. That got him back in class.

About a year after we'd started, I said to Greta, "You know, you ain't never made me call you 'Miss McKiernan' and I wish you would call me Sam. We are friends, aren't we?"

She thought about this a while, then said, "Well, I didn't want to presume on a false sense of intimacy, but you are a better friend to me than any I've known, save Wendy, so I will do as you say, Sam."

"Who is Wendy?"

"My bosom friend in school in Ohio. She is married by now perhaps I think."

"Well, that's fine. I'm Sam. 'Mr. Plunkett' makes me feel like I'm running a store. Call me Sam."

With this, Greta also became more at ease with Singing Night. But she could never wrap her tongue around Cheyenne names, though she did learn some of the basics of the language over time. My wife told Greta to call her "Misa", which was shortened down from "Missus Plunkett," and the nickname stuck. Singing Night could never manage more Englishing of her name than "Misa Lunke", not being familiar with many English sounds. So, for Greta it was Sam and Misa who were her hosts, and the Menoke Valley school grew like buffalo calf in summer.

Greta came to find uncomfortable but necessary compromises between the life in our valley and the schooling she'd had in what she described as a "convent finishing school." There, good Catholic orphan girls were raised to be prim and proper, and suitable to marry prosperous Catholic men. They were also taught the realities of motherhood and homemaking. Greta never did take to eating with fingers, so I carved her three wooden forks and wooden spoons, and gave her one of my smaller knives. Singing Night so admired this less painful way of eating—no more burned fingers—that I had to make her a set and then a set for all the children. And Greta did admit to me that she had been an orphan, who had been taken in by the nuns. I told her about the betrayal of my father, and the death of my mother, as well as all about Jack Rather, who'd loved me and saved me. She agreed with my thought that Jack was my true father.

Greta got a long strap of deerskin and belted in her deerskin dress at the waist. This was a revelation to me, because when I'd seen her naked and almost dead, she was skeletal, hardly identifiable as a woman. But after her health was restored, it became plain to see that I had been wrong about her being skinny. She had small to mid-sized breasts and hips that curved as nicely as any woman's. As her hair became too long to put in a bun, she let "Misa", Singing Night, braid it for her, making her look almost Cheyenne, but for her white skin. She much admired the beauty of Singing Night's beadwork, and sweet Singing Night two weeks later surprised Greta with a beaded Cheyenne-style deerskin dress, which Greta wore proudly from that day on.

But what really surprised me was when Singing Night told me, "She is a good second wife." I did not translate this to Greta, who would have been horrified at the idea of polygamy. But I knew that if I'd gone into Greta's room and lain with her, Singing Night would have thought it all normal. For all our common thoughts, the Cheyenne mind and the Spider mind are still far apart.

With the spring of '50, love blossomed in our valley. I caught Kathleen many times out among the trees talking to young Lucién Broussard. Once or twice they were kissing. I know some fathers might try to hold on to a daughter, but I knew this young man was as upright and smart as young men get. And I recalled how the hot blood of love was on me by that age. So, when Lucién came to me and told me he loved Kathleen and wanted to marry her, but that he had no horses to give for her, I told him I would accept another gift in their place. I said I wanted to preside over a ceremony of my own making, and I wanted to make them their lodge. He seemed relieved that this was all I asked. You think me a fool? No matter. With Andrew and Spirit I had learned the bitter lesson that life can end in a moment, and that waiting for happiness is a fool's game. Grab what you can in the moment, for that's pretty much all you'll get. I adored my little girl and when I talked to her, it was evident that she loved Lucién body and soul. I gave her my blessing and had the gift of a daughter's joyful embrace, which alone was worth it all. I was only sorry that Spirit did not live to see her eldest daughter marry.

Phillipe Broussard agreed with me that our children were both good folk and well-suited to each other, so we set a date for the following week for the ceremony. The other families in the village all attended mainly out of curiosity, for they all thought of wedding ceremonies as a funny thing that Spiders do. But I enlisted Greta's help, and though neither of us were priests, we racked our memories of Catholic wedding masses we may have seen, and came up with a short ceremony that included promises to faithfulness in good times and bad, me wrapping my mother's rosary around the young couple's joined hands, and me declaring them man and wife in the name of the Father, the Son, and the Holy Spirit. I even made the sign of the cross over them like a priest. Charette would have been proud of me.

I had most of the lodge materials on hand, the poles and the buffalo hides. Singing Night and I worked all week before the wedding to put it together proper, and at the end of the ceremony, I led the newlyweds over to their new home, kissed my daughter, and hugged my new son-in-law. I also told him that the taboo over talking to Singing Night would be nullified. Then they went in, and I led everyone else away to dance and feast at the fire pit outside my house.

After that big event, time seemed not to pass in our valley. Winter, summer, spring, and fall came and went, but life seemed to move on. We had almost no contact with the rest of the tribe for two years, until finally a group of five families we knew came up from the Arkansas to join our village. Their news was grim. The Unseen Killer disease had ravaged our people, both north and south, and had only just recently stopped. But almost a third of our people had died, including Deer Kicks and many of our friends. We were devastated.

Most of the families in our little valley band decided they wanted to see what relatives they had left and return to their families in the south. The Broussards and two other families decided to stay. The rest were longing to see their kin, and so the band of Ivistsinihpahs on St. Vrain Creek went south and reunited with the rest of the tribe.

Singing Night decided we would go south too. We built a second tipi, for Greta and most of the children, since we did not all fit in one. Greta was uncertain, but she told me she had confidence in me. Living with a few Cheyenne was something she had become accustomed to. But the thought of living with two thirds of the Cheyenne nation frightened her. I tried to soothe her with the thought that at Bent's Fort, I might be able to buy her some proper dresses. That did not do much. Kathleen and Lucién volunteered to remain behind and watch the valley. Phillipe Broussard stayed too, and I was glad, for I didn't know who might discover our little valley and try and take it from us. In the end, the two families that wanted to stay changed their minds and it was my daughter and the Broussards who stayed.

When our little band left Menoke's Valley and followed St. Vrain Creek down to the Platte, we were astonished to see an adobe fort at the confluence with the South Platte. I and our few warriors rode ahead to see what this was. When I came through the gates, almost no one seemed to be moving. A few Arapahoes were sitting around and they told us in hand language that this was Bent's Fort. A minute later, old William Bent himself stepped out a door, walked up to my horse and shook my hand.

"Well, hello, Cheyenne Sam. Why don't you come in for a talk?"

I dismounted and sent my young warriors to bring in the rest of the band. Bent took me back in his office, which looked more like a storeroom with a desk. He offered me a glass of whiskey but I'd lost what little taste I had for it. I said "no thanks" and settled in a chair. He put up his feet on the cold stove and helped himself.

"So, what are you doing at the bottom of my valley, Bent?" I asked.

"Well, if I'd a knowed that you and a band of Ivistsinihpah were living upstream, I'd a come to see you. Lots has happened since you last passed through on your way to Taos in '47. St. Vrain never did get over the murder of my brother by them Mexican bastards, and he sold out his share and is back in St. Louie. And by the way, you have my thanks for helping string up them murderers."

I nodded, and said nothing about my mixed feelings regarding that episode of my life.

"I reckon you know about the cholera."

"The what?" Lisa reminds me to say that this was the first time I'd ever heard the name of the Unseen Killer that had ravaged people everywhere and killed all the other people in Greta's wagon train.

"Cholera. You seen it, I'll swear. Diarrhea that won't stop and you die right quick of needing water."

"Oh, yeah. I seen plenty of that devil. Found a white woman in a wagon train full of corpses. Just barely saved her life. I figured the disease was in the water."

"You did, huh? That's pretty smart. Took all those edicated doctors in St. Louie three years to figure that out. What happened to that white woman?"

"She's with us. She'll be coming into the fort right now. But why did you move up here?"

"Shit. Our Cheyenne kin were dying like flies down on the Arkansas River. The survivors fled and left their dead, it was so bad. What's left of the tribe is now living on the Smoky Hill River. Wasn't no trade left, and I wanted to get out of the cholera as much as the next man. It killed almost all my women and young uns. I'm single again. My boy, George, is the only one left."

"I was there when it hit the Omissis. I helped save Tall Horse's village."

"Maybe you did. Maybe you didn't. It would start to go away, and then a new wave would hit. I wouldn't be surprised if the Northern Cheyenne aren't all dead. No way of knowing, but I figure it killed half the tribe."

"Holy crap," I cursed. "But why move here?"

"Wagon trains are coming through here every week. I sell 'em the things they need."

"Women's clothes?"

"Well, yeah. I have some of that, but why do you ask?"

"That white woman I found has been wearing deerskin and I think she'll feel better in a cotton dress and underwear again."

"What's her name?"

"Miss Greta McKiernan. She was a school marm going to Oregon with a train and only she survived. Ready to meet her?"

"Sure."

So, we got up and went out to the yard of the fort, and my village of Cheyenne was just pulling in. Greta was riding with Misa, and had a wide-eyed look of wonder about her, as if she'd just wakened from a dream. I must say I don't know where she learned it, growing up in a Catholic orphanage for girls, but Greta McKiernan knew how to sit a horse right, and rode with her legs on each side. Not only that, she moved fluidly with the horse at every pace, from a gallop to a violent trot. Give her a saddle with stirrups and she could post like an English lady. With all her concern for being a proper lady, I'da thought she would be trying to ride side-saddle. But damn, that woman could ride like a Cheyenne warrior. She was a proper horse woman.

Upon seeing me standing in a white fort with a white man, she looked at Misa, squeezed her hand, leaped off her horse and ran up to us.

"Bent, this here is Miss Greta McKiernan, from Ohio. Greta, this here is Mr. William Bent."

"So pleased to meet you," Greta bubbled, shaking Bent's hand.

"So, do I still have enough credit to buy some women's clothing, Bent?" I asked.

"Hell, Sam, you got so much credit, you could buy half my stock. Come with me, Miss McKiernan, and let's see what I got that might fit you." And off Greta went with Bent to the building opposite. I walked over to Singing Night, or Misa, as I too was beginning to call her. Her face was sad.

"What is it?" I asked in Cheyenne.

"Tall Woman will leave us and go back to her people," she said. "Tall Woman" is what the Cheyenne of my village had named Greta. When Greta found out, she was pleased with the name. But that was two years ago now.

I squeezed Misa's hand. "She is not second wife, my love. Only you are wife. She has been our friend." This made Misa smile. I added. "She will want to go home. This we can maybe do for her."

We did not see Greta for over an hour, but in the meantime, our people set up our village just outside the gates of the fort, and Misa and I moved back into our tipi for the first time in years. We set up the separate tipi for Greta and the children, our family being so big.

Misa was startled, when later, Greta walked into our lodge wearing a cotton print dress that buttoned up to her throat and high-laced black shoes, carrying her deerskin dress and moccasins in a bag. There was apology in her eyes, but you could see that she was more comfortable than she'd been in three years. Misa said she looked nice, and I translated, but I could see that Misa was already beginning to realize that she was about to lose someone that she loved.

"Well," I said, "What have you decided?"

Greta sat on the buffalo robes on the floor in front of us. "Well, I must thank you again, not only for saving my life, but for giving me a wonderful life these last three years. And I can't tell you how much I love the children. They are so dear. But, Mr. Bent tells me that wagon trains are coming through almost every week, and one of those trains to Oregon will want a school teacher for certain. And he says I can stay as his guest till then. So, yes, I've decided to stay here until the right train comes along, and follow my first plan to go to Oregon. But I shall be forever grateful to you both. I would have died but for your kindness, and I will never forget it. I hope you don't mind, Sam, but I not only bought three dresses, shoes, and underwear, I bought a proper saddle and bridle for the horse you gave me."

I nodded. "I'm glad, Greta. You'll do better in a saddle like you're used to." I then translated all this to Misa, who began to cry. Greta rose and sat by Misa and the two women hugged for a long time. When they both rose, we followed Greta to the other lodge where the children were and she said goodbye to each of them, and hugged them. Then we all walked her back to Bent's quarters, where she got another round of hugs, and then we returned to camp outside the gate. In the morning, the village packed up and began moving south.

We'd been going south about an hour when the young warriors who rode around the perimeter, looking for trouble, heard a horse galloping up behind us. They turned to face the challenge, as did I. But what we saw was Greta McKiernan, her face bent over her horse's neck, like a racing jockey, riding after us at a gallop. When she realized she had found us, she reined up like the expert horsewoman that she was. Her horse was breathing hard, as she trotted up next to me and Misa.

"You are my family. I can't leave you." And she began to cry.

Misa maneuvered her horse next to Greta and they hugged as best they could from saddle to saddle. So, on that day, my family remained together. And I thought to myself, though I did not have sexual relations with her, Greta was my second wife in fact.

18.

Jack's Vision Quest, and a Grandchild

1853–1855

By this time, my oldest boy, Jack, or just "son" to me, was almost 18 and a Cheyenne warrior to look at him. But he had no name. Generally, boys went on their vision quests at 14 or 15, but White Coyote had left our village by that time and there was no elder to guide Jack. When the cholera hit, we just laid low and did not contact anyone outside the valley if we could help it. So, part of my reason for going south now that the cholera had passed was to link up Jack with his grandfather in hopes that he, Jack, could find his name. And that included finding his peace. I could see the boy desperately needed it. He was past that restless age when boys don't know who they are and get mighty troublesome. Some boys in that space become contraries, a brilliant Cheyenne way to deal with troublesome young men.

A contrary warrior buys a Thunder Bow off another contrary and once he does, everything he does is backwards: yes is no, he washes in dirt, and walks backward when he can. I often thought a lot of young people in their teen years were contraries, whether they bought a Thunder Bow or not. But though Jack had been on some successful horse raids against the Crow, with my reluctant permission, he had not fought and killed an enemy, or stolen a horse by himself, so in the Cheyenne mind, he was not a man or a warrior yet. This troubled him greatly and often he would get sullen and not talk for the longest time. I knew he needed to find himself in his vision quest.

So, we went looking for our kin along the banks of the east-flowing Smoky Hill River, and Misa and I were looking for White Coyote. When we found the Ivistsinihpah camp, the third one down the Smoky Hill River, we set up next to White Coyote's lodge. He was much changed when I went into his lodge to see him. The size of the village had been a shock to Misa and myself, with half of our friends and distant family just plain gone. It seemed shrunken. We almost expected these people to arrive after us and set up their lodges. But they were walking the Hanging Road of stars to the Beyond.

White Coyote was also a surprise. His hair had gone gray and his face was lined with wrinkles I didn't remember. He wore a wide bone choker, and had wrapped himself in one of those white Hudson Bay blankets, with the green, blue, and red stripes at each end. There were a lot of those around, and the day was cold. He had also got himself a black, broad-brimmed hat, with the crown rounded up. He had decorated it with beads and a feather, but such a Spider piece of clothing seemed out of place at first. He must have bought it at Bent's Fort. Yet, after a while I noticed that even the young men wore these slouch hats, which is what most white folk called them. They were soft and wide and kept the plains sun off your head. After some years it became common to see Cheyenne and Sioux and Arapaho men wearing these soft, wide-brimmed hats, sometimes brown but more often black. It was my first sign that the white man's world was on its way to swallowing up the Old Ways of the red man's world.

I sat down across from him and he looked at me without speaking for a little while. He finally said, "Welcome my son. It is good that you are back."

"It is good to see you, father. I am startled by the change in our people."

"The Unseen Killer has taken many of us. We are not now the strong people that can stand up to the Spiders that are coming. But you know they are coming. Their wagons go up the Moon Shell River to the west by the hundreds and scare off the buffalo." 'Moon Shell River' was the Cheyenne name for the Platte.

"It will get worse, my father. Even before the Unseen Killer, the Spiders to the east are 100 times 100 as many as our people. They are as numerous as blades of grass on the plain. We do not have the warriors to stop them."

"That is as I feared. When you and Lost in Snow and the first Spiders came to this country, I thought you would not be many and it would not matter. But now we chiefs know that war is coming and we cannot win." 'Lost in Snow' was my father, Jack's Cheyenne name. But I was mostly surprised by "we chiefs."

"I am not a chief, my father," I replied.

"You are wrong. You are chief of a small band on Menoke's Creek. When the chiefs are next called to Council, you will be required to be there. It is not just I who have said this. The other chiefs have said this. And your friend, Many Horses, is now also a chief."

"Many Horses? Is he here? I thought he was with Tall Horse's village in the north."

"Tall Horse and many others died of the Unseen Killer. Your friend is now chief of that village, and is there now. But it is time for your generation to step up and take leadership. Chiefs like me and Black Kettle and others are now old. We do not favor war with the Spiders. The younger men do. And the Dog Soldiers have become their own band and speak for war.

Lisa tells me I need to explain the Dog Soldiers. There were about five sort of men's clubs in the Cheyenne nation. I had joined the Elk Warriors long ago, but except for occasional group hunts and feasts, it was not a really serious group within the Cheyenne nation. Bands were far more important. And when the tribe divided into northern and southern tribes, most of these societies split up and stopped meeting much.

But one of these men's societies was the Dog Soldiers, and they had more of a function. They acted as tribal police if there were a big effort like an all-tribe hunt, where a few hunters could start too early and ruin everything for the rest of us. Or they organized things, perhaps if the whole nation was camped together, as at the summer meeting and Medicine Hat Ceremony, what white folks called the sun dance. The Dog Soldiers would police the area and whip anybody with horse quirts, who was breaking the agreed-on rules for the hunt, or didn't camp in the traditional position for their band. With more and more Spiders moving into our lands, the Dog Soldiers increased this semi-police role. They came to be the group that had the most young warriors who would not compromise with the increasing flow of Spiders coming up the Platte River. White Coyote told me that they were now a separate band of the Cheyenne, and had their own village further downriver. My brother and friend, Laughs at Night, had always been a Dog Soldier till the cholera killed him. Red Mountain, Four Thunders, Many Horses, and I had been Elk warriors. So, I was a little surprised when White Coyote told me "Your friend, Stands to the Left, is a chief in their village".

We both fell silent at this. I had not known that Stands to the Left had gone to the Dog Soldiers, and returned to the south. Then White Coyote said, "You will be called to Council as a chief if a Council is called. You understand the Spiders better than any of us. Our people will look to you for wisdom. But there is something else I feel on your mind." I did not believe I deserved this. At this time I was but 33 years old. But White Coyote clearly could guess that I had brought Jack to him, though he politely waited for me to bring up the subject.

"I have brought my son. He needs you. He has no vision and no name, and he has 18 winters. The Unseen Killer interfered with his becoming a man."

"Bring him to me."

"I will call him now, and then I will leave you with him. We will stay at least three moons. Then maybe you will return to the Valley with us?"

"I will think on it. There are few chiefs who speak for peace. I may be needed here. But go, send me my grandson."

"I will and I thank you for this." I stood up to leave.

"He is my oldest grandson, and it is an honor to be his spirit guide."

"I will send him in." I stepped outside and as luck would have it, Jack was outside the young folk's and Greta's tipi, looking at me. I think he knew and wanted this chance. I beckoned him over and he came, looking into my face. "Your grandfather waits for you. He will help you as I cannot. Stay with him as long as you need to. He is alone and it would be good if you moved in with him and kept him company. Go to him now and I will get your bundle and bring it to you."

Jack nodded. He fully understood, and I think it relieved him to not have to attend to the rest of the family for a while and focus on his own manhood and the teachings of his grandfather. I could see gratitude in his eyes that I had given him this chance and freedom. I remembered all too well that I had run away from my Irish grandfather in St. Louis in order to grasp my own manhood and my own freedom. It was time to let the boy go and be his own man. His older sister had married; he needed to be himself.

When I had gone over and found his things and given them to him in White Coyote's lodge, I went back to the lodge of the children. Greta was standing out front, dressed in her deerskin dress and moccasins again. Inside, I could hear the other children playing, my three girls left: Charlotte and Clara, or rather Red Girl and Star's Child, the twins, were both 12 and just starting to look like women with their body shape. They were both growing beautiful, and I knew that in the next four years they would both attract men and marry. Young men would be giving me horses for their hands. Running Doe, or Anne, was only 8, and followed her sisters around everywhere, their little shadow. It was good for Jack to get out of there. His sisters were probably driving him crazy.

Greta looked nervous. Cheyenne women were milling about, doing their daily work amongst the cone-shaped tipis. Small children played, and an occasional warrior, tall and straight, walked calmly through the melee. She had been living in a Cheyenne village for close to three years now, but we averaged about 30 people or less. Here there were hundreds and hundreds of Cheyennes. I knew it was alright because they were all ignoring her. If they'd had a problem, it would have shown pretty quickly. That they merely accepted her because of me was enough.

"It'll be alright," I told her. "Everyone in this village knows us and knows that you are part of my family. The only danger here is if white men attack us."

She looked at me and I could see this was a real revelation to her. "Sam, I see why you love these people. Are all these . . . people like this?" She had started to use the word "savages" but had stopped herself.

"Yeah, funny ain't it. Having fine clothes and fine manners, and white skin doesn't make men civilized, and having buckskin clothes and mountain ways, and red skin doesn't make men savages."

She nodded. "It's the heart that counts," she simply said, and left me to go help Misa. I listened to them from a distance for a while and realized that Greta's Cheyenne speaking abilities were getting better. She was far from fluent, but she knew all the phrases that went with women's work in daily life, and communicated perfectly well with Misa. No wonder Misa thought she was second wife. I had become quite fond of Greta myself, but my feelings didn't cross over into love or sexual attraction. Still, I had to admit that she had a woman's shape and beautiful hair and eyes, though her face was plain. Her heart was great and that was more important. Then I pushed these thoughts from my mind, got my guns and went out to hunt.

I didn't see much of Jack in those next weeks. He came and went from White Coyote's tipi. When I did see White Coyote, he assured me the boy was doing very well. One day, about a month later, Star's Child touched my shoulder and told me that Grandfather wanted me to come see him. I came right straight away, and when I arrived, Jack was sitting at White Coyote's right hand, a look of serenity on his face. Only White Coyote spoke.

"My grandson and your son has found his self. He is Flies Straight and that is his name."

"Ha hou," I replied. "So it is." I nodded to Jack, so to confirm that I approved and accepted this act.

"And he has decided to stay with me and hunt from this lodge."

I paused. Of all the hard things I had to do in this life, this might have been the hardest. I swallowed and said, "Then that is his decision. In peace or in war, my heart will always go with you, my son."

I stood up. I wanted to hug him so badly, but I restrained myself. I said, "I will go tell his mother." Then I walked back to our lodge and told Misa, "Our son has found his name. He is Flies Straight. He has chosen to live with his grandfather from now on."

She looked in my eyes for a few seconds, but Cheyenne women have the freedom men often do not, and she rushed out and over to White Coyote's lodge, where she hugged our son whether he liked it or not. Such is a mother's privilege and freedom. Perhaps all women have that freedom. They're not so locked up like us men are.

When March came, wet and muddy, as we were too far south for any serious snow, Misa and I packed up. Only two families decided to come with us back to Menoke's Valley. So, I was hardly a minor chief anymore. I said this to White Coyote and he told me to accept my role. He also told me that if I heard of trouble with the Spiders, I was to rush to him, because a Council would be called. I knew he would not go with us, though neither of us said the words. Then the last part made me swallow and hold in my feelings. Flies Straight, my son, Jack, was there too. He asked to talk to me. We went to the banks of the river near camp.

"Father, I am staying."

I was silent for a good long while, pulling myself together. "I understand," was the best I could manage.

"I have been talking to your friend, Stands to the Left. He has asked me to join the Dog Soldiers." Stands to the Left and I had spent a lot of time together over the winter and I had told him about my son. But it had never occurred to me that Stands to the Left would want my boy for the Dog Soldiers.

I looked at him a long time. "What does your heart tell you to do?"

"My heart tells me to defend our people from the Spiders. The Dog Soldiers stand between the Spiders and our people. I must go where there is battle."

"Yes, son. So you must. Your understanding of Spider language and ways will be useful. But do this for me before we leave: go tell your mother yourself. That is not for me to do." And then I said to myself 'oh what the hell', and hauled off and hugged that boy. He was surprised but accepted it. "My heart always goes with you, my son, in war and peace. I too will have to chose if war comes. But like you, I will be at the front of battle for our people." Then I let him go. "Do not be fooled. The Spiders are many. Our warriors are few. We will not easily win this war if war it is. And whatever happens, stay close to your grandfather. I leave him in your care. He is growing old and will need help soon."

Jack nodded in acceptance of this. And, somehow, I had the courage to just stand there as he nodded to me and headed back to my lodge to tell Misa. I waited maybe another 20 minutes so that I did not interrupt that ceremony. When Misa came down and found me standing on the river bank, thinking, I could see she had been crying. She took my hand. Finally, after long silence, she said. "I have sent Tall Woman and our daughters downriver to look for roots and berries. I told Tall Woman not to be back before the evening meal."

Misa was funny that way. All that time in Menoke's Valley having a bedroom to ourselves, Misa had become private about having sex in front of others. The Cheyenne mental barriers weren't enough for her anymore. And Misa when she was sad, found deep comfort in our love-making. So, we went up to our lodge and made passionate love for about two hours uninterrupted by children.

In the end, when it was time to go, she had the hardest time. I think she accepted that Jack was a warrior now and had to make his own way. But she wanted White Coyote to come with us. He felt that the voices for war had to be countered, and with his Suhtai friend, Black Kettle, he had become one of the prime voices for peace. Laying low in a Front Range valley would not help keep the young men from war with the Spiders. So, he stayed. We rode away with a tremendous sadness radiating out from Misa's heart and demeanor.

But when we arrived at our cabin, the sight of Kathleen Yellow Bird, our eldest daughter, and her husband, Broussard, was some comfort, as was living in the warm cabin. I had spoiled Misa. She never wanted to spend another winter in a tipi again. We did not see White Coyote or our son again for four years. But we had a different sort of comfort. In the spring of 1855 Kathleen gave birth to my first grandchild, Lisa Asimoni Broussard, now the smart woman writing all this down on the porch of the ranch house she was born in.

19.

War Finally Comes

1857

'55 THROUGH '57 WERE quiet years. At least they seemed that way. But the whole Cheyenne nation could feel the conflict coming. Several more families moved to my village just to get away from the tension. My village was hidden and now that Bent had moved his fort back down to a new location on the Arkansas River, most of the Southern Cheyenne followed him. But altogether they were both strong against, and at the same time vulnerable to a big attack. So, a few who had lived with me before, came back to be inconspicuous in Menoke's Valley.

I rode out of my valley a lot, simply because I did not want to be caught off guard again. My old friend, Bent, had built his fort right downstream from me and I had not known it for two years. That was not only embarrassing for a mountain man and a Cheyenne to be caught off-guard like that— it was damn dangerous. I had been staying in Menoke's Valley and never going further than a deer hunt, and that was dangerous. I swore I wouldn't be caught off-guard again. But us old-time trappers were scattering. Bent's South Platte fort was now abandoned and a den for coyote pups. Lots of fellows, like me, had married into tribes and were becoming white Indians. Others were guiding wagon trains. Some had just gone to California or Oregon and were living quietly as hunters and farmers among all the new settlers. I heard that Kit Carson settled down in Taos and married a Mexican beauty.

My old and dear friend, Jim Beckwourth, was out in California and other places. He had always been too restless to settle anywhere long. I heard he was running a business in the new state of California, or that he'd opened a hotel in Santa Fe, and that he'd married some Spanish beauty. Never mind that he already had at least two Crow wives squirreled away somewhere. But wherever he put down roots, he'd cut those roots off after six months or a year, two at most, and wandered off on a new adventure. I heard he was leading around that Army officer named Fremont, that Kit had introduced to me. And I heard, like a lot of the old trappers, now that the beaver were all killed off, he was leading wagon trains up to Oregon along the Platte.

It was these wagon trains that caused the tension with the Cheyenne for the early part of this time. The people in the wagon trains shot buffalo and drove the herds off from their instinctive wandering routes, so our hunters had a hard time finding buffalo and feeding Cheyenne children. The anger was growing. And then it got worse. All sorts of Spiders, or white fellows who were definitely not trappers like me, were wandering all over my mountains. They were miners, and no, not cowboys. If they came into my valley, I could smell them and I turned them around, usually with my Hawken aimed at the middle of their foreheads. Thus began my reputation in Colorado for being the murderous, renegade, old fool that lived with "injuns" in the valley of St. Vrain Creek. I decided right off that such a reputation could be mighty useful. I got in the habit of taking the two Broussards, my friend and my son-in-law, and usually a couple more Cheyenne warriors from my village on something like a regular patrol. It was a lot of work, but it was necessary. Some damn fool had got the idea that like there was gold in California, there was gold, or maybe silver, in Colorado. And then that damn fool wrote up a newspaper article about it that got carried in every paper east of the Mississippi. And, of course, every poor son-of-a-bitch, or restless and greedy idiot east of the Mississippi got the notion to come to Colorado territory, which is what some white folks, Spiders, were calling the Front Range area where I lived. Actually, it went by three names at one time or another: Kansas Territory, Jefferson Territory, and finally Colorado Territory. This was prime Cheyenne and Arapaho territory, by the 1851 treaty. But just as soon as some fat Spider gets a notion of riches, or prosperity, which is the real American religion, and not Christianity, they all go mad, and all bets are off. Treaties, honor, and honesty go in the dung-hole when the American God, Wealth, rears his ugly head. The madmen were penetrating every corner of the Front Range, looking for gold or maybe silver. They swarmed my lands like maggots. None of them gave a damn about the treaty leaving all this land to the Cheyenne and the Arapaho. The Broussards, my warriors and I patrolled our valley every two to three days and over the years drove out probably a couple of hundred Spiders—white miners—from just our valley, all at gunpoint.

Lisa tells me to explain the 1851 treaty. The US Government got pretty much all the plains tribes together at Ft. Laramie in the spring of 1851, and drew lines on a map as to who owned what land. It was pretty generous, and at the time I think they did it to stop the tribes warring on each other and because they thought the plains to be such a godforsaken and useless mass of land, they figured the Indians could keep it. Within six years they changed their minds. A lot of Omissis chiefs and White Coyote and a few of the southern chiefs went. I didn't know about it at the time because we were in Menoke's Valley staying clear of the cholera, which was still raging here and there on the plains. But White Coyote told me about it later, when we went south. At first the US was pretty generous with us Cheyenne, and our Arapaho allies, giving us all the land south of the North Platte River, east of the Rocky Mountains and south to the Arkansas River. The eastern boundary was an imaginary line maybe two day's ride east of Bent's new fort, near the current Colorado-Kansas border, to keep us out of the Pawnee lands. The US promised that white men wouldn't hunt our buffalo and that wagon trains would pass quietly up the Platte so long as we left them alone. And we were supposed to leave the Crow and the Pawnee alone and they us. None of this happened, of course, except that the wagon trains got more and more common. Spiders continued to slaughter the buffalo and we continued to raid the Crow and the Pawnee and they raided us. And by 1861, the US Government came back and forced the Cheyenne and Arapaho onto a piece of land carved out of this that wasn't even a fifth of the size of the original. Those US Government Indian agents would find some elder men who might be one of the 44 peace chiefs, or perhaps just old men who could be bribed. They'd call these fellows "chiefs of the Cheyenne nation" and bring maybe five or so of these fellows to a ceremony, to make marks on a piece of paper that these "chiefs" barely understood. Then the army would enforce this new land reduction. It happened again and again. Chiefs like White Coyote and Black Kettle didn't like it, but they would argue for compliance. The young men, especially the Dog Soldiers, would laugh at the treaty and ignore it. Still, in spite of plenty of opportunities, the Dog Soldiers held back from killing the Spiders. Even when some Spiders killed some Lakotas over some stolen cattle that weren't really stolen, in '56, our People held back. And the Lakota were our allies. But we held back. I think even the Dog Soldiers knew in their bones, just how brutal all-out war would get once it started.

But you couldn't hold back the flood waters of greed. In 1858, some son-of-a-bitch panned out some gold on the South Platte, not far from the entrance to Menoke's Valley and Bent's abandoned fort, and the Spiders came swarming in like flies on a dead horse. My gunpoint patrols went from every three days to daily, from necessity. At Lisa's advice, before I start telling about fights between my two peoples—my God, that seems strange for me to say, and always has been—I need to explain something about the difference between the Cheyenne mind and the white American mind when it came to war. White Americans, or as I think of them, the Spiders.... (Lisa doesn't like me using that word. She says the Americans need to own what they did, and not hide behind a name. I can't help it. That's how I thought in those days). The Spiders inherited the European concept of war, that must go back to the Middle Ages, or even further, when dukes and kings and princes had vast armies of archers and spearmen who marched against each other in great numbers and performed bloody slaughter, often just over whether one lord had to kiss up to some greater lord, or who ruled some worthless piece of land. Boat loads of peasants died over lords and their claims of authority. It was a bitter game for power. And it was a bloody sport.

My Cheyenne kin valued young men much more highly than that. It was unthinkable to lose that many in any fight. That is why trappers like my father, Jack, learned to hole up and shoot one or two attacking Indians. Indians don't want to fight if their medicine is bad. And don't you get high and mighty looking down on the Cheyenne for being superstitious! I seen Spiders who gamble do the same thing, only instead of "medicine", they call it "luck."

Anyway, young men are too valuable to lose in great numbers, and when a fight is looking bad, we will get out of there if we can. We Cheyenne wanted to scare the Pawnee and the Crow out of our hunting grounds, but killing them wasn't nearly as important as scaring the crap out of an enemy so that they clear out and don't come back, as when Laughs at Night and our war party punished the Pawnee after they killed Menoke. If we could have done that without killing Pawnee, we would have. (or maybe *they* could—I, on the other hand, was thirsting for revenge that day and wanted blood). Counting coup, that is coming right up to an enemy and touching them and coming away unhurt, was the ultimate act of intimidation. Plus, young men were too valuable to throw into the meat-grinder the way Europeans did, and later, the US Army did. So, when surrounded and someone had the drop on you, young Cheyenne warriors were trained to bolt in multiple directions, and cause armed pursuers to not be able to follow you. We became like smoke, and all of a sudden, we were just gone. Better to flee and regroup than to take heavy casualties, like white Americans liked to do. And because of this, if you read the accounts of white on red fights, it's often big troops of US Army troopers bearing down on a few Indians, who vanish in every direction. Army troopers came to believe that all red men were cowards, afraid to stand and fight. Red men came to believe that all US Army troopers were insane.

So, when the fighting started, it was mostly like that. A troop of US Cavalry would bear down on some of our young men, who would vanish in ten directions, leaving gear and horses behind sometimes. The troopers would not pursue us, but rather scoop up our horses and gear, and ride back to the nearest Army post in triumph, having secured a victory in their minds, proved by their trophies.

The European kind of warfare, of massing large numbers of warriors and wiping out the enemy, claiming the field, was not tried by my people and our allies for another 18 years. And when my people finally tried it, they destroyed half a US Cavalry regiment. No, wait. It was tried before that. Red Cloud, a Lakota chief, did it successfully ten years later, and kept the Spiders out of the Powder River country for almost a decade. Yet, we couldn't keep it up. The Spiders, that is, the Americans could keep soldiers in the field and in the saddle because they had logistics. Lisa gives me that word. That means that they had constant incoming wagon trains of supplies, arms, and food, and hay for horses, that kept American soldiers on guard at strategic points, and ready to fight day after day, year after year. My Cheyenne kin and our Lakota and Arapaho allies never even dreamed of such things. We had to break into small groups because we had to have grass for our horses and places to hunt that weren't pressured by masses of mouths to feed. We had always lived in scattered villages so that the land could support us. Except for the Medicine Hat dance in summer, we never thought to mass together, at least not till '76.

So, the US Army picked us off in little groups and forced us onto the reservations. I have often wondered what would have happened if the Cheyenne, the Arapaho, the Lakota, the Comanche, the Kiowa, and maybe a few other tribes had banded together and figured out logistics, and kept several thousand warriors ready to fight at all times in a large mass, a standing army, like the Americans did. Maybe today, the Rockies and the Plains would all be an independent country of red men and women, who kept back the white invaders when it counted. I don't know. Maybe I'm wrong. 'Cause when the Americans really came on strong at us, after fighting their Civil War, they already had an experienced, standing Army in blue coats, ready to go. Maybe there never was any hope for the Cheyenne and the other tribes.

Actually, I was thinking it was in '57, but that's wrong. The troubles started in '56, the year after my Lisa was born. It started like a snowball rolling downhill, becoming an avalanche. More and more bluecoats were along the Platte, what was now known as the Oregon Trail, so odds of a run-in between Cheyenne warriors and US troopers increased. First, in the spring there was an argument over horses that we had "stolen," which, as with the Lakotas, were strays some careless Spider had lost. An Omissis man I got to know well much later, Little Wolf, was not willing to give back one horse and things got violent. One Cheyenne warrior, Wolf Fire, died imprisoned by the soldiers. The resentment among my people was great. The Spiders treated us like naughty children that they had a right to punish. All the talk at treaty negotiations about us and them being two nations dealing honorably with each other, was proved a lie. We were looked down on as ignorant and weak, to be pushed around as needed by the US Army. I think that angered people more than the death of Wolf Fire.

But it really came home to me that August, because my boy, Jack Flies Straight, was right in the middle of the next fight. He was in a Dog Soldier war party headed over to push back the Pawnee. The weather turned bad and they were all sitting in the middle of a ring of their horses, sheltering under buffalo robes, waiting out the rain on Grand Island in the Platte River. They were within sight of the so-called Oregon Trail when they saw a single mail wagon going west to Ft. Kearny. Bear Paw asked my son to walk over there and make "Spider talk" to ask the Spider driving the wagon for some tobacco. Everyone in the tribe knew that my children spoke English, which made them useful as translators in the days to come. Jack did as asked, with a few of his friends, and waved down the man, asking him in clear, Kentucky English (which he learned from me) whether the man had any tobacco to trade. That may have been part of what spooked the fellow, hearing an Indian warrior ask him a question with a slight Kentucky drawl. Whatever it was that scared him, the man driving the wagon pulled out his shotgun and fired it, missing everyone. Then he whipped up his horses and got out of there, but not before one of Jack's friends fired an arrow through his left arm. The older Dog Soldiers soon showed up and yelled at Jack and his friends for causing trouble, whipping them with their horse-quirts, a common technique for Dog Soldier discipline. Then they all returned to camp on the island.

The following morning, Jack and his war party were charged without warning, by a troop of bluecoats on horseback at full gallop, firing their M1841 rifles. Our men didn't have much time to react. The gunfire killed six Dog Soldiers and the rest scattered. If this had been a handful of years later, when carbines and repeating rifles were available, it would have been a lot worse for our young men. Jack was grazed by a bullet on his right upper arm. Firing at a gallop is not a very good way to hit a target, and Jack and those Dog Soldiers were lucky the Bluecoat commander was such a fool. If our people had had a little more warning, they would have shot half the soldiers out of the saddle. Instead, they had to run for it. If the Bluecoat commander had any brains, he would have dismounted outside our camp and surrounded it. Then all the young men would have had to surrender or die.

As always, the soldiers, stopped, gathered up the horses and equipment and marched back to the fort after their "victory." It was short-lived, for the Dog Soldiers and a lot of Omissis young men began raiding the wagon trains on the Oregon Trail without warning or mercy, since they killed us without warning or mercy. And I am sorry for it, because women and children died, both Cheyenne and American. I regret that deeply. The Indian agent for the Platte area and the Southern Cheyenne, some fellow named Twiss, told the government that the southern part of the tribe was at peace, which was only partly true. But it was what he believed. Operating out of a fort on the Platte, he really did not know much about the Indians he was supposed to govern, except the few fort Indians who hung out at his post. He was the first, but not the last witless fool the US Government sent to "handle" my people.

What he didn't know was that whatever was restraining us was broken by those attacks on our young men. That fall a Cheyenne warrior that used to live with my little village rode into my valley with a message from White Coyote. The whole nation, though it was late fall and not summer, was to meet on Turkey Creek, which is what the Cheyenne called the Solomon Fork River, at next full moon, for a council of war. I was needed to be there as I was a chief.

20.

The First Wave

1856–1859

The camp on the Solomon Fork was as big as any Medicine Hat Ceremony reunion. No time was wasted and in the center of camp, on the thick grass around a fire, the 43 chiefs and I sat facing each other in a circle maybe 20 feet in diameter. We all sat and when someone wished to address the whole body of chiefs, he stood and spoke. There were long periods of silence when no one spoke. Only one chief was missing, the chief of Wolf Fire's village, who was angry that there wasn't an immediate strike against the Spiders when his friend was captured.

But the Cheyenne weren't quite a democracy, though we were close. There was no federal government to enforce the will of a majority vote. We never did anything all together without a complete consensus. That had worked for us so far, from the days in northern Minnesota, fleeing the attacks of the Chippewa, to the days on the Missouri River when Lewis and Clark found us all in one village, to the days on the Cheyenne River in the Black Hills, till the days I knew, when the tribe had left the Black Hills to wander the plains. But I knew my people had never faced an enemy like the Spiders before. I was considering saying this, but I felt like it wasn't my place to say. It was Stands to the Left, who sat beside me on my right, a leader of the Dog Soldiers and my brother, who stood and said, "I want to hear what Red Hair might tell us." Then he sat. I looked to my left where White Coyote sat by me. He nodded in encouragement. I stood and cleared my throat to speak loudly and clearly.

"My brothers. I cannot speak for peace or war. That, I feel, is for you to decide. But I can tell you about the Spiders, for as most of you know, I was born among them. They are like red ants in a large anthill. You see a few now, but kick the anthill and many more will swarm out. They do not think like a Cheyenne. They claim to worship *Maheo* (Lisa tells me to explain that this is the Cheyenne word for the Creator, God) and his Son, but will abandon all Maheo's teachings and do anything for possessions and power, which is given by the shiny yellow rocks in our streams. Even now they scour this country looking for the shiny yellow rocks or the silver ones in the mountains. I have had to drive them from my valley again and again. If they find these rocks, it will kick the anthill and they will swarm over our lands like nothing you have seen so far.

"But as you have already seen, even if peace comes at the price of a treaty, they will not keep it. If their people want lands that their chiefs have given us, those same chiefs will take those lands and force us off with their soldiers, treaty or no treaty. Their treaties are as solid and lasting as the morning dew. And the many men they have means they can throw many, many bluecoat soldiers against us, swarming like red ants. We do not have an easy or obvious choice, and I will not tell this Council which choice to make. I do not feel it is my place to say anything about that. But I do not see a road ahead that does not have war, and my heart is full of sorrow. I only know that I will die in battle if I must, as a Cheyenne."

Then I sat down. There was a long silence and one after another, chiefs rose, thanked me for my honesty and loyalty to the Cheyenne people, and advocated different courses. The Southern chiefs, including White Coyote, advocated for moving toward the Arkansas River where the buffalo were still plenty, and staying away from the Spiders as long as possible. The Dog Soldiers, north and south, wanted to fight. And Many Horses, my brother, and the other Omissis chiefs wanted to fight too, but first wanted to return to the north, near and west of the Black Hills, which they considered their country and the country of both our allies, and our ancestors. I think they were hoping that the whole Cheyenne nation would return to the Black Hills and make its stand there, with our Arapaho and Lakota allies. A few of the Southern chiefs wanted to learn farming as the Spiders wanted us to, and to settle down on one piece of land. They argued that our grandfathers farmed on the Greasy River (Lisa reminds me to explain that this was the Cheyenne name for the Missouri), so why shouldn't we? But they were in a small minority. As I said, the Cheyenne didn't vote, nor have majority rule, and when a consensus couldn't be reached, we all stood up and returned to our lodges. The following morning the camp broke up. The Southern Cheyenne, except for the Southern Dog Soldiers, went due south, back to the Republican and the Arkansas Rivers, and all the Dog Soldiers went with the Omissis to the north. I chose to ride with Stands to the Left and the Dog Soldiers, and follow the South Platte to my home. My boy, Jack Flies Straight, rode beside me, which warmed my heart considerably.

Some miles up the Platte, some of our scouts rode back to us and told us a large force of bluecoats was coming and they were set for war. It was infantry, with cavalry in the lead. We figured real quick that that large force of bluecoats was marching out to attack us. It was then I spoke up. I knew a place close by, across their line of march, where we could spread out with rocks on our right and woods to our left that would guard our flanks. There was a shaman there, Coyote Cries, who predicted that his medicine would silence the bluecoats' guns and we would have an easy victory. Within two hours we were spread across this place, shoulder to shoulder, on our horses. There were easily 300 of us with warriors from several Omissis villages, and all the Dog Soldiers. We sent the women and children on horses to ride an evasive course to the north, around the soldiers by crossing the Platte and heading into Lakota lands. If all went well, we would overtake them and call them back. Then we got ready. I remember wishing that we'd all had rifles, and then this would have been a really challenging fight for the bluecoats.

The blue cavalry showed up in the distance, their column of dust announcing them long before we could see them. I figured that they wouldn't be smart and wait for their infantry to come up and attack us in strength. I loaded up my second Hawken gun, the .30, so that I would have two shots. But only me, Many Horses, and Stands to the Left had rifles. The rest had bow and arrow. I thought for sure we could at least bloody the noses of these troops, and that they would do the smart thing and dismount and fire on us at distance, where they had advantage.

But in 20 minutes, though they had that advantage, those bluecoats slung their rifles into saddle holsters, drew their sabers and charged. And thus I learned something about bluecoat commanders. They liked charging. I and a lot of other Cheyennes remembered this in '76 and used it. But this time, all my fellow warriors had placed their hope in Coyote Cries and his medicine. Without the guns, the medicine was no good, and as I've already explained, Cheyennes don't throw their young men into the meat grinder. Everyone kicked up their horses and got out of there. I didn't. I got off my horse and found Stands to the Left and Many Horses riding up beside me and following my lead. They dismounted and stood with me shoulder to shoulder. We aimed carefully and fired with our Hawken rifles. But we only had time for one round. Our guns barked four times. Four bluecoats went down. Then we mounted up and got the hell out of there. Some of our lodges and goods were captured by the bluecoats, who once again, having scattered us and taken our possessions as well, claimed to have killed many of us (as I found out later—that gave me a good laugh) and declared victory.

Afterwards I felt stupid. I realized that I could have set up an ambush with a few warriors for a decoy, and those stupid bluecoats would have ridden right into the middle of it. Red Cloud did exactly that some eight years later at the Fetterman fight. I circled around to the south through the open plains and rode straight west to the mountains. I stayed away from the army by approaching the south Platte from the south, and made it home to my valley two days later. Only my family and the Broussards were there. All the young warriors from my village had gone with the Omissis, being convinced that war was coming. Oh, I reckon I should say that two older couples stayed, but I had no more warriors in my village. Some chief I was. Still, what I had said at Council had been valued and praised. I figured I had done my job and thought no more about it.

The following year was when some damn fools found gold in the South Platte near the entrance to my valley. And as I had predicted, it kicked the anthill. I killed at least seven miners who refused to leave my valley, adding to my reputation as a crazy old mountain man. Every inch of those mountains was scoured for gold, except my land. But you couldn't scare some of these fellows off, so I sent them to hell, usually with a fifty-caliber hole in the middle of their chests. I reckon then, that my count at the beginning of this book of dead white men, is off. Add to that the two US Army cavalrymen I had certainly killed in the attack near the Platte, and my total was nine at that point, if you don't count the two trappers who tried to murder me back in '34, Powers and Morton. But those were killed by my brothers, so I won't count them.

Greta, on the other hand, was thrilled when she heard that the river-bank mining settlements of St. Charles, and Auraria, which got combined into something called Montana City, were a half day's ride south of us. The way she figured, sooner or later a boom town was going to draw a Catholic priest and a church. Looking back on it now, it was Greta that made it possible for me to slowly ease back into the white world. I didn't much like it at the time, but if she had not done that, I'd have been hung for murder and buried long since, and my children thrown to the dogs. God bless Greta.

Not long after this, they changed the name of the new town to Denver and Greta talked me into going there. This was '58 or maybe '59. She had a mission, and thank the Virgin, I trusted her. You see, when I killed those fellows, it was after warning them off. They all came back and took a shot at me. Like most white men from the east, they couldn't hit a barn at 5 feet away, but they took a shot anyway. Gold fever will do that to a man, drive him to madness, murder, and suicide. I shot back and I didn't miss, so

Greta never blamed me. But she did insist on checking the body and helping me bury it. She had the intelligence to go through their pockets and packs before we planted them 6 foot deep. And thus, without doing a bit of mining, we ended up with a nice collection of small gold nuggets and panned gold-dust. I didn't know what to do with it. I'd just as soon throw it back in the creek where it belonged. As far as I was concerned, the stuff was evil, and drove men to madness. I didn't even want it in our home. But Greta stopped me and collected it where I wouldn't see it.

So, when we rode our horses into the new Denver, Greta knew what she was looking for. Most of the town was hastily thrown up—half a dozen wood buildings, and there was already a saloon and a whore-house. Important things first. There was an assay office with men lolling around outside, discussing ore prices. Greta kept her chin high and ignored the drunks, gold-seekers, and wanton ladies weaving through the mud of the streets. She found what she was looking for like an arrow skillfully shot at a mark. It had a crooked sign over the door that read "Land Ofise". No, Lisa did not misspell that word. That's what it said.

We went in and there was a stout fellow behind a desk with lots of paper on it. He had curly black hair on his head that flowed down into his curly, mutton-chop sideburns. He wore a white, collarless shirt and a black silk vest. Greta was equal to his propriety. She was in her cotton dress and boots, looking like a proper lady. And she dressed up all the education she had and talked to that man like he was a naughty student at her school. She had also got from Bent enough cotton cloth to make a man's shirt, which I had never worn. But she told me this was the day to wear it. So, though I had buckskin breeches, I had a white man's shirt. She also cut my hair for the occasion. I objected, but she simply asked me if I wanted to save our home or not. So, I sat down and using my knife, she trimmed my hair as best she could. But it was no matter, there were no barbers in town at that point and no other man looked any better. Besides, my hair would grow out again.

The man behind the desk looked startled when we came in. I'm not sure, but I've always had that effect on white men, due to the scarring on the left side of my face.

"Can I help you folks?" he said, in a tone that made it clear he didn't think he could.

"Yes," Greta replied crisply, "We need to record our property deed. I am Greta Plunkett, and this is my husband, Samuel. We have been living up here for some years and have a ranch in the St. Vrain Creek Valley."

"That true?"

"Yup," I said, and that was almost all I said.

"Well, you'll have to fill out this paperwork here, including a drawing of the property and a description of the boundaries in miles, yards, and feet. And we will need two copies."

I'm sure my mouth fell open. I could write a simple message and sign my name, but not much more. Greta took to it like a beaver slipping into a pond. "Of course," she chirped, and after she borrowed two pencils and a ruler, we sat down at a table on the other side of the cabin. You could tell the fellow was disappointed. He thought we'd give up and go away. But Greta had been thinking hard about this. She took the two pieces of large paper and drew similar large rectangles on them, aligning the corners with easily visible peaks in our valley that everyone could see. And she made sure that St. Vrain Creek flowed for a long way down our property. She guessed the distances, consulting me on that and the basic geography of the valley, the lay of the surrounding ridges and the path of St. Vrain Creek. And she made a prominent drawing of our ranch house that no one could miss. Years later I learned how smart this was, especially after the Homestead Act four years after this. Building something on a piece of land went a long way to staking it out. How she learned this, I'll never know. But we finally finished up. It took us more than an hour. And I forgot to say, she went and made a third drawing for us to keep.

We stood up and Greta presented the drawings to the man. He looked them over carefully, making "hm-hm" sounds. Finally he said, "Well, these are in order. But there are fees you know."

Greta had been waiting for this moment. I don't know where she squirreled away that gold she'd taken off of dead trespassers, but out of her right fist she squeezed a small, gold pebble. The man's eyes got big. He clapped his hand down on it and swept it into a drawer at his desk, briskly closing the drawer. "And," Greta said, before he could speak. "We will pay extra if this deed is water-tight, something that will hold up in any court challenge. We might be inclined to be very generous, if this is a legally bullet-proof deed." At this, she let lose another gold pebble and the man swept that quickly into his drawer as well.

"Come back in a week, Mr. and Mrs Plunkett, and I'll have the deed ready to sign and file with the territory court. And I think you'll find that your generosity will be rewarded."

As we rode out of town I said to her, "You realize with that last thing that bastard said, he was demanding more payment on completion. I ought to go back there and cut his throat."

"You'll do no such thing, my friend. I expected that. We have plenty more gold and I anticipate as land becomes dear, thieves will attack every sloppy land deed in the records, in hopes of stealing ranches. I want us to be prepared. We will probably have to fight in court at least once, and I expect to win. And by the way, my friend, since we have legally claimed a ranch, I think you need to buy some cattle to at least give the appearance of us being ranchers."

"You told him you were my wife." The second I said this, I felt sorry to have mentioned it.

She only laughed. "Sorry, presumptuous of me, I know. But anything irregular would weaken our case before a judge."

And right there, I knew I would marry her if somehow she could accept it, being a second wife. But I knew that would not do with her, and I kept my mouth shut. Then she said something that astounded me. "My dear friend, Sam, I hope you don't mind, but as Americans come into this country, you and I will have to appear as man and wife. I know dear Misa is your real wife, but no American will take an Indian woman seriously and you know that. If I can do anything for you, my friends, it is that I can shield you from the legal beaver traps Americans can lay out for each other. They will be much less likely to attack a white rancher and his wife than a man married to a Cheyenne woman. I hope you don't mind my ruse. Anyway, when we go back next week, I need you to buy some cattle."

And we did. After reading the deed over carefully for almost an hour, while the man fidgeted and looked pitiful, Greta slipped the man with the curly sideburns a small skin bag with about two thimbles-full of gold dust, and he swore up and down that this deed was watertight and filed with the courts. We also went up the muddy street and gave a cattle dealer a tiny nugget, and I drove home four black and white cows, plus a young bull calf. Then Greta set me to building fences on our new property lines, not only to keep the cows with us, but to say in the Spider way that the land belonged to us. This hurt my Cheyenne heart, where I understood that the land belongs to Maheo, and we only borrow it. But I knew she was right and did everything she told me, with the help of the Broussards.

I will say that Greta was also right that in the next ten years, we had three legal challenges to our deed by greedy bastards. We went to court in Denver all three times, with me looking strange in a suit the last two. We won the first two hands down with the judge laughing the plaintiff out of court. The third one, the plaintiff never showed up and the judge dismissed it after ten minutes. It's a good thing Greta did this because in '59 some fellows, not satisfied with the chaos of Denver, put up some buildings right down from us where St. Vrain's Creek met the South Platte, a place that White Coyote's Ivistsinihpah village had camped in many times. Because there were some boulders in the creek, they called this new "town" Boulder. There went our privacy. Now a town was less than an hour's ride from my front door. Damn. But Greta had saved us in time. And if there is a Plunkett home on St. Vrain Creek today, it's all because of Greta and how damned smart she was.

21.

Sand Creek

1860–1864

I FORGOT TO MENTION, and Lisa reminds me, that in those last years before the Tragedy, our family grew by leaps and bounds. I had three more grandchildren by Kathleen and Lucién Broussard. Sam Wild Horse was born in '59, Vern Wolf Follows in '61, and Carrie Ann Leaves in the Wind in '63. There was some joy. And Jack married an Omissis girl named Leaping Deer, a beautiful young woman who we all came to love quickly, and had his first son, Andrew Rising Water in '62. My children followed my pattern of both a Spider and a Cheyenne name. We all knew that the children would have to walk in two worlds. They learned English and Cheyenne.

For Greta, her Christmas wish of 1860 came true. A Fr. Joseph Machebeuf built a log cabin in Denver, complete with wooden benches and a wooden cross on the peak of the roof, and started saying mass on Christmas of that year. Of course, we were there and not many others. Charlotte Red Girl and Clara Star's Child, my twin girls, had both turned into lovely young women. When we left the Council, though I had gone with the Omissis and Jack, Misa and Greta and the girls had gone with a different group that was going up to the west. This was because I wanted to leave early with my brothers and Jack Flies Straight, and the Dog Soldiers, but Misa wanted to stay longer with White Coyote. When she and Greta left, they took only our youngest daughter, Anne Running Doe with them. She left the twins with White Coyote, as they were old enough and skilled enough to care for him in his advancing old age, and she confessed to me, that if they were with a large village, their chances of finding good husbands were better than in our secluded valley. So, Charlotte Red Girl and Clara Star's Child became part of White Coyote's household. This was good thinking, but it did lead to the greatest Tragedy I have known.

Back east, the Spiders finally got down to the business of killing each other in large numbers. The bluecoat soldiers all vanished from our lands and went east, many of them deserting to form the new Confederate Army. The good thing about this for us Cheyenne is that one, the army just wasn't around to harass us for every missing horse or cow, and two, the persistent wagon trains up the Oregon Trail along the Platte River dwindled down to a mere trickle, and most of those were mail coaches that we didn't bother. The buffalo were left alone-that's all we cared. It really wasn't so bad all of a sudden, and the forces driving us to war with the Spiders got less and less. But what was stranger, the peace held, right up to '64.

Those years are a blur to me now. Several things happened. We did have a war, but it was my people and our Arapaho allies against Utes coming over the mountains and hunting in valleys like mine. Like I said, Indians fight over hunting grounds, over the ability to feed their children, not for conquest or slaughter. The odd thing about this was two villages of Omissis people came down to fill in the center of our tribal lands and drive off the Utes. And when they came, they didn't camp on the South Platte as they had in the old days, for that was now Denver. They came to my valley. All of a sudden I was head chief of 200 Cheyennes in Menoke's valley, off and on. They weren't always there.

This, I found out later, put a flame under the tensions in Denver, and any reputation I had as a mad renegade, crazy old mountain man, who was more than half Indian, roared into bright flame. But that is what started it all—and led to the most horrible thing that ever happened to me. But I can't talk about that yet, and to be honest, dear Lisa, I'm not sure I'll be able to.

I want to talk about friends. My dearest friend in these years was Phillipe Broussard. He stuck with me and worked with me, and guarded the valley with me, even though it was not his. When you think of friends, you think of men you can talk to. God knows my other dear friend, Jim Beckwourth could talk up a storm on any subject you might choose. Phillipe, or Broussard, as I called him, probably said no more than 40 words to me in all the years I'd known him. French was his language, and he was never comfortable in English. Over the years in our valley, his Cheyenne got pretty decent, but again, unless he absolutely had to speak, Broussard preferred silence. The most words I ever heard out of him were for his first grandchild, Lisa, who is writing this down. For her, he would talk in French and she learned quite of bit of the language that way. And he would sing French children's songs to her. But never did a man have a truer friend than Broussard, and I miss him to this day.

Speaking of Beckwourth, I ran into him in Denver, I think around '62. He was walking out of the whore house with a lady under his arm and I was riding away from mass at St. Mary's. Next day he showed up at the ranch, at a time when a whole Omissis village was in motion around our ranch house, preparing a war party to go up over the pass against the Utes.

When he rode up, I walked out to him. "Beckwourth!" I shouted.

He looked around him warily. "Damn, Sam, you got the whole Cheyenne nation here. You know, I've come to be more comfortable with your people. We've been doing some trading."

"Glad to hear it. Get off that horse and come on in for some vittles. The children will want to see you. And Singing Night." I took his horse to my stable, unsaddled and unbridled it, and found a stall for it. When I came back in the house, little Anne was sitting at Jim's feet while he wove some unlikely story. Greta and Misa were sitting nearby and entranced. I waited for him to finish. He looked up and said, "Where are the others? Kathleen? Jack? Andrew? Charlotte, Clara? I expected a flock."

"Well, that's because you stayed too long away, off making a fortune in California or some such fool thing. Kathleen is with her husband and children two buildings over. Jack is up north with the Dog Soldiers, and his wife and child. Charlotte and Clara are with their grandfather, in that village near Ft. Lyon. Andrew." I paused, the pain piercing my heart. "The cholera took Andrew." I quickly changed the subject. "Did you meet Greta?"

"Yes, I did. She says you saved her life."

"Ah, weren't nothing."

"Nonsense," Greta asserted.

"How's your wife?" I asked.

Jim paused and looked studious, as if he were ciphering arithmetic or something, and then cheerfully said, "Let's go for a walk, Sam!"

I showed him around the ranch and explained how cleverly Greta had got our deed registered, and all the patrolling I had to do to keep miners out of this valley.

"You'd better be careful there, Sam. I been running around Denver for a couple of months now, and there is fear there, real fear. The Dakotas rose up in Minnesota, did you hear? Killed hundreds of white settlers. The Union Army had to send troops up there to put it down. People in Denver are scared that you Cheyenne and the Arapahoes are going to do the same here. You having all these Cheyenne warriors up in this canyon scares the crap out of them. There's talk that several miners have vanished up this way and people think you killed them."

"I warned them off and they all took a shot at me. I had better aim."

"Well, don't go talking about that in Denver. I know you and that other woman you go down there to mass on Sundays. Be careful. She your wife?"

"No, we put it that way in the paperwork so that people would take us seriously about our rights to this portion of the valley. Greta don't hold with polygamy. Misa—Singing Night—is my wife. By the way, you didn't answer my question. I hear you have another wife. Just how many do you have?"

"Well, there's River Run, and her little sister, Wind Blows in that Crow village up on the Wind River where you stole my horse and I pissed on your head. I haven't been with them in a couple of years at least. Their brother takes care of them. Then there's Carlota in Taos. She understands me pretty well. And she likes to flirt without closing the deal. Being a married woman with no husband around suits her just fine. But she likes to tell them how I am a dangerous mountain man, to keep her advantage. I think she'd be pretty upset if I just showed up again and ruined her game. And then I think there was another one in California. Don't recall her name. Oh, Luisa! Did we get married? Don't think so. I know she wanted to after the baby. And then there's Shen Ee, my Chinese wife. I think we got married. The ceremony was in Chinee so I don't know. "

"I heard you were in all sorts of businesses and leading Fremont and wagon trains."

"Yessir, pretty much. Wherever a dollar falls from a white fist, I'm there to catch it before it touches the ground. Now I'm trading with your people. So, it will help me if you can put in a good word. But I'm serious, Sam, about Denver."

"What? Somebody gunna shoot me in the back coming away from mass?"

"Actually, it could happen just like that. And they'd be after your valley before you were cold. But more likely the bullies will get after you. I know you hate bullies."

"Who's gunna bully a free trapper like me?"

"Well, there's a group of about seven wealthy, influential citizens, men who have mentioned your name in my hearing more than once. They think you're a danger, second only to the Cheyenne and Arapaho nations. They think you will be a leader if the Cheyenne rise up and murder every white man, woman, and child in Denver, like happened in Minnesota. You know they've raised a militia. The Colorado Volunteers. Three regiments of them. And if they can't find anything to do out here in Colorado, they'll be sent east, which they don't want. The head bully has been made a colonel and is in charge of them. He's a horse's ass named John Chivington. They already fought off the Rebs down near Santa Fe at Glorietta Pass. They don't want to be shipped to Gen. Sherman's command. So, I think Chivington is spoiling for a fight here, just to keep them near home. For a man you've never heard of, he has sure heard of you. Curses your name five times a day in public speeches. Stay out of Denver for a while, Sam."

"What you doing mixing with a bastard like that?"

"Money, Sam. Money. He needs a mountain man for a guide. He doesn't like me, but he knows I guided Fremont, and he pays good. Thinks I'm a runaway slave, like most white men. He hates non-whites as a rule. Used to be a Methodist minister, but they figured out what kind of man he was and booted him. But he's like that. All that tent-preacher fire and wanting men to kiss his ring and make him a king, and follow him. And the Cheyenne are his target. And you're part of that target. Stay out of Denver."

He left not long after and though he was only a few miles away, I didn't see him again till after the Tragedy. I find now that I have to talk about it I cannot.

* * *

It's been two weeks since Lisa and I have left off. I will tell the story. One day in mid-November of '64, when the leaves on the aspens had gone gold, Jack came riding up to our village, once again small. I had long since convinced the chiefs of the Omissis village that was staying with us into moving out, as the Spiders were growing fearful and there might be war. Greta was my spy and she went into town and melted into the population, which was growing and growing. There she said little and listened. She also talked to Fr. Machebeuf, who could take the temperature of the community. She said that my name and our home wasn't talked about so much anymore, but that people were getting angry and saying cruel things about our people, our Cheyenne. Hatred was coming to a boil.

But Jack was there because he had a message. White Coyote was very ill. Charlotte and Clara were doing all they could for him, but they had no skill in healing. Misa packed up and rode out with Jack the following morning. I saw her look over her shoulder at me as she rode away, fear and love in her beautiful eyes. Oh, my God. Oh, my God. I cannot.

* * *

I think I can go on. It was exactly on the 2nd of December. I know, because I kept that buffalo hide calendar all those years. The day is cut deep in my memory. Jack had returned and gone on to the north, back to his family up north. It was a quiet afternoon. The trees were almost bare of golden leaves and the first chill winds of winter were coming up. I looked up from where I was rubbing down my horse at the hitching rail, and I saw Jim Beckwourth riding up slowly at a walk. There was a girl in front of him on his saddle, who buried her face into his chest, so that I could not see her.

He rode right up to me, and I could see she had dark hair and wore a ripped and torn deerskin dress. She was sobbing and trembling violently. Jim looked at me wordlessly and my blood chilled. I could feel that evil had come into our midst. Jim leaned over to help the girl down and I dropped my horse comb in the dirt and rushed to him to catch the girl, who seemed incapable of moving. It was my girl. It was Clara. Her face was covered with dirt and blood, and she shook violently. Her eyes were wide open, staring, and she sobbed softly. I rushed her inside. Greta rose to meet me and we took her into the girl's bedroom and Greta began to care for her. Anne joined Greta and they hovered over my trembling Clara.

When Clara was settled, I went back outside and found Jim standing by my horse, tying off his.

"Jim . . . What?"

"You can kill me, Sam. Just make it quick."

"What?"

"Those lying white men, Chivington, the rest. Those lyin' sons of bitches. They said they'd pay me to lead the volunteer regiments to Black Kettle's village on Sand Creek. They said they were going to move the village closer to Ft. Lyon." Then he could not speak more, but hung his head and wept.

"What? Tell me, Jim!"

"They killed everybody. Women, children, babies, old men. There were almost no warriors there to fight and one regiment held back. They knew it was wrong. But that ass, Chivington led the other two regiments in. They raped all the women and tore them to pieces like butchers making cuts of meat. They tore up the bodies and kept souvenirs. Oh my God, Sam. I done seen no evil worse than this."

"But Misa! White Coyote! Charlotte!"

"Gone, Sam. Gone. And I led them there. Just cut my throat quick. I deserve it."

I knew he meant it and I even in the flush of shock and anger felt for my Green River knife. Jim stood there and didn't move, waiting for me.

But I couldn't do it. I knew once again the white men had used him because he needed the money. "Tell me about Clara."

"I don't know how she got away, but as I was riding away in disgust and shame, I heard weeping in a bush. I dismounted and found her just as you saw her when I brought her. I put her up on my saddle and rode day and night for here. I had to get her out of there or they would have butchered her as well. She hasn't spoken a word, but she seemed to recognize her Uncle Jim, or I don't think she would have let me put her on my horse."

"But the others. Did you see them? Could they have gotten away too?"

He waited a long time before he could answer, struggling to make the words. Finally, in a raspy, cracking voice he said "I found Charlotte and Misa, raped and their throats cut. They did not get away." I think I started to collapse, but Jim caught me and walked me into the house, where he sat me down in front of the fireplace. I kept seeing the day that I rode off with Jack and the Dog Soldiers, and saw Charlotte standing next to White Coyote and waving. How was I to know that I'd never see either of them alive again? And when that image faded, I remembered Misa riding off with Jack to help White Coyote, turning back and looking at me with love, over her shoulder as her horse cantered after Jack's horse. I don't know how long I sat there unspeaking. These two images ran through my mind over and over. Charlotte and Clara were only 23, sweet, innocent girls who never harmed anyone. One tortured to death and the other driven wild. And my Misa, my sweet Misa, who only brought love and healing to all who knew her. Again and again, I ran on the bed of thorns of the agony of these thoughts.

Slowly, I felt Anne, Kathleen, and Greta moving around me, running the house. They told me later I sat there a day and a half without speaking. The first words I said they tell me were "Where? What?" I felt a hand on my shoulder. "*Éhane*" Anne said, the Cheyenne word for father. "We're here." The minute I spoke, Greta was at my side.

"Sam, my dear Sam. You are home safe and well. Misa and Charlotte are gone and all our hearts are shattered. But Clara has been saved. Sam, I need you to come out of this trance. Your daughters need you. I need you. Sam. Can you hear me, Sam?"

22.

Killing Chivington

1864

"Clara is saved?" I repeated, my head swimming.

"Saved, yes. But she has been driven to distraction. Anne and I are caring for her. We are safe. Broussard has taken over seeing to the ranch and the valley, dear man, and his son. Kathleen is here too. We are all worried about you. You've been in shock for a long time. Please, Sam, come back to us."

I think I nodded, stood up and swayed a little. Anne and Greta caught me, one on each side. All I could say was "tired." They led me to my bed and I am told I slept another two days. When I came out into my main room two mornings later, Anne and Greta were doing the chores and making a breakfast. They sat me down at the table and put a plate in front of me. Anne even sat by me and offered to feed me. I shook my head 'no' and realized I was famished and dug in. After a while, Anne looked relieved and got up to help Greta. For a while I watched Greta move around the house confidently. Misa had taught her well. I felt salt tears on my cheeks at the thought of Misa. I finished my meal and stood up. I felt steady.

"I'm going to go look after the horses," I said.

"Alright, Sam," Greta replied. "You do that."

I walked out. The air was crisp and cold and the winds blew so that I knew snow was coming in the next few hours or days. I expected to find my horse, Buck, hitched out in front of the house where I left him. Yes, my old horse, Ann Marie, had died sometime back. But there were no horses on the hitching rail. And yes, Buck was a pinto gelding. I always rode pintos. I heard raking sounds in the horse barn and walked in there. My son-in-law,

Lucién was raking out the last of the horse manure and had a load of fresh hay he was about to lay down. The horses were all in their stalls, munching on their breakfasts.

"Sam," he said, ceasing to rake. "It is good to see you. We were worried about you."

"Everything alright, round the ranch, round the valley?"

"Yes. Father is out riding the fences. No one has come up the valley since Beckwourth."

"Beckwourth still here?"

"No, he rode away the same day he came and brought Clara."

"Uh, thanks for taking care of things."

"You are welcome, Sam. We are grateful for all that you have done for us and are glad to help you for a change."

But he made me think of Clara. I walked around the house and the lands a bit. There were no tipis up now. All the Cheyenne had gone, mostly to the village at Sand Creek. I knew they would never return. They were elders and thought the Sand Creek village was safe, not wanting to risk the anger of many Spider soldiers. Sand Creek was the place for a Cheyenne to go if they wanted to cooperate with the Spiders and be safe. And now they were almost all dead. This brought Clara back to mind. I went into the house.

"Where's Clara?" Greta took my hand and led me to what had been the girls' room. It had only two beds now, where it normally had three. Clara was laying in Greta's best nightgown on the bed with the blanket pulled up to her shoulders, and her arms and hands loose on top of the blanket. Her hair was clean and not full of mud and sticks as when Jim brought her to me. She had been bathed and the mud and dried blood was washed off her skin. She stared at the ceiling fixedly and whispered words, falling silent. Then she whispered again. I sat down beside her and took her in my arms and hugged her. She let me, whispering "Papa, Papa, Papa." When I let go, she went back to her whispering. I could hear up close what she said. "No. Don't. Mama. Help me. No. Charlotte. Mama. Help us." She kept repeating these words over and over again. I stood up next to Greta, who whispered to me. "We bathed and dressed her. She's been like this since you brought her in the house. Anne looks after her constantly. What a sweet sister she is. You should be proud of how strong Anne is in the face of this horror."

"I am proud," I whispered. "Was Clara raped?"

Greta paused. "Almost certainly. We will know in two or three months if she is with child."

I thought of this a while and asked. "Did Beckwourth tell you anything?"

Greta looked at me, looked down at the floor, looked at me, looked away, and then fixed her eye on me. “Sam, I insisted and he told me in great detail the horror that happened at that accursed place. You can throw me out of this house or kill me, Sam, but I will never repeat to you what evil things he told me he witnessed. I will not pass that burden on to you, and you can never make me. I will only say, if you imagined every possible evil thing that could be done to the old people, women, and children in that village, it was done. I will, I hope to God, never know of such evil again in this life. It was a Hell on earth, and I know that as a Christian woman I should forgive, but I am afraid that I wish fervently that every soldier that went into that village rots in hellfire for eternity.”

I looked at her and nodded in acceptance of her resolve. “Ok, I won’t ask ever again.” I brooded for the next few days and slowly got back into the work routine with the Broussards. But they never let me do as much of the work around the ranch as I had done before. It began a pattern of allowing myself to need someone else on that level, something that as a mountain man I had avoided. But I thought a lot about what had happened in Denver that had led to this. As before, when I discovered that Bent had built his fort at the entrance to my valley and I didn’t know, I realized I could not hide up here anymore, that hiding would not keep evil from my loved ones. Up till now, I only went into town with Greta for mass, or to look around. And I had stopped doing even that when Beckwourth told me how rumors swirled around me, and danger was close.

I had all my adult life been a hunter. And a hunter learns patience and how to stalk the prey. I decided that I would hide in plain sight and not in my woods any longer. And I even felt that I had let my Cheyenne brothers and sisters down. What if I had had my ear to the ground when that raid against Sand Creek was getting ready to go? What if I had ridden down there and scooped up my wife and daughters, and my father, and got the hell out of there, and had warned everyone else, so that Chivington and his men had just come upon an abandoned camp? I felt that I had failed my people by not being watchful enough. It was time to be the hunter and not the hunted.

I thought a lot about how to stalk this prey, and I drew upon past knowledge. I already had a reputation in town for being a dangerous, crazy, old mountain man, even though at this point I was only 45 years old. What if I played on that reputation and got myself in earshot of the heartbeat of Denver? Then maybe I could save the next village, or my own ranch and family. I could not stay clear of the white, Spider world any longer. I had to stalk it like an antelope. And, today, at 83, I still stalk the white, Spider world.

I discussed this with Broussard as best I could. Lucién was with us, and he translated much of it into French for Phillipe. He agreed my logic was sound. I proposed to him that his job would be to take care of the ranch and its people. And my job would be to . . . I don't know the word. Lisa says I was being a spy. I'm not sure what that is, but now that she explains it, I think she is right. With Phillipe's help, I started doing something I'd learned back working Rendezvous for the Sublette brothers—making fake whisky. Their recipe used pure alcohol with coloring and flavoring. I wanted to look drunk and be deadly sober. So, I didn't bother with the alcohol, just water and the coloring. And I used one of my skin flasks and filled it with colored water. I then explained all my thinking to Greta, and she nodded but did not look happy about it. I think she knew that I was doing more than spying. But we'll come to that in a bit.

And I became a . . . what's the word, Lisa? A barfly. I found two or three saloons in town and I visited them all every week. I'd stake out a corner of the bar where my back was to the wall. And I'd order a whiskey. I'd drink off a bit of it, and when people weren't looking, I'd pour most of it into the spittoons. Then I'd top it off with my whiskey-colored water and act like I was getting drunk. As I said, I'd spend two to three days a week doing this. And it accomplished my ends. First, instead of thinking of me as a danger that they had to attack, the men of Denver began to think of me as a colorful old drunk, when in fact I'd never been drunk once. Second, I learned a lot from these varmints about what did happen at Sand Creek, and it was as horrible as Greta said. I understood why she could never speak of it to me. But I also learned just who was involved, and the names and identities of the men who disobeyed orders and refused to go into the village, as well as the butchers and rapists who went in and who still had body-part souvenirs. More on that later.

And I learned to my pleasant surprise that the feeling across Denver of the people was disgust at the men who had attacked the village, and a wide-reaching shame. Anybody who had a trophy, was now hiding them. When I learned that White Coyote's genitals were being held by a man by the name of Wilson, I went to his house one night and knocked at the door. His wife was terrified of me when she opened her door, but calmed down when I told her I'd never hurt a woman or a child in my whole life and wasn't about to start. I just wanted the trophy her husband kept. She said it was disgusting, but he wasn't home. I said I wasn't leaving without it. She gladly went and got the testicles and penis, wrapped in a bloody rag, and gave it to me. I wasn't sure it was really my father-in-law's genitals, but I buried it under Menoke's tree just the same. It was certainly Cheyenne and that was enough reason.

But the third thing I learned was that drunken men have no secrets. Spending two hours in a bar was better than reading a newspaper. And I learned of the evil that John Chivington was the focus of. Most of these men had been decent, but John Chivington had made them believe that to attack and slaughter Indians was the work of Christ. John Chivington told them that lies were the truth and that the truth was a lie. John Chivington made them believe he was the messenger of God. It was a kind hypnotism or something, so that when good men heard the madness of John Chivington, they went mad and followed his lies, calling the truth a lie, and doing unspeakable things in the name of God. No wonder the Methodist Church threw this guy out. Odd thing was, though many had seen through him, yet one man or woman out of five, still talked of him like he was an angel from God, or Jesus Christ himself. The madness was incredible. How can people be so gullible? So stupid?

I decided that he had to die. I went about it carefully. I told no one, especially not Greta. Chivington himself I'd seen in the bars a few times, always glad-handing everyone. But he was getting the cold shoulder a lot. And you could see it making him wilt. Still, his hunger for attention and adulation (Lisa gives me that word) wouldn't let him just ride out of town with his tail between his legs. Finally, after watching his patterns for a month, I got him outside in the dark in an alley. He was staggering along, drunk. I came out of cover and pinned him to a wall, with my Green River knife against his throat artery. One slight bit more of pressure and he would have bled out like a stuck pig.

"What?" he cried.

Looking at him up close, he was a lot different from the man you'd see in the podium, working up a crowd to hatred and murder in the name of Jesus with his powerful words. He was in poor physical shape, plump and with a considerable gut. Not your typical regimental colonel. No wonder he didn't want to go back east and stand up against all those professional officers. His sparse remaining hair grew in two clumps which stuck out diagonally from the upper curve of his head, just before it reached the top, and a little in back, like two stunted and wind-twisted bushes on a rock peak. Otherwise he was bald. His eyes were close together and black, like the face of a rat. And those eyes were filled with terror, and not just because I had a knife at his throat. I got the sense his eyes were always filled with terror and therefore the deeper his hatred for everyone and everything around him. He used Jesus like a club to beat back the frightening people all around him. And his eyes were deep and black, two holes into a vast bottomless pit. I wondered for a second if he was really human, or just some evil spirit, some twisted faery, as my Irish mother would have thought.

I put my hand over his mouth. "Listen, you son of a bitch, you and your murdering militia killed my family and it is going to be my distinct pleasure to take you out into the mountains and cut your throat and leave your filthy corpse for the coyotes."

He started yelling through my hand, something about the wrath of Christ condemned evil-doers who loved Indians, and I'd burn in Hell. There was also something about his murder being the greatest crime of all time, as if he was the most important person in the world, something that I'm sure he truly believed. He was the only and true Victim, and everyone was conspiring to get him. The man sickened me, and I got impatient to execute my plan. I figured I had to gag him and throw him over my horse. People would never find him, and they'd probably assume he'd finally high-tailed it out of there in shame. But maybe I should kill him first just to shut him up, or drive the faery-demon out of his sad corpse.

I was just going for my gag with my left hand when I felt someone off my right shoulder. It was Greta. How in God's name she knew where and when I would take the life of that faery-demon, I will never be able to explain. But she was there. I could tell from her horse breathing hard behind her, that she'd been riding hard to get here. That woman must have known what I was thinking. And damn, she was the best horsewoman I ever saw.

Greta spoke to me, softly yet forcefully. "Sam. You don't want to do this, Sam. It's a mortal sin, and this disgusting filth is not worth your eternal soul, Sam. Justice comes from God, and you know that, Sam. You've never murdered anyone yet. Don't start now, my friend."

At this, Chivington, who had been preaching through my left hand over his mouth, stopped talking.

Greta went on. "This is not who you are, Sam. Leave this man to his Hell. No matter what he says, Sam, he'll know for the rest of his life that he is a mass-murderer and a butcher of sweet, innocent lovelies like my Misa and my Charlotte. And he knows he is a master rapist. He knows, Sam. And though he won't say it aloud, his soul is already in Hell for it. Are you going to spare him that torment?"

I hesitated for maybe a minute, or was it a year? Then I leaned back, put away my Green River knife, and let him go. Chivington sighed and found a handkerchief to mop his brow. Then Greta did something else that totally surprised me, even more than her reading my mind and finding me. She walked right up to him, wound her shoulders up like she was about to throw a heavy sack, and slapped him hard on the face. The percussion of the sound was so sharp it echoed off the walls of the alley. Chivington almost fell over, the blow was so strong. He bounced off the wall behind him and put his left hand up to his face in astonishment.

"That's for my Misa and my Charlotte and my Clara! And if we ever hear another thing from you, you *wretched* man, I will personally come and cut off your miserable life!" And though it doesn't fall here in the timeline, I must say Chivington never bothered us again. I thought he might form a posse against us or incite a mob to hang me. But I think he could never admit to anyone that he was wrong, or that he'd been well ambushed, or worse, that a woman had slapped the crap out of him. He could not admit to losing anything—his pride wouldn't allow it—he was never a "loser." That, and at heart, he was a great coward, which explains why he was brave in battle so long as he was in the rear and his soldiers did the dying for him. To be entirely fair, I heard he led a charge at Glorietta Pass and took the Confederate supply train, so they had to pull out of the West altogether. But he must have come down from that bravery by the time of Sand Creek, when he would only attack women, and children, and old people.

So, he pretended he'd never met me or Greta. And thankfully, he stopped mentioning my name. He wandered around Denver for a few more months, maybe a year, until he had grown so hated with his whimpering defense of the action at Sand Creek, and his self-pity, and his perpetual sense of being the victim, that he finally did ride off with his tail between his legs. At first, he had some hard-core defenders who were not interested in facts. But eventually they dwindled away. I heard later that he never stopped defending himself for Sand Creek, and went through a series of business failures back east before dying a pathetic, despised, old man. Congress even investigated him and found him guilty of an atrocity. Greta was right. From the moment he ordered that attack, his life became a relentless hell.

Greta and I rode back up to the ranch in the moonlight. I kept looking over at her, but she did not say a word. We must have reached the ranch about one in the morning. When we reached the stable, we unsaddled our horses—I never did anything to a horse for Greta—and went inside. Anne was asleep on the wooden chair before the fireplace, book half open in her lap, exhausted from tending to Clara. Greta caressed Anne's cheek and woke her just enough to help Anne to her own bed. Then Greta headed to her own room without another word, her door closing with a soft bump.

I went to my room and threw off my deerskin shirt and pants. In the old days I liked to sleep naked when indoors. Pajamas were a revolution to me that I didn't surrender to until at least 1880. I had a small fire burning in my fireplace and I knew that Anne had lit it and stoked it, thinking I would be home sooner. Now it was dying down, giving off a soft glow. I laid down and could not stop the feeling of loneliness. At this point I had been sleeping with a woman for almost thirty years and my grieving for Misa was still raw. I started weeping and though I tried to keep it quiet, it was one of those shoulder-shaking sobbings, where every broken thing just comes heaving out of your soul. You lose all control. I had been going for a while like this and did not seem like I could stop. Then I heard my door open softly. Greta stood there in the firelight in her old night gown. Her long, black hair hung down, in silky, dark waves, and her eyes which were always pretty, reflected the dying fire glow, filled with empathy and sorrow. She reached down to her hem, and to my great surprise pulled her night gown up over her head and threw it to the foot of my bed. I had last seen her naked when she was near death and was almost all bones. But in health she had beautiful breasts and round, curved hips. She knelt down and got under my buffalo robes and became my lover.

23.

The War Begins

1864–1868

Oddly enough to me, the children seemed to accept that Greta and I shared the same room. Misa had always called her "second wife" and being raised with Cheyenne values, that was fine with Kathleen and Anne. The only reason Greta didn't know was because her Cheyenne was limited. But even Jack Flies Straight, when he next came by, thought the change not worth mentioning. Clara, of course, was lost in the chaos of her mind, something that made a deep rip in my heart that never, ever healed.

Greta felt differently, being raised a good Catholic girl and sleeping in my bed. She knew she was living in sin. I needed to help her, if I loved her as much as I knew I did. I made sure to kneel down and ask her to marry me. That kneeling business never seemed sensible to me, but I knew she needed it, after all her years of being an orphan, lacking family and self-respect, to be able to say that her husband has proposed on one knee. And considering all the other things she had done for me, for us, it was the least I could do for her. We rode down to Denver maybe five days after our first night, and Fr. Joseph married us quietly and properly in the Church. I think we were the first wedding at St. Mary's, which later became a cathedral in Denver. That made Greta happy. Otherwise, our life continued. But Greta was uneasy with my new role as a fake-drunk, and a spy. Still, she understood why I did it and realized it was not something I enjoyed, or even wanted to do. It was a necessity for our survival.

She was less accepting of the other thing I did. I bought guns, rifles and their ammunition, wherever I could. I even made a point of picking up the military carbines, a small rifle that you could reload in a second through the breech in the back of the barrel. I kept one for myself and put my two Hawken guns up over the fireplace for good. After the wind down of the War to Save the Union in the east, the black market was flooded with military surplus carbines that soldiers had kept in spite of the requirement to turn them in. I bought them sporadically—Lisa gives me that word—as I could. I spread my purchases out to different sellers and never too much or too many at one time. I should add that I also bought the new Colt revolvers and kept two for myself, wearing them in my belt when I went fake-boozing in Denver. It added to the effect and made people less likely to come after me. My reputation had grown to the point that men said I shot better drunk than most men did sober. Well, I wasn't drunk, but otherwise that was true. I always aimed and hit my target. As a mountain man, I'd been trained that to miss was an insult to the man who made your gun. I did nothing to hinder that reputation.

After Sand Creek, we were granted a sorrowful mercy. Clara, who never regained her mind in these months, began to grow big in the belly. At about four months of pregnancy, Anne went in to check on her one morning and found blood all over her lower night gown. She'd had a miscarriage in the night and had not even been conscious of it. Greta and Anne cleaned it up and put Clara in a new nightgown, burning the bloody one. I took the unfinished child—it was a boy—and buried him under Menoke's tree.

One thing that stuck in my craw, and still does to this day is that some of our people were able to return to Sand Creek and collect the remains of the dead there. Misa and Charlotte were never found—or so I had to believe for many years. Many of the dead were butchered, literally into cuts of meat, and spread around. It took time for Cheyenne and Arapahoes to return there and search for the dead, so that wolves and coyotes, vultures and crows got into the dead and made things worse before anyone could come. Or maybe some decent white folk—Spiders with real human hearts—came out and buried some of the dead, and perhaps buried Misa and Charlotte. In time I learned that this was true, but I'll tell that story in its place. But even with the revelation that came later, we never even were able to identify even parts of their bodies. White Coyote's genitals were the only parts I ever came across. In the Cheyenne way, I made clusters of colored beads and bright feathers, one for each of my beloveds, and tied the feather clusters to a low branch on Menoke's tree. That was all the grave I could give them.

Well, if there was a will to war amongst a small few of the Cheyenne before Sand Creek, afterwards there was a positive fury across the whole tribe to make the Spiders pay. Black Kettle was about the only chief who wanted peace. He and his wife somehow escaped the carnage at Sand Creek. But still, no one in the tribe wanted to listen to him after Sand Creek.

I did my bit. In the middle of March I rode into Stands to the Left's Dog Soldier village south of the Black Hills with two pack horses in tow. Many of the Dog Soldiers looked at me with suspicion. Sand Creek had embittered them. But when I stopped in front of Stands to the Left's lodge, he came out with a curious look on his face.

"I bring gifts," I said, dismounting. And then I uncovered the loads on my pack horses: rifles and ammunition, many of the rifles being carbines. There were whoops and war cries when the Dog Soldiers standing round saw this. "We must talk," I told Stands to the Left. He told a couple of elder warriors standing near him to distribute the guns and ammo and invited me in. Seated already was a man I knew as Roman Nose, another chief of the Dog Soldiers. Stands to the Left explained to him that the shouting outside was because I had brought guns and ammo. Roman Nose nodded to me and thanked me.

I sat down and spoke quickly. "I do not have time to stay, for I must not be seen by the Spiders. I have much to tell you. We were surprised at Sand Creek because no one was in the Spider city listening to their plans. I have changed that. I can fight with you in the saddle, but I think I can be more help to our people if I go and listen. Then they will not surprise us ever again."

Roman Nose spoke up, "Explain this to us."

So, I explained my whole pretend-drunk routine and how I listened to the Spiders and their plans. I had to do it twice, not because Cheyenne are stupid, but because the concept of scouting was familiar to them, but not spying. I talked about being a scout in hiding because Cheyenne language has no word for spy. Then a painful moment came to me when Stands to the Left asked. "We have heard that many lost loved ones at Sand Creek. I hope you did not."

I stopped talking and looked down at my hands. The whole tipi grew silent, waiting on me. I looked up. Both Stands to the Left and Roman Nose had looks of tremendous sorrow, as my silence had led them to guess the worst. I got it over with. "They raped my wife and two of my daughters, and slaughtered my wife and one daughter. The other I recovered, but she has gone crazy. And they killed my father and cut off his manhood. I was able to recover that and give it honorable sending off. But I could not find their bodies. My crazy daughter will not be well ever again." They all knew that White Coyote was my father-in-law, or my father in Cheyenne speech. The Cheyenne embrace relations by marriage, and do not push them away like many of the white folk I know, so they would not be meticulous about distinguishing father from father-in-law. Once I said this, any suspicion of my loyalties and motives that Stands to the Left and Roman Nose might have had pretty much evaporated. They knew why I was there.

"Does Flies Straight know?" Stands to the Left asked, referring to my son, Jack.

"No, I was hoping to find him here."

"He is out scouting and will not be back for some days."

"Then," I said, "Do not tell me what your plans are. If the Spiders capture me and torture me, I want to be ignorant of any plans. But I leave it to you to tell Flies Straight. His mother, Singing Night, is dead. Red Girl, his sister, is dead also. Star's Child, his other sister, is safe at home, but she is crazy. She lost a child, but it is better that she did. White Coyote, whom Flies Straight loved much, his grandfather, is dead but I did what I could for his remains." I stood up. "I cannot stay. My value to our people is that the Spiders think me a drunken fool with no contact in the Cheyenne nation. They suspect Red Tail Hawk and Beaver, but they think me lost in whiskey. They must not find out the truth. I will go now. Fare well in battle my brothers." And I ducked out of that tipi, mounted up, pulling my now-unburdened pack horses, and disappeared out of that village.

I should explain that there were others like myself, whites who had married into the Cheyenne nation or were half-breeds, or "breeds." Kit had been one briefly till his Cheyenne wife left him. White folks liked to use such people as interpreters, but this was a tricky role, because when white leaders lied in treaty negotiations, which they always did, the "breeds" were blamed by the Cheyenne. I had always worked to avoid playing any such role. William Bent had a son by his Cheyenne wife. The boy's name was George Bent, or "Beaver" in Cheyenne. And a French trapper had a son named Edmund Guerrier, or "Red Tail Hawk" by a Cheyenne woman. Both these men had nearly been killed at Sand Creek, a real eye-opener if you were ever inclined to trust white folk. And there were other trappers who had married into the tribe and either took their woman off to the settlements, or to Oregon. I was pretty much the only one married into the tribe who had stayed in the country after the fur trade died. And I was just about the only one who stayed true to the Cheyenne and fought for them. George Bent, after nearly being killed at Sand Creek, never went into the white world again, he was so bitter. I heard he rode with the warriors a few times. But I think he mostly hid and sulked. He died years later, another reservation Indian.

I was more practical. I always figured to do something, not just sit and brood. Red Tail Hawk, or Guerrier, like Beckwourth, let the Spiders use him and wound up scouting for Custer. His welcome in the tribe, in spite of his Cheyenne blood, dwindled down to almost nothing, even up into the reservation days. I'm sure he regretted it to his grave.

A couple of months after I delivered the rifles, the Cheyenne struck. And they struck hard. I'm sure my rifles made a huge difference. But first, days after my return, Jack came riding onto the ranch and said I was called to a meeting of the chiefs. I packed up and told Greta as little as possible. She asked no questions, but I could see she was worried and unhappy. I kissed her, mounted up, and rode off with my son. We had to take a winding route as the bluecoats had put an army camp not far from the ruins of Bent's Fort on the South Platte. Jack and I both looked Cheyenne, and I did not want to be picked off by some patrol. We went very carefully until we were far from Denver. As we rode along across the windy plains, staying away from the routes that most white folks would ride, we talked.

"Father. I received your message and am grateful that you came with aid. What more can you tell me about my mother and my sisters, and my grandfather?"

"Not much, my son. We could not find any bodies. Either the animals got to them, or some decent Spiders came out and buried them. Some man killed your grandfather and cut off his manhood. Then he bragged about it. I went to that man's house. He was not there, but his wife was disgusted by his act, and readily gave me the remains of your grandfather. This I buried under your grandmother's tree. You did not see your sister back at the house, but Star's Child cannot think. She mutters to herself in a daze, asking for help and asking for someone to stop. She recognizes me, but her mind has been poisoned, and I have no hope she will recover. Though, I think she would recognize you.

"Also, I counted coup on the man who led the raid. I wanted to kill him, but he was a coward and I think he is crazy. Even now the Spiders in Denver, many of them, will have nothing to do with him. And most of the people there are convinced the deed was cowardly and dishonorable. This surprised me. But there still are many in that city who think this man is sent by Jesus, or even is Jesus, and who believe all his lies no matter how many facts and how much evidence is produced. They have gone crazy with fear that our people will come and slaughter them in Denver." I thought it was perhaps wise not to tell my son that Greta had talked me out of slitting Chivington's throat. Even at that point, I was wondering if I might have saved some lives by doing so, and was wondering if I should go back and do it after all.

We talked more those two days of riding. I explained to Jack that Stands to the Left and Roman Nose had accepted that I would be a pretend drunk in Denver and act as a scout for the Cheyenne. Jack had a hard time understanding the concept, but if his Dog Soldier leaders had accepted my service that way, he would go along.

I could see that Jack's anger at this attack on his family ran deep. He told me that the entire Cheyenne nation, north and south, would meet at Cherry Creek in what is now the northwest corner of Kansas. And the Arapaho and the Brule band of Lakota would be there also. This was clearly a council of war. As I rode into the vast sea of tipis on Cherry Creek, beyond just amazement, two things entered my mind. One was that those white folks in Denver had no concept of just how badly they had erred when they slaughtered a village of peaceful Cheyenne and Arapaho at Sand Creek. And two, I wondered if at last, my people and our allies would embrace the Spider way of war, of building overwhelming force and destroying the enemy beyond recovery. I mean, dear Jesus, there had to be a thousand tipis here! We had the numbers to burn Denver to the ground and drive the Spiders out of this country for a long time. But as soon as I thought this, I realized that my story of the red ants was true. The Spiders would send an even bigger army against us, just as soon as their armies were finished destroying the rebel South. And we could not mass strength like this for very long, as I said before, because we had no logistics, no way to keep a vast army of Cheyenne, Arapaho, and Lakota in the field for very long. Still, I wanted my people to make a decisive stroke, rather than to fawn like a dog, as Black Kettle had done, only to be slaughtered anyway. I guess my mind was in agreement with the Dog Soldiers at that point. And me, a not-quite-upright citizen of Denver. I laughed at the thought.

I only heard about it afterwards, from folks in Denver, and later from my friends in the tribe. On January 7, on a cold day of slush and patches of melted snow, a thousand Brule Lakota, Arapaho, and Cheyenne warriors hit the town of Julesburg, on the South Platte River. Back when I went back and forth to St. Louis, all the length of the Platte River was a wide and shallow flow, with small groves of cottonwood trees at every side, and no sign of human habitation. But since the gold rush in the mountains around Denver, the whole route had become a series of ranches and stores and more ranches. The dangerous old Oregon Trail was now quite civilized and hardly a challenge anymore. The South Platte was a straight and civilized road to Denver from St. Louis and Julesburg was one of the biggest stops. I had hope that our warriors might cause the Spiders to rethink coming into our country, but when I heard the details later, I despaired. For Cheyenne, Arapaho, and Lakota were still fighting the Indian way. The Indian way included a lot of charges and fallings back, and a quick and violent sting against your enemy without risking many casualties. Defeating them decisively and destroying them was a European idea. Our forces had a good plan to ambush the bluecoats that would ride out of Ft. Rankin, but some exuberant young bucks tripped the ambush too soon, and half the bluecoats got away. Then our warriors, instead of following up with more decisive moves, fell to plundering the goods in Julesburg, finishing by burning all the buildings to the ground. For the next month, our warriors did manage to destroy everything the Spiders had built along the river, including the telegraph wire. I had urged them to do that. But the force and the focus were gone. Plus, in attacking Julesburg, some white women and children were slaughtered, which broke my heart. Small bluecoat units tried to attack the warriors over the next month, only to be driven off. The US Army at that time was concentrated east of the Mississippi, destroying the South. They couldn't spare many troops for the west. By February 2, the three tribal allies all broke up and went north. Most of the Southern Cheyenne went to join the Omissis in the Powder River country, as the Omissis chiefs had long wanted. The Cheyenne were one tribe again in one country. And when I next got to talk to my people, they seemed satisfied that they had avenged Sand Creek.

I could not make the chiefs see that we needed to sustain a powerful force if we were to push back the Spiders. Indian warfare was all about short bursts of intimidation and payback. The kind of strategic warfare that had developed in Europe was completely alien to their way of thinking. Plus, as I said before, we could not sustain a large body of warriors for very long in the field, as we had no logistics. The bluecoats had logistics.

When I heard about the women and children killed at Julesburg, it saddened me greatly. Yes, I understood the anger of the Dog Soldiers, perhaps even my son in that fight, knowing that our women and children had been slaughtered, and feeling that turn-about was fair play. But before this time, the Cheyenne, my people, never, never, never killed women and children in war. We might take captives, but they were welcomed into the tribe, and often chose to stay, even when they had a chance to leave. There are many stories of white women having been taken captive and married into a tribe, and finding they liked their life among the Cheyenne, or the Lakota, or the Comanches, much better than they'd liked life as a white woman. But our killing these woman and children was a falling off for my people. In our rage, we stooped to the evil behavior of our enemies. And I realize the evil of the word "All". 'All white men are . . . .' 'All Indians are . . . .' When we stop seeing individual people and just see a mass of enemies to be killed, we fall in the trap of the word "all" and lose some of our own humanity.

And I saw it in Denver. One of the things that disgusted me was the amazing popularity among a large minority for Chivington, even after he left town in '65. Some folks ignored facts with enthusiasm. They kept defending him and lying about Sand Creek. No, there hadn't been any rapes there. No, there hadn't been any women and children killed and butchered. Our boys in blue only fought evil Cheyenne warriors. No, it was a noble fight by a noble Colonel Chivington, a sainted man, almost Jesus Christ come back to earth himself. I knew better and I could plainly see these people were as mad as rabid dogs. I can only explain it by thinking that fear drives normal people to madness. Fear and the evil word "all." "All Indians are heathen savages out to destroy us." "All Spiders hate Cheyennes and are out to destroy us." Once you believe that, you can shed some of your humanity and kill without nudging your conscience.

The slaughter at Julesburg and the destruction up and down the South Platte was fuel to the fire of these mad people, and some of the folks that had been ashamed of Sand Creek reverted back to the madness of their fellow citizens and bought again the lies of Chivington and his followers. More than once I wished I had cut his throat when I had the chance. He didn't let me have a second opportunity and went about in large groups of armed "friends." I didn't go into Denver for a long time because I could not stand to listen to them reassure each other with their lies. I did sneak in with Greta for early mass and make a couple of journeys, but to be in the City of Lies and listen to the delusional fear being echoed between those foolish Spiders poisoned my heart.

But the thing that tried my heart more than anything around these years after Sand Creek, was that sometime in the end of '66 I heard Jim Beckwourth had died. He was always lively, popping up in some new place as a scout, or a businessman, a new husband, or something. (He must have married at least 10 times that I heard of) The white man never held him down, never quenched his spirit for very long. But when they used him to lead them to Sand Creek, they crushed his spirit at last. His last brave act was to rescue my Clara and bring her home before they butchered her. And I think he was convinced that I never forgave him for the rapes, and the deaths of Clara, Misa, Charlotte, and White Coyote. I know for a fact that the rest of the Cheyenne nation sure blamed him, and his business as an Indian trader dried up right quick.

But I knew he'd been lied to. They'd told him that they just planned to move the Cheyenne camp, the lying bastards. It wasn't his fault. I never blamed him. And he probably risked his life to bring my daughter back to me. I never hated Jim. But they say he went back to his Crow wives and brooded for two years, until one morning they couldn't get him to wake up. I ain't no doctor but I'd swear he died of disappointment and a broken heart. If I had known he felt that way, I'd have risked my life and ridden into Crow country to tell him he was wrong. Maybe I could have roused his restless spirits one more time. But I didn't know, and I only found out months after he'd gone and been laid out in a tree branch for the Creator to take Home. I said some rosaries for his soul.

24.

The War Heats Up

1865–1875

I HAVE ALSO FORGOTTEN to mention in all this turmoil, something wonderful happened. Greta became pregnant. It was a real surprise for her, as much as it was for me. She'd grown up believing that no man would ever love a plain-looking, shy, Catholic orphan. And she was Irish to boot. You have to remember that in the first 70 years of the 1800s and even beyond, to be Irish and Catholic was almost as "bad" as being black or an Indian in the minds of most "decent" white folk. Greta had gone west because there was no hope in the east. She was Irish, Catholic, poor, with no family or prospects. And she wasn't even good looking enough to overcome those things. It was either teaching or being a whore. She chose teaching.

And then she'd watched as one by one, the men, women, and children of her wagon train succumbed to cholera. As far as she was concerned, it had been just another piece of her usual luck that she was dying of cholera, or so she thought to herself as she lost consciousness. I was her first gleam of hope, and Misa, who nursed her back to life, was a miracle of love to her. So having a husband who loved her, and was Irish and Catholic, and having been married in the Church, and now to be pregnant was far more than she'd ever allowed herself to even imagine, much less hope for.

The boy was born in late '65 and she insisted on naming him Sam, after me. Samuel Connor Plunkett. Connor had been Greta's father's name, though that was almost all she knew about him. In time my boy earned a Cheyenne name, Red Coyote. He looked white, with blue eyes and red hair, but was just as Cheyenne as his brother and sisters. Around the ranch he was "Little Sam", or "Little Red Hair" in Cheyenne language. And he did much to make up to me for the death of Andrew, the big brother he never knew. I will talk more about him later.

One thing I want to get out into the open right here and now is about cowboys. Those fool books and magazines my grandson hungrily reads are a pack of lies. They are full of cowboys, with their lariats tied to their saddle horns, and Colt pistols in thigh-holsters, fighting the Sioux and the Cheyenne. What a lot of horse crap. I had cattle and I worked cattle for years, and I was no damn cowboy. I didn't get a lariat till years later, and the way I worked, I hardly needed it. Except for one brief day, the real cowboys never fought the Sioux, that is the Lakota, and my Cheyenne. When the Omissis fought their way back north, they stole horses from the white settlers in Kansas, and killed three cowboys in the business. But that was all of the Cheyenne-cowboy fights that there ever were. My tribe and the other plains tribes were all whipped, slaughtered, and the survivors living in misery on the reservation by the time the first Texans came up the Chisholm Trail, which runs along the eastern border of the Cheyenne-Arapaho reservation in western Oklahoma. All those miles in contact with my people and hundreds of cattle to watch. Cowboys had problems with rustlers, but those rustlers were all white people. My people did not rustle cattle.

What can I tell you about these years? My people learned that I was right and had warned them. We'd tap the Spiders lightly in warning, by raiding a ranch or a train, and they would pound us like an anvil falling. My people would rise up against the Spiders in small groups, paying out small reprisals. Then the bluecoats would come rushing through one of our camps in a repeat of Sand Creek. We'd strike back and teach them a quick lesson and the bluecoats would come back with a hammer-stroke and slaughter sleeping women and children. The list of fights kept growing: the attack on the Southern Cheyenne villages on the Arkansas in '66, which led to the 1867 Medicine Lodge Treaty. This treaty was broken quickly, in true Spider style. Whenever a new group of settlers wanted something that had been given to the Cheyenne, or the Lakota, the old treaty was thrown on the fire and commissioners would force a new one down our throats, taking away whatever it was that the new white settlers wanted. This way of acting led to the Beecher Island fight in '68, the raid on the camp at the Washita also in '68, where Custer and his men finally finished the job of Sand Creek by slaughtering the one remaining chief in favor of peace, Black Kettle, and his wife. Custer's men shot them in the back as they fled unarmed. With Comanche and Kiowa help, my people fought at Summit Springs in '69, and Adobe Walls in '74. Our people were attacked and chased, and though the Southern Cheyenne (who had unwisely returned to the south) tried to retaliate, after the Spiders of the north conquered the Spiders of the American South, they were able to turn their formidable bluecoat army on my people. The Southern Cheyenne by 1876 and our Arapaho allies had been forced onto a reservation in western Oklahoma. Many of them went north and joined the Omissis and the Northern Cheyenne became the largest and freest part of the tribe.

A lot of the leaders of the bluecoats were among the most brutal of commanders when the white men fought each other back east in the War to Save the Union. In command of the wars against the Indians was General William Tecumseh Sherman, who had burned his way through Georgia. His right-hand man was General Philip Sheridan, the man who had burned the Shenandoah Valley. They showed us no more mercy than they had shown the Southern rebels. Sheridan became famous when a Comanche or Kiowa chief at a conference, with limited English, tried to make out that he was a "good Indian." In the Indian mind that phrase only translated that he didn't want to fight. Kissing ass was foreign to the Indian mind. Sheridan was quoted as saying, "The only good Indian I ever saw was dead." Damn, if I'd been that Kiowa chief, I'd have shot that bastard and taken the consequences. Like I said, I still am not certain that I made an error in judgment by not cutting John Chivington's throat.

I need to say something about the Beecher Island fight. The fight was on the Arikaree Fork of the Republican River, two day's ride east of Denver. My son, Jack, was there and was badly wounded. But Roman Nose, who had been kind to me, and another of my dear brothers, Stands to the Left, died in that fight. They told me Stands to the Left was cut down in the first charge because the bluecoats were all experienced mountain men or scouts, with Spencer repeating rifles. Like me, they'd all been trained not to waste a shot by missing. They laid low in the grass and fired up into our horse-charging warriors, taking one out with each shot. Our people also inflicted a lot of casualties, but we lost more from the deadly and accurate fire of those experienced men. In the end, the small force of scouts was rescued by other bluecoats, and our people and the Lakota had to withdraw. And just like that, there was another hole in my heart. Cheyenne men generally don't weep. White men neither. Maybe it was because I am Irish. When I heard about Stands to the Left, I wept for days. Greta was very tender with me. I told her, "I can not stay back from this fight again." She looked concerned, but what could she say?

Then we heard about the Fetterman fight the following year, in '66. A Lakota chief named Red Cloud had done what I had been urging the Cheyenne chiefs to do. The Spiders built a road right through the area of the Powder River country they told us would be left to us by treaty. Instead of futile, small raids, Red Cloud controlled his warriors. He drew together every Northern Cheyenne, Northern Arapaho, and Lakota that would come to him. He forced them to wait and follow his strategy. A handful of warriors attacked a small wood-gathering party that had gone out from Ft. Phil Kearney, right in the middle of Omissis country, just east of the Bighorn Mountains. The wood party took a few casualties but scampered back to the fort with the news. But that was just the bait. When the bluecoat commander, a fool named Captain Fetterman, came charging out like bluecoat commanders like to do, leading a sizeable troop of cavalry, he got quite a surprise.

He had bragged that he could "ride through the whole Sioux nation." Red Cloud took him up on that brag. Red Cloud was waiting with thousands of warriors. Just about every Omissis warrior was there, under our Cheyenne chiefs, Spider Horse, Wooden Leg, and White Elk. Many Horses, and my boy, Jack, were there too. It was the ambush that Julesburg was supposed to have been. We slaughtered the bluecoats and paid them back for every warrior lost since Sand Creek and Beecher Island. The dead bluecoats were treated like the dead at Sand Creek, mutilated in insulting ways.

But the battle gave me a speck of hope, for the US Army withdrew from that country for several years and actually kept that part of the treaty for a short while. I could see that combined action, and disciplined strategy might push back the Spider wave that was overcoming our country. Red Cloud had proved it. If we had only done this at Julesburg and on the Arkansas and at Beecher Island, there might have been a different story. We might have fought them to a standstill, got some territorial respect. Or maybe that was a false hope. After Adobe Walls in '74, things got quiet for a while. But just before the massacre at the Washita, my daughters laid siege to me. And I must tell you, there is no more formidable opponent to a man's will when his daughters stand shoulder to shoulder against his plans.

On the ranch, in spite of the battles out on the plains, life in our valley was quiet. Sometimes our village swelled to twenty lodges as Cheyenne came to my "chief-dom" or whatever you'd call it, to find peace and safety, especially after raids like the one at the Washita River, where Custer slaughtered so many of our people. After that massacre was when I got twenty tipis up the valley from me. Then things would settle down, and some of those Cheyenne would go back to the reservation in Oklahoma, though most would leave the hated reservation behind and go up to the Powder River country and swell the numbers of the Omissis.

But I was confronted by two mighty warriors who conquered me. That year, 1866, Kathleen, my eldest was 32 years old and four times a mother. She was mother not only to her eldest, my Lisa, who is writing this down, who was 11 at the beginning of that fiery decade, but another little Sam, a boy named Vern, and a girl named Carrie Ann. My Anne had turned 21 that year. And both were beautiful young women who knew their own minds.

You're probably still thinking of the Kathleen I last described, her long, black hair in braids, wearing a Cheyenne-style buckskin dress on her wedding day. Well, she had changed. And you're probably thinking of 19-year-old Anne, dressed in buckskin, caring for her sister, Clara. But sometime after two years of me playing the drunk in Denver, and growing to hate it, they came to me in the main room while I was sitting in front of the fire. Greta, who I'm sure was in league with them, made it a point to be gone that morning. What stood before me were two beautiful young women, my girls. I do make beautiful daughters, I have to say. Kathleen, my little Meadowlark then at 32, looked Cheyenne, with long black hair, a full figure, high cheekbones, a small Roman nose, and deep-brown eyes. And yet there is a bit of my Irish mother's beauty in her face. She stood wearing a white blouse, bought in Denver and a long, black skirt. Her hair was done up on top of her head the way white women did it in Denver, like a rich, black cloud hanging over her ears and forehead, and you'd only know she was half Cheyenne by the color of her skin and her prominent cheek bones and nose. I knew for a fact that her husband, Lucién, after some 16 years of marriage, was more enchanted with her than ever.

Anne was equally lovely, and I felt a fool not having noticed. I did know that they had begun consulting Greta about the proper ways for young ladies to act and dress in Denver, but I had not seen the result till now. Anne had the dark, Cheyenne skin, and the long, black hair, but she had eyes that went green or blue depending on the day, and in every other respect, in face and form, she was the image of my Irish mother in loveliness. She was dressed much like Kathleen with her hair up also, very proper ladies for the mid-1800s.

They spoke partly in Cheyenne, partly in English, but I'll have Lisa write this all down as English. Kathleen spoke first.

"Papa, we need to talk to you." Her tone was like I was one of her sons being naughty. I was taken aback, but she did not let me recover.

"We know why you go to Denver and pretend to be a drunken, old fur-trapper. We understand your need to help our Cheyenne family. But we want you to stop. Right now."

"Yes," Anne agreed. "It is not necessary and it does not help our own family, here in this valley. And it's not fair to Mamagreta, who goes to Denver more often than you know, and suffers insult because of your actions. And we too, are constantly embarrassed by your behavior." When Misa died and Greta became my wife, "Mama Greta" is what my children called her.

Eventually the two words melded into one and she was now "Mamagreta," all one word.

I looked away from their eyes that drilled into me, and looked down at my hands. "Well, I have to admit I hate doing it and would gladly stop. But what if another Sand Creek is brewing? Who will warn our Cheyenne kin?"

Kathleen spoke, "We understand that, Papa. But we have begun to make friends in Denver. And everything that happens in that town goes into the gossip of the young ladies. If another Sand Creek is brewing, we will warn you in time. You no longer need to listen to drunken men in bars."

"Alright, then," I nodded. "If you can promise me that, I'll be glad not to go for a while and not to play the drunk any longer. It was disgusting, I'll own. But I have to have your absolute promise that this will work. I cannot let my people down ever again." I think they were prepared to get more of a fight out of me. But I was relieved to stop the play acting. They swore that they would do everything in their power to find out if anything dangerous was brewing.

Funny how things work out. My vanishing from the bars and then showing up a year later on Greta's arm, Sunday after Sunday, sober as a judge, caused me to become respectable, even admired for having conquered my "dipsomania." Through that decade, I attended regular mass in Denver and even wore white man's trousers, white shirt and suspenders in place of my buckskins. And true to their word, my daughters become respectable too—plus, by their listening skills, I knew every damn thing that happened in Denver almost before it happened.

That was only the first time my girls took me behind the woodshed for a stark word or two. They convinced me over a long time, that the survival of our ranch, of our family, meant all of us integrating into white man's society in Denver. Though privately, my heart cheered at the news of any and every Cheyenne victory and white defeat, I recognized their insight as true, and I hypocritically became one of Denver's most respected citizens, keeping my thoughts to myself. The white folks of Denver would say I'd been a renegade, but seen the error of my ways and left the murderous, heathen Cheyenne behind. I had overcome the demon, alcohol. I had married a respectable white woman and my only failing now was that I was a confirmed "Papist". Lisa tells me to say that the word Papist was an insulting term for a Catholic. What the hell. I let them think it and say it.

I should mention that even at the height of my "respectability" I kept my time in Denver to a minimum. I went to mass at St. Mary's with Greta, Little Sam, and the girls on Sunday mornings, driving the buckboard wagon. I went to the feed store and the lumbermill when necessary. And I went into town from time to time, driving cattle with Lucién, to sell at the pens where the Kansas-Pacific Railroad came to town. There I'd sell ten or so new cows from time to time, which was the income for the ranch. They'd put them in cattle cars and ship them to the meat factories in Chicago.

I was using money again. It was a strange thing, as I hadn't dealt with paper dollars since I was a boy in St. Louis. But the real hypocrisy of this that stung me was I knew men like William Cody were slaughtering the buffalo to feed the railroad building crews. Life is like that sometimes. You know right from wrong, but to survive sometimes you do things against your conscience. Still, the ranch had to survive and all of us on it. I sold my cattle to the railroad man, took my cash and rode off. I remember riding the miles back to the ranch from Denver and remembering how when my Cheyenne brothers raided Julesburg, they found a lot of paper cash and threw it to the wind, because they saw no good use for it. To them it was—Lisa gives me the word—confetti.

But in spite of my love and loyalty for my people, I had a primary goal. I, my family, our ranch, we were all going to survive. If I had to bullshit all of Denver to reach that goal, well, then I would. Jim Beckwourth would be proud of me, and I even more deeply understood his constant and endlessly creative re-invention of himself to keep white folks from attacking him, a free, black man.

One of the sadnesses of 1867 was that Phillipe Broussard, my friend and fellow worker on the ranch, grew deaf. Lucién insisted that he not work so hard anymore. Kathleen backed him and you don't cross Kathleen, as I learned. But old Broussard and I were both fluent in hand language of the kind that mountain men and Indians used. So, a regular part of my day consisted of me walking up on the porch of Lucién's and Kathleen's house and sitting down next to Broussard. We'd strike up a long and deep conversation with our hands. He couldn't hear but he could still laugh. So, we laughed a lot. And I found that I had missed the chance to really know him because he spoke little English and almost exclusively French. But when we both spoke sign, we had great and wide-ranging conversations, and I got to know his huge heart and his sharp mind in ways that had been closed to me as I knew little French. You might say we belatedly discovered each other. He was completely eloquent in hand language. And he became one of the dearest of my friends. I was only sorry that I had waited so long to really get to know him. We went on like that maybe a year and a half. Just as I was getting used to our silent talks, one morning he just didn't wake up. Kathleen found him and told her husband. That's the way Jim Beckwourth went. I miss them both dreadfully to this day.

Somewhere in that time, some of Menoke's bones were found below her tree, fallen from her platform, which was clearly about to collapse.

Lucién climbed up for me and brought the rest of the skeleton down. There was little else left after all those years in the elements. We dug a grave next to where I'd buried White Coyote's remains and planted Menoke, his sister, next to him. And I realized we had a cemetery on our ranch. Lucién helped me fence it off, leaving space for future graves. It is a sad place, and I have to admit, the tree above is as much a part of it as the graves below. Every few months, I renew the bead and feather pendants I hang in the tree branches for Misa and Charlotte. I added another for my beloved Asimoni, my Spirit, whose body I'd been forced to burn when the smallpox took her. Next to White Coyote was Andrew's grave, my sweet boy lost to cholera. And now there's a fresh grave for Phillipe Broussard, my friend. It occurred to me that at this point in my life I might have more dead loved ones than living loved ones. My Irish mother was buried in St. Louis. Grandfather and Aunt Mary probably laid beside her by now. That grew in me a deep, incurable sorrow. I know it's out of the line of time here, but in the '80s I even went into Crow country and found the tree in which we laid out my father, Jack, back in '33. His bones were still there and some of his gear. With the help of two of my grandsons, Kathleen's boys, I gathered it all, brought him home, and buried him with Menoke, his wife.

Maybe it was my sense in these days of how personal the ranch and the valley had become to me that made me all the more outraged when we found in '73 that the land to the east of us had been bought by some wealthy Denver lawyer. Greta went into town and charmed the land agent with a cake, so we learned the details. It was a fellow named Richard Lear. I spotted him with my field glasses a couple of days later. Tall, straight-backed, slender, with short blond-brown hair and a black suit and black string tie. He seemed to have pursed lips, like he'd been sucking a lemon, and a small, narrow nose that got lost in his face. I hated him on sight. He was driving stakes into the ground not more than a quarter mile from my ranch house. Of all the nerve. He'd bought pretty much the whole eastern part of the valley, running about four or five miles toward Boulder, Denver, and the South Platte. With all that land, why the hell did he have to put his house within sight of ours? Yes, the road to my place came west along where he was building, but there was plenty of road further east, out of our sight for him to build next to. And St. Vrain creek ran all the way down it.

By the way, there was no more gold in St. Vrain creek. Greta got herself some grubby man's work clothes and over a few months panned out the whole length of St. Vrain creek. She told me she did it for two reasons. First, it was our land and we could pay for a lot of things with that gold. Second, if the stream was panned out entirely, we'd lose the attentions of claim jumpers and I wouldn't have to be shot at and then be forced to kill them, as I had to do before now. So, the gold fever had died down in Denver, and no one bothered us till Richard Lear showed up and his crews put up this gaudy Victorian mansion with gables, and odd frills at the ends of beams. Greta said she was surprised he didn't add gargoyles. She found having neighbors less offensive than me, but she did not like the house. And then, one day as my girls, Kathleen and Anne, in their finery, were taking the buckboard wagon—yes, that was a concession I had to buy as well—to town, the young Lear was standing out on the front porch of that ugly house. He looked like his father and even walked like him, though the young man's hair was black. He watched my girls go down the road and he was riveted. Kathleen was safely married, but oh, Lord save us. I could just tell he was looking at Anne and had fallen in love. Shit.

But I needn't have worried. That rascal managed after some time to catch Anne near our east fence, our common fence, and engage her in conversation. She was not interested. Then one afternoon he came to call on her at the house, standing on the porch with flowers in his hand. Thank God I was up the valley and didn't come back for hours. I'd have kicked him in the ass and started a ruckus with our sole neighbor. But no matter. Anne refused to come to the door. She told Greta to tell him, she wasn't taking visitors, now or ever. She was much too busy caring for her sister. Nor did she care for store-bought flowers. She thanked him for thinking of her but begged that he not disturb the family again. Wow. That's my girl. Polite as polished silver and lethal as a .50 caliber round in the gut. About the only thing he got out of that was to leave his name: Glenn Lear.

But Glenn did not give up. He walked the fence almost every day, if the weather was good, and some days when the weather was lousy. Anne responded by taking her walks on the west end of the ranch, as far from the Lear-Plunkett fence as possible. You'd think he would get it. One day, he, dressed in an odd outfit with pants stopping just below his knees and a walking stick, struck out up our road, which was acceptable, to "hike" as he put it—a word I'd never heard of—in the hills at the end of our valley. He came back late in the day, exhausted, muddy, and scratched up from tree branches. He did not see Anne, but no matter. Three days later, he did it again. I figured after a week of not seeing Anne on the ranch, he would give up this hiking thing. I was wrong. It took three months and winter coming on. I actually begin to admire his determination, and I admit I followed him several times, mainly to make sure he didn't run into a grizzly bear or something of that nature. But he was like a little child in that dangerous world of the Rocky Mountains, in which I had been trained. And he had some sort of beginner's luck. He even ran across some deer at close quarters, though he made as much noise as a railroad engine, forcing his way through the brush. And oddly, the deer ignored him. They sensed that he was absolutely harmless, raised their heads long enough to look at him as an odd thing, and then went back to quietly eating. I was impressed. Deer never treated me like that. They fled if they scented me a mile away. It gave me something to think about. I will say that he never got into trouble the times I followed him. That was the first clue that I had misjudged him, but more on that later.

By '74 all of my people in the south had been forced onto the Oklahoma reservation with the Southern Arapaho. The Washita raid and the Adobe Wells fight had been too much for them. But they were angry and smoldering. Two years later, though the Omissis were on treaty lands given to us, the Indian agent at the Red Cloud Agency told the Lakota and our people would have to come in and then go live in the newly-drawn, and far smaller Lakota reservation. They were told not to leave the reservation, or the soldiers would come after them. And once again we knew that Spider promises set out in treaty were no promises at all, so long as there was land or anything that was ours that some Spider somewhere wanted. I could smell it. War was coming again though things had been quiet north of the Platte for nearly a decade. I got my gear together. I had gone from a Spencer carbine to the new Henry lever-action rifle. Seven rounds fired in quick succession. And I had two Colt revolvers, and two saddle-bags full of ammo. 21 rounds at the ready, and me trained to never miss. That was a lot of firepower to blow off before having to reload. But like I said, I could feel war on the wind and this time I planned to be in the center of it. I told Greta and the girls as much. I could tell they didn't like it, but they could see how deeply this ran in me. Not even my formidable daughters would stop me from going to war if war came again. I am a Cheyenne, dammit.

25.

Cheyenne Revenge

1876

In late May of 1876 two young warriors appeared like ghosts at my front door. I stepped outside to meet them. Three Moons and Shouting Horse couldn't have been more than 18, but they were warriors now. Elk Runs, the head chief of the Ivistsinihpah since White Coyote's death, sent them. They were Ivistsinihpah warriors I had known since they were some of the boys that watched the horse herd. They told me the Omissis had been reporting to an Indian agent at the Red Cloud Agency, near Ft. Laramie, up on the Platte. But the agent had ordered all the Northern Cheyenne to leave the Powder River and Bighorn River country and go live on the Lakota reservation. They had refused. The bluecoats had been called out, and many Southern Cheyenne were leaving their reservation down in Oklahoma and going to the Powder River country to fight. Once again, the three tribes were massing in force. Already, another Cheyenne village had been charged through (those bluecoat commanders sure loved charging through villages) up on the Powder River. The whole tribe was going to war with the Spiders. I could not stay behind this time and hear the news later. I dressed in my Cheyenne buckskins and breechclout, and got my gear together. Greta said nothing, but her face said it all. I simply told her, "For the people, I must go." She didn't like it. But not even Greta could hold me back. Kathleen and Anne said nothing, but made sure to be there when I left. They knew all too well that any farewell could always be the last one. I mounted my new pinto gelding, named Kit, with my Henry rifle in my left hand, and my Colt pistols in my waist band, and rode with the warriors over the ridge to the north so the Lears wouldn't see me go. I was 57 years old but was still spry, and I would be a warrior to the last. By nightfall the second day, we crossed the North Platte and vanished into the south end of the Black Hills on our way north.

We rode into a massive Lakota-Cheyenne-Arapaho camp of almost 3000 lodges five days later. There was a little tension among the Lakota when they saw me, because for all my Cheyenne finery, I still look like a Spider. Four Lakota warriors were lining up to kill me as a traitor when Two Moons walked by. He was a chief I had known since the first Council I had been invited to. He said I was a Cheyenne warrior and if the Lakota had a problem with that, the Cheyenne would leave. "Red Hair has fought for us before and will again," he said to some Lakotas who spoke our language. This was translated and the four Lakotas walked off sullenly, obviously not fully convinced. Once this tense moment was over, Two Moons led me to his lodge, where I found my brother, Many Horses, in the lodge with Spider Horse, Wooden Leg, and White Elk, along with maybe six other Omissis chiefs and leading warriors.

Now, what I'm about to say will change history, the history of this Powder River campaign. And I thank Kathleen and Anne, and their listening skills, plus the loose-lipped fiancés of several US Army officers. Because I was able to tell the combined chiefs that three large bluecoat forces were going to converge on us. A Colonel Gibbons was coming from the west. A General Terry was coming north-to-south from the Missouri River, down the valley of the Bighorn River, and a General Crook, whom we called "Three Stars", was coming up from the southeast, from Ft. Fetterman. Two Moons sent out a messenger for the two Lakota main chiefs, Sitting Bull and Crazy Horse, who came to our lodge, and I repeated to them, with others translating, what I had learned from the careless girls of Denver.

We all talked in two languages, with interpretation, for over an hour. In the end it was decided to wait where we were and keep scouts out. Some of the elder men advised against going against the bluecoats if they came in force, but the younger chiefs prevailed. The first bluecoat force that appeared, we would attack it.

About a week later, a young warrior I had also known as a small boy tending the horse herd, by the name of Little Hawk, with three of his friends, came howling like wolves into camp. I have told you a friendly comes into camp singing. Warriors having found a threat come into camp howling in order to raise the alarm. The camp became of whirlwind of motion, as a thousand, Lakota, Cheyenne, and Arapaho warriors, said their final prayers and donned their tokens of the spiritual power, their warbonnets for some, and their weapons and best horses for all. A swarm of bluecoats was coming up Rosebud Creek from the south. This must be General Crook's column.

I won't narrate the whole battle. Anyone who wants can look that up. I will tell you what I saw and did. I mounted up on Kit, riding close to Many Horses. I had determined that I would stay with him throughout the battle. I had lost four of my brothers when I was not around. I would stay with my fifth and last brother to the very end. I will tell you that it all took place out on the plains where some low, grassy ridges, almost too shallow to even deserve the name of 'hill', ran from northwest to southeast. The bluecoats came from the southeast and our people came from the north. There was some small advantage in terrain for us, but you have to understand the style of Indian warfare. We don't go in for big, dangerous charges and take huge casualties. We charge in. If we're opposed, or the energy of the charge dissipates (Lisa gives me that word), we fall back. So, the Indian battlefield is always surging back and forth. This pushes the enemy but reduces casualties. Like I said, my Cheyenne brothers didn't like to feed their warriors into a meat grinder. There were massacres of Cheyennes, the first and most horrible being Sand Creek. But these never happened on the battlefield. There was never anything like Two Moons' Last Stand, because frankly, we weren't that stupid.

So, most of what I can tell you is that the bluecoats were lined up south of us. They would charge from one side or another and we would fall back, only to charge and they fell back. I think if we'd had disciplined soldiers instead of individual warriors, we might have done something clever, like flanking them. But we weren't that organized. Our chief advantage was that we outnumbered them, and I don't think they were expecting that.

But I was determined to make a difference. When the group of Cheyenne warriors I was with stopped on one of the tops of the shallow, northern ridges, I dismounted with my Henry and got on my belly. There was a slight wind from the west I had to account for, but other than that it was perfect shooting weather. A group of bluecoat cavalry had dismounted about 50 yards or less in front of us, they were firing at us but only in quick individual bursts and none of them were really aiming. I've heard this called "suppressing fire", but I think it's just a waste of bullets. I sighted in on the one yelling at the others. I figured he was an officer or a sergeant. Many Horses got down on his belly beside me and asked, "What are you doing? We will charge them." Just after he said that I fired and that sergeant or officer pitched to the ground. Many Horses was impressed. A Lakota dismounted next to us and said in broken Cheyenne language, "What are you doing? You can't hit them from here." Just as he said it, I squeezed off a second shot and another bluecoat went down.

"He's already got two bluecoats," Many Horses laughed.

The Lakota got on his belly on the other side of me as I squeezed off a third shot. Another bluecoat went down, and they all pulled back to about 80 yards, out of my range. Just then, Comes in Sight, one of our war chiefs, shouted that we were charging. Many Horses and I mounted up quickly. I put my Henry in the saddle scabbard knowing I could not hit anything at a gallop with it, and pulled out one of my two Colt pistols. We rode down behind about 200 warriors, mostly eating their dust and got a few shots squeezed off before a bluecoat cavalry unit came at us, and we turned and retreated. I aimed my Colt before we turned and hit a bluecoat, who tumbled out of his saddle. That was 4. Then I spurred Kit and we got out of there. I remember wondering what might have happened if we had stood and fought, but that was not the Indian way. When the bluecoats reached us at the top of the ridge, another 100 of our warriors came up behind us and we turned. The bluecoats saw that it was a trap and turned their horses and fled. Then I pulled my Henry and swiftly got down on my belly again, with Many Horses kneeling beside me. As the bluecoats fled, I picked another one out of the saddle. I had 5.

I could narrate the rest of the battle for you, but it was pretty much the same. I was eating dust on my belly and then up in the saddle and then on my belly again for about 6 hours. Charge and retreat. Charge and retreat. The most exciting part was when one of our war chiefs, Comes in Sight, had his horse shot out from under him. His sister came riding into the battlefield and he hopped onto the back of her horse, and they got out of there without a scratch. My people were so impressed by that, they to this day call it "The Fight Where the Girl Saved Her Brother." In the end Two Moons and Crazy Horse decided we had punished the bluecoats enough for one day. We had lost maybe 20 killed or wounded. I'm sure the US Army lost more like 50 some from what I saw. I ended the day with 10 bluecoats to my credit. There was a big dance and celebration back at the camp, and none of the Lakota were questioning what side I was on anymore. Many of them had stopped and watched me pick off bluecoats with my Henry. That day I got my second Cheyenne name after "Red Hair". It is "Does Not Miss". The bluecoats held the field at the end of the day, but they had been whipped and they knew it. General Crook withdrew in hopes of connecting up with Terry or Gibbon, but it never happened. I learned later that he was close to running out of ammunition. And that was after killing maybe twenty Indians after blasting off maybe 9000 rounds or more. I'll bet you he was not happy. Still, our leaders thought we should not be so easy to find. The camp packed up lodges, and we moved a day's ride west to a river the Spiders called "Little Bighorn."

The Cheyenne called it "Little Sheep River," but no matter. Most folks know it by the white man's name.

Before we move on, I want to say that Crook was no fool. He was the only bluecoat commander I encountered who didn't have this suicidal need to charge Indians. His troops made advances, but pulled back when they were outnumbered. Later on, he dealt with the Apaches down south and was the only commander to get results, mainly because he had this funny notion that Indians were actually human beings. Imagine that.

But I think most of the officers they sent against us were fools. I'm thinking of Custer, yes. I know people disagree about him. Some think he was Jesus and others think he was a fool. I concluded years later that he wanted to run for President. And that was too bad for the unlucky bastards who had to follow him into battle at Little Bighorn. I think he was another Chivington, and only slightly less crazy. He was more ambitious and full of himself. Chivington, if you watched him carefully, was always desperate to be admired and never really believed all the fine things he said about himself. His dark rat eyes craved what they could not have. Custer, the one time I had seen him, had a cool demeanor (Lisa gives me that word) like he thought he was God's anointed and hadn't a single doubt. Down south our people called him "Long Hair" or "Yellow Hair". The Omissis had another name for him because he once chased some warriors in the saddle for almost a whole day: "Hard Ass."

Anyway, our camp was long and huge, running along the west bank of the Little Bighorn River, which ran almost due north and south. To the east of the camp, across the river, laid a fairly high ridge, though out on the plains, no ridge was really high. It overlooked us from the east bank. Unlike Rosebud, where our scouts warned us and we picked the battlefield, this time we were surprised. To be honest, the bluecoats had withdrawn to the southeast and we did not expect attack from that direction. Our scouts were out to the west and north.

But this battle has been discussed and discussed till I'm sick of it. I'm just going to tell you what I saw and thought and you can make of it what you want. Many Horses and I, sleeping in his tipi, awoke to sounds of gunfire to the south in the middle morning. There had been a celebration the night before and we'd stayed up late. We put on war paint—I did not want to look remotely like a white man—and grabbed our guns. He had a Spencer carbine he'd captured from a bluecoat in a battle sometime back, and my second Colt revolver, which I'd given him. I had my original Colt and my Henry. I loaded up a double saddlebag with ammunition for both of us, and we mounted up on our horses outside, where we'd staked them for the night, and rode south with a stream of almost a thousand Lakota, Cheyenne, and

Arapaho warriors, all sounding loud with the rustle of their war-feathers and the rattle of carried guns, and the clopping of hooves at a canter. We made a big cloud of dust, which I believe scared the bluecoat commanders. Almost all of us had one sort of gun or another. Many of us had captured guns at the Rosebud battle.

Not far ahead, I could see a column of bluecoats in the distance coming down from the hills from the south end of the ridge across the river. Already some of our warriors were trading fire with them and retreating. But as several hundred of us crowded up behind, the bluecoats stopped. I heard a bugle, and they started to retreat, backing up to the east, across the river to the south end of the ridge that ran east of our village. As our warriors pressed forward, the bluecoats reached the top of the hill and dropped down onto their bellies over the crest, their gun barrels the only thing visible through the grass at the top of the hill. Well, I thought, that bluecoat commander has half a brain at least. Custer or Sumner or Fetterman would have charged and led his men to their deaths.

I should add, Lisa reminds me, that before the celebration, the war chiefs met. Two Moons and Many Horses insisted that I be included. Sitting Bull and Crazy Horse readily agreed, after my marksmanship at Rosebud. I had argued that bluecoat commanders liked to charge and that instead of retreating, we should surround them when they do, and then wipe them out. At the time, I got the impression none of the chiefs understood what I was saying, but I was proved wrong later that day.

Anyway, our warriors dismounted in the best bush cover at the bottom of the hill and started pouring fire into the crest of the hill. Just as my horse rode up, I did see a few blue-sleeved arms go up in the air, as if a man had been hit, but as it proved later, the bluecoat commander, who I found out later was a man named Major Reno, was not stupid enough to sacrifice his men and held a defensible position till the next day when he slipped away with Captain Benteen and the other survivors. We got off our horses and let them wander back while Many Horses and I got down on our bellies in a strong-smelling bush, and I poured fire into the hill crest. I didn't shoot a lot of rounds, because I always waited until I had a solid target and the bluecoats were being careful. I'm pretty sure I got one fellow who must have panicked, and turned to run to the rear, leaving cover. He got three steps and I dropped him. That was 11. But, I'm afraid I must have wasted at least ten rounds on moving grass. First time since Jack taught me to shoot that I'd ever missed anything.

The bluecoats were doing what I was doing, saving ammunition, and only firing when they had a solid target. So, I don't know exactly how it happened. Many Horses and I were down on our bellies in dust and the bushes, not really visible. I think now it was just a stray bullet, lucky shot by some greenhorn bluecoat who in his death-terror fired off a round with his eyes closed. The bullet went through Many Horses' left elbow, shattering it, and then passed through my right-side pelvis, just missing the leg joint. All I knew at the time was that my right hip was burning and on fire, or so it felt. I screamed I think and then all was dark for quite some time while I wandered in dreams of pain. When I came to, two men were carrying me on their shoulders between them, one under each arm. The fellow under my right arm was an Arapaho I'd never seen before, and never saw again after that day. Under my left arm was my son, Jack Flies Straight. As I came to, we were already in camp and they took me into Many Horses lodge and laid me down, where his wife, Night Star, cut off my right-side legging and stopped my bleeding. The bullet went through and through, so I was lucky. Shortly after they laid me down, two more Cheyenne warriors brought in Many Horses, whose left arm was all askew at a crazy angle. Jack told me, "Father, I will be back," and dashed out again. I drifted in and out of consciousness with only one thought. No, no, not Many Horses. He cannot die. I could not bear it.

So, what does this mean? It means that I cannot give you an eyewitness account of the part of the fight that everyone wants to know about: when Custer came charging at the camp from the hills on the east bank of the river. But this much I know. From what Jack told me later, Crazy Horse, who led the fight against Custer's flanking attack on the village, I figure he must have been listening to me in Council. Because instead of running away from Custer's charge, he got all those warriors to form a pocket at the bottom of the hill, starting at the river ford. And Custer, damned fool that he was, charged right into the middle of it. And all those Lakotas, and Arapahoes, and especially, our people, remembering the slaughter that Custer had made at the Washita, by God, they created a hellish crossfire. Many of us Cheyennes slipped around the hill behind Custer so he couldn't get away. And the rest I figure the reader knows, how all those poor bastards that followed Custer were rubbed out. 210 men slaughtered because one man wanted headlines that would carry him to the White House.

I was unconscious or barely conscious the whole time. Some folks say, like Grinnell says, that if Custer had kept pushing, he might have chased all those warriors off and destroyed the camp after all. Had he done so, I would have been executed by bluecoats. But I don't agree. There were just too many of us. We had over 3000 warriors. I found out later that Custer had 210 men with him, and even if he'd had the other half of the regiment he left with Reno and Benteen, he would have had no more than 465 men.

The bluecoats were outnumbered almost 7 to 1. Custer and his men never had a chance in Hell.

And, what really riles all those folks that try to defend Custer, is that the damned fool knew it. His Crow scouts told him, but he ignored them. His defenders act like this didn't matter or the Crow scouts weren't clear. No, he was told he was vastly outnumbered. My guess is that he thought that beating overwhelming odds would make a good part of his stump speech on his way to the White House. Any sane commander would have known it was not possible. Plus, I found out later his orders were to find us, and keep us from escaping to the north and send for General Terry and reinforcements. But following orders doesn't get a man to the White House, and so he charged one last time. Look, we pushed back *seven* cavalry regiments at Rosebud. And you think Custer could have chased us off with half a regiment? Last Stand my ass. I call it Custer's Last Mistake. Or maybe Custer's Last Arrogance.

I don't want to talk too much about that part of the battle, as I did not see it. Sometime after Custer and his command were rubbed out, Reno and Benteen took advantage of a lull and pulled out, and just got the hell out of there. That's what I would have done. I found out later they tried to talk Custer out of the attack from the first, but he wouldn't listen to them. Anyway, we let those bluecoats go. We'd had enough of their blood. But the next day, leaning on Jack, I walked up the hill and looked at Custer's dead. It was pretty sad, I have to say, even though if I'd been there, I would have gunned down many of them myself. And yes, I saw Custer's body. It was not bothered any more than the rest; mainly they'd taken his weapons, ammo, and his yellow scalp, though I noticed his hair was thin on top and it probably wasn't much of a scalp. I'd seen photos of him looking like a young god. Dead, he wasn't very impressive. He was wearing a buckskin jacket, which was against Army regulations to be out of uniform. All his life he had made his own rules though, and his own mistakes. To Hell with army regs and orders. Custer only obeyed his own pride. That was on him. Like I say, I feel sorry for the bluecoats who had to follow him to destruction. I remembered the Scripture. "Pride comes before the fall." And it's even worse if you take all your men down with you. Idiot.

But what I heard later in Denver, by "experts" who weren't even there, was that we Cheyennes butchered the dead and that was less than human. Funny, it didn't bother those experts that Chivington had done worse at Sand Creek. He was a white man and that made it all right, I reckon. A lot of mainly bullshit has been said about this, and most of it was mighty stupid. Yeah, they were all scalped, and warriors had scooped up all the weapons and ammunition and tobacco they could find. I am sorry to say that it was true that many dead bluecoats were mutilated, though nothing as bad as what was done to us at Sand Creek. But I'll tell you now how they were mutilated, and you might just possibly understand it a little better. All that time when we Cheyenne were promised land and goods in treaty negotiations, those white negotiators seemed to talk over our heads. They weren't negotiating; they just wanted us out of the way. We weren't human enough to receive the dignity of real negotiations. They thought we were ignorant children. And then the Spiders violated the treaties and re-negotiated them again and again, breaking all their promises. We figured out that the Spiders did not consider Cheyenne people as fully human, with needs and lives and loves. We were like the blacks, and the Irish Catholics: lesser beings to be got out of the way. We were vermin to be either used or eliminated.

So, a few days later, when the bluecoats found the bodies on the battlefield, yeah, they were horrified by the mutilations. But they never got the message. For almost all the mutilations were the same. Ears were cut off and placed next to the body. Eyes were gouged out and placed next to the body. Any intelligent man would have understood what it said. It said:

"DO YOU SEE US?!!!!

"DO YOU HEAR US?!!!"

But no, they didn't get it. To them it was just more proof that we were savages. They were deaf and blind to us just so long as we had something they wanted for their own.

26.

Coming Home

1876

We had won a great victory, but our war against the Spiders was lost. For we could not stay together in this mass of warriors long. Grass had been eaten down to the soil; the local game had fled from our many hunters. We were forced to break up into small villages and go our separate ways. And I had a problem: I was badly wounded and I had to ride from our camp some 500 miles south to my home in Menoke's Valley. And there would be bluecoat soldiers all along the route, looking to round up Indians, and I was dressed as a Cheyenne.

Jack, my son, urged me to stay with him. His village, which was the village of Many Horses, was going north and east, trying to hide from the soldiers. I asked him why I had not seen him when I came into camp, but he told me he'd been sent to scout to the west and had only returned as the battle began. I think there was a time, when he was waiting to go for his vision quest during the cholera, that he became annoyed with me and distant. And that hadn't healed for years. But here in this battle, I knew I had his heart again. Jack had pulled me from the battle, exposing himself to fire. Jack had dashed back into the battle and recovered my guns and my horse. I thanked him again and again. I was glad for the victory over Custer, but for me, the biggest victory was to bask in my son's undamaged love.

Many Horses was recovering, but his left arm was useless, and would not move when he wanted it to. It hung limp at his side. At least he was alive, and I thanked God for that. I got my possibles together to ride out as camp was breaking up. As I said, Jack had found my Henry and my ammo in saddle bags and retrieved them for me. We had a silent farewell. I don't know why it is that men cannot say their feelings to each other. I did see his wife and son, who was in infant in a cradle board at the time. She was Leaping Deer, a sweet little Cheyenne maid. I did hug her and blessed them both. But then, with extreme pain, I eased up into my saddle and rode south. Many Horses loaded me down with as much pemican and jerked deer meat as Kit would carry and off I went, south, into the winding hills. The Bighorn Mountains were on my left all the way and I figured if I went south-southwest, into Crow country a little, my odds might be better. I was certain that in a week or two, I'd pick up the Sweetwater River, and avoid the bluecoats moving east to pursue my tribe. By day I kept the Bighorns to my left and at night I followed the stars.

The pain was constant and intense, but stopping did not help, so I just bore it and said endless Hail Marys in my mind. I did wipe off all the Cheyenne bear grease and war paint before I went, and sadly, even cut off the beautiful Cheyenne-style beadwork on my shirt that Misa had made for me. And I changed into my buckskin trousers. So, I looked more like a white scout and less like an Indian. After two days, I spent a day sleeping, as that was the only thing I could do that wasn't painful, and then rode in the night to avoid bluecoat patrols. I took a deer on day four and stopped two days to dry and jerk the meat. Then I set a pattern of riding all night and sleeping all day under some kind of cover, in a wood or under the shoulder of a hill. It was a miracle, but I only saw one column of blue cavalrymen riding away from me to the east. Looking back on it now, most of the villages went east and south toward the Lakota-Cheyenne reservations south of the Black Hills, so the army concentrated on them there. But that is not why I was not caught.

On day seventeen the pain was worse than ever and there was no sign of the Sweetwater. I was moving too slowly. But the traveling and the throb in my hip, which was beginning to numb somehow, made me exhausted. Sometimes I slept a day and a night straight. And now that I was not steering south by night stars, but following landmarks, I really needed to travel by daylight, so I didn't miss anything. Also, I was getting to the bottom of the deerskin pouch of jerked deer meat. And I was in too much pain to hunt. I might starve before I was caught. Plus, I was coming close to Ft. Laramie and riverside settlements—white people who might wonder why I was wounded and where a white man dressed as a savage was going and doing. That was when the Lady came to me.

It was on the night of the 19th day, where I had ridden five or six hours before I became so exhausted I was forced again to stop. I laid down by Kit in a small copse of pines. The stars to the south were brilliant and high overhead. I made no fire and ate my deer jerky silently, when in a moment I heard the swish of a deerskin dress to my left, and looked up to see a woman looking at me with compassion in her sweet eyes. She was clearly a Cheyenne, and my first thought was that she was lost, and that I might help her. Her deerskin dress was beautiful with much beadwork and little white cowrie shells. Her long, black hair was unbraided, and her brown skin clear and smooth. It was only then that I realized that she was faintly glowing. But I had no fire to cast a glow on her. Still, she glowed. All this confused me. She spoke in Cheyenne language.

"My son. You are weary and in pain. I am with you and will keep you safe the rest of the way. Ride in daylight and be at peace. I will see that no harm comes to you till you reach Greta. She worries about you deeply and is praying steadily for your return." Then she leaned over me and touched me on the right hip, right where I'd been wounded. The pain eased quite a bit, though it did not go away altogether. Greta? How did she know about Greta? And still she glowed. Maybe it was starlight. I don't know. I was fascinated. And it was in that instant that I finally realized that this was the Mother of God, the Virgin Mary herself. I became flustered and would have bowed if I had been standing.

She laughed softly and said "No, do not rise. I know of your love and have known for a long time. Sleep and have new strength in the morning." A moment later I was peacefully asleep. When I woke in the morning, my hip was less painful and I felt strong. I looked around in the dust but there were no footprints where she had stood, no sign at all. Yet, there was a single flower. It was a little purple flower that I could not name. But I had seen this flower on the northern plains in early May every year. But I was now well into July. These flowers usually showed up across the plains in the thousands, and then vanished by June. But here was a single flower where the Lady had stood. I plucked it gently and folded in the cleanest corner of my deerskin pouch.

I know what you're going to say. Most white folks will say I was hallucinating due to pain and exhaustion. But a Cheyenne would say that hallucinating would not mean the vision was not true. More than that, when I opened that deerskin bag with only a couple of venison jerky strips left, the bag was full again. The Lady had refilled my food bag. You can think what you like. I knew that my Lady had been there. I mounted up and found the Sweetwater later that same day. I then followed the north bank of the Sweetwater, down to the Wind River, riding east-southeast for three days.

While I was riding, I thought about the first time I took this route, with my five brothers and six or seven newly stolen horses. I was just about a boy in those days. And I thought about all that had passed since, and how I had lost four of my five brothers. I also thought about the time I took this route coming home from seeing Charette, and realizing I would never see him again in this life. You get a lot of time to think when you travel alone. When some settlements appeared in the distance, I rode around them and stayed well clear of Ft. Laramie. When I reached the Platte, which I remembered as a wilderness river, the banks were lined on both sides with ranches and occasional stores. This used to be the dangerous Oregon Trail. Now it looked like the road from Louisville to St. Louis. There I had to search quite a while to find an unpopulated stretch of river. I forded in the night and went due south to where I knew the secret pass that led into Menoke's Valley.

I came over the pass with difficulty, due to my hip and the rough trail. But as Kit and I dropped into my valley, I could see my ranch house and Greta in the yard, feeding the chickens. I was still a quarter mile away when she looked up and saw me. She ran into the stable, and came out on her horse bareback. I swear there was never a finer horsewoman. She galloped up the trail, narrow and twisting as it was, and met me.

"Sam! Sam! Oh, my Sam! You're wounded!"

I don't know how she could tell, but maybe I was sitting funny in the saddle and she noticed, or maybe it was the dried blood on my buckskin trousers. "Come on! Come on. We're going to get you in the house, now!" That woman grabbed my reins at the bridle, pulling them over my horse's head, and Kit let her lead him, even though she had no saddle. There wasn't anything Greta couldn't do on a horse. As we came into the yard, she yelled really loud, "Anne! Lucién! Little Sam!" They all three came running. Anne was in the house with her brother, Little Sam, and Lucién was in a nearby field. Greta dismounted and then the four of them eased me out of the saddle and I leaned on Lucién and Little Sam while they took me inside and got me into bed. They listened carefully as I told them how I was shot and what had been done. Once they knew the bullet went through and through and the bleeding stopped, Greta made great effort to keep the wound clean, but basically I was in bed for three weeks straight.

That first night I told her everything that had happened, about the battles and the death. And I told her how I wasn't going to survive to make it home, but the Lady came and visited me. Greta was listening carefully to every word of that part, especially when I told her how the Lady had mentioned her specifically.

"Oh, Sam you could not count the rosaries I've said for you."

"Well, she heard them. Say, fetch me my food bag. I have to show you."

Greta went and got my deerskin bag from the other room and brought it to me. I opened it, and all the venison jerky that had mysteriously appeared and had kept me alive for some two weeks, was gone. The only thing in the bag was the little purple flower the Lady left behind. Surprisingly, it was in perfect shape, like I'd just plucked it. When I told Greta that part of the story, she took it in her hands with tears streaming down her cheeks.

"As a girl, I learned how to dry and save flowers. I will save this as one of my most precious possessions." And she did. Years later, some biologist fellow gave us the name of the flower: it is a Few Flowered Shooting Star, growing in Montana only in early May. And I had found this in July. After Greta had dried and preserved it, she framed it and it's still on the wall today.

So, for three weeks I was pampered by Kathleen, Anne, Greta, and even my boy, Little Sam. I felt so useless, but they wouldn't let me lift a finger. But I didn't fight it. My energy had gone with the wound and it took a long time to come back. When I finally got up, walking was still rough. My right leg seemed shorter somehow and after enough walking, my hip began to hurt. Lucién carved me a good, solid cane, which I walk with now and have ever since that day. This meant that Lucién took over just about all of the ranch work from that point on. I was the old man limping along on a cane. But I don't feel bad about it. I feel like I gave all I could give to my people. This was the price of my sacrifice and the cane reminded me of that honor. And Hell, I was getting old. Couldn't be a young fool forever.

My people, as I had feared, were all scooped up by the army as they fled the Little Bighorn, and disarmed and dismounted. Warriors found with bluecoat scalps were hung on the spot. With no horses or weapons, my people could not hunt and became beggars waiting for the US Government food rations to arrive, *if* they arrived. Then to add to this indignity, the final indignity was that some damned fool in Washington decided to make his paperwork easier by ordering the Army to ship all the Northern Cheyenne to Oklahoma, with the rest of the tribe. This bean-counter wanted all the Cheyenne beans on one place on his tidy map. To get them to go, they were promised they could look it over and come back north if they didn't like it in Oklahoma. They did not like it at all. And they were told that they were staying, like it or not. So, they were lied to one last time. And the remains of the mighty Omissis band, who had never once gone south, were forced to live there.

It was about a year before I rode into Denver again. The word was that old Sam injured himself on his ranch and couldn't walk very well. That was half-true, but Greta let it stand. But something happened to me while I was lying there. There was an article in some magazine out of Chicago that Greta had picked up in Denver and left for me to read. And it was an honest article, about the prejudice against the Irish, how they couldn't get jobs and so many of them had gone into the Army because it was the only way to earn an honest living for an Irishman in America. In fact, a large percentage of the enlisted men in any US Army unit, the bluecoats, were Irish immigrants. This connected to something I'd heard back in the Mexican War, where whole American Army units, being Irish and treated like crap by their white, non-Irish officers, deserted and formed a unit to fight for the Mexicans, calling it the "St. Patrick's Brigade." Most of them had died in that fight or had been hung as deserters when captured.

This really stung me, for here I'd been counting the 11 bluecoats I'd rubbed out, and chances are that most if not all of them were my Irish brothers. And from that day on, I never was tempted to make war again or shoot at anyone. I remembered my thinking about the word "All" and how evil it is. 'All Cheyennes are savages.' 'All Irishmen and Catholics are stupid and lazy.' These "Alls" made me furious. But was I not guilty of the same thinking? 'All Spiders are against us.' 'All white people are Spiders.' 'All bluecoats are the Enemy and need to die.' 'All white people are bigoted and evil.' I was disgusted with myself. I realized the simple truth that all men are a mix of good and evil, white and Indian both. That's how God sees us, not in terms of "good guys" and "bad guys" like them fool dime-store novels my grandson reads. I told Greta about it and she listened without speaking. Finishing up, I said, "I ain't going to war ever again." She crossed herself and thanked the Lady.

But one last thing I'll say and then I'll have done with that war in the Powder River country. Actually, two things. The most decisive and important fight was the Rosebud on July 17, 1876, where at least a thousand Indians defeated a whole US Army corps. Hell, if we'd pressed the attack, Crook would have had to run for lack of ammunition. We might have slaughtered his men in a rout. The second thing was that the battle everyone talks about was hardly a battle at all. One arrogant bluecoat commander took his vastly outnumbered regiment, and to further his stupidity, he split it, and charged us. If we'd had as few men as Custer had, the historians would have called it a skirmish. And this glory-hound got himself and his men killed. For folks back east, he was their pretty, golden boy, a darling of the press, and he made their newspapers. The death of pretty-boy Custer got the focused attention of all those ignorant folks east of the Mississippi, who were looking for heroes and villains. And that's why here in 1902, everyone has heard of the insignificant skirmish, the so-called "Battle" of the Little Bighorn, on June 25, 1876, and almost nobody remembers the vitally important Battle of the Rosebud, on June 17 of that year. Why, hell, Little Bighorn was just a mop-up operation for Rosebud. And Lord, we did mop them up right smart.

27.

The Omissis Return to the North

1878

Somewhere in the dreary days of mid-January of '78, with the air bitter cold and the snow on the ground in refrozen and crisp, crunching patches, there was a knock on our door one evening. We never had visitors at this time of night. But we had heard of the breakout of the Northern Cheyenne from the Oklahoma reservation, and the girls told me that tensions in Denver were high. I had two Henry rifles by this time, and when the knock came at the door, Greta took up one from where it was leaning in the corner, much to my surprise. I swear that woman might have fought off the whole US Army in defense of her family. And any discomfort she had as a result of knowing that I'd fought for the Cheyenne at Rosebud and Little Bighorn had melted into her fierce sense of protection, as if she'd fought there with me. I watched her release the safety and work the lever to chamber a round. Damn, she was one hell of a tough woman.

I put my cane up against the wall, picked up my Henry, chambered a round, then opened the door with my Henry cradled in my left arm. Out in the dark and the snow stood my son Jack and nine other Cheyenne men and women and children, wrapped in blankets and shivering. I only paused maybe half a second and said in Cheyenne, "Get in here!" Greta, Anne, and I got them in front of the fire as quick as could be, and Greta and Anne got extra blankets to wrap around them all, taking away their wet blankets to dry elsewhere. Then the girls dug out roasted venison from a kill I'd made that very day. I built the fire up into a big blaze and got more wood. Our Cheyenne guests ate silently. When Jack had time to warm up and eat, I knew he'd tell me what was going on. While they did that I took stock of the nine other people in my main room. I recognized his wife, Leaping Deer. Besides these two were two other young warriors, three other women, and a young boy and two little girls. I don't remember all their names now. One of the young warriors, Running Cloud or maybe Running Rain, was husband to one of the women, whose name I can no longer even guess. One of the boys was their son. The other young warrior and young women were just following Jack. I can't begin to remember their names, they were with us so briefly. The other boy and girl I remember well, for Jack told me, his teeth chattering, "Father, these are your grandson and granddaughter, Andrew Looks Ahead and Anne Winter Dove." I was stunned for a moment there. Then Jack turned to these children and told them that me and Greta were their grandparents, and Anne was their aunt. I looked at Greta, who understood enough Cheyenne to have comprehended the news. I was unable to think what to do next, but Greta knelt down and hugged and kissed each of the children, as did Anne, who especially introduced herself to her younger namesake. Greta was all love. No wonder she and Misa saw eye to eye on nearly everything. And to think that the world back east had tossed her aside as a homely orphan, a person of no worth. And Anne was the imitation of her mother.

Within an hour my guests were all warm and fed. Greta, Anne, and I broke into our store of buffalo robes and laid them all out before the fire. They were soon all asleep except for Jack, who talked to me for hours, and Anne, who stayed up to hear what her brother would say. I can't remember his exact words, but he told us that Many Horses' village had been overtaken by the bluecoats after three days running northeast from the Little Bighorn. The bluecoats did not hang any of their men, so maybe that was only true in some places. But all their guns and weapons of any sort were taken, except for a few the women hid under their skirts. They were allowed to keep their horses just as long as it took to escort them back to the Ft. Robinson reservation, where the victors of Rosebud and Little Bighorn were prisoners of war. There, all their horses were taken. The following year some white commissioners came by and spoke glowingly of the good life their fellow Cheyenne had on the reservation down south in Oklahoma. Damned liars, all of them. They told Little Wolf, Dull Knife, Many Horses and the other surviving Omissis chiefs that if they did not like Oklahoma, they could return north. Then, with bluecoat soldiers all around them and few horses, they moved the almost 800 miles to be with their kin in the south. At first, it was good to see family and friends. All the Hevataniu and Southern Cheyenne who had managed to survive were there, including Jack's Ivistsinihpah kin, and the few surviving Dog Soldiers he had fought beside so many times. But the welcoming feast was a weak soup. And the Omissis soon learned that the promises to provide for the tribes, which had been part of the deal for surrendering, were frequently broken and that food was scarce. I learned years later that the agents in charge were selling some of the food they were supposed to give to the Cheyenne and Arapaho in order to make themselves rich. Also, the air was warmer and the mosquitos brought disease that was unknown in the north, where it was too cold for mosquitos most of the year.

The Omissis asked to be returned to the north and were told without explanation that they were staying. Sickness and hunger became their constant companions. Many of the children were sick and dying. In the midst of winter, some 200 of the Omissis, led by Little Wolf and Dull Knife, headed north in the January night. They raided farms and ranches on the way, though they went too far west to hit the Chisholm trail. So no, they only killed three cowboys, despite what you read in the dime-store novels. Thousands of bluecoats were called out to capture them. They took losses, especially to the young warriors, who sometimes fought to the death to cover a retreat. And people from time to time could travel no more and were left behind for soldiers to capture. When they came to the Platte, Little Wolf and Dull Knife were just beginning to disagree. Dull Knife wanted to go to Ft. Robinson, and find the Lakota chief, Red Cloud. He hoped Red Cloud would intervene with the Spiders and let our people remain there. Little Wolf had no faith in the Spiders and wanted to go back to the Powder River country and hide out there if possible. The remaining Cheyennes were divided as to who to follow.

Jack decided to lead himself, and with these two friends, their wife and sister and child, and Jack's own family, they slipped into the night and headed west up the Platte, aiming to come to me and Greta. It was a difficult journey, for not only were the bluecoats swarming everywhere, but ranches along the Platte were guarded by men with guns. Jack and his family and friends had only the horses they had raided and the guns they had taken in those raids in Kansas. Those raids were the story Greta and I were hearing about "savages ravaging the ranches going north, raping white women and taking everything." I don't think our people had the time or energy or even interest in raping anyone. They were in need and as the Spiders had taken from them, they took from the Spiders on this last, desperate journey. And that meant a few white ranchers died trying to stop them. That was my people's "savagery."

Near the junction of the south and north Platte, a squadron of cavalry had started to follow them. Jack and his companions knew how to vanish in the prairie, and being so few, they did it well. Jack told me the bluecoats had ridden as close as ten feet from them on three occasions, and missed them.

But the bluecoats were hot on their trail when Jack found St. Vrain Creek past Boulder, and made their way here.

I looked out my window to the east and saw the porch lamps lit on Lear's house. That was unusual. Why were the Lears awake? Fear welled up in my heart. I told Jack and Anne to stay low and quiet. Greta was asleep, thank God, and had taken our grandchildren to bed with her to keep them warm. The other boy was sleeping with my son, Little Sam, in order to keep warm. I was planning to sleep with the others on the robes on the floor.

But I had a bad feeling about Lear's porch lamp. I got on my heavy, buffalo-fur coat, my black slouch hat, picked up my Henry, after having given Jack my second Henry, grabbed my cane and slipped out the front door. I made my way to my east fence, maybe a hundred yards, the fence that borders on Lear's land. After about 20 minutes, I could hear the clatter of maybe ten to twenty horses and then they appeared in the light of Lear's north-facing front porch along the road. "Column halt!" some voice ordered and they came to a stop, their horses blowing and stamping in the biting cold. The bluecoat officer stepped up and knocked on Lear's door. After a while the door opened. Lear himself stepped out, dressed warmly. They were so close, I could hear every word.

"Hello sir. I'm Major Robbins, 13th Cavalry. We are pursuing a group of hostiles who may have come up this valley."

I could see that Glenn, Lear's son, had stepped out with him. I knew I had a chambered round. And I knew the people in the ranch house would need time to get away. I could do my own Cheyenne last stand right here and now. I planted my cane firmly in the crisp snow beside me, raised the Henry and got a bead on the Major. He would be the first to go.

Then I heard Lear say, "Thank God you're here, Major! Those savages came on my land but I fired a few shots and they turned around and disappeared up the ridge to the north. I think there's a trail up there that goes up over the mountain and into the country of the Platte."

"Trail? Where? Finding a trail in the dark . . . ."

"I can show you!" Glenn volunteered eagerly. "Let me get my horse." And soon Glenn Lear led the cavalry straight to my ridge-crossing trail that I thought was a secret. I stood there for another hour, getting mighty cold. Finally, I went in to my house where Jack was waiting with the Henry at the ready. Anne stood by him. She had taken down my old Spencer carbine and had loaded it. That's my girl. I told them what had passed and they were both amazed. Anne especially seemed unable to speak. Was this that foolish boy that had been trying vainly to court her? We all sat at the ready for the next few hours and I built up the fire. But the night remained silent. Anne fell asleep about 3 in the morning and Jack and I waited till daybreak.

Greta came out of our room and took one look at me. I told her about the Lears and Glenn Lear diverting the bluecoats. She looked out the window to the east and said, "He's just now riding back. He's by himself. There are no soldiers." Jack and I stood up to look and it was true. Glenn Lear was riding into the family stable all by himself. His father came out the front door when Glenn stepped onto the porch and put his arm around his son. They went inside. Daylight grew.

Greta said, "I'm making a big pot of coffee."

I can say the day passed with us feeding the Cheyenne refugees again on eggs and bacon, and Anne waking up, startled at the sounds of people talking in Cheyenne, my Spencer still across her lap. I unloaded it and put it up above the fireplace for her, kissing her on the forehead. I told her, "Go get some sleep." She went into her room and slept for about 6 hours.

The following day it was clear that the Army had lost the trail of our Cheyennes. Jack was uncertain about moving on. So instead, there being a building on the ranch that was the extra stable, we moved our Cheyenne refugees in there. It was far on the west side, close to Kathleen and Lucién's house. Kathleen, on learning her brother was there, took over feeding our refugees, as her house was out of view of the road and higher up the valley. Greta and I went up there often, and got to know our new grandchildren, who played with their cousins, Kathleen and Lucién's younger children.

And so my son and his family and friends lived there for about six months until the idiots at the US Government finally figured there was no point in trying to force the Northern Cheyenne to become Southern Cheyenne. They allowed a new reservation to come into being, along the Tongue River, not far from where we whipped the bluecoats at the Rosebud. It was called the Tongue River Reservation. In time, the small Cheyenne town of Lame Deer grew up in the middle of that reservation. When we heard about this, Jack was able to lead his family and friends north to the new reservation, where Jack built his own ranch house. He lives there today.

But the thing that most amazed me was that two days after our close call with the bluecoats, Anne dressed in her best finery, got herself a heavy wrap for her shoulders, and put up her hair like a white woman. She announced she was going out for a walk, and I watched her out the window as she intentionally walked along the east fence. I thought to myself that it might take a couple of days for young Glenn to notice. It took no more than half an hour in fact, and he was out there, walking along on his side of the fence. At a gate they stopped and talked for quite a while. I was about to go out there when Greta caught me and said sharply, "You'll do NO such thing!"

Long story short, the walks along the fence soon became walks together on our side of the fence, and then sitting long spells under the pines near the creek.

Meanwhile, a few days after our close call, I swallowed my damned pride and walked up the road with my cane to the Lear porch. I knocked on the door. After a time, Richard Lear came out with a puzzled look on his face. "Come in, come in, Mr. Plunkett. I believe I have the name correct?"

I came in and he led me to a fancy parlor with fancy furniture. I took a seat at his invitation, cleared my throat and said, "I wanted to come over and thank you for what you did."

"What I did?"

"That night last week when the soldiers showed up."

"Ah, what did I do?"

This seemed funny to me. "I think you know."

"You know, Mr. Plunkett. In my line of work, it's pretty difficult to get in trouble for something you did not say." And he made a small smile and I realized what he was doing.

"Well, you have my and my family's thanks all the same. And you can call me Sam if you like. Mr. Plunkett always sounded strange to me."

"That's fine. Call me Richard. I'm afraid you've caught me in a day of confusion and frustration. I have bought twenty cows, hoping to get this ranch started, and I have so much to learn and am making so many mistakes. Perhaps you could advise me. I'm told there isn't going to be any calves or a drop of milk until those cows spend some time with a good bull. But when I inquired into the cost of renting the services of a good bull, I found them incredibly expensive."

"I have a good bull," I offered.

"Oh? What might you charge me?"

"Nothing."

"Nothing?"

"Richard, in my line of work, when a friend helps you out, you return the favor with thanks. When do you want the bull and where?"

"Oh. Well, how kind. I didn't think . . . . I suppose in the south pasture where the cows are, and any time you might be able . . . ."

"I'll have the boys herd the bull over there this morning. I think a couple of weeks with your cows would do the trick. Just don't go walking in that field while he's there or he'll get onery." I stood up. He stood and walked over, shaking my hand. I said, "You are not the man I thought you were. I misjudged you. And for that, I apologize."

"Well, you needn't. I should mention that my boy has taken a fancy to your daughter, as I'm sure you've noticed."

"He's a fine boy," I said. "We'll see what the young folks make of it."

"Yes, I'm sure that's the right approach. Thank you for stopping by."

"My pleasure, and my boys will be driving that bull through your south gate about 10 o'clock if that works for you."

"That's fine, Sam. Nice to have met you at last. They say you were one of the first people in this country."

"That's true. But I won't bore you with stories today."

"Well, I doubt they'll bore me, and I'd like to hear them someday."

I left soon after. As the winter turned into spring, Anne's long walks with Glenn continued. Greta threatened that she'd shoot me with my own Henry if I interfered, but I told her there was nothing to fear, that I was determined to let things take their own course. My holding back paid off well because one cloudy spring day with the wind whipping the trees, Anne asked me to walk with her. We walked up the valley toward Lucién and Kathleen's place. She didn't speak for a long time and I waited for her to speak.

Finally, she said, "Papa, Glenn has asked me to marry him."

"Oh, well, he seems a fine young man and kind and generous, as well as brave."

"So you approve?"

"If it's what you want, yes."

"Papa, I'm not sure what I want. The fact is he has become very dear to me. He is kind, and considerate, and brave as you say. But Papa, I'm not in love with him."

I thought for a while and said, "Do you love him at all?"

"Oh, yes, yes. He's as dear a friend as I've ever had outside my family."

"You know, my girl, I think all this talk of 'falling in love' ain't all it's cracked up to be. Do you know how I met your mother?"

"No, you've never told us."

"Well, she was the wife of my Cheyenne brother, Red Mountain, and a cousin to my first wife, Asimoni. When Red Mountain was killed fighting the Pawnee, she was homeless. As you already know, our people allow a man two wives, usually if they are sisters or cousins. Asimoni came to me and asked me to take Misa, your mother, as second wife. I hardly knew her. But I agreed. When Misa and I were first alone, I was gentle with her. Kindness goes a long way, as I think you know. I told her that I would never force her against her will. She thanked me and gave her whole heart to me.

"After a year, the love that radiated out of that big heart of hers had totally conquered me and I loved her with all my heart. I still do. Your young man may not excite you, but I think falling in love has led as many people into bad marriages as it has into good ones. You say he's good and kind. If you can find just one young man who's mature and good and kind, I think that's better than any falling in love. With me and your mother, love came later. It might well do so for you. But I'll tell you one thing for sure. You might look at all the young men in Denver or Lame Deer and never find one with so kind and brave a heart. Then you'd be sorry to have passed him up."

"But Papa, he is leaving this summer for Chicago. His father is paying for him to go to read law there under his uncle on his mother's family's side. He wants me to go as his wife."

"What did you say?"

"I said I didn't know, but that I have sworn to care for my sister till the day I die. I have to be where Clara is. He said that was fine with him and he'd have enough money to care for Clara there in our home in Chicago, that he could hire her a full-time nurse. He's waiting for my answer. I must tell him something soon."

"My girl, you know I love all my girls, but you are different from your sisters. Only you have the heart of Misa, your mother. It's what makes you stand out from all my other children. And I betcha anything that is what young Glenn has fallen in love with. And I don't blame him. I fell in love with that heart in your mother." I stopped walking and took her into my arms, kissing her on the forehead. "It's up to you, my girl, but if I were you, I'd go tell that boy you'll marry him."

"But Papa, I'll be taking Clara away from you and Mamagreta."

"You've made up your mind to care for your sister when Greta and I can no longer do so. That is a noble burden, and Misa's heart in you has taken it on. I will not fight that. In fact, I support it with all my heart, and your mother would have loved you all the more dearly for doing it, if I know her. I will come see you and Clara both in Chicago if you want. Now, go to that young man before you break his good heart."

She stepped away from me a little, tears streaking down her cheeks, smiling, as she kissed me on the cheek.

"Go on," I said. "He's probably all on fire waiting for your answer. Put him out of his misery."

Smiling and happy she turned and almost ran east toward the Lear ranch.

So, we had a ranch wedding that summer. Glenn converted to the Catholic Church so that Anne could have the Catholic wedding she wanted. Fr. Joseph wed them at St. Mary's in Denver and we saw them off, the newly-made Glenn and Anne Lear, and my Clara with them, on the train to Chicago.

One last thing I wanted to mention is that as a wedding present, Richard Lear bought the remaining unclaimed land at the top of our valley, between my ranch and the mountains, and gave it to Anne and Glenn. They arranged for Lucién and Kathleen to manage and use the new land. So, all the land from our east fence to the top of the valley will come to the young Broussards and Lears in time and will remain in our family. I cannot tell you how grateful I was.

Those years from '76 to '78 were incredible to me and still are. I fought for the Cheyenne against the white man in a major battle and a skirmish, and was wounded. I had a vision of the Mother of God. I rescued some of the Northern Cheyennes and sent them on to Lame Deer. And yet I also made a deep friendship with a white man, Richard Lear, and saw my youngest daughter well married. But most importantly, I came to realize that I had to give up the evil word "All". I cannot figure how all those things came together in less than 36 months.

28.

The End of the Old West and Lisa's Revenge

1880–1882

Come the new decade, I turned 61 and my long red hair started to quickly become long gray hair. Kathleen and Lucién became prosperous on their part of the ranch. Lucién did less and less of our ranch work, and found a local man named Dan Cameron, with three strong sons to hire as ranch hands. Lucién and Kathleen's eldest daughter, Lisa, who writes this down, was and is a particular favorite of mine. She was sharp and her parents had sent her to school in Denver, paying for her to live in a boarding house through the last four years. She was and is also a lovely young woman, and was much admired by the young men of Denver. Yes, my dear. You have to write that down too. The other three children also needed schooling: another young Sam, Vern, and a little girl whose white name was Carrie Ann. They are ten and twelve years younger than Lisa. The education of the children caused Kathleen and Lucién to buy a home in Denver, and leave me to manage Cameron and the ranch hands. It was in 1879 that the city of Denver hired Lisa to be the school teacher. The first year went well, and Lisa proved to be a natural-born teacher. But the fall of 1880, we had a disaster. The disaster was a young fool by the name of Kyle Garran.

All right, we'll start again. It has taken me a week to talk Lisa into letting me tell this story. But it is my story too, and it has to be told. Garran was the arrogant son of a Denver store owner who had sold supplies to gold miners in '58, and when Colorado had a silver strike up in the mountains in

'79. By the way, we were a state now and had been since the year I fought at the Rosebud. Money was rolling through the town and old man Garran got rich. His boy was a bully. Yes, you have to write that down. It's true. He had a crowd of worshippers, young fools that followed him around. He treated most people like crap, while his worshippers looked on and laughed. Sad to say, he saw our Lisa girl one day and followed her back to the school. She was proper but polite and sent him away. Any sensible young man would have got the message. But Kyle figured the world was his for the taking. He kept pestering her for a month, telling her she would go out with him—he never asked for anything, only demanded. On the second day of October in 1880, his frustration with having this pretty, poor, schoolteacher, who should be worshipping at his feet, turn him down, caused him to force the issue. For Lisa's sake, I will not describe in detail what happened in that empty school room. The reader will be able to guess. When he was done, he buttoned up his pants and walked out laughing. Lisa pulled herself together, and after about an hour, locked up the schoolhouse and fled to her mother and father in their home. She wrote a letter of resignation that same day and sent it to the City Council, who'd hired her. But that was just to keep things quiet. She knew that once they found out she'd been raped, they would blame her and fire her. It's always somehow the woman's fault, even though Lisa did what she could to cry for help. I wish to God I'd been there with my Green River knife.

After a time, Lisa could not go out even on the streets in fear and shame. Lucién drove her up to me in the original ranch house and explained to me what had happened. Plus, we were certain by that time that she was pregnant. I told Lisa that my home was her home for the rest of her days, and Greta and I took her in as another daughter. She moved into Anne's old room. Meanwhile, Greta helped her through what proved to be a difficult pregnancy.

When she was six months along and really showing her swelling belly, I had had enough. She had been vomiting for about three days and Greta was much taken with caring for her. That's when I slipped out and got Lisa some justice. I . . . .

* * *

It is now a month since we last wrote. Lisa, upon learning how I avenged her, has not been able to continue until today. But she has built up her courage and overcome her shock. So, we proceed. I will say again what Lisa was not able to write down the first time. As I had with Chivington, I went to Denver and spent a few days just watching this young fool strut around with his friends. I've long been a hunter and know that you have to stalk your prey for a long time if you want to make the kill. Like with Chivington, I waited till he was weaving home, alone and drunk one afternoon and caught him in a different alley. I cold-cocked him and bound his hands and feet, gagged him, and dragged him off to an out-of-the-way cove of that alley.

I had a bandana over my face like a cattle rustler, so he never knew who I was. I didn't want any of this to come back on my family, as much as I would like to have told him Lisa's grandpa was paying him back. I hitched down his britches and made two shallow, clean cuts behind his manhood. There was almost no blood. He did not wake up while I was there. I cleared out as soon as the job was done.

And I knew I'd done it right because I had gelded a lot of stallions and young bulls by this time and knew just how to do it right and with as little damage as possible. Hell, I even doused my Green River with whiskey before I started so as not to cause infection. I figure he was a lucky bastard because some other enraged Denver father was going to shoot his ass with a shotgun one of these days. I guess you can say I saved him from that fate, and I saved some Denver father from the noose.

I thought of it as revenge at the time, and there certainly was some sort of justice to it. But really, thinking about it now, I suspect Lisa was not his first rape, and probably would not have been his last. Lisa told me some years back that he changed after this date, and no one, including his family, could understand why. He stopped bullying folks and actually turned into a quiet and studious young man who showed no interest in women. Shortly after, he moved to New York City and vanished. I bet you anything there was a collective sigh of relief from the young women of Denver the day he stepped on the train and waved to his bewildered parents for the last time. His daddy thought he'd inherit the store and become a rich and aggressive businessman. But all the fire seemed to have gone out of young Kyle Garran. Gelded studs are a lot easier to break and ride. And I have to add, this was the only time I did anything like this that Greta never found out.

In June of 1881 Lisa had her baby at my ranch, whom she named Lucién Phillipe Plunkett. I took a shine to that boy the first time I held him at ten minutes old. I told Lisa I'd help raise him and be his father. Shortly after, I sat down with Greta, Kathleen, and Lucién, and we hammered out an understanding. Later on, my friend, Richard, made it legal in documents. Except the original ranch house and about 10 acres, including the cemetery, all the ranch would go on my death and Greta's death, to Kathleen and Lucién. The original ranch house and the 10 acres would go to Lisa and her son. Kathleen was grateful and the family agreed to the partition. We all knew that in white society, Lisa was a "fallen" woman and no man would marry her, nor would any school ever hire her again. She needed some form of provision, and I took this on. I had to do it because the idiot belief of white folks in something they called "feminine purity," but what really meant that an unmarried mother was treated like used goods, even if she'd been raped, something totally against her will. It still makes me angry. I'll talk about something else. I'm going to talk about something sad, but it has to be said.

Two years after this, I lost Greta to cancer in '82. It still hurts like a raw wound, damn it. Lord, what a fine woman she was. Some fellows go looking for a good woman and take years, and never find one. I ran across Greta dying in a wagon at the worst of the cholera plague. I had no idea what a fine person I was carrying away from that scene of death, wrapped in a buffalo robe. Just one day we both noticed that she was losing weight way too fast. We rode into Denver on the buckboard and went and saw the doctor. He sent us to a newly-arrived surgeon who ran a lot of tests. Then he took us into his office and sat us down at his desk. That scared the crap out of me, and I wasn't wrong.

"It's cancer," he said. "It's in your esophagus and around your abdominal cavity. We could go in and do a surgery, but there's more than a 90% chance the surgery will kill you, and less than a 10% chance we'll get it all. As it is, you have something like 3 to 6 months. I'm very sorry. I could offer you morphine when it gets close to the end." Greta turned down the morphine. She wanted to die with her mind intact.

We both rode home in a daze, not speaking. That night we just held each other and slept little. In the morning we had to break the news to Lisa, and my boy, Little Sam, who at 17, wasn't so little anymore. Lisa cried and hugged Greta, who was her beloved grandmother, the woman who had carried her through her fiery trial. Sam took a long walk and didn't come back till dinner.

So, Greta grew thinner and soon looked twenty years older. And what tore me up, is she began to look like she had when I pulled her from that wagon of death all those years ago. She was skeletal again and could barely speak or move or eat, going in and out of consciousness. It all happened so fast. She didn't even make three months, and was barely able to eat shortly after we saw the doctor. She was in our bed at the last. (She'd had me build a proper bed because she was tired of sleeping on the floor). Her bright eyes shone out of her gaunt and wasted face. "I have loved you from the moment I saw you. And you have made me so happy," she told me. Minutes later she stopped breathing.

I felt like a horse had kicked me in the gut. Lucién came back from Denver for a few weeks and took over running the ranch again while we grieved. Since then, I have learned to accept it. And I have learned to sleep in a bed alone for the first time in 52 years. And I also came to be just grateful for the three good women that all came into my life by accident and made it good. I can't find words to say how good Spirit, and Misa, and Greta made my life. I have been awful damned lucky. Thanks be to God.

I dug her a grave in the cemetery with space to one side. I charged Lisa to bury me next to Greta when the time came. Lisa agreed and promised she would. Fr. Joseph came and said the service over the grave after a funeral mass at St. Mary's. And life became so quiet. All my days I had worked from sun up to sun down. But for about four months there I sat in front of the fire or walked around the ranch and just thought. Lucién and Cameron and his boys did the work for me. What finally broke me out of it was Richard Lear, who seemed to become a better and better friend every time we met.

Well, that's not entirely true. Lucién discovered that some of our cattle were missing. He confronted Cameron and his sons one day and it looked like Cameron was ready to fight. But I was standing on the porch with my Henry aimed at Cameron's head. "Clear off. And don't come back!" I told him. My reputation for never missing a shot was pretty well known by this time. They cleared off. Cattle rustling by this time was big business. All these poor Spiders coming west that didn't get rich, well, they got unhappy and decided to take what they could not earn. It was the only thing people wanted to talk about in Boulder and Denver. Fortunately, Cameron and his boys decided they'd rather clear off than have me turn them over to the law, which would have hung them in under 48 hours. We never saw them again, thank God. But now Lucién had to do all that work himself. We needed to find reliable ranch workers.

Richard had inherited land in Lincoln County, down in New Mexico. One day he found me wandering around my ranch and asked me a great favor. His brother had died in some particularly violent range war down in Lincoln County, New Mexico the previous year. His ranch went to Richard, as the brother had no wife or children. Richard wanted to go see the ranch but didn't know the country well enough. Plus, he thought it might be dangerous and though he had a Colt pistol, he'd never really had to use it. He wondered if he could hire me as a guide and guard. I was glad to go, though I told him he didn't have to pay me. He could feed me and put me up for the night at our stops. Otherwise, it was to be a trip for two old friends, and I wouldn't charge him a penny over expenses. He found this arrangement agreeable.

We considered riding the train down, but it didn't go far enough and eventually we'd be on horseback anyway. And if things might possibly be dangerous, I'd rather be on horseback and not in a buckboard or a surrey.

I'd want to be able to get the hell out of a scrape, and quick. So, Richard followed my lead and we mounted up like a couple of fur trappers. I left Lisa, and her father, Lucién in charge of the ranch and we rode out one fine morning in late May. The first day we went as far as Denver and stayed at his townhouse there. I hadn't been to Denver in a while, almost since I performed that delicate surgery on Kyle Garran. Little Sam went with us. His heart was sore from the loss of his mother and while I was away, he had agreed to stay with his big sister, Kathleen, in Denver.

I was very worried about him. He seemed to have lost his way and could not talk about it. Well, maybe he could talk to his niece, Lisa, who was eight years older than him. (Things like that happen in big families.) But her sad fortune and closer age made him able to talk to her a little. Still, I felt he needed to spend some time away from the place his mother had lived and died. I was certain that the same was true for me.

The second day Richard and I went on, as far as Colorado Springs, where Richard booked us a comfortable room. I was stunned. I had made this journey, between my ranch and the Arkansas River, more times than I can count and I had to camp each night. I was fully prepared for Richard and I to do so this time, with warm buffalo robes to sleep in and saddlebags full of jerked venison. But the third night we dropped down into the shallow Arkansas River valley and found a hotel in Pueblo, a town I had never seen before. It was just a river bank last time I'd been down this way. But here was a town, growing like a weed after a rain.

Finally, on our fourth night, we made it to Eagle Nest and there wasn't a town there. But as we sat around the fire, I told Richard about the time I was ambushed near the spot we were camping in. That led him to ask me all about my past, and over the next few days, I pretty much told him all the stories in this book, and how I first came to the Rocky Mountains as a boy.

The following night we pulled into Taos and Richard got us a room at the hotel. I knew where Kit Carson's house was, and we walked over there. I knocked on the front door and after a while it opened. A young Spanish woman answered the door. She was beautiful, with long, black hair. I asked after Kit and told her that I was an old friend, Cheyenne Sam. She looked at me for some time and said, "My father, he die fourteen year ago. I am sorry."

I was shocked. Kit not in Taos? Kit dead? Impossible. "I'm sorry for disturbing you, Señorita," I replied and we walked back to the hotel. Richard noticed that I didn't head to the bar and asked why. That led to my story of faking being drunk in Denver for years. Richard said he'd buy me a cup of coffee if I'd go with him to the hotel bar, and that was fine. He had a glass of wine. And while we sat there, I told him about my natural father and how I grew to hate whiskey at the Rendezvous. Finally, when I'd told him about Sir

William and Doc Ben, I said, "You know, Richard. The old west is dead. That world where there were no towns, no trains, a million buffalo, proud tribes in their 300-lodge villages, that whole world is dead. And I don't know if I fit in this new west."

He nodded and thought for a while. "Well, Sam, I know of no one in Denver who more lived that old world than you. And I even remember hearing tales about you as the town drunk. To think you were sober the whole time. That's a good laugh. But the west still needs people like you. If nothing else, to keep us honest. I wanted to tell you something, but I haven't had the courage till now. Sam, I've been to Sand Creek. I was there."

"What?" I said, sitting up.

"No, don't get me wrong. I did not ride with Chivington, thank God. My sweet wife, Cordelia, and I had just taken the train from Chicago and bought a small house in Denver. There were no other lawyers in town, so my business started growing pretty fast. Glenn was only eleven at the time, just a little boy. We heard Chivington going around town, rallying the volunteers and I remember watching a long column of horsemen following Chivington out of town one day to the cheers of people on the street. The Volunteers had whipped the Rebs a couple of years before at Glorietta Pass and now the word was that Chivington was ready for a showdown with the Cheyenne and the Arapaho. People cheered as the soldiers rode out of town. When they rode back in some days later, there was joy, and the word was that they had slaughtered the Cheyenne and Arapaho warriors in a pitched battle.

"It was only after a week or so, when some of the Volunteers were showing off body parts they'd cut off dead Cheyennes, that the truth started to leak out. There were almost no warriors at the fight. They had slaughtered old people, women, and children. Then it came out that the Indians were camped there near Ft. Lyon as a gesture of peace. A lot of folks started to speak up about this being a crime. I did. I lost a lot of clients for speaking my mind. But about ten of us men heard that the site had been abandoned and the dead left. Doc Danson, you might remember him, got us together and we took cloth masks, gloves, and digging tools and at least two wagons. I was mounted, so this isn't my first trip down to the Arkansas on horseback. We rode down river and up past Ft. Lyon to Sand Creek and found absolute horror. Sam, I want you to know I have nightmares about it to this day. You've told me how mad you get when people lie about Sand Creek. My friend, you're not alone there."

"But what did you all do?"

"We dug a big trench and laid all the bodies and body parts we could find in the trench. Then we covered it up. I'm sorry, it's all we could do.

Animals and insects were attacking the dead, and the smell was ungodly. I'm sorry."

"My wife before Greta, she was there. And my twin daughters. You know Clara. Her twin sister was there too."

Richard looked horrified. "Oh God, Sam. Don't ever ask me to tell you what I saw. I cannot speak of it, it was so horrible what those Volunteers did. Ever since that day, even if the fellow landed up in jail or hung, I have refused to do law for any Colorado Volunteer. I lost a lot of business that way, but I do not regret it."

"My wife. She was a Cheyenne woman."

"There were so many dead Cheyenne women, Sam . . . ."

"You'd know her by her left hand. She had a thumb, but when she was born, all her left fingers were merged together."

Richard's eyes got big and red. "Oh God, Sam. I saw that woman. And now you mention it, there was a girl's body next to her, that was the spitting image of your Clara."

We were both weeping like women at this point. I said "That was my wife and daughter. Clara managed to escape but it drove her mad, as you have seen. Clara was raped. I figure they were all raped. That woman you buried was Anne's mother, your daughter-in-law's mother. The other girl was Anne's big sister." He looked stunned.

"It's a strange and cruel world, Sam. I had no idea."

I stood up and reached out my right hand. "Thank you, Richard, for burying my women. I am eternally grateful. When we head home, if you're willing I beg you to show me where that grave is."

It was really too much for both of us. Richard finished his wine, stood up, shook my hand, and we went upstairs and slept even though it was 3 in the afternoon. Grief does that.

29.

Gunslingers and Cowboys

1882–1889

Leaving Taos was sad for me, though I did have one startling moment. A grand old lady, Spanish, with a fine red and green dress and expensive saddle, was riding down the street on a big, showy palomino horse as we left town by the south end. Her hair was finely combed, long and silver, flowing over her shoulders, and even with wrinkles in her face, she was beautiful. As we rode past her, with her proud chin in the air, she did not give us a second look, I recognized her as the girl I'd known as Lupita, who tried to seduce me all those years ago. If she recognized me, she did not let on, nor was I interested in striking up a conversation.

Richard and I talked as we rode along, mostly him wanting to know stories about my past. At one point, he asked, "So Sam, you never told me about that time you hurt your hip back in '76."

I paused, and then said "In my line of work, Richard, I'm told by a wise man that you can't get in trouble for something you didn't say."

He looked over at me and laughed. "Point taken, counselor. I withdraw the question."

But I knew that he could guess that I had been at Little Bighorn. Yet I had another question on my mind. "You never told me about your wife, Richard, Glenn's mother."

"Well," he said, "I think you know how hard it is to talk about a good woman who has gone before her time."

I nodded. Oh, I knew that pain far too well. "Well, then I withdraw the question."

He sighed and began. "Cordelia was beautiful and adventurous, and as good-hearted as a woman can be. I see some of her in your daughter, Anne, which is why I supported Glenn's decision to marry her. She passed from a case of pneumonia that came out of nowhere, in '72, and I never knew what pain really was until that year. After some time, I knew I had to get out of Denver for a while or go mad. By this time, money was no problem, so I bought that piece of land next to yours and built that house. I think you know the rest."

I reflected on this and said, "Sometimes, moving on, taking a journey is the only cure for that kind of pain. I want to thank you for taking me along on this trip. I feel a little . . . oh, what's the right word? . . . more free, each day we ride."

"Yes," Richard nodded. "I feel that too. I've taken many more trips since I lost Cordelia. It's not a perfect medicine, but the only one I know that works, if only a little. Rambling down the road makes you realize how big the world is. That somehow makes your pain just a little smaller."

I nodded. I couldn't think of anything to say to add to that.

So, we talked and rode. By nightfall we made it to Santa Fe. We followed the Rio Grande and by next day made it to the tiny village of Albuquerque. I asked some of the *Mexicanos* for directions, and three days later we rode into a town called Lincoln. I think in all the journey down, we only camped one more night. Ain't that an amazing thing. My west was dead and gone.

Lincoln was a damned war area when we rode in. Oh, we'd heard the stories, but that's not what I'm talking about. I'd seen many small settlements like this one. But this one was full of tension, even four years after all the gunfights. We rode to the hotel and booked a room, stabling the horses. After a bit, we headed uptown to find the land office or maybe a lawyer's office. Normally, in a town like Taos or Santa Fe, I would not feel the need to carry my Henry on an errand. But I could feel tension like lightning waiting to strike. On almost every corner there were armed men, deputies we were told later, standing around, guns at the ready. We found no land office, but there was an attorney in town and we went to see him.

"Can I help you, gentlemen. I'm afraid if you're here to see the gunslingers, you're about four years too late." Then he laughed. I could tell that Richard was not amused.

"No," Mr. Urukwart . . . "

"Ah, that's pronounced Urkirt. So, what brings you to Lincoln?"

"I am Richard Lear. Perhaps you knew my brother, John."

The attorney's eyes opened wide. "Ah, I am so sorry about your brother. Most unfortunate that he got caught by unintentional gunfire."

"Yes, yes. I'm interested in selling his ranch, which I inherit."

"Well, I shall have to look at the documents . . . . "

"No, you won't. I am an attorney, sir, and everything is in order. However, you might earn a reasonable fee if you can find me a buyer and quickly."

"Ah, well, that should be mighty easy. The Lear ranch abuts to the Dolan ranch, and I'm certain that Mr. Dolan will be happy to acquire the property, at a reasonable price, of course."

"I and my friend are staying at the hotel. I have the deed with me and have even drawn up a bill of sale. If Mr. Dolan will offer me a good price, we can sign the same day, and I'll be on my way."

"That sounds most agreeable, Mr. Lear. If you'll permit, I will close up the office and ride out to the Dolan ranch this very hour. Where can I find you at the hotel?"

"Room 10. I will wait there to hear from you."

As we walked out of the office I said, "That's one greedy snake."

"Oh, I'm sure. Lawyers like him give the profession a bad name. I will bet you twenty horses he's in deep with Dolan. I'll probably get an offer for half it's worth, but since the war here, everyone is afraid to stand up to that king, or they're dead, so I'll take what I can get, and we'll ride out of here with our scalps."

I had a good laugh at this. Sure enough, two hours later, Lawyer Urquhart showed up at our door with an offer that Richard later said was reasonable, if a bit a low. Urquhart said we were to ride with him to the Dolan ranch to sign the papers and get the pay-out. We went to the livery stable, got our horses and followed the lawyer through some canyons dotted with scraggly pines and brushwood, on a well-worn road. I thought to myself that this looked like poor eating for cattle. No wonder they felt the need to have lots of land. When the house came into view, I thought it was a palace. Though it was all one story, it must have had ten rooms, with big porches all around it. I think it covered almost an acre. Ranch hands stationed at strategic points looked at us as we rode through the front gate to the enclosed house and pastures. All of those men were heavily armed, like they were soldiers and not cattlemen. When we got to the house, one of them spoke up and told us we had to leave our guns with him before going in. I didn't like it much, but we were heavily outnumbered and heavily outgunned, so I handed over my Henry and my Colt pistols. Richard handed over his Colt and we went in to the well-furnished house. Fortunately, my shirt in back went down far enough so that they never saw my Green River.

We were shown into a parlor by the ranch hand who took our guns, where a big man with dark, black hair, wearing a fine tan suit, was much too friendly for me to believe he was sincere. There was hand-shaking, and smiles, and offers of a glass of whiskey. I declined, but Richard played the part well, accepting every courtesy and smiling like it was the best day of his life.

And I learned something about his profession. He was an actor as much as anything else. You'd think Dolan was his dearest friend, and not someone who was a murderous and greedy, self-made king. The papers were signed quickly and Richard declined any further hospitality as graciously as possible. Dolan gave him a burlap bag filled with greenbacks, and off we went. Our weapons were returned and we mounted up. We rode back to town.

On the ride, Urquhart seemed quite at ease and narrated the recent war. I'm sure he meant to make his patron, Dolan, out to be a wronged man who stood up for his rights, but in fact it sounded to me like a story of three powerful men, Dolan on one side, Tunstall and McSween on the other, who used all sorts of hired men, rustlers, and bandits, to make war on each other over land and domination of the town and county. But Urquhart assured us that all was safe. All those armed men in town told me another tale. Indeed, after bidding the oily attorney farewell, putting up our horses at the livery stable, and heading into the hotel, I saw motion and instinctively pushed Richard behind a stack of barrels. Gunfire erupted. Some fellow in dark brown clothes had walked toward us across the street, with his hat pulled down over his face.

One of the armed men shouted "Regulator!" Bullets started pinging off every wall. The man dived away from us behind some crates, from where with a Colt pistol, he returned fire and killed one of the armed deputies. From there he dashed away from the main street and out into some buildings on the far side of town with the deputies in pursuit. We lost sight of him and his pursuers, but heard the gunfire for another ten minutes. It stopped abruptly and we never found out the fate of the young man. The bartender said he must have been a Regulator trying to sneak into town for food. The Regulators were the personal army of Tunstall and McSween, both deceased. A few survivors were in hiding, but occasionally they tried to use the services in town, which was why deputies were armed and watching. One of the Regulators had been Billy the Kid, but the word was that Dolan's men had finally killed him.

Now, I mention this sad scene in detail because my grandson and his fool dime store novels, where he reads about gunfights in the "Old West." In those fool books, two men come out into the middle of the street, wearing some weird kind of combination of gun-belt and holster on one or both of their hips. The two men stare at each other, out in the open, until one moves and they see who is the fastest to draw and shoot. The other one dies. That horsecrap may sell dime store novels, but it never happened. If men had holsters, they were small, only one, and it was stuck diagonally in the front of a man's belt. If someone went for the draw, like the young man we saw, the first thing they did was duck for cover and then return fire. They didn't stand still in the middle of the street like a damn fool target. It didn't have nothing to do with speed, but instead, how close you were to cover, and how bad your opponent's aim was. Years later, the dime store novels had cowboys standing in the streets like idiots, blasting away at each other without a thought of taking cover. Horseshit! Plus, in my grandson's novels, every man is a cowboy. More horsecrap. There were cattlemen there surely, but they weren't cowboys, not like the ones out of Texas. And yes, there was a difference.

Speaking of Texas, that's where we went next. I wanted to go up through Indian Territory and the Cheyenne Reservation. Richard had agreed. He was very grateful I kept him out of the gunfire the day before, as that was how his brother died as an innocent bystander. This was confirmed by the bullet holes we saw in the wall right where we had been standing. If I hadn't shoved Richard behind that stack of barrels, we both would have died like his brother. So indulging me on visiting the Cheyenne came easy to him.

I kept thinking about how not even a full generation ago, traveling through this land would have been extremely dangerous unless the Comanches permitted you to do so. Now this land is full of ranches, and these Texas cowboys need only fear rustlers, who are cowboys who want to set up for themselves and figured that for them to steal from these large herds was no bad thing. It was considered a crime and it made me think of my old ranch manager, Cameron, who was a close, quiet fellow, and perhaps a sneaky bastard, but in the end all he wanted was to have his own cattle and spread, which he couldn't afford, except to steal from me. But the Comanches are no longer a danger—a mighty tribe converted to a group of poor farmers.

We rode several days east and had to camp twice, something I was familiar with. We found a hotel in a Spanish town called Santa Rosa, on the Pecos River. Then we were out on the plains again, Comanche land, but no longer. On the third day out we made Amarillo and had a second hotel. While in Amarillo, to Richard's bewilderment, I bought two fat steers and took them with us on lead lines. We traveled 4 days east, camping all the way, and I began to realize that Greta had spoiled me when I built her that bed. Sleeping on the ground wasn't all that comfortable anymore.

On the fifth morning we came on *real* cowboys. It was almost evening and I was looking for a stream or river to camp on. There was a vast herd of longhorn cattle on the prairie, more cattle than I'd ever seen in one place. They were settling in for the night. We saw a campfire and I decided to ride up, shouting "Hello!" Like the Cheyenne, most folks in the west figured if you came up silently, you were fixing to fight them. Those cowboys were a friendly bunch of fellows, eight of them, all sitting around their camp fire. And they looked like cowboys.

Now let me explain that, because in my grandson's fool novels, every man west of the Missouri or the Mississippi is a cowboy. I'm afraid he was bewildered when I saw the drawings in his books and laughed at that. He's a good boy, Robert, and smart. And I think he's got some of my spirit of adventure in him, which is why he is hungry for the "Old West." I try to be gentle with him. "It's gone, my boy," I say, and there is a sadness in his face. I feel that sadness too.

Anyway, cowboys. I've worked cattle for some years now, so I can be called a cattleman. That's not the same as a cowboy. My cattle are all in enclosed pastures, so we don't worry much about branding them, or roping. Real cowboys are experts at managing cattle in the open country, where a thousand things can go wrong. And they ride through heavy brush I can usually avoid. So they wear "chaps", leather coverings to their legs to protect them from brush. And they can do magic with a long rope, that they call a "lariat." And their horses are specially trained to "cut", that is to switch directions real fast to direct cattle. They wear long-sleeved shirts for sun and brush protection, and big, floppy hats with wide, round, soft brims. The crowns of their hats are usually left with no crease, so they are tall and round. Occasionally one fellow won't like the brim in his eyes, and will pin up the front of the brim up vertically to his crown, but other than that, the hats are soft and take on odd shapes over time, like they had a personality. Cowboys do carry a Colt in their belt and often a Henry or a Winchester in the saddle scabbard, like I do. I never saw a Colt holstered on any man's thigh until I saw it in those silly drawings in my grandson, Robert's, dime store novels. The thigh holster and the one-on-one, stand-in-the-street-gunfight were invented by some imaginative writer or illustrator in Chicago or New York. And very few men in the West were ever cowboys. Certainly, the man I saw in the gunfight in Lincoln was no cowboy, though he probably had been a ranch hand. Now, I figure he was a corpse underground.

These cowboys turned out to be a friendly bunch of guys and they even shared their bacon and beans with us. Two of them were Mexican, as was very common. And I learned that the Mexican *vaqueros* had taught these cowboys most of what they knew about riding and roping and herding. One, their leader, a friendly blonde kid named Billy, admitted it out loud. "Yeah, Carlos and Ramón her taught us how to be 'buckaroos,'" he beamed, quite proud of himself and his grasp of the Spanish language.

"That's '*vaqueros,' pendejo*," Carlos corrected.

"That's what I said. Buckaroos."

I learned that not only the chaps and the roping with the "lariat" were Mexican, but so were the words, from *chaparros* for chaps and *la rieta* for rope in Spanish. So, all the skills and gear they'd learned from the Mexican *vaqueros*. That's part of the laugh to my way of thinking. So many people here in 1902 think that a cowboy is so very American, when all of his technique and gear was invented by Mexicans. Lisa says the cowboy these days is an American icon, whatever that is. Anyway, like I said, they were a friendly lot and I asked them how to find the Cheyenne in Oklahoma.

"Well," Billy volunteered, "just ride due east about three days and stay on the south bank of the Canadian River and you'll hit their town. You know how to find the Canadian?"

"I do. Much thanks." In fact I'd camped on the Canadian many times with my Ivistsinihpah kin.

"Say, Don," Billy added, looking at the one older fellow, who was at least thirty. The rest of them couldn't be older than 22. "Isn't that where Johnny White Cloud and Hank White Man come from? They're good cowpokes."

"Cheyenne cowboys?" I asked.

"Some of the best," Don said, with very few words. I liked that. More of what I was used to. The conversation fell silent, which was no problem for an old trapper like me. Billy seemed to be embarrassed by the silence. He added, "Don don't speak much. He was at Gettysburg with the 1st Texas. Got wounded in the Devil's Den, he was."

"I totally understand, friend. No offense at all. I'm used to silence," I replied.

Don nodded in appreciation and added, "The agent at that rez don't like to let injuns off the rez to work. Got his head up his ass, if you ask me."

The conversation drifted to girls up in Nebraska that they hoped to find there and soon we all rolled up in blankets or buffalo robes and were asleep.

In the morning it was an impressive sight to see them rise, cook bacon, then pack up. They rode into the herd and within minutes had all those hundreds of cattle on the move. I saw one cow break away and Billy's horse went after it in an instant. Billy swung his lariat around his head and caught the cow's two hind legs, bringing it down. When he reached the cow, Billy and his horse were on the side away from the herd to the cow, so that when he loosened his lariat, the cow ran back to the herd. It was impressive.

"You know Richard, I think I know what to do about ranch hands back home."

"I'd like to hire some myself but after your experience, I'm not sure."

So, waving goodbye to the cowboys, we headed east. On the fifth morning, following the Canadian, we came on a village of sorts. Twenty or so small cabins were clustered loosely in the space of a square mile. I rode up to the biggest one and we tied off our horses and the steers. When I knocked on the door, a Cheyenne woman answered it. She said in astonishment "*Maovese!*", which, of course, is my Cheyenne name. After a minute of looking at her, I realized that she was the little girl I remember, Horse Calls, daughter of Spirit's cousin on Deer Kicks, her mother's side, and therefore my cousin. Now she was grown. She wore a dirty cotton dress and a blanket wrapped around her. She opened the door to me and Richard and showed us to the back of the house, where a weak cow chip fire burned in the chimney. There sat a man my age, wrapped in a blanket. He stood up, walked over and embraced me. It was Silent River, not only my cousin, but my Ivistsinihpah kinsman and a man I had fought beside both against the Pawnee, and at the Rosebud and the Little Bighorn. We were welcomed and the Cheyenne language flowed like a rushing river. I would translate to Richard from time to time, but he told me not to bother, and to go with the flow of the words. What a damn gentleman he is. I swear to the Lord God that Richard Lear was the finest white man of my generation I've ever known. I can't even think to call him a Spider.

Anyway, there was at least a half an hour of family news back and forth, when Silent River said to me "We are poor and have little to offer you. I am chief now, but there is little I can do for the people. And the Government does not always deliver the food they promised."

"Well," I said, "I am the guest who brings a gift. I have two steers outside and I think they need to be prepared for a meal."

This caused excitement, for most of them hadn't had fresh meat in a long time. Two of the young women and one of the young men went outside and took the steers to butcher them. After a while they brought in some slabs of beef and built up the fire to cook it. Silent River said there was too much meat for just his family and that he would invite the kin. I said that I had hoped for that. An hour later the whole room was filled with about 40 Cheyennes all eating and talking at the same time. Richard got many friendly nods and one older woman, who knew some English, sat down next to him and talked to him as best she could through the meal.

After everyone had eaten their fill, I got down to business. I learned about how badly the reservation was run. They suspected that the agent sold some of what came to them, and I made a point of translating this kind of information to Richard. Then I asked if I could hire six young men who had experience with cattle. "Johnny" White Cloud and "Hank" White Man were both at the meal and got excited when they heard my offer. But White Cloud said the agent would not let them leave the reservation anymore. He said that too many Spiders remembered the escape of the Omissis, and he couldn't do it. I translated this back to Richard, who surprised me. "Sam, let me go see this agent. You know I can negotiate with scoundrels. You've seen me do it. Let me help these people, and help myself by hiring decent ranch hands."

It was about noon when he said this. White Cloud and White Man understood enough English and offered to take Richard to the agency. I said in Cheyenne that we needed six young men, four more besides White Cloud and White Man. Four more volunteers raised their hands, and it looked like we had our ranch hands. But White Cloud pointed out that they all had wives and children. I translated this back to Richard. He requested that they write the names down of each of the people he would request, so that was done by a small boy who had been going to school.

The paper in Richard's hand, he stood up, put on his hat and told me he'd be back. Then he and Johnny White Cloud and Hank White Man went out the door and mounted up. I got more family news while we waited for over two hours. Then the door opened, and Richard looked at me, smiling. "Sam, I got 'em."

We rode out of there next morning with 15 Cheyennes added to our number. As promised, I rode up to the Arkansas River, we forded to the north bank and then rode to the Sand Creek site. Richard showed me where the trench had been. It was overgrown with grass, and the only sound was the wind blowing. You wouldn't know the trench was there, except Richard knew where it had been. I fell to my knees at the spot where Richard said my Misa and my Charlotte lay. Richard fell to his knees beside me. Behind us I could hear my Cheyenne kin weeping and chanting the death song softly under their breaths. It was very affecting to be there, even though there was no sign that this had ever been a Cheyenne village on the landscape of windswept grass and soil.

Our ride home took longer than I had thought it would, because we stayed out of Pueblo and Colorado Springs and Denver. I figured a route around the edges of settled country that took us home. And we therefore camped for several nights with my Cheyenne friends and family. We didn't dare take them into town. That agent had been right about people still fearing the Cheyenne. On the way I asked Richard how he had gotten the agent to cooperate.

"Well, Sam, I figure he was another of what you like to call 'greedy bastards.' I spent almost half an hour painting a picture of investment opportunities in Denver for him. Then I said it wasn't going to happen because I needed reliable ranch hands, but that I'd heard Cheyenne cowboys were the best to be had. Then I shook my head and said it was too bad I couldn't get any. He practically begged me to hire some Cheyenne. I'll have to let him in on some investment opportunities, just to keep things going, but it's hardly a strain for me. Basically, all I promised him were some contacts in Denver. If he fouls it up, it's not on me."

"You know, Richard, maybe you are a Spider. You caught that man in your web pretty neatly."

"Spider?"

I explained the Cheyenne word and its meaning.

Richard laughed, "Well, it certainly fits the legal profession, if not all Americans. But I hope a day comes, Sam, when your people can be proud again and at peace. I've been to many rich and expensive social events in Denver. But I've never been among people so happy and kind and warm-hearted as at that cabin on the Cheyenne reservation. Just one question. All those people were so friendly, but I wondered if any of those men fought at Little Bighorn. It just doesn't seem possible."

I thought for a minute, then said "Well, Richard, you can tell me if I'm wrong but, doesn't a lawyer have to keep anything a client tells them a secret?"

"That's true, Sam. It's called 'attorney-client privilege.' I cannot divulge anything a client tells me on pain of being struck off as a lawyer, as well as the possibility of jail time. Every judge in this country would back me. But I'd never do it, even without those penalties."

"And you've done some legal work for me, it seems. So does that make me your client?"

"Actually, yes, it does."

So, I told him the whole story of Rosebud and Little Bighorn and my wounding. And I told him, that except for the young men who were following us home, every one of those older men we feasted with in Oklahoma was at Rosebud and Little Bighorn. The victors were reduced to poverty and starvation.

"My God," was all he could think of to say.

30.

I Grow to be a Cantankerous Old Man and Other Matters

1900–1902

LET IT BE KNOWN that I insisted on the title of this last chapter. Lisa says I've been cantankerous for many years and she loves me all the more for it. Well, that was a surprise, but I did laugh.

Those Cheyenne boys worked out well on the ranch and on Richard's ranch. I had them all build cabins up beyond Kathleen and Lucién's house, and it seemed to me that the old Cheyenne village on my ranch was back again. When we expanded our herds and needed more men, I was able to get them from the Northern Cheyenne reservation at Lame Deer (called the Tongue River Reservation) and here in the heart of Ivistsinihpah country was a small but united Cheyenne village again. Richard and I kept it quiet, and the boys agreed not to go near Denver. All those white folks in Colorado believed they had driven the Cheyenne out of Colorado forever, when in fact, I was running a small and unofficial reservation in the canyon just west of Boulder. Only Richard knew outside the family and he said "attorney-client privilege." After about 1891 it didn't matter anymore and no one in Denver cared if we used Indian cowboys.

In a lot of ways this was an evil decade. Some well-meaning "friend of the red man" named Senator Dawes decided that Indians all needed to be civilized and the reservation was holding them back from full American citizenship. All the greedy bastards who still wanted to snatch Indian land told him that his cause was holy, and in 1887 they passed the Dawes Act.

Basically the reservation was given away to white buyers except bits of farm given to each Indian family. Of course, lots of whites came roaring in and traded Indian farms for whisky. So the new state of Oklahoma, once almost all reservation, became all white with a few scattered Indian towns. It hit the Southern Cheyenne and Arapaho right in 1890. Some Cheyenne were even killed if they refused to sell. It was one vast robbery. It's a good thing I wasn't there, or I'd have hung for several dead white men. So far it hasn't hit Tongue River, but Jack and everyone is afraid.

Speaking of Jack, he has become a chief among the Northern Cheyenne. He knows how alcohol has destroyed many a young Cheyenne man and woman, as it destroyed Little Wolf, who along with Dull Knife brought them all home to the north. So, Jack as a chief, fights reservation alcoholism any way he can. He came south to visit me in '92 and told me that he has taken the legal name of "Jack Flies Straight" to honor his Cheyenne blood down through the generations. Like I saw in the south, our people are finding that the Spiders place great store in family names, last names. So many warriors have given their own names to be the 'last name' or family name. All of Jack's descendants will be of the Flies Straight family, just as Johnny White Cloud and Hank White Man had sons and daughters that used 'White Cloud' and 'White Man' as their family names. Jack thought I might be hurt by his not using Plunkett for his family name.

"No boy," I told him. "You have chosen the way of wisdom. Keep the memory of our people strong with our own names."

"Father, I am glad you like this. I have misjudged you in the past. I thought you were too close to the ways of the Spiders and that you did not want me to find my name in the Cheyenne way. I was angry at you for many years. But I was wrong. And I began to see that when you fought at the Little Sheep River. I came to say I am sorry and . . . ." here he stood up.

I stood up.

My son came over and embraced me. My goodness, I am a very rich man.

But that's the news about Jack and his family. His oldest boy, Andrew Flies Strait, has married and his wife is pregnant, so I will be a great-grandfather soon.

But I've forgotten Jack's younger brother. Little Sam, my son by Greta. Shortly after Richard and I returned from New Mexico and Oklahoma, Little Sam came back home and was restless for a while. I suppose this part should have been in the previous chapter, since it goes back to 1883. But Anne and Glenn begged me to come visit them in Chicago, and with their approval, I brought Little Sam, who since his mother's death could not seem to feel comfortable in the world. We boarded a train in Denver and for the first time since I went back to St. Louis in 1832, I went back east to what I still thought of as the American nation, which in my old man's mind, was far different than the West.

Chicago was the strangest thing I have ever seen. Tall buildings are all shoved together. A man can barely see the sky. There ain't no horizon. And people, thousands of people, are walking around everywhere. My Lord, I didn't realize there *were* that many people in the world! Glenn and Anne had a big, two-story home on a grand street lined with old trees. There were horses and wagons going up and down every street and even something that looked like a small train car pulled by a horse, called a trolley, so you didn't even have to have your own horse to get around. I could describe more strange doings, but I'll just say the place staggered me. I would never want to live there.

Little Sam was fascinated with the place. And Glenn at dinner one night told Little Sam about his work in law. The boy was even more fascinated, so that after three days, Anne came to me and asked me if I would consider leaving Little Sam with them. Glenn said he could be apprenticed in Glenn's law firm and make a fine career. I told Anne I wanted her to ask him, but I was fine with that if it was what the boy wanted. She did talk to him, and he was excited. He came to me and I said "You know, your mother would be right proud of you working in the law. She would be so happy if she could hear this now." That decided it for Little Sam, so when I got back on the train to Denver, I waved to Glenn, Anne, and Little Sam on the platform. I rode that train alone. When I got home, Lisa and I packaged all his remaining clothes and possessions and shipped them to Chicago.

It turned out to be a good decision and the boy is now a man and an attorney. He moved out of his sister's house a few years back, and bought his own home after marrying a sweet girl named Annette. And in Chicago today, Sam Plunkett is the name of a young attorney, and not a cantankerous old mountain man. His first boy, Robert, is the grandson that asks me about the Old West whenever I go visiting in Chicago. I try to be gentle with him and set him straight about cowboys not being every white man west of the Mississippi, about gunfights being something that came late in the century and did not involve two fools standing in the middle of the street. And I try to tell him about the real Old West, the fur trappers like his great-grandfather, Jack Rather, who was among the first white Americans in the Rocky Mountains. And I tell him about the *Tsistsistas*, the Beautiful People, the Cheyenne, and how Cheyenne blood runs in his family. That got him excited.

Before I forget, when Little Sam and I first went to Chicago, I saw Clara. She was clean, well-dressed and fed. A nurse was with her constantly.

She has stopped her whispering, but she does not speak, except when one of us hugs her. Then she repeats our name at a whisper. Anne walks in the park with her nearly every day, and except for her silence, no one would know she was mad. She stares vacantly into the distance and seems to see almost nothing. So, there is some small improvement. After that first visit to Chicago, I started going out every summer, to see my children. Clara continued to live quietly, but never improved beyond what I've already described. Something in her mind just broke on the evil day, and it will never be healed. Thank God Sam and Anne are doing well. Clara is a wound in my heart that will never heal.

There is little good left to tell about these years. I went to a Buffalo Bill show about '88. I had met Cody in Denver once and given him a piece of my mind about his buffalo hunting. But I'm sure he did not remember me. I was just another face in the crowd. The show itself was a circus, only all the performers were cowboys and Indians. And the cowboys stage-fought the Sioux at an imaginary Little Big Horn, and a heroic Custer died for his country, leading the cowboys into battle. I was laughing so hard through the whole two hours of bullshit that people sitting next to me got up and moved. They seemed to think I had no respect for history. Well, that's why I was laughing—because this show had no respect for history, true history. It told that audience that white America had fulfilled its God-given destiny to conquer the continent and bring the light of civilization to the Indians. Some fool announcer at the end even said those very words. That's when I got up and left, much to the relief of anyone sitting near me. As I was walking out, cussing under my breath, I heard my name in Cheyenne from one of the tents to my right, not too far from me. "*Maovese*" it said again. I stopped and turned and looked to my right. A man came out of the dark of the tent opening. His long gray-streaked hair was braided and he worn a gaudy buckskin shirt, leggings, and breechclout. He was old, and sadness radiated from him.

At that moment I realized that when the Lakota warriors rode out in the show, the feathers in their warbonnets fluttering, that those were *real* Lakotas, and not white actors in face paint. And when they announced "Chief Sitting Bull!" and everybody booed except me, that really *was* Sitting Bull. I walked up to him and took him by both hands.

"What are you doing here?" I asked in English.

"I need money to feed my grandchildren," he replied.

I nodded and understood why he put up with the repeated humiliation. "I heard about Crazy Horse. I am sorry that all this has come to pass."

He nodded. His English was limited, but even if he'd spoken it fluently, what could anyone say to such appalling loss? We talked a little more and he said he remembered me from the battle, that my words and ideas had been used by Crazy Horse to catch Custer in a trap. I said I was glad I was able to give something. After that, he looked down. There was nothing else to say and memory was painful for us both. I wished him well and left. Two years later he was gunned down as they tried to arrest him for being dangerous. The white folks feared the Lakota long after my Cheyenne kin were penned up in Oklahoma and Montana. They slaughtered a whole village at a place called Wounded Knee in '91 for not much more reason than that they were Lakotas, and they were dancing the Ghost Dance, or so the Army thought. To my heart it was Sand Creek all over again.

But they didn't have to gun down all those Lakotas at Wounded Knee. My people and our allies were already defeated. It was the 7th Cavalry that did it and some folks say it was payback for Little Bighorn. Except for the Apaches, who had been resisting the Spiders since 1849 and didn't give up till 1886, the American Indian was defeated by '77. Funny thing, it was General George Crook, whose Army corps we defeated at the Rosebud, who finally defeated Geronimo and the Apaches at last. I guess he needed at least one win.

But looking back on everything that Lisa has written down, I feel sad. The Old West was a wonderful, and beautiful, and dangerous place. When I was young, I used to hear old men mourn their lost youth, and claim that the world they used to know was better than the one they now lived in. I swore I would never do that.

Yet, here I am, looking back on that beauty and freedom of roaming the Rocky Mountains and the Great Plains, where the only thing to really worry about were grizzly bears and the Blackfeet. I don't know if it was a better world, but it was more exciting and awe-inspiring (Lisa, like so many times, gives me those words too). I'm not sorry that I'm wiser than when I was young. But if I could work my will, perhaps the Lakota and the Cheyenne and the Arapaho would have organized, and held the Black Hills and the Rockies and the plains near the Rockies as their own country. Then I could have said that the new world was as good as or better than the old one.

Like I told the Cheyenne Council of Chiefs, the white man, the Americans, were like a hill of red ants, that only got angry if you kicked it. I'm not sure we could have ever stopped that swarm. I will say that I have prospered on my ranch and regularly have through the nineties paid my Cheyenne ranch hands to run small herds of cattle down to Oklahoma or up to Montana to give to the people, so that they did not starve. And any young Cheyenne, Northern or Southern, that wanted to go to school but didn't have the money, if I heard about it, I paid for it.

As for Richard, he has retired from law and we spend our days mostly sitting, watching our ranch hands from either his porch or mine, telling stories and laughing. Johnny White Cloud manages both ranches and I never worry about a thing with him running things. Lisa scolds me if I try to do any real work. She says I've already done my share. I don't see how that can be when the world is so full of hate and racism even today. But it's not so bad here on the small and unofficial and only Cheyenne reservation in the State of Colorado.

Epilogue
by Lisa Broussard

At risk of distracting the reader from the pure and true ruminations of my beloved grandfather, I, with trepidation, add this epilogue. I will say briefly that I have taken significant editorial liberties to make my grandfather's Kentucky English more formal, though in places I let his more vulgar diction stand, because it seemed necessary to give the full flavor of the event. For the same reason, I have preserved his profanities, or some of them anyway. I did modify the title from the rather blunt one he had chosen, though I kept the gist of his meaning. Grandpa's speech could be quite colorful when he was angry. I had to remove many profanities from the section on Sand Creek, and his encounters with Col. Chivington.

More importantly, I hope the reader is able to ascertain the depth and purity of my grandfather's loving heart, even through the contradictions of his life. He was overflowing with kindness and love, and yet, raised on the frontier, far from American civilization, he learned to be quick, and violent, and at times lethal. For Grandpa Sam, killing in order to survive, whether it be hunting or self-defense, was something to be done quickly and without feeling. A fight man to man was something you ended quickly, and you made sure you won. He was trained to understand that these things were the only alternative to dying.

In his years when he played the drunk in Denver bars, spying for the Cheyenne, he tried to stay out of fights. He would put up with a lot of humiliation before he would engage in fist fighting. But some fools were drunk and insistent, and Grandpa Sam would teach them a lesson if they persisted on attacking him. From the reports and eyewitness accounts I was able to gather, he was known for a quick blow to the throat or the cheekbone, or perhaps both, that left his opponent retching and choking on the floor, if they were lucky enough to still be conscious. Or, if the opponent meant serious harm, in a flash they found Grandpa Sam's razor-sharp Green River knife at their throat, and heard him asking if they were ready to quit for now. They were always quite willing, given that inducement. He was never forced to kill anyone in Denver, though as this account will show, he came extremely close to murdering John Chivington after Sand Creek. Only Mamagreta stopped him.

Yet, I have heard stories of how he cradled his young son, my Uncle Andrew, as the little boy was gasping out his last from cholera. And the story of how he rescued Mamagreta is family legend. Perhaps it was his Irish blood, but in spite of any of his words to the contrary in this manuscript, he was a man quickly moved to tears. And he has loved me as much as he loved any of his cherished daughters. We have had a special bond that still pains me now, when he comes to my mind on the ranch, as he often does. Then I go visit him in the cemetery, lying next to Mamagreta, with the feather and bead pendants for Misa, Auntie Charlotte, and my grandmother, Asimoni, fluttering in the wind above his grave. I talk to him for maybe a minute or maybe an hour, but always come away feeling better for having visited. He believed that the dead can pray for the living, like many a Catholic, and I can to this day feel his prayers floating around me.

Yet, he was a man of swift violence, there is no doubt about it, and he admits to having killed at least thirteen US Army soldiers in clean battle both at Rosebud and Little Bighorn, and in the Sumner fight. But then, as he would have told me, the Rocky Mountains—like life—were both beautiful beyond imagining, but also violent and dangerous. He told me that he had almost been killed by a grizzly bear at least five times, though in this memoir, he could only clearly place two of the attacks: first, the one that scarred him forever as a boy, and second, the one where Jim Beckwourth saved his life. The only other attack he could remember at all was when he somehow found himself on the back of the bear with his Green River knife. Of how he got up there, he had no memory. But he did recall saving his own life by cutting the bear's throat. When I asked him if he was terrified, he only commented, "You know, there's good eating on a grizzly bear. It would surprise you how tasty they are." He was trained to survive. Emotions were a luxury in the heat of a fight, and no sensible mountain man would throw away a large portion of fresh bear meat. He was trained from the youngest age to first and foremost, survive.

He was in fact, because of his training in marksmanship, a sniper, though he would not have recognized that word. And he was not trained in the Army in the war between the North and the South, because he thought it a foolish war, and would not have gone with the Colorado Volunteers, who after all, were the very people that followed Chivington to Sand Creek and murdered Grandma Misa and Auntie Charlotte. I'm afraid Grandpa Sam had a poor opinion of the US Army and an even poorer one of the Confederate Army. I think he always believed the Cheyenne and their allies could have won, if they had learned how to keep warriors in the field and changed their tactics, as they did at the Fetterman Fight and the Powder River campaign.

Grandpa was a Cheyenne sniper, perhaps the only one ever. And yet he was the truest Christian I have ever known, devoted to his Lord Jesus Christ, and Holy Mother Church, as well as extremely devoted to the Lord's Mother, to whom he was constantly praying, with or without great-grandma's rosary in his gnarled fingers, and which he kept with him at all times. The reader may struggle with reconciling these seeming contradictions, but I find there was more of the Spirit of Christ in my Grandpa than many a flashy preacher or sanctimonious fool I have met in Denver, or Boulder, who throws the name of Christ around like they were old pals, all the while ignoring Christ's teachings. I will refrain from a rather long and dishonorable list of names of "religious" men I've known in Denver that meet this description.

We finished this manuscript in the winter of 1902. His mind was sharp and his memory good when we worked on it. And as the reader may have perceived, I was shocked and surprised by some of the things I learned that had been family secrets till then. In March of 1903, I rose one morning and found he was not out and about his usual chores. His cane was still resting in the corner by the fireplace and the sun was well up. I went to his room and found him still in his bed. He was muttering out of the left side of his mouth and was in distress and unable to move the right side of his body. I sent little Lucién riding hard for Denver to fetch Mama and Papa and a doctor. Between us we cared for Grandpa Sam through the spring and summer of '03.

In September, Auntie Anne wired from Chicago, pleading to take over the care of her father. She was already caring for Auntie Clara, who had gone insane in the horror of Sand Creek, and needed constant attention. Uncle Glenn and Auntie Anne had hired a full-time nurse for Auntie Clara and offered to do the same for Grandpa Sam. Mama and Papa and I were doing our best, but we had responsibilities to our own homes and children and Uncle Glenn and Auntie Anne were childless, as well as wealthy, Uncle Glenn being a highly respected federal judge in Chicago. Mama and all the aunts and uncles agreed that it was time for Anne to care for her father on his last journey. Uncle Jack, who had ridden down from the Tongue River Reservation, thought that Grandpa would not want to leave Cheyenne lands. But when Anne promised that he would be brought back to rest here, Jack agreed with his sister and the decision was made.

I last saw Grandpa Sam as we made him comfortable on the train to go from Denver to Chicago. Auntie Anne sat by his side, holding his hand. As we stepped out of the train car, and the whistle sounded 'all aboard', I looked over my shoulder for the last time at his dear face.

But for me my true last day with him was the afternoon before his stroke, when he and I sat out on the porch and watched the early evening sky turn to stars and the Rocky Mountain night. He reminded me that the Milky Way was the "Hanging Road" to the Cheyenne, the bridge souls walked on their way to eternity.

In 1906, in April, never having recovered from his stroke, my Grandpa Sam, my second father, as he would have agreed, walked that Hanging Road. I am firmly convinced that when he reached the far end, he looked upon the face of the Mother of God, and she took his hand and led him home. Auntie Anne was in the room when he passed. She said that he suddenly became awake and clear minded. He looked all around the room, which held only Anne and himself, and started to clearly call the many names of all his lost loved ones, as if they were all walking into the room. I firmly believe they were actually walking into the room. You cannot convince me otherwise. After a minute of this, he looked up and said at last, "Jack. You came." Then he breathed his last breath. Auntie Anne had to gently close his eyes.

Richard Lear helped him draw up a will years before. At Grandpa's insistence, his body was placed in a simple pine coffin, with no stain or color. His body was dressed in his worn Cheyenne buckskin shirt, breechclout, and leggings. His long, gray hair, once red, was gently combed over his shoulders. He was always sensitive about what he unjustly thought was the ugliness of the scars that covered the left side of his face, and the fact that the bear had torn off his left ear, so he never cut his hair. Plus, a Cheyenne man traditionally wore his hair long as a sign of spiritual power. We sent him off with his hair long and proud. Uncle Glenn and Auntie Anne rode with his coffin on the train from Chicago to Denver, where the family gathered at the station. The men of the family shouldered his coffin and placed it on the back of the buckboard wagon. It rode to the ranch, where a fresh grave had been dug beside Mamagreta. And with old Fr. Joseph presiding over the graveside service, there he was laid to rest beside his third wife, not a quarter mile from our home, in the valley that he loved best and for which he sacrificed for over 60 years. All the family was there—only Auntie Clara was missing: my mother, Kathleen, and my father, Lucién, and my brothers and sister; young Sam out from Chicago with his wife and sons; Uncle Glenn held Auntie Anne, who sobbed and leaned on her husband; Richard Lear was there, standing tall and ramrod straight, in a black suit and white hair, weeping silently. Uncle Jack was there, with his wife and son and daughter. And he brought an old Cheyenne chief with him, translating for him. The man had long white hair and his left arm hung limp. He wore a fine, blue silk shirt and a beaded vest, obviously his best clothes. I knew it must be Grandpa Sam's remaining brother, Many Horses. Jack and I brought him into the house and I welcomed him as my guest for four days, asking him to honor my house in good Cheyenne language, as my grandfather had taught me. At the end of the four days, Jack drove him and Jack's family back to the reservation. It was an honor to meet the man who was not only Grandpa's dearest surviving Cheyenne friend, but who had been wounded together with Grandpa Sam at the Battle of Little Bighorn.

The will stipulated that I was his principal heir, except for the land that went to my mother and father. The family all agreed, since I had become his closest companion in his last years, especially during the writing of this memoir. So, the ranch house comes to me and is my home. When I pass, the heir will be my son, Lucién Phillipe Plunkett, "Little Lucién", whom he raised as his own son all these years.

But I don't want to end with these sad thoughts. My Grandpa Sam fought not only for the Cheyenne all his life. He fought against rape, on several occasions. The reader will be aware that one occasion was my own. And he learned the lesson first by becoming aware of the rape of my great-grandmother, Kathleen MacCready Plunkett, his Irish mother. His sense of Christian honor, and his fierce sense of justice somehow combined with his training in swift, frontier violence, as this book will have shown. And secondly, long before any white man I can find record of, he rose up against racism. It started in an unlikely way: he fell in love with an Indian girl, my grandmother. But from that, and his deep friendship with Jim Beckwourth, he learned that the racial assumptions of most of the people around him were evil and had to be fought. It's to this that I attribute the fact that he fought at Rosebud and Little Big Horn on the side of the Indians. He befriended Jim Beckwourth when other men scoffed at the notion of a black fur-trapper. On the occasions where I asked him about conditions in the South for black folks after the Civil War, he just shook his head. I do not know if I ever will, but I hope I live to see the end of Jim Crow. I know my Grandpa would have felt the same. He was a Cheyenne warrior for justice, and a fighting Irishman. And though he was uncomfortable with much that this nation stood for, especially racism and the shabby treatment of Indians, I have to finally say that he stood for the very essence of all that is worth fighting for in America. I one time dared to share my opinion with him that women should be allowed to vote. To my surprise he retorted, "Why the hell not? Most women I've known were far more sensible than their menfolk." He was truly a man who did not lean on the common opinions of society in determining what he believed to be right and wrong. I think I can safely say that if there were more people like my Grandpa in this country, it would be a far better place.

Now, as I move around the house he built, I see signs of him everywhere: his Hawken guns and powder horn that hang on the wall over the fireplace; his hand-made cane rests in the corner by the fireplace, that he walked with everywhere after Little Bighorn; his certificate of his "college degree" from the so-called "University of the Rocky Mountains" that his companions bestowed upon him when he first came to the Rockies on his own, and which I have proudly framed and hung on the wall; his "fooforaw" as he called it, thinking it of little value, but these combinations of gorgeous colored beads and feathers that he made, that I consider profound Indian art; the framed Shooting Star flower the Lady left him; his Bible, the binding all falling apart from wear; his worn copy of *Lyrical* Ballads, which I still read a little from every day; Great-Grandma's rosary, which he treasured and fingered for decades; and finally, the hundreds of pages of manuscript, painstakingly written in my hand, that open the door to his life for you, our readers. It is, after my loved ones, my greatest treasure.

I cannot find words to say how much I miss him.

Lisa Asimoni Broussard
March 12, 1907

www.ingramcontent.com/pod-product-compliance
Lightning Source LLC
LaVergne TN
LVHW050618100826
845148LV00011B/1644

9798385267217